THE
FORBIDDEN
PLANET

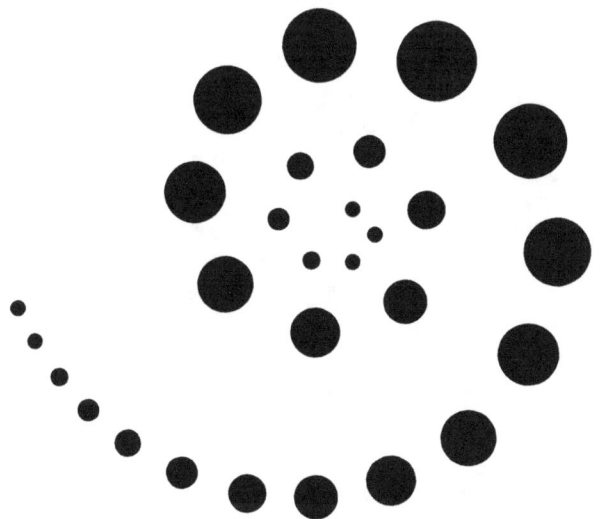

C.A. HARTMAN

5280
PRESS

Published by 5280 Press
PO Box 12477, Denver, CO 80212
www.5280Press.com

ISBN 10: 0990391949
ISBN 13: 978-0-9903919-4-4

Printed in the United States of America

Cover design by Chris Voeller (chrisvoeller.com)

CHAPTER 1

The bonds of sentient creatures should never be underestimated. A Sunai has his wives and his children. The Calyyt have their liqqat, or domestic units. The Derovians have their brothers and sisters, the humans their nuclear families, the Korvali their lifemates. The arrangement differs, but the bond itself is nonetheless more powerful than even the laws of physics.

- Dr. Layla Jalal, anthropologist

Catherine Finnegan stared at the mottled tangle of rich blues and greens, painted with such delicacy onto the large flat seashell. She saw something different in the abstract piece, something she'd never seen before. It seemed to reflect not so much water or sky now, but perhaps an internal state, maybe that of the Derovian artist who'd created it.

How Eshel had returned the piece of art to her quarters, to its rightful spot on her bulkhead—after it had gone missing for well over a year—still mystified her. Tom said he knew nothing about it. She might never know the truth; but right now, its presence gave her solace.

Catherine sat on the deck, resting against the bulkhead, strumming the beautiful handmade guitar that Koni had given her as a gift for aiding the operation that had lured eight biocrackers into the hands of the Sundani. The caramel wood's odor wafted up to her as she practiced the little tune the Sunai musician had taught her at the music festival, just days after they'd arrived on Suna for the first time. She was surprised she remembered it after that long.

Yet the music, instead of reminding her of the festival or Koni or even Suna, reminded her of Eshel. Despite the reserve between her and Eshel in the past year, and despite his only having been gone a week, the void of his absence seemed gaping, as if he'd taken half the ship's crew with him. Eshel had gone into hiding on Suna for the safety of all, and she didn't know when she would hear from him again.

Her contactor chirped.

"Where are you, Finnegan?" Tom's voice said.

Catherine glanced at the time. "Sorry. Lost track of time. On my way."

She sat for a minute more, then put her guitar in its stand before dragging herself to her feet. When she arrived at the mess, the cacophony of clanging dishes and chatting crewpersons assailed her. She overlooked the ornon and sea vegetables in favor of chicken and potatoes, and sat down with Tom and Snow. The fourth chair at their table remained empty.

"Poker tonight?" Tom said before stuffing a forkful of chicken into his mouth.

Snow nodded as he chewed. Catherine curled her lip, recalling the last game she'd attended, including Middleton's remarks about Eshel and all that had happened. She had no more tolerance for Middleton's whining, and could withstand no crowing about Eshel's removal from *Cornelia*. During their mentoring sessions, Yamamoto had focused on teaching her to respond rather than react, especially to those who triggered her anger. But she knew that, right now, her cushion of patience had dwindled to its thinnest.

Tom gave her a disapproving look. "What's with the face? Middleton said he'd keep his mouth shut about Esh. And now that Esh is gone there's nothing for him to complain about."

"He'll find something," Catherine said.

"You busted his ass pretty good," Tom said.

"Yeah," Snow said, with a chuckle. "He's pissed at you."

"Good," she said.

Tom scowled. "What's with you, Finnegan? It's nothing new, and a lot of people feel like Middleton does."

She looked at him coldly. "Are you one of them? Eshel's our friend, Tom. Middleton is just some twat you let hang around because he's Zander's friend, and because he works in Engineering," she added, glancing at Snow.

"Ah, quit your whining," Tom said.

Snow elbowed Tom. "Knock it off, man."

Just as Tom went to retort, something grabbed his attention. Tom stared beyond Catherine for a couple of moments before he broke into his usual grin and winked. When the object of Tom's focus reached their table, Catherine glanced over. It was Maria Trujillo, the woman Tom had fallen for and lost to Lieutenant Commander Ferrars, an outcome that had pained—but perhaps not surprised— all of them. Maria passed on by and went to sit among her own friends, one of whom included Ferrars.

Snow turned to Tom. "Oh, look who's quiet now."

"Shut up," Tom muttered.

Catherine ate a few more bites before she stood, picked up her tray, and left without a word.

Glad to be back in the haven of her quarters once more, Catherine flopped down on her bed and turned on her reading pad. Barely two paragraphs in, her door sounded. Tom's mug was on her display. She rolled her eyes and voiced him in.

Tom entered, his swagger a bit muted and his expression more serious than usual. He pulled out one of Catherine's chairs, turned it around, and sat down near her bed. He paused for several moments, as if, for once, thinking carefully about what he would say.

"It's weird without Esh here," he said.

She nodded.

Tom stood up again, stretching his arms as he paced. "Look, C. A lot of shit has happened… with the clone attack and the loss of two of ours. It's taking a toll on the crew… you, me, even Middleton. Yeah, he's an asshole. But excluding him won't solve anything. He knows we love Esh, he knows Esh is ten times the man he is, and he keeps coming back anyway. If we keep him around, maybe he'll learn something."

"Maybe," she said, putting her reading pad aside. "I just can't take it right now."

"Esh had to leave. Hopefully it's only temporary."

She shook her head. "It's not temporary. You said yourself that even if they go after Elisan, it will take a long time. And before you say it, I already know: involving myself with him was a big risk from the start and it's my own damned fault."

Tom sat down on her bed. "It's not your fault, C. Sometimes people grow on you, no matter how hard you try not to let 'em."

Catherine blinked a couple of times to discourage any tears that threatened. She sat up, and she and Tom hugged one another.

"Come play with us when you're ready," he said. "In the meantime, don't stay in here alone anymore. It only makes it worse."

And he left.

Tom shuffled the cards one last time before dealing them to Snow, Zander, Middleton, and Shanti. They all picked up their cards. Shanti, first to act, placed a bet with a dark hand adorned with strands of pale green jewels like those worn by Sunai women.

"Where's Catherine tonight?" Shanti said.

"She's taking it easy," Tom said. "I think this situation with the clone, and Esh leaving, has taken its toll on her."

"I miss Eshel," Shanti said, her dark eyes forlorn.

Tom nodded, glancing at his cards. "We all do. Well, most of us do," he added, giving Middleton a look.

Middleton, his head freshly shaved, made a face. "Oh, come on, man. What the fuck?"

Tom eyed him, daring him to take it a step further. But Shanti chimed in.

"How long will Eshel stay with the Sunai?" she asked.

Tom shrugged. "Don't know. Could be a while." He tossed in a bet.

"But why here?" Zander asked, folding his cards. "I mean, he's Corps now. Why not send him to Earth, to Headquarters?"

"Don't know that either," Tom said. "But I get the feeling there's a lot of disagreement at Headquarters about this situation with the Korvali. And, realistically, he's easier to hide here."

"So what happens now?" Zander said. "What about the Korvali and what they did to our people... and to Doctor F?"

Tom sat back in his chair. "Hard to say. I don't know any more than you do right now."

"They're not going to let them get away with that shit, are they?" Middleton said, folding his cards after Snow bet.

"I don't know, man," Tom said. "It's not that simple. We've already had a taste of what the Korvali are capable of, and Eshel says it can get much worse. And the real problem isn't the Korvali; it's their leadership. Some of the others want what Eshel wants, to join the Alliance and keep the peace. If I had to guess, Esh is working with the Sunai to come up with some kind of plan."

"But our mission ends in, what, ten weeks?" Shanti asked. "What happens then?"

"Good question," Tom said.

Fog escaped Catherine's mouth as she breathed the chilly air of Jula, the pungent odor of the shrubs muted during the moon season. Heat and sweat began building under her layers of warm clothing while she trekked up the steep path. The altitude slowed her down and made her feel heavier, and she wondered how long it would take her to readjust to Colorado when they returned from duty.

"Are you warm now, nonaii?" called Koni's strong, guttural voice ahead of her on the narrow trail.

"Definitely," she said.

She followed her Sunai friend, working to keep pace with him. Koni's fitness levels were at their peak, as required for any Sunai military officer. Her boots crunched over a light snow that had become thin enough to reveal occasional spots of rusty volcanic soil. Highland shrubs rose on either side of the trail, their coppery branches bare from winter dormancy. As Catherine passed a small tree with wandering limbs, she spotted long spines—the spiri tree, the one that had punctured her shoulder nearly a year ago while training with Tom, leaving her in pain for days along with a story-generating scar. She marveled at how much more easily she could see the wicked spines during daylight and without leaves to obscure them.

The trail rounded the corner and the woody foliage cleared, giving them a view of Jula below. The tall black buildings rose from the snow-blanketed city and the culverts that snaked throughout had become even more prominent, now bright rust from the spillover of a recent eruption. Bits of ash still hovered in the cold, unmoving air, but Commander Ov'Raa had informed the crew that levels were now safe for humans.

"What do you think of our great city?" Koni asked, raising his chin as he peered at Jula with his big amber eyes.

"Other than the one incident, I like it here. I'm glad we're back."

"Do not let such scum color your views of Suna, nonaii. Every people has its filth."

"I know," she said, gazing upon the metropolis. It seemed still and lonely that day.

He turned to her. "Something troubles you, nonaii. Perhaps it is that Eshel has left your ship and come to live among the Sunai."

She looked down. "I'm grateful that your people would protect Eshel, Koni. But..." She paused, shaking her head. "I don't know when I'll see him again."

"None of us does."

"You and he seemed to be making progress. Is that ruined now?"

"It is difficult to say, nonaii."

Catherine nodded, wondering if Koni still had access to Eshel. She knew there was a chance he did, but she didn't want to ask. Not yet. Koni had already done so much for her, and she doubted that his connection with Eshel—the one Koni had sought for so long and that Catherine had fostered—had yielded enough to satisfy him. It certainly hadn't produced enough to give Koni what he wanted most, to reach the next rung in the Sunai military hierarchy.

"What did Eshel say when he told you of his leaving?" Koni said.

"He said only that it was safer for everyone, that he didn't know when he would return, and that he was sorry he didn't tell me in person."

Koni's chest puffed up. "He conveyed such a message over communications?" he bellowed, gesturing wildly with his hand. "Bloodless fool!"

Catherine, taken aback by Koni's reaction, burst out laughing.

"What amuses you?" Koni asked.

Catherine, still laughing, said, "For the first time, I'm not angry that you called him that."

Koni began to laugh as well, a guttural guffaw that echoed upon the towering mountains behind them.

Once their laughter subsided, Catherine spoke. "Thank you for bringing me here, Koni. I feel much better."

"You are welcome, nonaii. Now, we must return. I am needed."

As they turned to leave, Catherine heard the snapping of branches behind them. Compared to her previous experiences in the highlands, the snapping was loud. A knot formed in her stomach. When she craned her head around, she saw what she'd expected to see.

A gogooi stood only meters from them.

The dark brown creature was the size of an elk, but with much shorter legs. Its coat was smooth, its musculature bulky, and it had three thick horns that protruded from its head. Golden brown eyes stared at them as the gogooi snuffed, fog spewing from its mouth.

Shit, Catherine said. But the word came out silent as she slowly reached for her weapon, not taking her eyes off the creature. But her hand found nothing. She'd left her weapon behind, knowing she'd be out with Koni. The gogooi snuffed again, this time more aggressively. Suddenly the beast came charging at them.

Koni lunged in front of Catherine and grabbed the gogooi by its horns while letting out a long growl. The creature's progress ceased as it fought the control Koni had over it, snuffing with even greater ferocity and revealing rows of spine-like protrusions from its open jaw. Koni spoke to the creature in Sunai, his orders commanding but with a bit of soothing and even reverence as he sustained his grip on the horns. Within a few moments, the gogooi stood still except for the jerking of its head, still trying to regain its freedom from Koni's meaty hands. And finally, the gogooi's headjerks and snuffs diminished, and eventually ceased. Koni spoke to the animal, stroking its hide and muttering something that Catherine didn't understand.

"You may touch him before I release him," Koni told her.

Catherine, still in awe at the spectacle, approached the beast, steering clear of its menacing jaw. She reached out and touched its flank; the hide had a smooth sturdy feel that reminded her of cow leather, but perhaps oilier. Koni spoke to the beast again before releasing him. The gogooi remained for a moment before trotting off into the brush.

"Where did you learn that?" Catherine said.

"My father taught me, as a child," he said, his eyes still on the animal. "Before my acceptance, before I left my family to serve Suna, we lived in a highland region like this one, but far from here."

They watched the gogooi disappear up the mountain before they turned and made their descent into Jula.

Once off duty, Snow left Engineering and went to his quarters. He stripped off his dirty uniform, revealing his pale, thin body with its many tattoos. He was due for a new tattoo, one that reflected this mission in some way, one that would tell a story. He hadn't gotten around to it on the Thirty, and the art of inking hadn't reached the other worlds. Except for the Korvali, whom Snow suspected could create a tattoo worth having, at least based on Eshel's intricate and impeccably executed marking.

"Yeah, you're probably not getting a Korvali tattoo anytime soon," he muttered with a chuckle. He'd have to ask Eshel about offering inking as one of the services the Korvali provided in exchange for Alliance membership. Hell, after this long, Eshel might even appreciate the joke. But then he remembered… there would be no asking Eshel anything. Not anymore.

He took a shower, scrubbing himself quickly before the water snapped off when his timer told it to. He'd programmed it that way, knowing that he'd otherwise exceed his allotment to take the long showers he missed so much.

Coffee. He began heating water to make a cup. He would never dare imbibe this late under normal circumstances. In the past, he suffered for it with sleepless nights thinking about too many things. About Jooni.

Through Catherine's wrangling, Jooni had come to visit him when she found out *Cornelia* had returned to Suna. The relief he'd felt at the sight of her under that ridiculous blonde wig was immeasurable, and he realized then just how stupid he'd been for walking out on her after she ended their relationship. She was only trying to protect herself, her powerful uncle, and him. They'd talked: he apologized for storming out, she apologized for not responding to his delayed message of apology, delivered to her secretly with Catherine's help. And since then, they'd surreptitiously spent more time together, the thorny topic of her emigration put aside for now.

Snow sipped his coffee while he dressed himself, donning a pair of boots and a warm coat. He polished off his cup before leaving his quarters, hoping the MAs wouldn't give him any shit for going out alone this late. But when he saw a couple of friendly faces standing guard, he knew he'd have no problem.

As he walked through Jula, Suna's many moons lighting the way, the frigid wind tore through his coat while he kept a vigilant eye on his surrounds. It was late enough that even the scum wouldn't be out. Tom would give him hell for going out alone this time, but Snow wasn't too worried about safety. So much time had passed since that incident with the gumiia... and Jula's moon season meant he was too bundled up to be recognized. And he'd found different routes to Jooni's home once Catherine gave him a full schematic of Jula's old tunnels.

After weaving his way through the seeping tunnel and brushing away the occasional drip upon his hood or face, he arrived at Jooni's. When she opened her door, she stood before him in her winter gowns.

"You wear your ear jewels!" she said in delight.

He touched one of his metallic earrings. "Yup. A beautiful Sunai woman gave them to me." He put his arms around her delicate frame, inhaling her unique blend of spiced tea and her own scent as he began unbuttoning her gown.

Later, they sat upon Jooni's cushions and played for hours, until Jooni announced that she must begin work at her shop. Snow offered no argument, knowing he would see her soon.

"Snow," she said, re-buttoning her gown. "I have important news. You must no share this, and you must no speak of it to your leadership. If you do, you will ruin it."

Dread came over Snow at what this news could be, news so dire that he couldn't even go to Catherine, or Yamamoto.

"I have gone to military consulate and requested permission to join your Space Corps," she said.

Snow broke into a smile.

CHAPTER 2

Eshel awoke suddenly, his eyes surveying the area, searching for any sign of trouble. But everything appeared as it had when he'd entered his slumber: the Sunai craft's instruments still showed them heading in the proper direction, the desolate space around them had no problematic phenomena, and Ashan sat quietly, keeping watch while Eshel rested. Eshel checked their position; they were getting close to Korvalis. He stood up to remove the sleep from his body.

"I was just about to wake you," Ashan said. "It is time to send the transmission to Station Fourteen."

"You are certain of this?" Eshel said. "Many years have passed since you served at the station."

"I am certain," Ashan said. "Those in the vokalis, those I worked with before my escape, acknowledged the transmission from Grono Amsala and await our arrival."

Eshel paused for a moment. "Send it."

Ashan did so. The message would route through Grono Amsala and the response, if they received one, would do the same. They had agreed to wait one hour. If they received no response within that time, they must abort the operation and rendezvous with the Grono at a location determined by him. But before long, they received word.

They were cleared to proceed.

In silence they continued on. After Eshel engaged their clandestine device, only one thing captured his attention: there, in the distance, was his homeworld. Today it remained entirely enshrouded in clouds, with not a patch of ocean to be seen. It gave him unexpected pleasure, as did the prospect of taking in its oceans and perhaps swimming in them soon. However, his pleasure quickly gave way to apprehension about breaching the border and arriving at the surface without incident.

He glanced over at Ashan, who stared at the planet. His face appeared colder than usual, his blue eyes murky and a hint of a sneer at the edge of his mouth. Thirteen months had passed since Eshel last stood upon Korvalis. For Ashan, well over six Earth years had passed.

In the distance, Eshel saw Station 14 and even Stations 15 and 16. When they crossed the border, the two men remained quiet, watchful eyes looking for Guard ships. Slowly, they inched their way toward the cloud cover. And as expected, two Guard ships deployed and headed to the border to examine the disturbance their ship had created by invading Korvalis's net. Eshel slowed the ship even more as they drew closer to Station 14, his eyes focused, along with Ashan's, on the one bay door that remained open.

Eshel still had his doubts that such a ploy would work. After his abduction and rescue from Korvalis, and after Catherine having been detected on Fallal Hall's surveillance, the leadership would have learned. They would have learned that Catherine had some type of cloaking device, deduced that the craft which had brought her and Tom to Korvalis had generated the disturbance in their net during that time period, and likely discovered that the cloaking device exploited the genetic differences between human and Korvali, resulting in the Korvali inability to detect a narrow segment of the visual range that humans took for granted. If he and his father had figured this out, they could as well, given such clues.

Yet, despite Eshel's protestations, Ashan, who knew the details of Eshel's rescue, still insisted that the vokalis—their allies—would protect them in this instance, that there was a reason they must contact those they contacted and that they must go to the station Ashan once supervised, rather than any of the other 20 stations. Eshel wondered at the power Ashan would have, especially after all this time, that would render him able to achieve such a feat. However, Ashan's best argument was that merely discovering the nature of the cloaking device, assuming they fully understood it, did not mean they had the means to quickly develop technology to counteract it. For that, they would need the humans, or even the Sunai. Such facts did not guarantee Eshel and Ashan's success; but they kept the risk at a level that Eshel found acceptable.

Beginning to feel hope that his risk estimates were correct, Eshel navigated the Sunai craft into the narrow bay door and set down, disengaging the clandestine device as he did. Two Guard in black robes entered when the bay door shut.

Eshel and Ashan exited the craft and stood before the Guard, placing their left hands upon their right shoulders to reveal their crests. The two Guard, a male and a female, peered at them for several moments, examining their hands, their faces, and their brown makeshift robes, before finally revealing their own circular tattoos.

"You will take this," the woman said, motioning to another craft nearby, a small shuttle.

Eshel and Ashan retrieved their belongings from the Sunai ship and put them in the shuttle. The woman followed them into the shuttle and handed them two dark gray robes, the color worn by the Moshal. They changed into them and put their brown robes in the Sunai ship. She gave a brief primer on the functions of the shuttle, to which Ashan gave acknowledgement.

"You have the coordinates," she said to Ashan.

"Yes," he said.

Once she exited, Ashan started the shuttle's engine, directing it out of the bay and toward the bright cloud cover.

But before they reached the clouds, the console emitted a high-pitched sound. Eshel's eyes darted to the display; two Guard ships headed their way and were soon upon them. Eshel closed his eyes for a moment. When he opened them, he saw a bright flash of light. He blinked a couple of times, wondering if they'd been attacked. The shuttle slowed.

"What was that?" Eshel said.

"A warning," Ashan said. "We must follow them back to the station, or the next flash will be the last."

Ideas for attacking those who detained them, each more violent than the last, convened in Eshel's mind. But each would have consequences even more dismal than what they faced now. In great frustration, he waited while Ashan came about and followed the two ships back—not to Station 14, but to Station 15. Eshel quickly sent a transmission to Grono Amsala.

After docking, Eshel and Ashan emerged from their shuttle. They refrained from putting their hands to their shoulders, which Ashan had told him would suggest, along with their dark gray robes, that they belonged to the Moshal clan and thus did not need to show their crests. Four Guard surrounded them, one aiming a weapon at them. Two of the Guard led them away while the remaining two trailed behind.

Once inside the station, they proceeded down a stark white hallway until they reached a door. A Guardsman opened the door, and Eshel and Ashan entered. The room had only a polymer bench along its white walls, and a window that looked out upon the darkness of space. The door shut, leaving them alone.

Eshel turned to Ashan.

"I do not know what is wrong," Ashan said. "We had authorization to leave the station. Perhaps there is an informant among the vokalis."

Eshel sat on the polymer chair, the feel of the chair strange to him, having only sat upon wood and stone on his homeworld, rather than the manufactured materials that had proven practical in space. He began to consider each possible way to remedy their situation, including their backup plan. Their backup plan would require Grono Amsala's assistance, a last resort that Eshel had not yet determined was necessary. His other ideas... they would involve him utilizing his improved self-defense skills. However, Eshel dreaded this even more than their backup plan. To utilize such methods, on his homeworld, with his own people... would be ignoble indeed.

After some time, the door opened, and in walked a Guardsman. Older than Eshel but younger than Ashan, he was thin and gaunt, a mottled scar on his cheek. As they stood up, he looked at both of their faces, then at their hands. His gaze lingered on Eshel's hand before giving Eshel an unsettling stare.

"I know you, Volen," Ashan said to the Guardsman. "Do you not know me?"

"I know you," he replied coldly. "I know you both. You are the traitors."

"We stand with Korvalis," Ashan said, just as coldly. "Not with Elisan, nor his violation of our Doctrine."

"What do you know of Doctrine?" Volen asked. "You have not lived amidst your people for years, after your trickery took you to the lands of the others."

"I do not need to live amidst our people to know our Doctrine," Ashan said.

Volen glanced at Eshel. "Why do you bring this Shereb oppressor here?"

"He is no oppressor," Ashan said. "It is he who has spurred the vokalis to gather in this way, to plan in this way. You would be wise to remember that." Ashan paused. "You risk everything by detaining us, Volen. We are authorized to proceed to the surface."

Volen raised his eyebrows. "I received no such authorization."

"Then go find it," Ashan said.

Volen hesitated for several moments before leaving. After a short while, he returned, giving Eshel another onceover, perhaps with a slightly less critical eye, before turning his gaze to Ashan.

"You will be safe to deploy shortly," Volen said. "Take your craft to the surface, to the location discussed with those you communicate with." He looked at Eshel, his blue eyes making contact. "You knew Mosel, who aided in your escape and accompanied your party of absconders."

"I did," Eshel said.

"Did you witness her passing?"

"Yes."

"I am told you used the science to secure your own survival, Shereb," he said. "Why did you not share this with Mosel, with the others who would perish with her?"

Eshel, disliking the questions almost as much as he disliked Volen, said nothing.

Volen took a step closer to Eshel. "You will answer."

"Mosel and the others are not your concern," Eshel said.

"The others are not," Volen said. "Mosel is. She was my sister. I still see her."

Eshel, now understanding Volen's hostility, softened his tone. "The opportunity to leave Korvalis revealed itself before I had tested the therapy. I had only enough for myself." Eshel paused. "Mosel passed peacefully."

Volen broke eye contact for a moment. "I believed you only behaving with the self-interest of a Shereb."

"We are all self-interested, Guardsman," Eshel said. "If we were not, you would not distrust me simply because I wear a leaf on my hand."

The Guardsman stared at him for some time before he stood up. "Go," he said. "Do what you must."

Ashan landed the shuttlecraft beneath the canopy of a seshac tree, its weeping branches reaching the ground and hiding the craft. Eshel and Ashan donned their gear and began walking.

Eshel took a deep breath of humid air, feeling immediately refreshed after so long a period in the dry airs of Suna, of Calyyt-Calloq, of *Cornelia*. Gone was the minor but persistent worry that he would overheat and become ill, as he had come close to doing on many occasions offworld. He looked around him, basking in the familiarity of the great tree, its weeping leaves, the soft light of the hidden sun, and, perhaps most of all, the vast gray ocean surrounding the island they stood upon. Other than the sea lapping against the rocky shoreline, it was all so quiet. How he'd missed that.

Nearby, Ashan also took in his surroundings, a look of wonder on his face as he appeared to inhale the smell of the ocean and tree. But along with the wonderment remained clouded eyes.

They began searching for a sea vessel, one that would take them to their destination, to the large body of land north of them, where many of Korvalis's clans resided. They soon found two wooden boats: one small, for a single person, and another that would fit both of them.

Eshel studied the roiling sea. A storm was coming, but likely a small one. "The tides do not favor us."

The two men waited in the ship until the storm passed and the tides shifted to take them north. They stepped into the boat, carefully protecting their gear, allowing their robes to become wet on the bottom. Eshel recalled the brown robes he and Ashan had worn for so long. The Sunai fabric, while sturdy and reasonably comfortable, had no ability to repel water or moisture, and the brown would have attracted attention. He was glad to wear a true Korvali robe once more.

They picked up the oars and began to row, the tide not fully thrusting them north, but not fighting them either. Eshel wielded his oar, chagrined at how his technique had slipped and his strength had waned, despite his training on *Cornelia*. They wove between small islands, some only large enough for a fluff of green sea grass or perhaps a jutting dark rock. How strange the ebony rocks appeared to him, having grown up with the gleaming white rock of the west. The rain came down upon them, and Eshel felt better than he had in a long time as the drops landed confidently upon his face and dripped into his eyes. He recalled the reactions of the humans at boot camp when the rain fell hard, how they'd cowered from it, blinking their sensitive eyes and wiping their faces. It was perhaps the only time in which his drill instructor appeared impressed with him, at least until something unusual occurred, a story he'd still never shared with anyone.

They paddled for some time until, in the distance, Eshel spotted them. First, a boat with a single person in it. Then another. Then two sets of arms, stroking through the water, swimming in another direction. And finally, many of them, in the sea and along the shoreline, stopping what they were doing to notice the two strange, gray-robed men intruding upon their territory.

Eshel and Ashan docked their vessel and stepped ashore, webbed hands open and in front of them to indicate that they carried no weapons. The villagers only watched them. They were nude and wore a dotted marking on their hands; on many of the older villagers, the marking went beyond the hand and up the arm. It was the marking of the southern Shemal. Before Eshel could speak, a group of patrollers surrounded them, spears in their hands.

Perhaps a full head taller than him or Ashan, the patrollers stared down at them with green eyes, greener than any he'd ever seen, with the exception of his father. His father had told him of the southern Shemal, of their long spears and their great stature. Ashan put his hand to his shoulder, and Eshel did the same. As Eshel had expected, the towering patrollers shifted their green eyes to the magenta leaf that indicated his belonging to the Shereb clan, their gazes lingering on it before raising their spears. Before they could make any move, Eshel spoke.

"I am a friend," he said in Old Korvali, the ancient tongue of the primitives that the civilized clans rarely learned, much less spoke. "My father was Shemal. He was Othniel, of the Elliptical Isles. Koriel expects us."

The patrollers ceased their progress.

"Koriel spoke of no Shereb," a man said.

"Koriel expects two outsiders," Eshel said. "Myself, and a Moshal."

The patrollers stood in silence, spears still raised.

"Come," the man said.

Later, Eshel and Ashan still followed two patrollers along the shoreline, the sea to their right and bright green sea grass under their feet, as the rest of the Shemal patrollers trailed behind them. They passed many wooden huts and numerous other unclothed Shemal, all of whom stared at Eshel and Ashan. Eshel, who like most Korvali had spent little time outside his own clan's territory, still found it strange that he would encounter as much staring here as he had when he traveled to the outside worlds. They turned and entered the cool darkness of the forest. When they encountered a fire pit surrounded by flat slabs of gray stone, the patrollers halted.

The man who'd spoken to them disappeared behind one of the huts. Soon, he reemerged with an old woman in a woven robe, her hair faded and her stride slowed with age. The woman spoke quietly to the messenger, who came over and took Eshel and Ashan's gear. Eshel looked over at Ashan, who gave a Calyyt sign indicating that he offer no resistance. The messenger walked off with the gear and disappeared.

The old woman approached. Once only a couple of meters away, she brought her hand to her shoulder, revealing a tattoo with a different dotting pattern than the others. When Eshel and Ashan did the same, the woman eyed Eshel's crest before turning her attention to Ashan.

"Why do you bring this Shereb here?" she said in Korvali, rather than Old Korvali.

"Who are you?" Ashan said.

"Answer my question," she said.

"He is with me," Ashan said. "Koriel was informed there would be two of us."

"We were told of two men, but no Shereb."

"This Shereb's father is Othniel, of the Shemal. Look at his eyes; you will see the green in them. He is the other who left, who lived among the outerworlds." Ashan gestured to the sky.

She turned to Eshel. "Tell me of Othniel."

Eshel spoke of his father, listing his kin, when he'd left the clan to mate and pursue science, even offering a detail his father had shared with him about his own mother, about her ability to remain submerged underwater longer than any other native of the Elliptical Isles.

The old woman listened to all he said, gazing at him as if searching for a resemblance. "So you are Eshel." When Eshel gave his acknowledgement, the woman added, "And where is Othniel? Does he know of your return?"

Eshel hesitated, not expecting the question. "He is dead. Murdered by the malkaris's eldest son."

The woman's face paled. "Elan is dead."

"I killed him, by tradition of the sher keltar."

She raised her eyebrows. "Since when does a Shereb follow the ancient ways?" she said in Old Korvali.

"Since his Shemal father taught him the ancient ways," Eshel responded in the same tongue.

The woman said nothing, her expression unreadable. She looked at Ashan, then back at him.

"I am Koriel."

CHAPTER 3

Eshel and Ashan sat upon the gray stones near the fire pit, the crackling blaze illuminating the others who sat nearby. Darkness had come. The villagers, adult and child, had donned their robes. Their robes were made not from the sophisticated fabric Eshel and Ashan took for granted, but instead from a coarser, woven fiber without dye. All drank water from wooden cups and ate large wooden bowls of mollusks and sea plants with their hands. They ate in silence, until a small child spoke. Several of the others turned an eye on the child, while the male next to him briefly placed his hand over the child's mouth. Eshel relished the taste and texture of the food, which had more pronounced salinity than Derovian ornon and sea vegetables. He glanced over at Ashan, who focused intently on the food he'd gone without for so many years.

The Shemal villagers allowed Eshel and Ashan to eat with them, but none sat near them. When they'd finished eating, none spoke to them, either. But before Eshel could speak, something captured the attention of the others, who moved their gazes to the forest. A woman emerged from the trees, her mate at her side. Her mate held an infant, a child still small enough to be carried, which meant it had been born very recently. Many requested permission to hold the quiet infant, to which the mother and father agreed, and each held him for a few moments before passing him to the next suitor. Eshel stood up and approached the scene, knowing his presence would bother them but not caring, knowing that years had passed since he'd seen a newborn, and that soon the child would begin to walk and seem more like them. Eshel would not deign to ask if he could hold the infant; he only wanted to see it, to be near it. He stood back just a little, catching a closer glimpse of the child, its body plumper that it would be in a few more weeks, its greenish eyes huge as it took in all that was around it. Once the others returned the infant to its parents, the crowd dissipated and Eshel rejoined Ashan, who still sat with his empty bowl.

Earlier, they'd met with Koriel and seven other men and women, most of whom Ashan's contacts had mentioned and instructed them to rendezvous with. They'd talked at length about what was to come. Eshel informed them of plans they'd made thus far; he also requested that exceptions be made for certain approved individuals to trespass in Shemal territory from time to time, with appropriate escorting by Shemal patrollers. The Shemal had grown to hate Elisan and the malkaris, and they resented the diminishing of their voice within the assembly, as well as the voices of all the primitive tribes in the remote territories. Thus, the Shemal began to show more receptiveness to the plan that Eshel and Ashan had laid out. Based on what his father had told him, their eating together afterward was a very good sign, even if nobody sat near them or spoke to them. Yet, despite such progress, a pack of Shemal patrollers stood nearby during the entire gathering, spears in hand.

It was time to sleep. Koriel's granddaughter led Eshel and Ashan up a tree ladder and into the crown of the tree, where they'd built a wooden hut upon the tree's thick branches, its architecture cleverly adapted to the tree's structure. Similar huts sat within most of the trees, strung together by an elaborate network of bridges. The girl opened the door, revealing a narrow room containing only two wooden platforms, one on each side. Eshel and Ashan chose their sides and lay down. Eshel wondered where his belongings were, feeling more unease at the thought of his gear—the items necessary to do what he and Ashan needed to do—in the hands of strangers. But he was told to trust the Shemal, to honor their ways. He would say nothing until morning.

When Eshel awoke, the other platform lay empty. Eshel stood, put on his robe, and left the hut. A mist hung about the trees—not the dense, blinding sort, but a thin hint of a mist that made everything seem quieter. He descended the ladder and spoke to one of the villagers, who carried a woven basket of mollusks.

"Where is my Moshal comrade?" he asked.

The green-eyed man stared at him for several moments before he gestured south. It was as Eshel had expected: Ashan was at sea, swimming. When Eshel arrived at the shoreline and removed his robe, carefully setting it aside on a rock, he entered the cool water, the spectacular coolness of it invigorating him. He submerged himself and began to swim out to sea. And while the number of strokes he could take before coming up for air was again quite low, he cared not, for the pleasure of it, the sheer vastness of the sea and how it felt to him, was more than enough to satisfy him.

Eshel swam for some time, past boats with Shemal who eyed him and his magenta marking, past others who swam in pairs this way and that, and past tiny islands of dark gray rock and salty earth. He submerged himself completely numerous times, taking in the small dark fish that simultaneously flitted from one direction to another, the larger bulbous green fish that stung him if he got too close, the bright multi-branched diaphanous structures that lined the sea floor, and even, from a distance, the giant flat creature that would periodically leap from the water, soar a vast arc, and submerge itself again. Once so far out that he could see nothing but gray sea and uninhabited islands enshrouded in the mist, he perched himself on a rock. And instead of thinking forward as he had for more days than he could recall, he thought back. To Catherine.

He had left her. Left her aboard *Cornelia*, not only with the lie of his whereabouts and doings, but without her having heard the news from his own voice. Ferguson and Yamamoto had ordered him to remain quiet about his plans and keep them from her. He didn't fully support this order, but understood it just the same. Grono Amsala had said nothing when Ferguson issued the order; looking back,

Eshel realized such restraint was out of character for the Sunai man who opined on everything with great fervor. Now Eshel understood that perhaps the Grono had also preferred another way, probably because he too knew that Catherine was intelligent, resourceful, and, most of all, trustworthy. Yet Eshel knew that such orders could be overlooked later, if necessary.

Eshel could hardly believe that he'd learned to tolerate being near Grono Amsala for any length of time, much less entrust such crucial information to him, to have him part of something so important. Under normal circumstances, regardless of Catherine's persuasions, he would never place trust in any Sunai. But he now knew, as Catherine always had, that enlisting Grono Amsala was perhaps a wise move, and that it would work for two reasons: first, Grono Amsala wanted to be Gronoi more than he wanted anything, and thus would go to considerable lengths to ensure the mission's success. And two, Eshel had come to learn that gaining the support of the Sunai was just as important as gaining that of the humans.

Yet, order or no order, Eshel could have said goodbye to Catherine in person, and chose not to. He could not face her, could not lie to her when he knew the truth. He could not, not after what she'd suffered at the hands of Elisan and the despicable abomination Elisan's scientists had made in his likeness. But as he sat there among the misty sea, he knew the truth… that he'd avoided such a difficulty for more selfish reasons. Perhaps that made him no better than Tom, who'd lacked the courage to face the woman he cared for and tell the difficult truth. Tom had eventually found that courage, however, had spoken to Maria and said what needed saying. But, cowardly or not, Eshel had made his choice, and he must live with it.

Now it was time to face the future, the one he had discussed with his father and mother, the one for which he had risked his life, for which he had made sacrifices. Opportunity had come sooner than he had expected, and he would do whatever necessary to make the most of it.

When Eshel swam back to shore, Ashan stood waiting for him, after which they dressed and went to speak to Koriel and the others. Eshel was relieved to see a patroller emerge with their belongings. It was time for them to leave and go west, to the place where everything would begin.

Eshel and Ashan took one of the two-person sea boats and began paddling west. Despite there being a sizable uninhabited region between Shemal territory and the industrialized regions to the west, by sea they could travel more swiftly, they were less visible, and they would reach their destination with minimal intrusion into foreign territory for both of them.

As they paddled, the mist lifted and the sun emerged, warming them in the chilly oceanic breeze. The tides of the southern sea were vastly more predictable than those of the more remote regions to the east, and wouldn't work against them to any notable degree that day. They rowed west for some time, their pace good but perhaps slower than it should have been; a former Air Guardsman and a scientist had neither of them grown up with oars in their hands. They travelled through the day and rested at night. Near dusk on the second day, they began to see it.

Islands. White rocks jutting from the sea. And a large crescent-shaped bay. Beyond it all, a cliff rose from the sea. Built within the cliffside were numerous metal and glass structures. Similar but smaller structures stood just above the sea, resting on sturdy metal piers, protected in part by the tall rocks that sheltered them from the incoming swells. The giant windows in these dwellings did more than allow sea vistas; they curved in such a way as to encourage deflection of seawater away from the structures. Narrow suspension bridges linked many of the dwellings together and, in some cases, stretched all the way to the shoreline. Wooden boats became far fewer, replaced by more sophisticated boats powered by technology. They headed into the industrialized region... into Osecal country.

Eshel had seen this place before, having swum here in the past, during his longer swims that had begun at the western shores. He'd always admired the unique design of the sea dwellings, built after the Osecal were banished from Fallal Hall and made feasible by the protection of the region's cove and rocks. To Eshel, the Osecal did not quite compare with the Shereb when it came to scientific innovation; but in architecture, they stood above all. Even Ashan, who stared at the buildings in wonder, admitted as much.

Back then, the Osecal would spot his magenta tattoo and eye him with suspicion, but never accost him. They would only watch, ensuring he did not bring trouble with him. Now, those they passed noticed their gray robes and did the same, as Eshel kept his hood on and his tattoo hidden. He marveled at the size of the industrialized region, how small it seemed when compared to the vast territories of the primitives. So few the industrialized clans were, yet so much power the few had over the many, and it took only one shift in leadership to begin ruin of what his people—industrialized or primitive—had spent millennia building.

Eshel and Ashan paddled past the islands, beyond the dwellings, and under the bridges, until they arrived at their destination. Ashan secured the boat to a small dock built below the structure. They gathered their things, climbed a ladder to a deck, and opened the door.

Inside stood a woman with gray eyes that gazed at them both. Ashan abruptly halted. When Eshel followed Ashan's gaze, he saw what had given him pause. The woman's hand bore a magenta leaf.

CHAPTER 4

Catherine's door sounded. Tom, arriving to accompany her into Jula. And on time, even. She voiced him in while securing her boots. But when she looked up, the man in the black Space Corps parka wasn't Tom.

"Mahoney," she said, standing up.

"Hey, C," Mahoney said, his fair hair recently cut. "Tom got called up. He said you needed an escort into Jula, and I need off this damned ship. Care to join me?"

She smiled, unexpectedly happy to see him. "Sure."

They exited the ship and stepped into the cold that grew milder every day as the frozen snow began turning to slush.

"Where do you need to go?" Mahoney said.

"Nowhere in particular," she admitted. "I just wanted to get outside. I wouldn't mind some dried gogooi for my quarters, though. You?"

"I want to check out one of the music shops. I'm not much of a musician, but I've always wanted to try a few of their instruments and never got the chance last time we were here. Maybe afterward we can get some lunch?" he asked.

"Perfect. And I know a good music shop."

Catherine led Mahoney through the streets of Jula, walking swiftly to keep warm. As they entered the shop, the familiar smell of wood and unfermented kala flooded her, reminding her of the op that brought down the biocrackers. Catherine removed her hood and smiled at the Sunai woman who emerged from the back.

"Jooni!"

Jooni smiled in return. She wore jewels around her neck, and her thick, fur-lined wrap seemed to dwarf her thin figure.

"Jooni, this is Michael Mahoney, a friend of mine." She turned to Mahoney. "Jooni helps me with my guitar."

Mahoney approached Jooni and held out his palm to meet hers.

"Mahoney wants to try some of the instruments," Catherine said. "And I need a new song for my guitar. Do you have any Sunai songs that are good for beginners?"

"Of course, Catherine," Jooni said, pointing. "Those are for beginner. Press button for sample." She gestured to Mahoney. "Follow me. You will try guitar first. Human male always like guitar."

While Jooni selected a guitar for Mahoney, Catherine listened to the samples and picked a few. She paid Jooni while Mahoney fumbled out a warbled tune on his four-stringed instrument.

"Now that's talent, right there," Mahoney said, grinning as he placed the instrument back on its mount.

Catherine laughed. They thanked Jooni and left. After looking at some other shops and purchasing snacks to stow on the ship, they found an eatery and ordered their meals.

"So how are you doing?" Mahoney asked, holding his clay cup of kala. "Any residual effects from the clone attack?"

"Some minor headaches, fatigue… but it's better now." She sipped her spiced tea.

"How do you feel about Eshel being gone? I didn't even know him, but it seems weird."

Her face grew hot. "Yeah. I think a lot of people feel that way. At least those who liked him," she added. They sat silent for a moment, until Catherine set down her tea. "Look, Mahoney… I'm sorry. For what happened between us."

He shook his head. "It's alright."

"I… I liked being with you. A lot. I don't want you to think otherwise."

A Sunai woman, neck and hands adorned with metallic jewelry, set their meal in front of them, a pile of seared gogooi over a heap of grains, along with two bowls of thick soup. They scooped some food onto their plates; Catherine took a sip of the spicy soup, its steam warming her face, before she took a bite of gogooi.

"Why did you end things?" Mahoney asked.

Catherine stopped chewing.

"Look, C, it's fine. I wasn't looking for anything serious anyway. I just… I want to know the real reason."

She finished chewing, glad for a few moments to consider what to say. "Um… I guess… I guess I didn't see it having a future." In truth, she'd gotten tired of hiding so much from Mahoney when they'd dated—her work as COO, her project with Holloway, even her brief encounter with Eshel. A future, considered or not, seemed impossible under such circumstances.

"A future?" he said, his eyebrows raised. "That's important to you?"

"I suppose it is. You?"

"Someday." He cocked his head, like he had more to say. "How do you think you're going to have a future with Eshel?"

She looked down, her face growing hot again. "I never said I did."

"That's not what I hear."

Irritated, Catherine made a face. "You believe everything you hear?"

"Look, C, I don't mean to be an asshole. But I suspected even back then that you still cared about him. Just because we didn't go anywhere doesn't mean I want to see you waste your time on a guy who puts his political agenda before his personal life."

She sighed, twirling her soup in its bowl. "Mahoney, you're preaching to the choir."

Mahoney smiled.

Relieved, Catherine returned the smile and grabbed another handful of food.

Varan Mel'Kavi flashed a big Derovian smile as he gestured with a six-digit hand. "I'll be next door if you need me, Lieutenant Finnegan!"

"Okay, Varan," Catherine told her subordinate as he shuffled out to perform his duties alongside a fellow Derovian in Anka Henriksen's lab, rather than endure a day of working alone. She turned to Holloway. "You still have the data hidden in our special place, right?" she said quietly. "Steele hasn't said a word, but I don't trust him and you shouldn't either."

He made a face. "Balls to him. Of course I don't trust that old bastard. The data are safe."

"Made any progress on it?"

He glanced around, lowering his voice more. "I finalized the mouse model, the amended version that ended up working. And I've made a lot of progress adapting the model to the human genome."

"Great!" she whispered.

"You did that entire mouse experiment by yourself… it's the least I could do. I've run into snags… there are several areas where the human genome just doesn't map well to that of a mouse."

She nodded. "Let me work on it for a while. I have a lot more time these days." Holloway's brows furrowed. "Hey, we got the model to work in the mice. Making it work in humans is just one more step. We'll get there."

"It's not that," he said, looking around again. "I've been on edge ever since that situation with Steele. That bastard stole our data and used it to blackmail me, and he tried to corner you. We're both lucky that I can hack and you can fight. Next time, he could really hurt us."

"I don't see how," Catherine argued. "He did all that because he thought he had the better hand. Now he knows he doesn't. If he tries something, we can take him down."

He shook his head. "Now he's checking on us every day, making sure we're working. I'm not comfortable with this, Catherine. The mission is almost over… it's not worth getting it stolen again or getting caught. Can't we just wait a little longer? Once back on Earth, we can work without anyone knowing."

Catherine sighed. "Holloway…"

Holloway's cheeks flushed. "I'm tired of looking over my shoulder, yeah? I've got to think about my girlfriend, my future. And you should too. You take more chances than you used to."

Before Catherine could respond, the lab door opened. Steele entered, his gaunt face glancing at Holloway before turning his gaze on her. A flash of him touching her hair went through her mind, and she made an effort to ensure her face didn't match her feelings. They saluted.

"Why aren't you both working?" he said.

"We are, Sir," Catherine said. "Just finishing a meeting."

Steele looked around the lab. "Where is Private Mel'Kavi?"

"Next door, Sir," Catherine said.

"What for?"

Catherine gritted her teeth. "He works better with Dorel to talk to, Sir."

"He doesn't need someone to talk to, Lieutenant. He needs to shut his mouth and work." He handed Catherine a portable. "Another project for you both. Have it completed by the end of the week. And I want Private Mel'Kavi back in his seat immediately."

"Yes, Sir," Catherine said as Steele turned and left.

The door buzzed just as Tom finished putting on his pants. He glanced over at the screen.

Maria.

Tom raised his eyebrows, a mixture of nervousness and anticipation coming over him. Other than greeting one another in the mess, it was the first time he'd seen her since he'd told her the truth, the truth that had surprised her as much as him. He grabbed a t-shirt and glanced in the mirror before voicing her in. Maria looked fresh-faced, like she always did just before beginning duty, her still-moist hair up in its bun.

"Hey, Beautiful," Tom said, grinning.

"Hey, Kingston. I'm on duty soon… but I wanted to talk to you."

Tom motioned to his chair, pulling it out for her. As she sat down, he turned his chair backward and did the same. He wanted to say all kinds of stuff—tell her how glad he was to see her, make a few jokes—but something told him to shut his mouth and listen.

"I'm glad you came and talked to me," she said. "About how you felt, about us. That took a lot of guts."

He shrugged. "It's the truth."

Maria's face contorted briefly as she glanced away for only a moment. And that's when Tom knew he wouldn't get the news he'd hoped for.

"I'm with someone else now," she said. "I can't just…"

"Can't what?"

"It's better this way," she said.

"Why?" Tom said disdainfully.

"Don't start," she warned.

"Don't start what, Maria? You said it's better this way and I want to know why."

"Because it is."

"That's not an answer," Tom said.

"That's the only answer you're getting," she snapped.

Tom sighed in frustration. "Why are you digging in your heels? I'm just trying to understand why you want to be with him. I'm just not seeing it."

"I'm not digging in my heels—"

"Yeah, you are."

Her dark eyes bore into him. "You interrupted me."

He put his hands up. "Sorry."

"I'm not just being stubborn," she went on. "You think everyone's stubborn when they won't give you what you want, when you want it."

Tom wanted to argue again, but knew that doing so would only make things worse. "Maria, I accepted a while ago that I'm probably not getting what I want out of this situation. I guess… I just want to understand why Ferrars. But maybe there's nothing to understand. I fucked everything up with you, and he didn't."

Maria sat for several moments. Finally, she uncrossed her arms and leaned forward. "He wants what I want, Tom. He wants a family."

Tom stared at her. "A family? What... what about your career?"

"You can have a career and a family, Tom."

"You can't bring kids on space missions. You know that."

"I've been on plenty of missions," she said. "Long, short, and in-between. I'm ready for a career at Headquarters, for short missions. I'm ready... for something else."

Tom, still flabbergasted at Maria's admission, shook his head. "How long have you known this?"

"It's something I've thought about for a while. I've already talked to Headquarters about making a change when the mission ends, and they're game for it." She paused, watching him. "Have you ever thought about it?"

"Working at Headquarters?" he said. "When I'm older, maybe."

"No. I mean about having a family."

Tom made a face. Then he chuckled. "No."

"Why not?"

"Come on. I'd be a terrible father."

She gave him a dubious look. "How can you say that? After the way you've looked out for Snow, for Catherine... and Eshel too, when no one else wanted anything to do with him?"

He shrugged. "So? I'm a soldier and I look out for mine."

"That's what fathers do."

He cocked his head in acknowledgment. "It's not just that. You know I like people—all kinds of people—but I'd never bring a child into the world we live in."

Maria looked at him with disapproval. "It doesn't have to be like military social services, like what you grew up with. And you're a service kid and you turned out okay."

He shook his head. "You don't know everything, Maria. Kids are vulnerable, to all kinds of shit, whether they're service kids or not." Tom, hardly knowing what to say next, sat in silence for several moments. He glanced at the clock. "You're on duty, darlin'. Don't want to make you late."

Maria nodded and stood up.

"Thanks, M," Tom said. "For being honest."

"You too." Maria left.

Catherine sipped kala as the aroma of roasted gogooi lingered in Koni's home. His servant gathered their empty plates and took them away as Catherine and Koni took in the view of Jula.

Koni's expression changed. "I must speak of a difficult topic, nonaii, so that I may issue warning."

"Warning?" she said. "What happened?"

"This comrade of yours, with the markings... Lieutenant Jebediah Snow. He has again attempted to consort with the daughter of Gronoi Okooii's brother. She claims they participate in friendship only, but now she asks to join your Space Corps. I am ordered to speak with her now, to say she shall not join, and that she must cease this liaison with the human male."

Catherine set down her kala. "Koni, they're friends, no different than you and I. And I don't see why she can't join the Corps—"

"She is Sunai," he growled. "The humans have no say in this."

"I know," she said, trying to reason with him. "The Sunai are great explorers, Koni. Maybe Jooni wants to explore, too."

"She can go to other provinces, to our sister moon..."

"Maybe she wants to explore farther than that, Koni. Some of us do." Catherine knew Jooni's desire to leave Suna was less about exploration than it was about escaping a society whose oppressive rules didn't work for her. However, knowing Koni wouldn't tolerate the truth, she opted for other persuasive tactics. "I know her leaving Suna could reflect badly on Gronoi Okooii, and she doesn't want that. If she joined the Corps, she'd be doing something good and she'd be protected."

He grunted. "Such a desire... it is not the way of our females. They do not live on the other worlds without their families, without their husbands." He paused, his large pupils contracting. "I am not so obstinate as Gronoi Okooii, but even I see that this shall not be."

Catherine sighed. "Let me come with you. You'll only scare her. She's my friend too and she might take it better if I'm there."

Koni eyed her for several moments before grunting in agreement.

At Jooni's home, Koni approached her as Catherine stood aside, his bulk making Jooni appear even smaller and more vulnerable. Though Jooni seemed intimidated, she nonetheless raised her chin just a bit, giving Koni a daring glare before casting her eyes down. It made Catherine uncomfortable to watch, but she refrained from showing any displeasure, knowing that Koni's peripheral vision would catch it.

"You will not consort with Lieutenant Snow," he told her in his guttural voice.

"He is my friend," she said, her eyes still lowered.

"You know the rule," he growled. "Suna's females do not consort with human males. You will attract no husband if you associate with humans."

"I want no husband."

Catherine almost gasped, wondering whether her presence had emboldened Jooni, or if Jooni was as gutsy as Snow had said.

"All Sunai female want husband!" Koni said. "You are the daughter of Gronoi Okooii's brother, and that means you shall have only a superior man of Suna!"

"So I am told."

Koni grunted at Jooni's impudence, walking closer to Jooni. Catherine watched closely, hoping she wouldn't have to step in. "If you believe these words I speak are not important, perhaps you shall hear them from Gronoi Okooii," he growled at her. When that silenced Jooni, he went on. "I offer only warning, Okooii Jooni, so that you shall avoid Sundani arrest and avoid Gronoi Okooii's anger. You will not see this Lieutenant Snow again! And whether you choose to marry or choose not to, you will receive no permission to join the human military. The Sunai only enlist in Suna's military."

"The Sunai do not allow women in military, Grono Amsala! Earth female join Space Corps, Derovian female join Space Corps… Suna leaves little choice for women!" Jooni looked down, her face scrunched in pain.

Koni put his hands upon Jooni shoulders. "Jooni, you are Sunai. Even if Sunai could join the human military, such an act would dishonor Gronoi Okooii. You have your excellent music shop. You may select a husband of your choosing, or not marry. If you desire exploration, the consulate can arrange for you to see the provinces, our sister moon, and even the other worlds if you are accompanied by those who would protect you."

After several moments of silence, Jooni, her eyes still downcast, thanked Grono Amsala and escorted him and Catherine to her door. When transporting back to *Cornelia*, neither spoke a word. Catherine waited for Koni to bring it up before she would offer her opinion. But Koni remained uncharacteristically silent, only saying goodbye to Catherine as she exited the transport.

Just as Catherine adjourned her meeting with Holloway and Varan, her contactor chirped.

Report to the Captain's ready room, immediately.

She stared at her contactor for a couple of moments, her hands beginning to sweat.

If Yamamoto had an assignment for her, he'd call her into his own office. She didn't know what could be wrong this time, but getting called up to Ferguson's ready room wasn't a good sign. By now, there was plenty she could get rung up for; most recently, she'd secretly worked on her and Holloway's data. Tired of speculating, Catherine did a quick check of her uniform and hair, told the guys she'd return soon, and left.

When she arrived, she saluted and took a seat once Yamamoto indicated she could. Ferguson sat quietly, her dark hair in a neat bun, her expression showing its usual sternness. Catherine waited for someone to speak. When Yamamoto didn't jump in to begin, her hands began to sweat more.

The door opened. Koni walked in, his bulky rust-colored uniform crunching as he moved. He met palms with the Captain first, then Yamamoto, before he held up his big mitt for Catherine. She met his palm, sitting back down while entertaining a whole new set of concerns.

Yamamoto turned to Catherine. "You are aware of Eshel's having taken refuge on Suna, and you are aware of the reasons for this decision."

"Yes, Sir," Catherine said, both relieved and excited that the conversation would involve Eshel.

"Catherine," Yamamoto said. "We have questions for you. You may be frank in your answers. Grono Amsala can hear anything you have to say."

"Yes, Sir," she said, glancing at Koni.

"Have you had any contact with Eshel since his leaving *Cornelia*?"

"No, Sir."

"And that is your word, to your XO and mentor?"

She began to worry. "That is my word, Sir. I've heard nothing."

"Did Eshel leave you any information of his whereabouts, or any other information about his reassignment?"

"No. He gave Tom a short message to give to me, stating that he was going to live among the Sunai because it was safer for everyone."

"What else did the message say?" Yamamoto pressed.

"That he didn't know when he'd return." Catherine paused. "And that he was sorry he didn't tell me in person. That's it."

Yamamoto took a deep breath and sat back in his chair. "Everything discussed from here forward is classified, Catherine." When she nodded, he went on. "Eshel isn't on Suna. He's on Korvalis."

A chill ran through Catherine. *Korvalis.* Her mind began to race with possibilities.

"He's there as part of a larger operation, one that benefits him… and us," Yamamoto said.

"Who's in on the op?" she said.

"Only the people in this room," he said.

Catherine blinked a few times. An op that involved them, but not the Alliance or Headquarters? "Is Eshel okay?"

"We received a transmission that he arrived safely on the surface. The plan was that he'd move to another location and contact us after two days… but we've heard nothing."

"How long has it been?" she asked.

"Two weeks."

Catherine shook her head, anxious feelings creeping in. "If you were able to communicate with Eshel, the messages would have to be relayed through someone on Korvalis. Perhaps they know something?"

Yamamoto shook his head. "They've lost contact with him, too. He's missing in action… and we need you to find him."

CHAPTER 5

Why does everyone want to see the Forbidden Planet? Is it the oceans? The forests? The fact that the sun never shines on the damned place? I don't think so, people. We want to see it because we're not allowed to. It's that simple.

— Commander Valery "Val" Petrovsky, Space Corps, retired

Catherine awakened, and for a moment felt unsure of where she was. But the ship's strange interior and spicy odor clued her in as she glanced out the window into darkness. She was on a Sunai science ship, one of the smaller but still impressive crafts designed for shorter missions. Koni, refusing to sleep during any part of the long trip, had insisted that she rest and prepare herself. She raised her seat to a sitting position.

"You slept well, nonaii," Koni said. "Good. You will need your strength for the operation."

"Did you do this for Eshel, too?" she asked. "Take him to the border and then serve as decoy while he crossed it?"

"It is better that you don't know such details," Koni said, his big amber eyes scanning the console, looking for any abnormality.

"I still wish someone would've told me the truth. I know how to keep a damned secret."

Koni raised his chin. "Your rank does not afford you such knowledge, nonaii. Such a plan of secrecy carries risk, and it is better for those in power to incur this risk and include subordinates only when necessary."

Since Yamamoto and Ferguson had let her in on Eshel's true location, two concerns had dominated her thoughts: worry for Eshel, who dared to return and face those who would harm him, and a strange indignation that Koni and the others had known the truth and kept it from her. But as much as she'd come to feel a sense of ownership regarding anything involving Eshel, particularly when his safety was involved, she knew Koni was right.

After offering her the assignment, they'd questioned her more. There was the usual concern that Eshel had gone rogue, although this time that concern seemed to come mainly from Koni. "He does not abandon a plan and replace it with his own?" he'd asked, his chin raised. Catherine understood Koni's suspicion. Unlike Ferguson and Yamamoto, who'd developed at least some trust in Eshel, Koni and Eshel's mutual understanding was still in its tentative stages. She could hardly believe that the two men, who'd once detested one another, now collaborated on something this big. She'd put Koni's mind at ease, reassuring him that while Eshel had his own way of doing things, he would do all he could to ensure the plan succeeded, given that this seemed to be the sort of plan Eshel had sought all along.

Yet, it was that thought that unsettled her. Eshel's missing in action didn't mean he'd changed the plan to suit him; it meant something was wrong.

"You won't face all the complications you did last time," Ferguson had said. "No prisons, no palace, no surveillance."

"Where am I going?" Catherine asked.

"Beyond the developed areas," Ferguson said.

"How will I cross their border without being detected?"

"Leave that to us," Yamamoto said.

Catherine sat quietly for a while, reviewing the plan over and over until it began to sound routine. Once they dropped out of FTL, she gathered her things and got into the Pokey.

"Be safe, nonaii," Koni said.

Catherine, nervous as hell, just nodded and closed the hatch. As the ship's bay door opened, Catherine engaged her clandestine device and navigated the Pokey away from Koni's ship, on a heading toward Korvalis. The planet hovered in the distance, pockets of vivid blue ocean peeking through openings in the cloud cover. Soon, a boxy Guard station appeared, the one she would creep past, unseen to the Korvali eye.

"Do not question Eshel about the mission," Yamamoto had said sternly. "You will have the information we give you, and no more."

He'd given her that look, the one everyone recognized, the one that meant disobeying him would have more severe consequences than she could imagine. She'd learned that Yamamoto knew how to lean on people, knew how to persuade them in ways that made them think twice about their actions. That gift, along with his many other abilities, made him the number one XO in the Corps, the one all Captains wanted to work with. But he always chose to work with Ferguson whenever possible. No one knew why, not even Tom. Some at the poker table had made jokes about their having romantic feelings for one another, but Catherine shook her head at that. Somehow, Yamamoto understood Ferguson better than others did.

Catherine approached the border, leaving Koni and his ship behind. And when she crossed over, she cringed a little, as if waiting for an alarm to sound. She realized she'd been holding her breath, reminding her of the first time she and Tom had traversed the line, the line that must never be crossed, lest one would, as with Yamamoto, suffer consequences worse than imagined. At least Yamamoto and Ferguson would place more trust in her this time. And this time, she would have no secured doors to decode, no tiptoeing through narrow hallways, no dodging robed government officials, and no unknown force to drain her clandestine devices. She would trek through uncivilized country on foot… something she'd grown up doing.

She scanned the area again, waiting for some unsophisticated little ship to detain her, having figured out their ruse. Her hands began to sweat at the thought of deploying Plan B. However, patrol ships whizzed past her, instead heading to Koni's science ship to issue severe warning to him. The presence of a Sunai ship would nettle the Korvali but would not surprise them. The Sunai periodically skirted Korvalis's borders in order to observe and make near-futile attempts to collect data, getting as close as they could without creating incident.

And when she broke through the clouds, she was mesmerized by the beauty of the planet, the deep blue of its massive oceans and the bright green of its lands. Unlike Earth, with its immense continents, Korvalis's landmasses—at least in the lower latitudes—were much smaller, breaking into peninsulas and archipelagos that seemed to go on forever. How one navigated all the tiny islands was beyond her. She glanced westward, where civilization occupied the western region of one of the landmasses. However, she instead headed east, even beyond the river valley, with its tributaries weaving past one another and reflecting the gray sky above until eventually spilling into the southern sea. She flew until civilization and its capitol were out of view, where forests stretched as far as her eye could see.

She heard pelting—rain hitting the Pokey. As she drew closer to the interior of the landmass, she headed to the coordinates that her superiors had given her, an unpopulated region east of industrialized territory and the riverlands, but still west of the remote eastern shores that were inhabited by the Shemal. Soon, she slowed the Pokey, looking for a good place to set down. Spotting a small opening in the forest, she hovered over it and slowly lowered the Pokey before proceeding forward again. Tom would make fun of her crude, rookie-like maneuvering, but it got the job done. Among the tall thin trees, she spotted one that stood out, a grand beauty of a tree with a broad crown of branches that arched curvaceously toward the ground. When her instruments told her she had enough room to fit under the tree's crown, she took the Pokey inside and set it down.

Catherine stood up and engaged her clandestine device before stepping out of the Pokey. She peeked through the foliage from all sides, seeing nothing but forest. Recalling Yamamoto's instructions, she sent off a short coded message, conveying that she'd arrived safely. That was another thing they wouldn't tell her—how such a message would get to them at all. After checking her gear, she put on her waterproof field uniform and emerged from the tree's crown. And it was then that she recognized the tree; it was the same species as those dotting the gardens of Fallal Hall. Recollections returned, of ducking under the great trees with Eshel to avoid a gale, to argue over festering misunderstandings, to plot what would turn out to be Elan's death. It seemed so long ago.

She first noticed the air, cool and humid as it moistened her skin and breathing passages. She smelled dampness, particularly damp wood, with just a hint of sweetness, as if something bloomed. Her positioning device—a primitive one that appeared to do little more than specify direction and rough coordinates—steered her west, the direction in which she would continue for some time.

As she hiked through the forest, she examined the trees—exceedingly tall, leafy, noble creatures so dense in their foliage that little grew beneath them. The trees' broad crowns made it so they stood reasonably far apart, making it easier for her to weave her way through the forest. The ground felt soft under her feet as she walked upon damp leaf litter, her steps making almost no sound. Such freedom she felt compared to that of tiptoeing around the prison at Felebaseb or avoiding collisions with blue-robed Shereb at Fallal Hall. Yet, she still watched with a vigilant eye, as her directions were vague and she had little knowledge of what sort of creatures or challenges she would encounter in the forest. Eshel had never mentioned any lurking dangers; but then again, Eshel had spent no time in this region.

Eshel. Would he be at the coordinates they'd given her? If so, would he be surprised to see her? Or would he expect that they'd send her, a trusted friend, to offer aid? She was glad, perhaps gladder than the circumstances warranted, to be off *Cornelia* and helping Eshel with the plan she knew so little about.

It would get dark soon. Their plan to get her on the surface as close to sunset as possible, offering her more travel time under the cover of darkness, had appeared to work. And when darkness descended, she glanced around with greater vigilance, suddenly feeling like a child who feared the dark, as if daylight would render her safer on a planet where she had no damned business being, where the people would have no problem killing her if they detected her.

Pushing such thoughts aside, she kept at it, sipping her water and nibbling some dried food, until she stopped to relieve herself. As she squatted down, she felt self-conscious and even guilty doing her business on someone else's land, wondering if her urine would have some property that could harm their flora or soil. How did the primitives handle their waste, she wondered? Something told her the Korvali, primitive or not, would never allow their waste to pollute their rivers or stink up their living areas. They would find some use for it.

As she buttoned her pants, Catherine heard a crunching, like feet upon leaves. Before she could even turn around, something yanked her sideways until she slammed into a tree trunk, almost knocking the wind out of her. As she went for her weapon, she found that she couldn't move. Twine had bound her to the tree. Adrenaline flooded her as she strained her hand toward one of her pockets, the one with her knife. She grabbed it and flipped open the blade; but before she could make a cut, something struck her hand and the knife fell to the ground. When she looked up, she froze.

A group of Korvali had formed a tight circle around her. And each of them held a spear, the tips of which pressed against her neck.

CHAPTER 6

Catherine remained still, even breathing with great care as the spear tips aimed so near her arteries. She felt pressure upon her chest; more spears, pressed hard enough to make her wonder if they would pierce her field uniform and then her flesh.

They were tall, far taller than Eshel, towering over her and making her feel tiny. Numerous pairs of eyes—eyes so green that they almost seemed to glow in the nighttime forest—stared at her. But there was something odd about their eyes, their gaze. She realized they made no eye contact with her. They seemed to look beyond her. Except one of them, whose eyes bore into hers.

"I am a friend," she sputtered, speaking the Old Korvali greeting. Their spears remained, as did their cold expressions. "I am a friend for Eshel, son of Othniel," she added.

Still no reaction. Catherine closed her eyes momentarily, preparing to have her neck punctured and her heart and lungs impaled by wedges of dark stone. When the pressure upon her vital organs ceased, she opened her eyes. The spears had retreated. With the flick of a spear, the one who'd made eye contact with her cut the twine that bound her to the tree, then used the broad side of the spear to coax Catherine forward. Catherine stepped away from the tree and she was bound once more, pinning her arms and hands to her.

Catherine finally noticed that the tall person who'd bound her had breasts. They were small, even smaller than hers. The woman's face had the softer, large-eyed quality she'd seen on the woman she almost collided with outside Fallal Hall, during her previous visit. She glanced at the others, noticing that several were female.

Then, Catherine had another realization: her clandestine device was still engaged. How the hell could they see her at all?

The nudge of a spear urged her forward again as the others began walking. When they headed east, opposite of where she needed to go, Catherine, in no position to argue, muttered a curse and followed along.

They wore nothing. They were thin, with longish torsos like Eshel, all sinew wrapped around long bones. Their skin appeared moist, giving it the appearance that deceived one into thinking it would be soft. Their hair was light brown, like Eshel's. They maintained at least two meters of space from her, and perhaps half a meter from one another. None spoke, nor did they look at her.

After perhaps an hour, Catherine spotted a flickering orange light. Fire. As they drew closer, a group of Korvali huddled around a fire pit, sitting upon wooden stumps. Many sat unclothed, impervious to the cool air that made her glad for her jacket. Simple, neatly crafted log huts with sloping roofs stood nearby, almost reminding her of her father's home. One of the spear-wielders called out to the villagers: one word, in a voice far louder than she'd ever heard from Eshel. Those who sat fireside stood and looked their way before scurrying in other directions, disappearing into the darkness. One of them gracefully scaled a tree ladder until he too disappeared from view. Her eyes followed him up… and she gasped.

Above was an entire network of tree huts and wooden pathways that connected one tree to another. Something thudded her back; when she looked over, the woman who'd bound her gave her a penetrating stare. Catherine stared back, partly out of annoyance, but also hoping the woman would say something—anything. When she didn't, Catherine looked back up. A group of Korvali peered down from a bridge. A thud to her back again, harder this time.

"Okay," she muttered, lowering her eyes.

When they stopped walking, Catherine halted. They faced her, forming a circle around her, their faces illuminated by a torch that one of them carried. Again, they made no eye contact. They were ignoring her, refusing to acknowledge her. It was what the Korvali did when they didn't like you.

The same female approached her, her chilly expression shadowed from the flickering torchlight. She motioned with both webbed hands to her shoulders. Catherine sighed, removing her pack and handing it to her. The woman took it and passed it off to another before turning back to Catherine. She flicked Catherine's jacket with a spear. Catherine shook her head, crossing her arms and rubbing them, attempting to convey that she would be cold without it. The woman's chilly stare remained and she speared the jacket again, a bit more impatiently. Beginning to feel stirrings of anger, Catherine removed her jacket. When she tried to reach into a pocket for her communication device, a spear reached out and slapped her arm. Uttering a curse, Catherine tossed the jacket to her. The Korvali woman caught it midair and handed it off. She then motioned to Catherine's pants, whose pockets contained the remainder of her gear. Catherine removed her shoes and socks, then her pants, her clammy feet stepping upon the leafy forest floor. When the woman handed the pants to another spear-wielder, he only stared, making no effort to take them. The woman inspected the pants for a moment before hanging them on the man's spear herself.

Soon, Catherine stood completely nude, the damp air giving her goose bumps, her personal items dangling from the others' spears, as if they had no desire to touch any of it. With nothing left to take from her, they merely stood there, studying her. A chill ran through Catherine as she hugged her arms to herself, wondering if they would now run their spears through her. And then, for the first time, they no longer looked past her. Their eyes met hers.

"I am a friend," she repeated, more desperately than before. "For Eshel!" She switched to regular Korvali, gesturing to her jacket. "I need my device. To communicate with Eshel."

They only stared.

Then, the woman motioned to a hut, its door open. Another thud to her back. Catherine swatted at the offending spear, giving the woman a surly look before entering the hut. It had platforms along each side, long enough for Korvali to lie upon. Before she could say anything else, the door shut, leaving her in darkness.

The hut smelled of damp wood, slightly reminiscent of cedar. It had only one window, a narrow swath cut horizontally into the wood, illuminated by the flicker of firelight and higher than she could reach even when standing on a platform. She tried the door, to no avail. Hugging her arms to herself, she felt around for the bench, sat down, and began to think.

Assuming her transmission had reached its recipients, they'd know she was here. But if they didn't hear from her soon, they'd begin considering their options. If they sent Tom, he would have no more information to work with than she'd had, and even less knowledge of the Korvali. Given how easily she'd been captured, and in territory that was supposedly uninhabited, Tom would face capture as well, or worse. And with Eshel and two operatives missing, things would get ugly.

Catherine took a deep breath, quelling the panicky feeling that rose in her. Who were these people? This far west, maybe they understood standard Korvali. She needed a way to convince them to let her go, to prove she meant no harm, to get her belongings back. So she sat in the dark, considering all her possible next moves.

Some time later, the door opened. The woman appeared in the doorway, carrying a torch. She stepped aside while a smaller Korvali, shorter and thinner than the others and wearing a robe, stepped in, carrying a stack of neatly folded garments. Her clothing. He placed it upon the bench, giving Catherine a long gaze with greenish eyes until the woman spoke to him, after which he turned and left. Before Catherine could say anything, the door shut. She began dressing herself, feeling warmth and security return to her. But when she felt her pants and jacket, she discovered that they'd emptied all her pockets.

She paced for a while, preparing what she would say when they came back, including addressing more immediate concerns such as her full bladder. However, no one came. She sat on the platform, legs stretched out, her back nestled in the corner. As she drifted off, images of the tall, strange Korvali appeared, spears in hand, never quite looking at her until she disrobed. Many would assume they looked with such focus because she was naked, but she knew better. Something else had triggered their interest.

Tired of the assault of too many thoughts on her weary mind, Catherine began clearing it all away, as Yamamoto had taught her. And after she reached that quiet place she rarely visited, it hit her. When she'd removed her clothing, they hadn't stared out of curiosity; they stared because they could finally see her. Once she'd removed her pants, her clandestine device went with them. The man hadn't taken her pants because he couldn't see them. And the woman, who'd somehow deduced what was happening, had inspected the pants, knowing that what hid Catherine from the others' eyes was concealed within the pockets.

Yet, the woman. She could see Catherine the entire time. And that thought pervaded her mind until she drifted off to sleep.

Catherine woke, sitting up with a start. The door had opened. It was light out, and rain pattered on the rooftop. The woman held the door while the same young Korvali quickly placed something on the bench. Her food and canteen. Catherine caught a quick glimpse of his left hand: a dark dotted marking that she couldn't decipher.

"Let me out, and I take you where I go," she blurted out. But the young Korvali ignored her and closed the door behind him.

Catherine stood, her back and neck stiff from sleeping against a wooden wall. Her bladder made her grimace. She looked around, hoping for some indication of where one could relieve oneself. After all, Korvali elimination wasn't that different from that of humans; this she knew from spending time with Eshel. And, sure enough, in the back of the hut was a wooden bowl sunk into the floor. She grabbed it; it came up easily, revealing a hole in the flooring. She inspected it, hoping it was what she thought it was. She undid her pants and relieved herself.

After eating some food, she paced again, growing more impatient and promising herself that next time they came, she would be ready. She knew what to say this time, what might make them listen.

But as the hours dragged on, no one came. Day turned to dusk, then to darkness. Other than periodic rainfall on the rooftop, she'd heard little all day: no talking from villagers, no chirps or growls from animals, no sounds of people living their daily lives, except the occasional loud banging, which sounded like hammering on stone. Perhaps they were making more spearheads with which to carve her up and roast her over the fire, or impale her and hang her from an obliging tree for all to hate. Or perhaps even to perform live vivisection, honoring their scientific natures and desire to understand the inner workings of the alien creature who'd invaded their lands.

Stop it.

She shook her head. Yamamoto would chastise her for indulging in such morbid thoughts.

They returned your clothing. They gave you your food and water. They sheltered you. They probably wouldn't do that if they planned to eviscerate you. Sleep, woman.

Catherine curled up on the damp bench, her thoughts going to Eshel. Where was he? Why hadn't he communicated with them? If the spear-wielders ever let her out of this goddamned hut, would she find him? Suddenly, she recalled Eshel walking into sick bay after the clone attacked her, her breaking down in tears upon seeing the real him. She knew then how much Eshel had become an indelible part of her life, only to soon face his leaving *Cornelia* without a word… not to hide on Suna, but to provide her a startling reminder of the truth, the truth she'd known for a long time: that Eshel would eventually leave her and their friends to pursue that which mattered most to him. And with that thought, Catherine drifted into a troubled sleep.

She woke to a noise that rang loud and clear in the night. An animal of some kind… crying out nearby. A mating call? It didn't sound like one. It was too much of a wail, as if the animal were in pain. Then it ceased. She looked up at her tiny window: no flickering. Only darkness. The sound repeated itself in her mind's ear, one long loud wail. Something seemed odd about it… until she realized why: it wasn't an animal making that sound. It was a person.

She sat there, frozen. The wail suggested great pain, perhaps a victim of the sort of torture she'd imagined earlier. Perhaps the victim was also a prisoner, an interloper from some other place who'd wandered into their territory. Then a terrible thought occurred to her: what if it was Eshel? What if he'd been there the entire time, imprisoned, and now they killed him because an alien wandered onto their lands, speaking his name?

For the first time, fear consumed her. *Kick your way out of here, Finnegan. Run east, to the Pokey.*

Stop it.

Catherine shoved such thoughts away, shutting her eyes. And although it took a while, she eventually fell asleep. When she woke the next day, she waited for the sound of the door, fully prepared to address the woman who oversaw her. However, no one came that morning. Or the rest of that day.

Facing a third night of dark solitary, she considered new thoughts. Thoughts of how long it would take her to break out of her wooden prison and what sort of damage she would incur. How easily she could surprise those who visited her next and dodge the spears that would inevitably find their way to her. How many hours she'd trekked before capture and how much more quickly she could get back to her ship. From the risky to the preposterous, she considered every possibility.

Sleep. Tomorrow, you'll know what to do.

A noise awakened Catherine. The door again.

She shot up from her lying position and immediately began

shouting in Korvali, imploring them to listen to her. But when her sleepy eyes cleared, she went silent.

A man in a dark gray robe stood outside the door. Among the naked spear-wielders, the robe seemed strange and out of place. He was closer to Eshel's height, and his darker hair and blue eyes only confirmed that he didn't belong.

Not knowing how to interpret his strange look, Catherine charged out the door and spoke loudly in Korvali, rushing her words, hoping to get each persuasive argument out before he too turned his back on her. The gray-robed man put his hand up.

"Be silent," he said.

Catherine ceased her tirade as the robed man spoke to the others in words she didn't understand. As he did, she realized he'd spoken to her in English. When finished, he turned to her again.

"Who are you?" she said.

"You will come with me, human."

CHAPTER 7

Snow sat down at his viewer, waiting for the video feed to engage. When Jooni's face appeared, he cracked a smile, still aware that she was one of the few who could even get him to smile. But his smile faded when he saw her furrowed expression. He knew that look.

"What's wrong, Jooni?"

"You must promise you will not get angry."

Snow hesitated. "I won't."

"Say it. Say the words."

"I promise I won't get angry."

She hesitated. "I cannot join your Space Corps."

Snow gritted his teeth. "Did they give you reasons?"

She looked down. "Sunai enlist only in Sunai military—"

"But not women."

"That is not important, Snow! Grono Amsala… he say what I feared, what I told you before… that my living among the humans, even serving in their military, dishonors my uncle."

Snow heaved a sigh. Grono Amsala. He felt irritated at the Sunai Catherine had spoken so highly of, never understanding why she would befriend one of those assholes. But he refrained from saying what he really wanted to, attempting to keep the promise he'd made. "There has to be another way."

"I no see it," she said, her eyes cast down.

"Let me talk to—"

"Say nothing," she said, looking at him. "And Snow… you cannot come here again."

Snow scowled. "Oh, come on, Jooni!"

"They do not like our friendship, Snow. And if they learn the truth, that you come to my home, or if my uncle know… terrible, Snow! Terrible! It is better that I receive warning from Grono Amsala, and not my uncle."

"Grono Amsala has a friendship with Catherine… she just had dinner at his home!"

"Grono Amsala is male, and Grono," Jooni said. "He shall do as he wants. And that is not same, Snow, as Sunai men no want to consort with human female."

If they wanted to, they would allow it, he thought with disgust, noting to himself once more that rules always seemed to conveniently favor those in power. Snow sat there, shaking his head, hardly believing he was here again, fighting an uphill battle to see the woman he wanted to be with.

"You said you would not get angry."

Snow rubbed his face with his hands. "Well, I'm fucking angry, alright? I don't like my life being dictated by stupid rules made by stupid people. And you're not even fighting them… you let them push you around!"

"You face Grono Amsala, Sundani officers, or my uncle!" she cried, gesturing with her arm like the males did. "You face… and you tell me how strong and brave you are, Lieutenant Jebediah Snow of the Space Corps!"

And with that, Snow's viewer went dark.

Yamamoto sat quietly in his chair, waiting for Snow to speak.

"Sir, I… I ask that you don't share anything we talk about here."

"That depends on what you have to say," Yamamoto said.

"I don't think you'll need to report anything I say, Sir."

"You aren't involved with Jooni again?"

"No. We've had contact, but we're only friends."

Yamamoto said nothing, watching him. Snow knew he suspected the truth, that he'd probably noticed Snow's morose mood over the last few days. At this point, Snow didn't care about getting rung up. However, angry or not, he couldn't put Jooni at risk. Fortunately, if Yamamoto had any real evidence of his relations with Jooni, Snow would've known by now. After the measures Yamamoto and Ferguson took to cover up the relationship the first time around, they wouldn't tolerate a second violation. If caught, to appease the Sunai and avoid diplomatic incident, the Corps would issue nearly any punishment the Sunai demanded. Somehow, such a dim prospect was quickly forgotten when he'd reconnected with Jooni, and he wondered at his temporary stupidity. However, his anger at Jooni's situation remained.

Snow shifted in his seat, tapping his legs with his hands before making himself stop. "Sir, Jooni tried to get approval to enlist in the Space Corps. They denied her."

"I heard."

"Permission to speak freely, Sir." When Yamamoto gave the nod, Snow went on. "It's stupid. We let the Derovians enlist, male or female. We'd take the Sunai if they wanted to join. I mean... if the Sunai don't want women or anyone but the biggest and smartest men, what do they give a shit if their rejects choose to go elsewhere?"

"Snow, you aren't thinking like a soldier. No society with a strong military presence wants their own joining the enemy's military. We have excellent relations with the Sunai, but it wasn't so long ago that my own parents fought and died in the wars against them."

"I know, Sir. But the Sunai call the Derovians their brothers and sisters, and their military protects them... and they still let Derovians join the Corps."

Yamamoto shrugged. "The Derovians have their own government and laws. And their citizens always take non-combat roles: service, administration, science..."

"Why couldn't Jooni do the same?"

"She's not Derovian, Snow. She's Sunai, and Okooii's niece."

Snow slumped in his chair. "Why do they say they allow emigration, women included, if they're only going to complain that their leaving will dishonor the men? Why don't they just admit they're no better than the goddamned Korvali and don't want their people leaving?"

"Snow, what do you want out of this situation?"

Snow hesitated. "For her to be happy."

"For her to be happy, or for her to be yours?"

Snow scowled. "What difference does it make? I can't have either."

"It makes every bit of difference. If you want Jooni to be with you, you'll find the list of obstacles endless. You know how the Sunai are about such things, and that won't change anytime soon. However, if you want to help Jooni remove herself from Sunai society, there may be ways to explore that."

"How?"

"The Sunai allow offworlders to live among them for a limited period, to enroll in their music programs or to teach… a Sunai could do the same on Earth, as part of the interplanetary exchange program. That may offer a more palatable alternative to the consulate, and to Gronoi Okooii. Speak with Ov'Raa; he has influence with the Sunai… and with the Alliance."

"I can't see Ov'Raa convincing them of anything," Snow groused. "The minute they raise their voices, he'll back down."

Yamamoto's eyes narrowed. "Snow, do you want to help Jooni?"

"Yeah, of course."

"Then stop complaining and stop expecting things to be what you want them to be. Change does not happen quickly or easily. Do your research and earn it."

Snow blinked a couple of times. "Yes, Sir."

"You're dismissed."

When Snow returned to his quarters feeling even worse than he had, he grabbed his bass and sat down on the deck, his back to the bulkhead. He sat for some time, ignoring the chirps of his contactor while his bass lay unplayed. Hopeless thoughts passed through his mind, each one making him slump a little more.

Finally, he reached for his contactor. One of the messages announced plans for future missions, encouraging the crew to apply for assignment as early as possible. When he imagined what he'd do once this mission came to an end, he become aware of the options he had before him: a nine-month mission on the *Victoria*, a two-year on the *Alexandria* with the whitecoats, or take an assignment at Headquarters for a while, or even cease service altogether and go travel for a year…

Snow put his bass aside and got to his feet. And then he sat down at his computer and began to work.

"Kovsky," Tom shouted.

"Yeah," Kovsky called back, looking up from his screen.

"I'm grabbing a bite. And I have a meeting after that. You're in charge."

"Yes, Sir," Kovsky said.

Tom left Weapons, feeling just a bit uneasy. He'd never liked leaving others in charge, especially now, during shaky times. Eshel was the only exception; he knew Eshel would take care of things if shit went sideways. He entered the stairwell and took the steps two at a time before reaching the sixth deck, annoyed at his feeling a little winded. *You're out of shape again, Kingston.*

At the mess, Tom grabbed a plate of chicken and potatoes and scanned the noisy room, spotting a couple of empty chairs at one of the longer tables. He passed dozens of black uniforms, nodding at several of them. And despite knowing he shouldn't, he glanced over at Maria at a nearby table, sitting next to Ferrars. Ferrars was yammering on as usual, probably regaling them all with yet another story about one of the kids he'd mentored. Tom had no issue with the mentoring; he'd mentored some kids himself when he wasn't deployed. Although in his case they were service kids, and they had challenges well beyond those of the privileged youth that Ferrars taught to play sports. But maybe that was the kind of guy Maria needed, someone from a cleaner background who could teach his own kids to play soccer instead of how to defend themselves against angry drunken fathers or bigger kids with bigger weapons.

Tom hadn't taken more than a couple of bites before Snow joined him, sweat still on his forehead.

"Engine room again?" Tom said.

Snow nodded.

The two men ate in silence until Snow, half finished, spoke up. "Heard from Catherine?"

"Nah. They don't want her communicating from wherever she is on Suna unless absolutely necessary... for her safety and all."

"You think she's with Eshel?" Snow said.

Tom chuckled. "I wondered that, too. But I doubt it. They haven't told me his location... they aren't going to tell her." Secretly, Tom strongly suspected that Catherine was doing an op of some kind, and it bugged him that they hadn't included him.

When the crowd began clearing out, Tom stole another glance at Maria, who caught him looking and gave him a quick wave. He returned the gesture.

"Anything new?" Snow said, tilting his head toward Maria.

Tom shook his head. "It's done."

"Did she say that?"

"Yup. Turns out she wants a family."

Snow scowled. "Really?"

"That's what I said. Like I told her, I wouldn't bring a kid into this world."

"Why not?"

"Why not?" Tom said. "You don't want kids any more than I do."

"Not now. But down the road, maybe."

"Really?" Tom said, chuckling. "And how'd you think that was going to happen with you know who? Humans and Sunai can't reproduce."

Snow shrugged. "I don't know. Adopt. Maybe take on a kid like us, so they don't have to grow up like we did."

Tom made a face. "Are you kidding me? You don't know where that kid's been, what kind of shit he was exposed to..."

"So, what, leave him to be raised by neglectful drunks, like your folks? Or religious zealots like mine?"

Tom took his last bite and pushed his plate away. He wasn't sure why exactly, but the prospect of any kids, and especially adopting them, seemed like a bad idea.

"I thought you liked kids," Snow went on. "You always looked after the little ones when we were growing up."

"I like 'em, alright? I just don't want any."

"I could see you with lots of kids," Snow said, giving a crooked smile. "Like, three or four. All girls."

Tom shook his head. "No thanks."

When Tom and Snow stood up to drop off their trays, Tom found himself face to face with Ferrars.

"Hey, how you doin', Tom?" Ferrars said.

Tom stood up a little straighter, although he still came up a few centimeters short of Ferrars's stature. "I'm alright. What's up?"

"You got any room for another player at your poker game?" Ferrars said. "Maria said you probably didn't, but I figured it couldn't hurt to ask. I miss the game. Used to play with my buddies back in New York."

"Sorry, man. We're pretty full these days," Tom replied, starting to walk away.

"Let me know if you get an extra chair," Ferrars called after him.

Tom gave a faint nod, rolling his eyes as he caught up to Snow.

"We're too full?" Snow chided.

"Shut up."

Yamamoto took a seat in Ferguson's ready room.

"Any news?" she asked, her forehead crinkled.

"I'm afraid not," Yamamoto said. "Grono Amsala hasn't heard a word since Catherine landed safely, and neither have his Korvali contacts."

"Shit," Ferguson muttered.

"How long do you want to wait before we reconsider?"

"Another thirty-six hours, no more," Ferguson said. "Without a detailed map or a proper positioning device, our travel time estimates were pretty rough. It's possible the journey took longer than we expected, or she encountered bad weather or some other natural barrier. You know how it goes in the field." She sat back in her chair. "But after another day or so, we're out of excuses."

Yamamoto nodded. "Which leaves us only one option: briefing Tom and sending him in."

Ferguson stood up, heading over to her window. "We'll have to come up with a different route for him to take. It's riskier, but if we can get Tom close to the coordinates Eshel specified and then get him out quickly, it may work. Otherwise, people are going to start asking questions about the loss of two operatives and two Pokeys, and we'll have no way of retrieving them if Eshel fails."

"Let's meet with Grono Amsala first, to see if we can get intel on Catherine's whereabouts from his contacts on Korvalis. They may have ideas on how to proceed."

She nodded, turning to face him again. "What about her cover?"

"She's supposedly working with the Sunai on a confidential scientific project. Commander Steele is unhappy with his 'exclusion' from the project, but this seemed the best solution, given the situation. Derovia is unsafe for her, there was no reason to send her to CC, and we couldn't justify a transport back to Earth."

She made a face. "People think she's visiting Eshel. But I suppose there's no way around that."

"Agreed," Yamamoto said. "However, there is another problem. Commander Steele is angry about Catherine's extended absence and is insisting on getting in touch with her. I reminded him to relay the messages through Grono Amsala, but he has received no reply and has issued complaint with Headquarters about the 'commandeering' of one of his scientists."

Ferguson rolled her eyes. "Remind me to never let that asshole serve on my ship again. Work with the Grono to create some text replies, and make them seem like they're from her. You're good at that. I'll talk to Steele." She paused. "Is that all?"

"No. The Admiral contacted me, asking about Catherine's absence coinciding with Eshel's. He suspects something."

Ferguson took a deep breath. She stood for a moment, leaning against the bulkhead. "We'll get court-martialed for this, and they'll have every reason to convict. We'll lose everything we've worked for."

Yamamoto paused, understanding her need to state the worst-case scenario. It was her way, the way she dealt with problems that had become larger than she'd hoped. Those who didn't know her well labeled her a fretter, someone incapable of handling pressure. But it was her ability to acknowledge the worst that gave her strength, that allowed her to move forward.

"We have not arrived at that place yet," Yamamoto said, standing up. "Thirty-six hours. If we do not hear from Catherine, we'll go to the Admiral first and tell him the truth."

She nodded. "Keep me posted."

CHAPTER 8

Catherine stood before the gray-robed stranger, dumbfounded. After a moment, the young Korvali who'd delivered her clothing and food arrived with her pack and a wooden bucket. He set them down a couple of meters from her and left. The spear-wielders stood at a distance, watching her.

She approached the bucket: it contained the items that had once taken residence in her pockets, including communicator, her clandestine device, her weapons... and even the knife she'd dropped when they'd captured her. She peered inside her pack; everything was out of place. Kneeling on the forest floor, she emptied her pack's contents upon the leaf litter, checking off each item to ensure they'd returned all of it. They had, and everything appeared to function as it ought. Relieved, she repacked everything and put her pack on, stuffing the other items into her pockets before she turned to the gray-robed stranger.

She glanced down at his left hand, hoping to spot his marking. If he wore the gray branches, the circular design, or something else, she would follow him. But if he wore the magenta leaf, she would follow him until she could devise a way to escape. She motioned to the top of her left hand.

The man placed his left hand to his right shoulder briefly, then turned and began to walk. He wore the circular crest, like the ones she'd seen in Vargas's cold chamber so long ago. He was Moshal.

Catherine glanced at the others, waiting for someone to bind her with twine or urge her in some direction with the smack of a spear.

But they merely stood there, eyes on her. So she started walking, picking up her pace until she was a meter or two behind the blue-eyed stranger. He moved swiftly, never looking behind him. When she checked her positioning device, it indicated that they headed west… the direction she needed to go. She took out her communicator and sent off a transmission that specified her rough location and that she was en route with a Moshal man. It probably wasn't the news they'd hoped for, but at least it was news.

She followed the Moshal beyond the village, her guide confidently navigating a pathway through the maze of tall trunks. A cool breeze roamed past them, bringing the scent of foliage and damp soil. They crossed a couple of streams; Catherine hopped the narrower one, but her guide made no such effort and traipsed through the water with ease, not minding that his robe had gotten wet along the bottom. When the next waterway proved wider, Catherine attempted to traverse the rocks across the burbling stream. However, as in the past, she eventually slipped on one of them and the cool water found its way into her boots.

Before long, light appeared ahead. When they drew closer to it, the tall narrow trees gave way to enormous, gnarled things with thick gray trunks and stout branches that sprawled in every direction, their oval leaves a curious shade of silvery green. Something about them intrigued Catherine, as if hobbits would emerge from their trunks. As they wove through the forest, soft grass beneath their feet and showy, dark-petaled flowers brushing against her, she recalled roaming through spruce forests as a child, imagining a fantasyland with friendly creatures hidden away. Then, as if sensing her wonder, the sun made its first appearance since she'd arrived on Korvalis, and the tree's leaves began to sparkle.

Her guide, now much farther ahead, finally stopped, disapproval on his face at her dillydallying. Just as she sped up again, her communicator emitted a strange, warbled sound. When she checked it, the display showed unintelligible readings, as if confused or bombarded by some electromagnetic phenomenon that interfered with its functioning. She looked around, wondering what had caused the disturbance.

"It is the trees."

The Moshal's voice startled her. As before, he'd spoken in English.

"The trees cause my device to malfunction?" she said, skeptical.

"Yes. The koshac tree... it has unusual powers."

Catherine raised her eyebrows. Unusual powers? She was so used to Eshel's empirical mind that it hadn't occurred to her that other Korvali, if not educated, especially in the sciences, might be prone to thinking in magical terms. "I see. And how do these powers work?"

"I do not know."

"There must be some scientific explanation..."

"Perhaps," he replied. "But I am Moshal. We are protectors, not scientists." He resumed his course, his robe flowing behind him as he marched ahead.

Catherine jogged a little to catch up and walk at his side. "Did you say they're koshac trees? Like the one at Fallal Hall?"

"Yes."

She eyed their silvery leaves. "Why do they look so much healthier here?"

"The malkaris... she does not provide proper care for the tree." He paused. "You like the Gernoly star. You showed pleasure when it appeared."

The Gernoly star? Then she understood: the sun. "Yes. It doesn't make an appearance very often here."

Again, as if knowing her thoughts, the sun ducked behind a cloud. After a while, it began to rain, and it wasn't long before the temperature cooled and the wind blew with greater ferocity.

Her guide stopped and looked up, his eyes narrowed. "A gale comes."

Once beyond the koshac forest, when the rain began to fall harder, the Moshal led her into another dark forest, where the dense canopy would offer some protection from the storm. He easily climbed to a branch and sat upon it. Catherine did the same, putting her hood on and zipping up her jacket.

She turned to her guide. "Who are you?"

"I am Moshal."

"Do you have a name?"

"Of course."

She gave a tiny smile and said no more about it, knowing he'd offer his name if he wanted to. "Well, Moshal, I don't suppose you'll tell me where we're going, or when we'll get there, or why we're walking the entire way."

"No craft is allowed east of the river valley. We will arrive after nightfall."

Catherine ran the mental math; that meant they would trek for less time than she would have on her own. However, some time ago they'd begun heading southwest, away from where she'd been instructed to go.

"Those people, the ones who captured me... who were they?"

"Shemal."

Shemal. Even that far west. "I never saw them coming."

"No one does. One cannot enter Shemal territory without the knowledge of their patrollers, even with your devices of invisibility. They probably tracked you for a great distance."

She shook her head. She could infiltrate Fallal Hall—filled with people, technology, surveillance—without anyone knowing, but she couldn't walk silent and invisible through the great open without a horde of spear-wielding primitives sneaking up on her. She wondered at how much this Moshal knew: his speaking her language, his recognizing her reaction to the sun, his mentioning her clandestine device. Eshel, or someone, had schooled him.

"I assumed you would talk more," he said, sipping water from a tube that lay hidden under his robe. "They say humans talk even more than Sunai."

She shrugged. "You aren't the first Korvali I've spent time with."

After the torrent let up, they climbed down from their perches and resumed their trek. Eventually, gray sky appeared in the distance, signaling the end of the forest, and perhaps the beginning of the riverlands. But as they drew closer, she noticed shimmering. The gray span wasn't sky... it was the ocean. When they emerged from the forest, a giant expanse of water appeared below the hill they stood upon. They'd arrived at the southern sea.

The Moshal led her down the grassy hill until they nearly reached the water, the sea at rest for the moment, only tiny waves crashing upon the rocky shoreline. Her guide surveyed the region before leading her to a cluster of tall gray rocks. Nestled within the rocks was a wooden boat, long and narrow, its design simple but sturdy. The Moshal untied the boat and picked up one end by a hook, glancing at her. Catherine did the same, and they carried the boat to the shoreline.

Suddenly, a loud shriek came from above them. Catherine instinctively covered her head with her hands. When she looked up, a giant bird headed their way, its body and wings completely white, its long dark beak protruding from its small head. Wings made a "foom, foom, foom" sound as they flapped, the bird's wingspan reaching at least four meters in length and its beak nearly a meter. Catherine gaped at the creature, its shadow darkening everything momentarily before making its way toward the ocean.

"Holy shit," she murmured.

Something nudged her pack. She looked over; the Moshal had bumped her with an oar. When he motioned to his shoulders, Catherine took off her pack and handed it to him. He stowed it in a box at the far end of the narrow vessel. She took another glance out to sea; the bird was gone.

The Moshal motioned to the boat and Catherine stepped into it. He pulled the boat further into the water and eventually climbed in, rowing a few times before reaching into his bag and retrieving a dark gray garment. "Wear this."

Catherine began removing her jacket.

"Leave it," he told her. "You will get cold."

Catherine re-zipped her jacket and took the garment from him. It was a hooded robe, the same dark gray as his. She put it on over her clothing, leaning to one side to get the robe under her behind, the length of it puddling at her feet. The Moshal handed her an oar and they began to row.

They headed west, and at a greater clip than Catherine expected. Her guide had a powerful stroke, and she did her best to paddle when he did and avoid impeding him. From under her hood, she looked landward: the trees had ceased, replaced by a delta where river met ocean. The river valley. After rowing for some time, Catherine's arms got tired and she rested her oar along the boat's edge. The Moshal, sensing her lack of effort, spoke to her.

"You may rest," he said.

As the hours passed, the light began to dim. And that's when Catherine spotted them. Islands; white rocks and stark glass structures rising from the sea; boats of varying types; a tall cliff in the distance. They approached the industrialized region.

Her guide turned to her. "Does your invisibility device function?"

Catherine pulled them out and tried each. "They're dead."

"Keep your head down, as if you sleep. Do not let anyone see your face, your hands, or your hair."

She took one last look at the beautiful twilight scene before she pulled her hood down further and tucked her hands into her sleeves. Soon, she heard things: a splash here and there, a voice in the distance, the sea lapping against solid objects, whether islands or structures… She longed to look, to take in all of it, but knew her face would cause the worst sort of trouble.

By the time their vessel veered right, toward the shoreline, it was dark. The Moshal ceased rowing and put his oar back in the boat, and they soon came to a stop. After securing the boat, Catherine heard him open the storage box and remove her gear before stepping out of the boat. She wanted to look up, but dared not until he gave the word.

"Come up," he said.

Catherine spotted a ladder. She gathered her excessively long robe in one hand and climbed the ladder with the other until she reached a landing above the sea. Her guide led her through a door and into a dwelling.

Three gray-robed Korvali stood inside, staring at her.

The white stone table felt smooth against Catherine's hands as she sat upon a stool fashioned from a tree trunk. The room had windows on three sides, one of which included the doorway she'd entered, while the fourth wall had two doors that led somewhere unknown. The sea rested only meters beneath them.

It was the first time Catherine felt cold, other than perhaps the period she spent nude inside the Shemal hut. Too many hours exposed to maritime weather. Too many hours with soggy socks. Even her dry underclothing felt damp. She was hungry, too, having rationed her food, not knowing how long she'd be at large.

Her Moshal guide had disappeared. She sat upon the trunk, separated from her gear once again. The three who'd met her at the door stood at the other end of the room, talking quietly amongst themselves, occasionally turning to stare at her. One of them was a woman, whose stare seemed especially probing. Catherine returned her stare, feeling a strange sense of familiarity, as if she'd seen her before, possibly at Fallal Hall. She was older, perhaps 50 in Earth years, with fair hair, grayish eyes, and an unblinking gaze.

Catherine shook her head. She couldn't possibly know that woman, or any of these people. Fallal Hall was Shereb terrain, and her guide had brought her to the territory of some other clan. She'd done what all humans did when encountering foreign peoples: perceived that they all looked alike. They certainly behaved alike, at least in their tendency to disregard her. Catherine glanced down at the woman's left hand, but her sleeve covered her marking.

"Remove your clothing," the woman said coldly, her English smooth and her accent less pronounced than her Moshal guide's.

Catherine rolled her eyes and stood up, peeling off her layers for another inspection. Goose bumps formed on her arms and legs as she began shivering. Once naked, she removed the contents of her pockets, folded and stacked her clothing, and stood there.

One of the men picked up her garments. As he did, his sleeve came up, exposing part of his marking: it was the circular crest of the Moshal. He disappeared through a door.

The woman picked up Catherine's pack and set it upon the table. "Remove your other belongings and tell me what each is."

As Catherine unpacked her gear, the man who'd taken her clothing returned and extended a long arm toward her, something dark and folded resting on his webbed hand. Catherine reached for the item and inspected it. It was a woven blanket. She unfolded it and wrapped it around her, feeling immediately better as she sat down. The woman eyed him, almost as if disapproving of the gesture. The two men turned to leave; when the second man reached to open the door, his sleeve fell back and revealed his hand. But instead of the circular crest, he wore the branched marking of the Osecal.

The woman listened while Catherine explained each item in English. At last, she picked up Catherine's communicator and examined it.

"Why does it not function?" she said.

"It needs recharging," Catherine said. "I think the koshac trees drained it."

The woman stared at her for a moment. Then, she gathered all of Catherine's belongings and began putting them into the pack.

"Don't you want to know why I'm here?" Catherine said.

"I know why you are here."

"Then where is he?"

"Where is whom?" the woman said, her eyes steely.

"Eshel."

The woman paused before replying. "You will have no information now. You must wait."

"I've been waiting," Catherine snapped. "For days."

"You will wait more."

The woman took Catherine's pack and left.

Catherine gathered the heavy blanket around her and approached a window, peeking out from the edge of the woven shade. But she saw only darkness, heard only waves lapping against the abode's piers. Her superiors would wonder where the hell she was, what was taking so long. Her cover would buy her some time; but the longer she was gone, the more likely people would become suspicious, including Steele. And once Steele grew suspicious, he caused trouble.

When the door opened, Catherine turned around. The man who'd taken her clothing entered; he set a neatly folded stack of garments upon the table with one webbed hand, and a wooden bowl and her canteen with the other. He disappeared again.

Ignoring her clothing, Catherine picked up the wooden bowl. It contained a slimy concoction of pinkish sea flesh and bright green sea vegetables. But before she could take a bite, the Korvali returned, hastily snatched the bowl from her hands, and left. Muttering a string of curse words, she tossed the blanket away and began dressing herself.

If you ever show your damned face, Eshel, you're going to wish they'd sent Tom instead.

She glanced at her food supplies. They'd dwindled considerably and she still had her return journey to consider. She cursed again, allowing herself to eat only a small portion.

Once dressed, she sat down on her tree trunk. She recalled that some time ago, a trio of Korvali—two men and a woman—had transmitted a video message to the Alliance, offering to make an agreement with them while circumventing Elisan and their leadership. The trio included one male Moshal and a male and female Osecal, all of whom spoke with authority, as if they represented leadership among those who opposed Elisan. Now, she'd stood before two men, one Moshal and one Osecal, and a woman. They'd seemed to expect her arrival, had asked no questions of her. Perhaps they led the vokalis, the multi-clan faction of Korvali who'd formed the rebellion.

Her stomach grumbling and a headache on the horizon, Catherine laid her head upon the blanket and closed her eyes.

Catherine awoke to the sound of quiet voices. Robed figures stood at the other end of the room. As her eyes focused, she saw the woman, standing with upright posture, listening to what another said. Catherine felt that sense of familiarity again, like she'd encountered her before. And as if knowing Catherine watched them, they turned and peered at her.

Rain pattering on the roof made her aware of her full bladder. She said as much to the others. The woman stared at her for a bit too long, before finally motioning to the narrow second door. Catherine opened the door, grateful to see a toilet-like contraption. When she finished and emerged from the lavatory, the woman was engaged in conversation. As she gestured with her left arm, her sleeve shifted, revealing a glimpse of something Catherine hadn't expected to see.

A flash of a leaf. The Shereb crest.

Then she knew. The Shereb gray eyes, the strange familiarity of her… the woman wasn't from Fallal Hall, or from the video message. She was Eshel's mother.

Catherine took her seat and waited for whatever came next. The lot of them ceased talking and looked toward the door. Catherine looked too but saw nothing. Then, footsteps. Only one person, climbing the ladder. For whom did they wait? Who would arrive in the darkness, in the rain? One of them opened the door, and a gray-robed figure appeared in the doorway, a hood obscuring the figure's face as he shook off remaining raindrops. Once inside, the figure removed his hood, his gaze immediately meeting Catherine's.

It was Eshel.

CHAPTER 9

"Catherine."

"Hey," Catherine said, a smile reaching her lips despite the many eyes that watched them.

Eshel stared at her for a moment, his expression unreadable other than appearing unsurprised to see her. He turned to the others and spoke a few quiet words in Korvali, after which they disappeared through the internal door. Eshel's mother lingered behind, giving Eshel a look that Catherine didn't understand, but that put her on edge. The woman began to speak.

"She understands the language," Eshel said, cutting her off. And with the slightest tilt of his head, his mother exited. He sat down across from Catherine. "You look unwell."

"I'm starving."

Eshel rose and left the room. Soon, he returned and set a wooden bowl in front of her. The pinkish fish and green sea vegetables again. She took a bite, and then devoured the rest, after which she took several gulps from her canteen to quench her thirst from the salty food. She breathed a sigh of relief as her headache began to wane.

"I am told you were captured by the Shemal," Eshel said.

She nodded. "I was told that area was uninhabited."

"It was," Eshel said. "I have since learned that the Shemal expanded to that region because it has good land for farming. The leadership granted them the territory to assuage their anger for having so little voice in the assembly."

"I wore my device. I was quiet. I don't know how they detected me."

"Their patrollers are extremely vigilant. I too encountered them when I arrived."

"Did they imprison you?"

"No."

"I thought they were going to kill me," she said.

"If you had not spoken the old greeting, they would have."

"Esh," she said, leaning forward. "One of them could see me. She could see me even with my device on."

Eshel's eyes narrowed. "You are sure."

She nodded. "Do you think she was genetically altered, like you?"

"That is unlikely," Eshel said, his expression one she'd seen before, a mixture of perplexed and intrigued.

Catherine stirred in her seat. "Why haven't you been in contact with Koni? People are worried."

"The patrollers inadvertently disabled my communicators before they understood their purpose. Did you bring more of them?"

"Yes. Two extras." she said. "They're dead, but they're rechargeable."

"Why did they lose their charge so quickly?"

"My guide said the koshac trees have some kind of effect on them. That must be why they failed so quickly at Fallal Hall." She paused. "Esh, I need to get word to Koni and so do you. If we don't do it soon, they'll send Tom or do something that will harm whatever it is you're trying to achieve here."

"Where are the devices?"

"Your—I mean, someone took them."

Eshel got up and left the room. After a short while, he returned with her gear.

"I have sent word," he said. "I recommend you send no transmission unless absolutely necessary."

She nodded.

"Thank you for bringing the communicators," he said. He remained standing. "Catherine, you must leave. The longer you remain here, the greater the risk to yourself, and to us."

"I know," she said. But despite having done her job and knowing Eshel was right, a wave of disappointment came over her.

"Your guide will take you to your craft and ensure you have clearance to leave our space. You may sleep here for the remainder of the night. In the morning, you will go."

He motioned for her to follow him through the internal door, which led to an empty hallway. To the right, at the end, was another door. Inside was a small room with a platform, thick blankets on it. Catherine entered the room and set down her things.

"Sleep well," Eshel said. And he shut the door behind him.

Catherine stood for a moment, alone in the tiny room, staring at the door. Finally, she sat down on the bed and took off her boots. A keen desire came over her to leave this soggy place, filled with secretive people who ignored her. And if her Moshal guide had shown his face, she would've asked him to leave right then. Shaking her head, she lay down and covered herself with a blanket.

The next morning, Catherine stood near the stone table. Dawn hadn't yet come. She was rested and repacked to leave, her devices fully charged and her belly full of slimy sea sustenance. Her Moshal guide appeared from the internal door and handed her a gray robe. Eshel stood aside while she put it on, the material again pooling at her feet.

Her guide looked down at the extra fabric. "You are tall for a human female, but perhaps not tall enough."

Catherine looked up at him, recognizing his attempt at humor. She gave a half smile. "It seems I don't fit in here." She put her hood up, picked up the excess fabric, and walked out the door.

They descended the ladder to the boat that awaited them. As they pulled away, Catherine craned her head around. Eshel stood on the deck, watching them leave, his eyes meeting hers. She watched for a few moments before she faced forward again, pulling her hood down and hiding her hands within her sleeves as the Moshal rowed them east. And once he said the word, Catherine picked up her oar and began to row.

Eshel emerged from the internal door and sat down at the stone table, where his mother waited for him. Outside, the daytime skies grew dark and the gray sea roiled and heaved as the waves lapped upon the windows.

"A gale comes," his mother said.

Eshel nodded.

"Why was she here?"

"You know why. Ashan and I must communicate with the others if we are to succeed."

"Yes," Fashal said, her gray eyes boring into his. "But why her?"

"She has been here before. She knows the language."

"Because you taught it to her. Because you shared that which you shouldn't have."

A wave of irritation came over him. "We cannot achieve our goals without sharing with outsiders. Why do you resist?"

"Because I know the truth. You did the unspeakable, with her."

Eshel said nothing, as the sea rose up and partially consumed their dwelling, causing the room to darken briefly. He'd planned on telling his mother about Catherine, about his relations with her, at the appropriate time. But it seemed that someone had already informed her.

Upon hearing no argument or denial from him, his mother looked away. After several moments, she spoke again. "You put us all at risk with such behavior, and her too."

"That is why I severed our romantic relationship."

"And yet you watch while she leaves this place, until you could no longer see her." When Eshel gave no reply, she went on. "How could you do this… with a human? You cannot bond with them like you can with your own people, so why do this?"

"I do not know."

"That is no answer."

"That is the only answer I have," Eshel said angrily. "What did you believe would happen when we decided that I would escape? Did you believe I would live among the others—eat their food, drink their beverages, and learn their ways—and not change?"

"No," Fashal said. "But this… this is no small change. To do the unspeakable with an Inferior—"

"Do not call her that," Eshel said.

"To risk bonding with her, to risk creating an abomination, to connect yourself with humans in such a way… to defy our Doctrine!"

"I know," Eshel said. "But if not for Catherine, I would not be alive, we would have no bridge to the outsiders, and we would not sit here now. She is intelligent, and she has never betrayed me."

"Not yet. She is human, and we have not established trust with them yet."

"You haven't," Eshel said. "I have."

The room darkened again as a giant swell overtook their dwelling.

His mother gazed at him. "Your father… he was more liberal about such things. He would have gone to significant lengths to connect with outsiders. You cannot expect me, or others, to show such liberality."

"I do not," Eshel said. "But Father does not sit among us because we have allowed this leadership to harm us. That is why we are here. I do not need your chastisement. We must focus on our goal."

Fashal remained silent for several moments. "Yes," she finally said. "It is time to take the next step."

That evening, Catherine and her Moshal guide reached the rocky shoreline just before a big storm generated heavy rains and unusually large swells. Her guide had told her to paddle swiftly, likely knowing the squall was coming. They'd stored the boat behind the rocks, sat out the storm, and began trekking once more, taking a different route to avoid the ancient koshac forest and its inexplicable effect on Catherine's newly charged devices. Catherine followed the Moshal, lagging ten paces behind him as their footsteps fell silently on the forest floor. Finally, her guide stopped, allowing her to catch up to him.

"You are silent today," he said.

Catherine kept her eyes forward, on the path ahead. "What is there to talk about?"

"I am unaccustomed to interacting with humans," he said. "But you appear… angry."

Catherine glanced at the Moshal, taken aback by his unexpected and uncharacteristic interest in her. Maybe she had a narrow view of the Korvali, based on her time with Eshel. Maybe other Korvali, or perhaps the Moshal, weren't so standoffish or cold. Yet, the number of Korvali she'd encountered had grown significantly, and all of them had seemed far more like Eshel than like her guide.

"Am I correct?" he pressed. "Are you angry?"

"Yes," she muttered.

"Perhaps at the cold treatment you have received here, from my people."

"Perhaps."

"You are part of this human Space Corps," he said. "You must know that the Korvali do not like outsiders. Your very presence here violates our Doctrine."

"I was sent here, to help," she said. "I'm on your side; I don't want Elisan in power, either."

"The outsiders want Elisan removed for their own gain."

"Maybe. But so do you. And I've worked hard to protect Eshel and his interests."

"I know this. But the others do not."

"They would if you told them. Or if Eshel did."

He raised his eyebrows. "Do you believe the words of one or even two men would convince them of the appropriateness of an alien trespassing on our planet? If so, you have much to learn about us."

She looked down, feeling foolish at her outburst. "Maybe you're right."

"In this, there is no maybe."

"You sound like Eshel," she said with a chuckle.

"I will tell him you said that. Perhaps I will also tell him that you believe I am correct even more often than he."

She cocked her head. "Where did you learn your humor?"

"Perhaps I have always had it."

Catherine laughed at this, her dark feelings beginning to recede.

"And what of Eshel's treatment of you?" he went on. "Perhaps it bothers you as well."

Her smile faded. "Most of all."

"It is how he must behave. Not everyone knows of his past relations with you, nor would they approve."

Catherine looked away, embarrassed. If her guide knew about that, his mother probably did too. No wonder they hated her.

After trekking east for some time and crossing many a waterway, they returned to familiar territory. Shemal territory. And this time she saw them coming. She and her guide made no effort to camouflage themselves, and neither did the patrollers. They approached and formed a semicircle around them, twelve men and women, nude and spears in hand, their imposing stature and stares again making Catherine feel small and powerless.

Her guide put his left hand to his shoulder and spoke the Old Korvali greeting. He then talked for some time, none of which Catherine understood. Finally, one of the patrollers spoke. Her guide answered at greater length. After this went on for a while, the Shemal put their dotted hands to their shoulders and disappeared into the forest. Catherine, relieved that there would be no incident, followed her guide as he resumed heading east.

"You told them who we were?" she said.

"They knew. I relayed other information, about our plan."

"They know what's happening?"

"They must know," he said. "The Shemal are the largest of the primitive clans, and the most dangerous. They are the sentinels of the eastern and remote territories. One cannot achieve such a goal without their aid."

A thought came to her. "When they imprisoned me, before you arrived, I heard a noise in the night... a voice, crying out. It was terrible, like someone was being tortured or killed."

He lifted his chin, and called out briefly.

"Yes!" Catherine said. "Like that. But longer and much, much louder."

"That was the wail of the sher memeshar."

"Which rite is that?" she said, knowing she'd heard the word before.

"The death rite. The wailer was not dying, but honoring the death of a genetic relative, or a mate."

Someone had died that night. She shook her head. "I'm the only outsider who knows anything about your culture, and even I know so little."

The Moshal wove around a cluster of tree trunks. "We know more of the others than they do of us."

"Because the Korvali visit our worlds."

"Because we observe," he said. "The legends say that the Korvali have known of the others for centuries."

She turned to him, eyebrows raised. "How is that?"

"It is believed that the ancients travelled to the outerworlds and observed them, but made no contact."

"Huh." Catherine hadn't expected that, hadn't expected that the Korvali would have such legends, especially of such supernatural proportions.

Later in the night, they reached the Pokey hidden under the weeping tree, just as sheets of rain began pelting the forest floor. However, the Moshal refused to let her leave.

"It is not safe, since you are not an experienced pilot. Eshel insisted I ensure you did not depart during severe weather."

She sighed. "Then come and rest in my ship before you return." He made no argument. Once inside, Catherine turned to him. "I know you can't tell me anything about your plan. But… how do others feel about Elisan? Do they want change?"

His eyes remained forward, peering out the window. "The malkaris and Elisan have gained power due not only to cleverness and the trust of our people, but through deviousness and violation of our Doctrine. Such methods require punishment and cannot continue."

"And others agree with this?"

"They agree since discovering the truth."

"The truth?"

Her guide paused, turning to face her. "Your leadership trusts you to offer us aid and to come to our planet; thus, you must know of the first to escape Korvalis."

"Ashan," she said. "Yes, I've read his report."

"Do you recall the history of the Shereb ascension to power?"

Catherine thought for a moment. "The Osecal clan ruled for ages, until their malkaris died. His sister died too, and before either could produce heirs. Some disease... the report didn't specify. A cousin took power, split from her Osecal mate, and then mated with a Shereb. This cousin is the current malkaris, and she and her new mate appointed Elisan and cleaned out your assembly, both of which violate your Doctrine." She paused. "You're saying this isn't true?"

"It is true. However, evidence has arisen suggesting that the Osecal leaders died unnatural deaths. This was not questioned for many years because both siblings suffered a heritable disease that can strike during youth. However, science has revealed evidence of murder, of a Shereb plot to usurp power."

Catherine nodded at this, not surprised by it, but also wondering how a people so scientifically advanced couldn't prevent heritable disease within their royalty. However, knowing Eshel would be a better person to ask, she moved on to another question. "Why would Elisan and the malkaris do this, when it's created such unrest among you?"

"They believe they protect us. The Shereb have excellent scientists and good genetic stock; they believe forcing their ways on us will make Korvalis greater. Before the Sunai discovered our existence, there was talk of making contact with them. Some did not approve of this, including many Shereb."

"And how does bridging with outsiders benefit you?" she asked.

"You are a geneticist; you know that an insulated group will experience inbreeding of genetic material, and the disease that accompanies it. The same can happen with ideas."

Catherine looked at the Moshal in wonder. How similar he was to Eshel… and how different. "It sounds like you've given this a lot of thought."

"More than most, perhaps." Her guide looked out the window again, listening. "The rains have let up. You are safe to depart." He stood up from his seat, ducking just a little to avoid hitting his head. Catherine opened the hatch, watching as the Moshal went to exit the weeping branches.

"Wait," she said.

He turned around.

"Thank you. For guiding me, and for your kindness." Knowing he wouldn't know what to say in response, she went on. "I would fly you back to the house by the sea, but I imagine that's not a good idea."

"It is not," he said. "However, I will not return there. I have another destination, in the north, where my clanspeople live."

She nodded, expecting him to leave without another word. But he hesitated, gazing at her, as if looking at something.

"Your hair," he said. "Such an unusual color. May I touch it?"

"Sure," she said, surprised at the strange request.

Her guide took several steps closer to her and took a handful of hair with his webbed hand. It was the closest any Korvali, other than Eshel, had ever come near her. He examined her hair closely in the light from the Pokey before gently setting it down. And with that, he turned away again.

"What's your name?" Catherine blurted out.

He turned back around, his expression chilly, and Catherine cringed just a little, knowing she'd likely annoyed him. However, instead of ignoring her or refusing her request, he said, "I am Ashan."

And he left.

Catherine paused for a moment, the name echoing in her auditory memory. *Ashan?* A series of thoughts flooded her. The fact that he spoke such good English, despite being Moshal. His strange curiosity, his sense of humor, his willingness to talk with her, his passion about their cause. How different he was. Eshel hadn't schooled him…

years of living off Korvalis had. She let out an incredulous laugh. After so much time together, any human would've leaked some key piece of information that would give away his identity to the astute. Yet, the signs were there the entire time, and she'd overlooked them all, never having considered that Ashan was even alive, much less escorting her through unknown lands.

Another thought occurred to her: How did Ashan get back to Korvalis? Perhaps he'd returned with Eshel, had been part of the plan all along. She shook her head and resumed her place in the Pokey. Just as she went to start the engine, a robed figure appeared.

It was Ashan, his expression troubled.

She reopened the hatch. "What's wrong?"

"Leave your spacecraft," he said coldly. "You must come with me."

Catherine stared at him. "Why?"

"Elisan has discovered the vokalis, that Eshel is here. And he has told your Alliance."

She blinked a couple of times. "What happens now?"

"We must hide you," he said.

"I mean, what will become of the vokalis? Of your mission?"

"It has failed."

CHAPTER 10

Commander Yamamoto sat at his desk, scrolling through the latest string of complaints from crewmembers. His door sounded.

"Enter."

He glanced up, wondering who'd come to bother him without first setting up a time. Commanders Marks and O'Leary stood before him and saluted. Judging by their expressions—a combination of embarrassment and smugness—he had a strong suspicion about why they'd paid him a visit.

"Sir," Commander Marks began, jutting out his square jaw. "We know about the op... with the Korvali, with Eshel. Headquarters has asked us to place you under arrest... and to relieve you of duty. And the Captain, too."

Yamamoto sat back in his chair, letting out a breath. He turned to O'Leary. "You will take command?"

"Yes, Sir," replied the Chief Engineer in his deep voice. "Sorry to do this, Sir."

"What happened?"

"We can explain that at the briefing, Sir," Marks said.

Yamamoto stood up and followed the two men to the bridge ready room, where he'd sat through countless briefings with those who would now take command of *Cornelia*. Elisan found out. He and Janice had talked about this, had considered that this could happen. Eshel too had acknowledged the risks. Unfortunately, with Catherine having experienced unexplained delays and not returning to duty as quickly as they'd hoped, and Eshel not having received his new communicators in time as a result, he had little information with which to plead their case to Headquarters and to the Alliance. And now, it was too late. Their discovery meant that all communications with Korvalis would shut down indefinitely, leaving Catherine marooned there. Yamamoto hoped only that their precautions had guarded her from detection. Elisan discovering Eshel's presence was one thing; discovering Catherine's was quite another.

When they arrived at the ready room, Ferguson sat in her usual chair at the head of the table, flanked by Commanders Ov'Raa and Steele. She shot him a wry smile as he sat down.

Marks went to speak, but O'Leary cut him off. "Sorry to do this, Captain, Commander," he said, glancing at them as he sank his heavy body into a chair. "Admiral's orders. Headquarters has deployed the Starship *Victoria* to assist. I'll take command until she arrives in three days."

"Who's in command of *Victoria?*" Ferguson said.

"Dunno, Ma'am," O'Leary said. "Headquarters only mentioned that the Admiral is also aboard."

"What happened, Commander?" Yamamoto asked.

"Elisan contacted the Alliance," Marks chimed in. "He claims that Eshel is on Korvalis—not Suna—and that he's plotting with others against the leadership. I assume that all of this is true?"

"Yes," Ferguson said. "It's true. I coordinated the entire thing, and I take full responsibility for it."

Before Yamamoto could join in Ferguson's admission, O'Leary spoke again. "Elisan believes the Alliance orchestrated this, that they're in on it—"

"The Alliance had nothing to do with this," Ferguson said. "We acted outside their wishes, and I'm prepared to say so to the Korvali and anyone else who needs to hear it."

"The Alliance has denied their involvement, but Elisan's not convinced," O'Leary said.

"Not surprising," Marks said. "He's a liar, so he assumes we are, too."

"We will do what is necessary," Yamamoto said. "What's most important is showing Elisan that we acted out of turn."

"So this leaves an important question, Captain, Commander," O'Leary said, glancing at each of them. "Is the geneticist, Lieutenant Catherine Finnegan, with Eshel on Korvalis?"

Yamamoto turned to Ferguson.

"No," Ferguson said. "She's on Suna, on scientific assignment."

"I ask because it's an interesting coincidence that she happened to get assigned off-ship not long after Eshel left," O'Leary went on.

"I agree, Commander," Ferguson said. "It looks suspicious. But it's the truth—"

"Then why doesn't she respond to messaging in a timely fashion?" Steele demanded.

"Like I already told you, Finnegan can be contacted through Grono Amsala," Ferguson replied. "That's the way he wanted it, something to do with the nature of the project. If you want to know why there are delays, ask him."

Commander Steele's eyes narrowed. "It is unacceptable for you to reassign of one of my scientists to a dubious project that I have no knowledge of. I am Chief of Research and such a decision shouldn't be made without my permission."

Ferguson gave Steele a stern look. "We may utilize her as we choose, without your permission or your approval."

"You are in no position to make such a declaration now," Steele said.

Seeing Ferguson's dark glare, O'Leary stepped in. "Let's stick to the point. We've got much bigger concerns here. Elisan suspects we're somehow involved in Eshel's rebellion against him. He's demanding we stand down… and that we relinquish any rights we have to Eshel."

Yamamoto sighed, but remained silent. Now wasn't the time to argue.

"That sounds reasonable," Marks said.

"That's not all," O'Leary said. "He's threatening retaliation. And it appears they have the means to follow through on the threats." O'Leary clicked a remote, and an image appeared on the main viewer: a human woman with a blank look in her eyes stood expressionless next to two robed Korvali, their faces obscured. The woman had Janice Ferguson's face.

Yamamoto closed his eyes momentarily. He then glanced at Ferguson, whose face paled. A silence fell over the room.

"Was the image falsified, perhaps?" Ov'Raa said, his face bluing as he clasped his six-fingered hands together.

"Technology already checked," O'Leary said. "It's genuine."

"We can detect clones now," Marks argued.

"We can," O'Leary said. "Jula can. Not every spaceport on Earth can. The other worlds can't."

"We can give them the technology," Marks said.

"If it's not too late," O'Leary said. "For all we know, they're already here. And once they deploy one of their weapons, thousands will die before the disease control organizations can get their arms around it."

"What's Headquarters' take?" Ferguson said.

"Mixed, as usual," O'Leary said. "Some want war, others want to wave the white flag."

"And the Alliance?"

"The Alliance wants the latter, of course. They're also talking about suspending our membership in the Alliance, along with punitive measures."

Ferguson let out a sigh. "Look. Whatever our punishment, Suko and I are prepared to help. We must do whatever is necessary to calm Elisan down."

"I'm glad you feel that way, Ma'am," O'Leary said. "Because we've already decided to revoke Eshel's commission and return him to his people." He paused. "In six days, the Alliance delegates will gather, along with their respective leaderships. Captain, Commander, you won't represent Earth—those arriving on the *Victoria* will—but you'll attend to report what you know of this mess so they can come up with a plan to deal with it. In the meantime, the Alliance worlds have received warning to be on alert and allow no ships to enter or leave their space. With luck, the Korvali can't work their magic through gumiia or other hired agents who act on their behalf."

"We need to talk to Grono Amsala," Yamamoto said.

"I can't allow that, Sir," O'Leary said.

Yamamoto leaned forward. "If we want to get in front of this, Commander, I strongly suggest you find a way to allow it."

"Are the Sunai involved in your plans, Commander?" Ov'Raa said.

"Of course they are," Marks said. "Whether they admit it or not."

"I cannot speak for the Sunai," Yamamoto said. "And I would be cautious about leveling accusations," he added, eyeing Marks.

O'Leary took a deep breath. "We'll do what we can, Sir. But the Sunai haven't given us much. For now, Captain, Commander…" He paused, clearing his throat. "To show Elisan we're serious, we're sending you to Jula."

"What for?" Ferguson said.

"For imprisonment."

Yamamoto finished his last combination of maneuvers and inhaled a deep breath of air, a thin layer of sweat covering him. He picked up his towel and wiped his brow before pouring himself some water from a russet clay pitcher. After drinking a cupful, he paced the windowless room, lit to its maximum level for the benefit of his human eyes.

The room, with its ochre cave-like walls, was at least comfortable and cool. It had one bed, one chair, and a toilet with a design that could accommodate the needs of nearly any person, Sunai or otherwise. Yamamoto nodded in approval. The Sunai, for all their blustering and aggression, did welcome alien peoples to their lands, so much so that even their prison toilets accommodated all. He paced some more, letting his body cool, preferring not to sit for long periods, unless necessary. Too much sitting invited laziness, passivity, atrophy.

He'd given considerable thought to the situation they faced. He'd presented his recommendations to those who would consider them.

In his mind, there remained only two major concerns: first and most important was preventing Elisan from acting. They'd begun taking measures, but with Elisan there was always risk. He'd hoped to communicate with Eshel through Grono Amsala, imploring him to do what he could to assuage Elisan for now. But the Grono reported that communications were at a standstill, and would remain so until the vokalis identified the mole who'd betrayed them.

And the second concern: Catherine. While such a concern paled in comparison to that of Elisan, Yamamoto disliked putting Catherine at such risk, and not a day passed in which he didn't think of her, didn't hope that his training would help ensure her survival. He took solace in knowing that Eshel would do his best to protect Catherine. If necessary, and with the right measures, Catherine could survive on Korvalis for months, even years.

Voices outside his door interrupted Yamamoto's thoughts. He heard a loud guttural voice, along with a quieter, smoother one. A Sundani guard and a human. Someone had come to visit him. When the door opened, it echoed throughout the small room while a gray-haired man in a spotless decorated uniform entered and closed the door behind him.

"Sir," Yamamoto said, immediately giving Admiral Scott a salute, after which he motioned to his single chair. The Admiral sat while Yamamoto took a seat on his bed.

"I just briefed Janice," the Admiral said. "We meet with the delegates and their leaderships tomorrow. The Sunai guards will escort you both there."

"Yes, Sir."

The Admiral looked at him with shrewd eyes. "We could've found a better way if you'd consulted me, Suko."

"You wouldn't have granted us permission, Sir."

The Admiral shook his head. "So having your way and disrespecting your organization was worth facing court-martial, being stripped of your rank, and putting our people at risk."

Yamamoto stood up, pacing for a few moments before answering.

"Not consulting you was never out of disrespect, Sir. It was to protect you, to protect the Corps. If it succeeded, everybody wins. If it failed, you would punish your rogue command and continue on as before."

His admission had the effect he'd hoped it would. The Admiral seemed to relax.

"Before we meet with the Alliance," he said, "do you have anything you want to tell me? Such as how the Sunai are involved in this? Other than Grono Amsala coming clean and losing his rank, they've been unusually tight-lipped."

"I assume it's safe to talk here, Sir?" Yamamoto said, looking around him. The Admiral nodded. "I know no more than you do, Sir. I imagine tomorrow will reveal more of the Sunai stance on this issue."

The Admiral shifted in his seat. "How are you doing, Suko? They treating you okay in here?"

"As well as could be. Any news?"

"Nothing good. Elisan has located Eshel and plans to press him to reveal any co-conspirators."

Yamamoto shook his head. "I would not trust Elisan's threats any more than his promises. And you shouldn't either, Sir."

"You've put us in a position where we don't have much choice. Part of me is impressed by your audacity here... but the risks don't justify the rewards."

"We don't know that yet, Sir," Yamamoto said. "We've had problems with communications, but we don't yet know—"

"Stow it," the Admiral said. "Elisan knows and he's found Eshel. It's over." He paused. "Janice told me about the geneticist. You shouldn't have involved a subordinate in this, especially a whitecoat."

"She's a COO, and necessary to the mission," Yamamoto said. "She can handle herself."

"If Elisan finds her, they'll use her to punish us."

Yamamoto pressed his lips together at that, at being reminded of the thing he feared.

"Can we get her out of there?" the Admiral said.

"It's too dangerous. Eshel will protect her, even if he must genetically alter her to look Korvali."

The Admiral made a face. "Is that possible?"

Yamamoto shrugged. "Probably not. But then again, we didn't believe it possible to create a live adult replica clone, either."

"I still don't get it, Suko. Risking it all, including war with an enemy whose defensive powers are a threat to us... for what? To convince a reticent race of people to join an Alliance they've shown no real interest in joining?"

Yamamoto stopped pacing and turned toward his superior. "With all due respect, Sir, that's a very limited perspective. This... all of this... began long before Janice and I sent Eshel back to Korvalis. It began the moment we, as an Alliance, decided that we would house any Korvali who escaped the planet where its leadership has not honored the Doctrine that represents the foundation of their world. We can appease Elisan and send Eshel to his demise... but the problem remains. Another Korvali will escape, someone will give him shelter because they can't resist doing so, and Elisan will devise more ways to punish us. This mission... it was to put an end to this cycle."

"That's not the way Janice put it."

Yamamoto raised a finger. "Janice and I have never seen eye to eye on this. But we agree that Elisan must be stopped."

"And the words of one Korvali are enough to convince you that this cycle will end, that the new leadership won't pull the same shit once they get into power?"

"Not one, no. But the words of two have."

The Admiral's eyes narrowed. "What do you mean, two?"

Janice hasn't told him yet.

"You recall the Ashan Report." When the Admiral nodded, he went on. "Ashan is alive, I have met him personally, and he accompanied Eshel to Korvalis."

The Admiral let out a breath, shaking his head. "I'll be goddamned. Why didn't you mention this sooner?"

"Because I do not believe Elisan knows of Ashan's existence. Ashan has considerable influence with the Korvali Guard, many of whom support the rebellion. That is how we were able to achieve any of this."

He stroked his jaw for several moments. "Well, that's the best news I've had in a while. Maybe there's hope in this after all."

"I believe there is, Sir. However, I ask that you say nothing of Ashan for now. He may serve as leverage." When the Admiral gave the nod, he shifted topics. "What's the overall feeling at Headquarters?"

"They want your heads. But they're also still chafing over that clone nightmare and the loss of two soldiers, so if you'd succeeded without getting caught I think you'd both be decorated, rather than court-martialed. Now, they're looking at more aggressive tactics, but thanks to you and Janice the Alliance isn't interested in discussing them."

"They were never interested in discussing them," Yamamoto said. "Two of ours is nothing compared to convincing Elisan that he can put limited trust in us, a goal that I've become long convinced is futile."

The Admiral stood up. "Save your arguments for the Alliance meeting, Suko. Because after that, you and Janice head home."

"Yes, Sir."

Tom followed the hulking Sundani guard down a dimly lit hallway, its subterranean air stale but cool. They'd scanned and searched him, but Tom had known not to stow any weapons on him this time. After stopping at a door, the guard entered a code into the console and the door released. The eyeshaded guard turned to him and grunted.

Tom gave him a nod. "Thank you, Gro."

Tom entered the small room, squinting at the brighter light. Yamamoto stood, holding a reading pad. He motioned to the chair. Tom gave a salute before handing Yamamoto a metal canister and a portable.

"I thought you could use some refreshment, Sir," Tom said with a grin, taking a seat. "And some new book files."

Yamamoto studied the portable. "Thank you, Tom. I don't suppose you brought any for the Captain…"

"Already gave them to her, Sir." Yamamoto nodded, a hint of gratitude in his stoic expression. "Sorry this happened, Sir. Captain told me everything. I had a feeling something was up when you all sent Catherine to Suna for scientific reasons."

Yamamoto gave a slight tilt of his head. "It was the best cover we could muster, given the circumstances."

"Any news you can share?"

"I'm afraid not, Tom."

Tom hesitated. "Any news on Catherine?"

"No. Communications with Korvalis have ceased."

Sensing worry in Yamamoto, Tom waved his hand. "Esh will never let anything happen to her. She's not much of a swimmer, but at least she can eat their food and drink their water. She'll be alright." Tom paused. "You could've sent me, you know. Eshel trusts me now."

"If you'd learned the language and culture, I would have."

"Touché, Sir."

Yamamoto finally sat down. "Since we're on that topic, I need you ready for deployment, if it comes to that."

"Always ready, Sir."

"Good." Yamamoto paused. "Tell me what you know, Tom. About the crew, about what's happening."

Tom shrugged. "The crew's been on edge since the clone attack. O'Leary's announcement about you and the Captain was pretty brief—you know O'Leary—so everyone's suspicious. They think it has something to do with Esh and with Catherine being gone."

"How are they responding to the change in leadership?"

"Most don't have to deal with the new brass," Tom said. "I think they're just shook up about not knowing what's going on."

"Hopefully that will resolve itself soon, one way or another. Any progress with Jooni's proposal for interplanetary exchange?"

"Snow's spending his spare time doing research on it. He pissed and moaned at first, but once he got going... I don't think I've ever seen him work so hard on something. I think Earth will have her... it's just a matter of getting the Sunai to agree to it."

Yamamoto nodded. "And have you made any headway with Maria?"

Tom, not expecting the question, hesitated for several moments. "You want to know about Maria?"

"I've been confined to this cell for five days, Tom."

"Of course, Sir. No progress there."

"Why not?"

Tom shrugged. "She's with Ferrars. She says he wants what she wants."

"And what is that?"

"A family."

Yamamoto cocked his head, his expression one of curiosity.

"You look like I felt when she told me that, Sir," Tom said with a chuckle.

"What else did she say?"

Tom told Yamamoto what he could recall of his talk with Maria. "You know me, Sir. I'm a soldier, not a family man."

"You can be both."

"I know. But I'd miss out on the real missions, the long ones. I like being out here."

Yamamoto reached for the canister Tom brought him. "Tom, do you want my opinion?"

"Yes, Sir."

He opened the lid to the canister, inhaling its contents briefly before taking a drink. "You are approaching the age at which you must consider the path you will choose. You can seek command, forgoing children in lieu of a life in space, as the Captain and I have. Or you can spend your youth in space, after which you find your place at Headquarters and have a family, and take extended deep space trips when your children are grown... as Marks, Ov'Raa, and many others will. I don't see you taking the first path."

"Wha…" Tom sputtered. "Why not?"

"I don't believe field command would suit you in the way that fatherhood would. And I don't want to see you miss that opportunity for the sake of… this." Yamamoto motioned to the room they sat in.

"This," Tom said, motioning as well, "is part of the adventure."

Yamamoto took another swig from the canister. "When one takes field command, things look very different."

Tom, hardly knowing what to say, merely sat in silence, wishing he too could drink from the canister.

Yamamoto stood and began pacing. "It seems to me that you seek field command not to further the goals of the Corps, but perhaps as a way to avoid fatherhood and the responsibilities that come with it."

Tom scowled, crossing his arms. "When did I say that?"

"You didn't have to."

"I'm not afraid of it, damn it. I just… I don't want kids."

Yamamoto waved an arm at him as he sat back down. "If that's your choice, then so be it. However, if you change your mind, I believe you would do well at Headquarters, and that you would find fatherhood more rewarding than you imagine. And, if you choose to see things this way, I would not give up on Maria."

Tom raised his eyebrows. "Why not?"

"Maria cast you aside for Ferrars. If she then returns to you when you've had a change of heart, she risks appearing capricious. No one seeking command can afford that, particularly if female. You must maintain your friendship with her, and wait for her current relationship to dissolve on its own."

"What if it doesn't?"

"It will."

Tom, despite his confusion, grinned. "I like you when you're relieved of duty, Sir."

"You're dismissed, Tom."

CHAPTER 11

I am told the people of Calyyt-Calloq have their deserts and moyyt-toq, the Sunai their volcanoes and kala, the Derovians their shorelines and rallnofia, and the humans their diverse languages and their ale. The Korvali, however, have only their oceans and their Doctrine. Without these, Korvalis is no longer.

- Ashan, from the Ashan Report

In the room that overlooked the southern sea, Eshel sat with his mother at the white stone table as rain drummed upon the rooftop.

"This betrayer…" Fashal said. "I admit I have no suspicious person to investigate, much less indict."

"Nor do I," Eshel said coldly.

"This was always a risk."

"We used such caution… not revealing more information than necessary, hiding Ashan's identity, bringing Catherine here rather than to our other gathering places…" Eshel stood and approached the window, watching the gray sea heave beneath them.

"It only takes one, son. Many have difficulty with what we plan, and we are working with the other clans, all of whom have their own notions of what is correct." She paused. "Now that the Alliance has discovered the truth, they will disseminate it. They will punish the human and Sunai collaborators and seek to appease Elisan. We will no longer have allies among the others."

"Unless we identify the betrayer. But without evidence, such a feat is like finding a single leaf upon a seshac tree."

"Even if we find the betrayer, without secrecy we are defeated."

Eshel remained at the window, considering their options. "Do not speak of the betrayal or acknowledge defeat to anyone. Not yet. Elisan will begin pursuing us, so we must leave here."

"We must warn the others, son. Elisan may seek them instead of us."

"No. Each of us knew the risk of discovery and each must accept that risk."

"That is dangerous."

"It is dangerous to tell them without knowing who the betrayer is," Eshel said. "This way, Elisan does not know where they go."

"What will you tell them?"

"To scatter, that I will pursue an important operation. That will buy us time."

Fashal eyed him. "What do you plan? You cannot infiltrate Fallal Hall. They will expect it."

"I will go to Guard Headquarters and establish contact with the others at Station Fourteen."

They remained silent for some time, the rain still coming down outside. Finally, Fashal stood.

"What of this human?"

"Catherine," Eshel said coldly. "I will deal with her."

"She is a liability. If Elisan knows of her presence here…"

"He has issued threats of war to the Alliance. If he knew she were here, if he knew how large we are, he would be far more cautious, wanting to convey weakness. He bluffs."

"Bluffs?"

"Pretends he will act drastically, in order to instill fear. When he is truly affronted, he is silent."

"You merely speculate. If he finds her, it compromises us."

"He will not find her," Eshel said. "I will ensure it."

"And where will you take her?"

"Far from here," Eshel said. He turned away from the window. "Leave this place, and do not tell me where you will go. I will contact you soon."

Fashal approached Eshel and stood face to face with him. She leaned over and put her cheek to his before she turned and left.

As Catherine walked, the rains pelted her hood and spotted up her protective eyewear. Ashan plodded on, seeming not to mind the drenching of his robe or the water in his face and eyes. He didn't even blink.

Elisan had found out. She couldn't imagine how, given Eshel's usual caution, his attention to detail, his careful planning. However, Eshel now worked among his own people, rather than alone or with one or two trusted humans, who were more easily hoodwinked. Elisan may have had agents, those who claimed allegiance to the rebellion but who, like Eshel's childhood friend Elan, secretly believed Eshel was no more than a traitor. Perhaps one of these agents had ratted them out.

With that thought, she gave a sidelong glance to Ashan, who walked silently beside her. She began wondering what she'd told him, if she'd revealed anything that would make things worse for Eshel. She didn't want to believe Ashan would betray Eshel and their cause, and it made little sense considering Ashan's escape and strong stance on the leadership. But if she'd learned anything about the Korvali, it was that they could turn on you quickly, that loyalty and personal bonds stood no chance against one's beliefs about their Doctrine and how Korvalis should be governed. And while it seemed absurd for Ashan to go to such lengths to escape and hide, just to reconnect with Elisan, it was possible that he served as Elisan's agent, as part of a long-term plan that would, in the end, benefit Elisan. Letting Ashan walk a bit ahead of her, Catherine began redistributing the contents of her pockets, ensuring her weapons were more easily accessed.

She then put such dismal thoughts aside, in favor of slightly less dismal ones. She was stuck on Korvalis, and for an indefinite period of time. Days ago, the prospect of remaining on the planet, of being in such an undiscovered place, would have pleased her. Now, it made her uneasy.

Cold had seeped in again, a soggy chill that seemed to permeate every part of her. How was it possible that she felt so cold after growing up in a place where, during winter, temperatures plummeted to those that put the current ones to shame? Up ahead, the dark rainclouds and ensuing fog only filled her with more trepidation. She peered up at the sky; just an hour of sunshine was all she needed. One hour. But it hadn't appeared since they'd traversed the koshac forest days ago, and it seemed that today would be no exception. Now, they'd return to the house on stilts, sit at the cold stone table, and eat cold fish while everyone ignored her and Elisan hunted them down.

Knock it off. This is your job, the one you signed up for. Tom would call it an adventure... and that's what it is. Catherine took a deep breath, her thoughts going to Tom's grinning face, wondering what he was doing and if he knew where she was. She stood up straighter and continued marching behind Ashan.

She wondered what Yamamoto and Ferguson would think of her now. Sure, she'd done the most important part of her op by allowing Eshel to reestablish contact with them. But it was also possible she'd somehow jeopardized Eshel's plans by being here. Then again, maybe it no longer mattered. If the Alliance knew of Eshel's plans, that meant Headquarters also knew. Which meant that Ferguson and Yamamoto would face court-martial.

The fog came. It was so thick that it reduced their visibility to no more than a couple of meters. And when darkness descended, the fog seemed only thicker and more ominous. She tripped several times and even fell to her knees once. She glanced up at Ashan again, his tall thin figure traveling swiftly and smoothly through the forest. For reasons she couldn't pinpoint, she suddenly felt glad for his presence, and even more flabbergasted at his being alive, at his having hidden himself for that long without anybody—or most anybody—knowing. When did Eshel find out? And how? How long had Eshel kept that secret from her? She had so many questions now, more than she could keep track of.

"You have looked at me several times as we have walked," Ashan said. "You are weighing the possibility that I am the traitor who informed Elisan."

Her face growing hot, Catherine searched for a response.

"It is a fair suspicion," he said. After a pause, he added, "We are only minutes from leaving the forest, after which we will cross the river valley. We cannot stop in the river valley. Is there anything you require before we go?"

"Maybe a beer," she quipped.

He looked down at her, his face expressionless. "I don't believe any Korvali would allow such a foul-tasting substance on our lands."

Catherine, despite herself, began to giggle, and she was sure Ashan gave a tiny smile. She snuck behind a tree to relieve herself, after which she put on the robe Ashan had given her. This time, however, instead of puddling at her feet, the robe fell to the top of her toes.

"Did you get this robe from a child?" she asked.

"No," he said, beginning to walk. "It is the robe you wore previously. I merely shortened it for you."

Under the cover of misty darkness, Ashan led them toward the river and its numerous tributaries. Some of the tributaries could be hopped, others resulted in wet feet, and still others required submerging to her waist. The river itself required a boat. Somehow, Ashan had known where to go and where the boats would be, despite the dense fog. He moved at an even swifter pace, probably seeking to get them under the cover of the forest as quickly as possible. And once they made it, Catherine breathed a sigh of relief.

Then, she heard something. A light crackle, as if someone had stepped on a branch. Ashan halted his quick pace and sidestepped behind a tree. Catherine did the same. Ashan slipped his hand into his robe pocket, and Catherine slowly retrieved her own weapon, glancing around to ensure no one snuck up behind them. She heard noise again. It sounded like footsteps, quiet on the leaf-littered forest floor. They could see nothing beyond the blinding fog, but the noise grew louder. Someone was coming.

Only one set of footsteps.

A dark mass appeared in the fog. As it got closer, she realized it was a person in a gray robe. After several more moments, in which Catherine held her breath, Eshel emerged.

When Catherine and Ashan came out from behind their trees, Eshel peered at her for several moments. Catherine, prepared for whatever chilly treatment might come, turned to Ashan, waiting for him to speak.

"You made good time," Eshel said to Ashan in Korvali.

"She is a fast walker," Ashan said.

The two men gazed at one another for several moments, but the fog and darkness made it difficult to read their faces. Eshel too would wonder about Ashan. But he would remain silent, giving away nothing until he'd gathered all the necessary information.

"You will keep her safe?" Ashan said.

"Of course."

"Send word when you can." Ashan turned and left.

Catherine watched him go, his tall figure blending into the fog, his robe swaying gracefully until it too disappeared.

"Will he be safe alone?" she said, still watching the path Ashan had taken.

"Yes." He paused. "You appear perturbed."

"Eshel…. tell me what you need from me."

"Need from you?"

"Yes," she said. "I'm here, I can't leave, so tell me what you want. If you want me to help, I'll help. If you want me to stay hidden inside a Shemal prison for a while, I'll do that too."

Eshel stared at her, appearing unsure of her motive. "I need your help," he finally said.

"Okay. Lead the way."

And Catherine began following Eshel through the forest.

Hours later, Eshel stopped at one of the mighty trees with the weeping branches.

"We will sleep here," he said. "Tomorrow, we will begin."

Catherine glanced around. "Is it safe?"

"This is uninhabited territory."

"What if the Shemal come wandering through?"

"They won't. The Korvali do not leave their territories except in very unusual circumstances. Especially now, when we are at war."

Catherine ducked under the branches, realizing how tired she was. She kneeled near the trunk, pulling out her waterproof blanket. She would curl up there, using her pack as a pillow and covering herself with her blanket. At least the ground was soft and the tree offered cover.

"Catherine," Eshel said. "What bothers you?"

"What do you mean?"

Eshel only looked at her.

"I'm just tired." She began arranging her pack next to the tree's trunk, pushing away the question that nagged at her.

"And?"

She sighed, stopping what she was doing and rising to her feet. "Why didn't you tell me the truth? About going to Korvalis?"

Eshel hesitated for a moment. "I was ordered not to."

"That never stopped you before."

"I could not afford to disregard the order, when the Captain and XO had placed their trust in me."

Catherine sighed, feeling like there was more to the story but knowing she probably wouldn't get it.

Eshel went on. "I do not believe it fair for you to chastise me about not speaking the truth. You have lied to me, many times."

She looked down, all of it coming back to her at once: the painting, Mahoney, the biocracker op... the lies she told. "I had to. I suppose you did, too." She paused. "Look, Esh... it's not easy, being here. One of those men at the sea house brought me a bowl of seafood, the same stuff you gave me. But then he took it away, and I just..." She trailed off, not knowing what else to say, the memory of it still angering her. "I know I'm not welcome here, but I'm just trying to help."

"He took the bowl not to punish you, but because the others told him you might become ill by eating our food. They thought it better to wait until I arrived."

Embarrassment came over her. She hadn't considered that.

"Catherine… someone has betrayed us, has significantly harmed our mission. Until I discover who it is, I cannot trust anyone. Except you." He paused, his sea eyes gazing at her. "You are welcome here, if only to me."

Catherine softened. "Thank you."

"Remove your field gear. You will sleep more comfortably."

She stripped down to her base layers while Eshel retrieved a thin blanket from his pack and spread it on the ground. Catherine kneeled upon it, brushing the leaves from her feet before allowing them on the blanket. Eshel pulled his robe over his head and hung it, along with her gear, on a tree branch. He joined her on the blanket and spread a second blanket over them, maneuvering himself next to her. Her chill driven away by Eshel's warmth, she closed her eyes.

Catherine woke, her back moist from Eshel's heat. She inched away from him, realizing they were still inside their willowy haven, where the faint light of dawn crept in.

Eshel stirred. "We must go."

They got up and dressed themselves. Eshel pulled out a thin metal box and opened the lid, holding it out to her. It was filled with pinkish white strips, and the odor that wafted up confirmed that it was dried fish. She selected a piece and took a bite; it was salty, but far less chewy than dried meat. Eshel reached into his pack and produced a greenish yellow sphere. She examined it, smelling its skin. It had a citrusy odor. She took a bite; her mouth immediately puckered from the intense sourness of the fruit's flesh, but then it gave way to a pleasant tart sweetness. She handed it back to Eshel.

"Finish it," he said. "I have another."

After leaving their tree, Eshel led Catherine west until they reached a river tributary within the forest. He set down his things and indicated for Catherine to do the same.

"If you are to help me, we must first perform the sher mishtar," he said.

"The ritual of secrets? Is it that important?"

"Yes."

She glanced at the trickling stream. "We're doing it here? In the river?"

"The rite should be done at sea. But you will be too cold, and we risk being seen there. This will suffice."

Catherine began removing her boots and socks, glancing over at Eshel, who gathered up his robe and tied it off, baring his thin calves and webbed feet. She waited for Eshel to step into the water. Once he stood calf deep, she followed, glad that the water wasn't as cold as she'd expected.

"We do not have much time," Eshel began. "Remember, Catherine, what is said here must remain secret always, never to be shared."

She nodded. "Of course."

"I know you serve as operative for the Space Corps, that you are a COO. You do not have to acknowledge this or speak of it, nor will I share this information with anyone. However, I believe it important that you know I have discovered this."

Catherine, not expecting this revelation, said nothing for some time as her mind scrambled to adjust to the new information. Her first instinct was to resist, to do as she was taught and offer no information to confirm or deny Eshel's statement. But she quickly realized that keeping up that ruse was pointless with someone like Eshel, and could even work against them at some point. Then, her annoyance returned.

"If you knew, why did you give me a hard time last night about the lies I told?" she said.

"You didn't have to lie about giving away the painting, Catherine."

She looked down at the clear water that rushed past her legs. "I was ashamed."

"As was I, when I left *Cornelia*."

Catherine let out a breath, feeling a strange relief. She went to Eshel and hugged him, and he put his arms around her. When they separated, she looked up at him. "How did you find out? About my being a COO?"

"The evidence was there, but it was not until Grono Amsala spoke of your role in the capture of the Sunai information thieves that I began to 'put two and two together,' as Tom would say. Then, I had only to seek one more source to confirm my suspicion."

"What source was that?"

"It seems we share a common friend."

A common friend? She went through everyone she knew... until it hit her. Herr Sycophant. That explained those comments Herr made about Eshel, just before he signed off for good. Catherine began to laugh. "How do you know Herr?"

"That is a story for another time."

"Can I share a secret?"

Eshel nodded.

"Before I do... you should know that I hated hiding things from you, lying to you. But it's part of the job."

"I know."

She took a deep breath. "I told the clone the truth about being a COO, when I thought he was you. I broke my vow." Admitting it aloud elicited a wisp of shame in her, especially knowing now that she'd confessed needlessly.

"Do not chastise yourself," Eshel said. "I too have broken important edicts, with you. And I regret none of it."

She looked back up at him. "Then I won't either."

Eshel went on. "The other secret is this: I believe I know who the traitor is. But I will need your help, and your new skills, to confirm it."

"Of course," she said, glad her knowledge would help Eshel in some way. "This person you suspect... does he know I'm here?"

106

Eshel's face paled. "It is a she. And she knows."

"A she?"

Eshel merely stared at her. Suddenly, Catherine's mind returned to the gray-eyed woman.

The rat was Eshel's mother.

CHAPTER 12

As they stood in the stream, water trickling past their legs, Eshel's expression looked hard, cold... angry. But she saw something else in him. Pain. A pain that made Catherine think that if Eshel were capable of tears, they would fall from his eyes at that moment.

"Jesus, Eshel," Catherine said. "She kept eyeing me. She wanted me to explain the function of every piece of gear I had. I just thought... I thought she didn't like me because I was the human her son had been involved with."

Eshel's eyes narrowed.

"Come on, Esh. It took me some time to see it, but she looks like you, talks like you, and she's Shereb. She's your mother." She paused, Eshel appearing even more pained now. "Are you sure it's her?"

"Yes. She went through all your devices, read all your messages, saw every place you travelled. And she lied about having done so."

Catherine grimaced. "Maybe... maybe she was just being sneaky. You lie when you're up to something..."

"I have other evidence. She was seen speaking with Elisan on at least two occasions."

She shook her head. "But why? Why would she do this, when they killed your dad?"

"I suspect she seeks not to harm me or the others, but only to override our plan with her own. She will seek compromise with Elisan. She is the only Shereb among the vokalis, other than myself, and she served on our assembly... she is a likely candidate for such a move, and I hoped—rather than believed—that she would not pursue it."

"How can she trust him? Does she know about the clone, what he did?"

"She knows. She does not trust Elisan; she merely chooses that which she believes has the best probability of success. She has often argued that even if we unseat the leadership and charge them for their many violations of Doctrine, our people will only then rebel against us."

"So, in her way, she's looking out for you."

"She believes she is. But she acts outside the vokalis, instead of within it, and puts us all in danger. This… it is the Shereb way."

"What do we do now?"

"I told her a false plan, that I would send you away and go to Guard Headquarters." He paused. "But I have another plan."

Catherine followed Eshel as they headed southwest again, to what Eshel had told her was Osecal territory. The rain that had followed them all morning eventually ceased as they trekked through forests and across waterways. Curious, and hoping to distract them from the long trek and the difficulties they faced, she asked Eshel about Herr.

"How do you know him?" she said. "Did he teach you how to crack? Is that how you obtained those emails between Steele and Vanyukov?"

"I will share the truth. But you must keep it secret." She agreed, and Eshel began. "When I attended boot camp, our drill instructor continually rebuked me for having missed the first five days of the training, despite the Captain's obtaining approval for this. He then made several offensive remarks about my being Korvali, about my people, and many other comments that I will not repeat. Finally, I told him his teaching methods were stupid and ineffective."

Catherine began to laugh, recalling Tom's warning that Eshel keep his mouth shut and not argue with his instructors.

Eshel went on. "I spent that evening cleaning all the bathrooms in the camp. When nearly finished, I turned around, and my trainer was standing there, waiting for me…"

Master Chief McAlister stood perfectly rigid, holding a heavy metal device, his dark skin and hulking build reminding Eshel of a Sunai. A Sunai at his angriest. McAlister eyed Eshel with disapproval and looked him up and down, as if assessing how much damage he could inflict. Eshel prepared to defend himself, wondering if his skills, despite having advanced, would be enough against a large male with a metal weapon.

"You come here, Korvali, and insult how I teach them young pieces of shit how to be soldiers?" he said, his already booming voice even louder when echoing off the white tiles.

Eshel said nothing.

"Don't stand there like an idiot, Korvali!" he shouted.

"Yes, Sir," Eshel said. "I offer my apology, Sir," he added, wondering if McAlister would detect the disingenuousness of his apology and bring even more harm to him.

"How big of you!" McAlister said, his nostrils flaring as he stood even closer to Eshel. "It's only because you're our precious little refugee—and part of *Cornelia*'s crew—that I haven't sent your pale subordinate ass back and delayed your commission. But I don't need Ferguson or the goddamned press all over me about it."

At that moment, Eshel understood the purpose of the metal weapon. His instructor couldn't attract harmful publicity, so he'd issue his punishment there, where no one would witness it. Eshel waited for any sign of attack, ready to make an offensive maneuver that would take McAlister by surprise. But instead of making his move, McAlister only glared.

"How them toilets look? They'd better be goddamned spotless!"

"They are clean, Sir."

McAlister approached the toilets, meandering by each and inspecting them. "Your friends back on *Cornelia*, assuming you managed to make any, which I find difficult to imagine… didn't they warn you about how things work around here?"

"They did," Eshel said. "Sir. But I am unaccustomed to crude sexual language, and I believe I showed considerable restraint for many days."

"For many days?" McAlister cried, appearing almost amused. "For many days? Maybe the life of a soldier ain't for you, Korvali, if you can't even tolerate a few insults about your mama!"

"Perhaps not," Eshel said. "I am a scientist, not a soldier. However, I must serve as soldier because the Alliance has banned me from conducting science."

McAlister's eyes narrowed. "You one of them Mutant geneticists?"

"Yes, Sir."

Eshel braced himself, this time for insults or other ignorant commentary about science. However, McAlister's tired eyes and angry face seemed to change.

"How much you know about colorblindness, Korvali?"

Eshel raised his eyebrows. "I have read about it. A friend on *Cornelia* is red-green colorblind."

"Can you people fix something like that?"

"Of course," Eshel said. "I have altered my own vision, for other reasons."

"That right?" McAlister said, eyeing him again. He gave Eshel the metal weapon. "Some of them heads got bolts that need tightening. When you're done… my office."

When Eshel arrived, McAlister's viewer displayed a host of what appeared to be scientific articles and diagrams.

"What about this, Korvali?" McAlister said. "Ever heard of this?"

Eshel read through it all. Unlike Catherine's commonplace colorblindness, the particular sort he read about was far rarer, so much so that the humans hadn't developed treatment or even correction for it. Eshel, still unsure of McAlister's motives and especially of what punishment he could face, continued reading. The anomaly was genetic in nature, but it was minor and conferred no ill effects upon those who had it. Eshel glanced around, wondering if McAlister played some trick on him. However, as he read on, he found something interesting: if one tested positive for this anomaly, he or she could not pilot air- or spacecraft.

Eshel turned to his drill instructor, who stood aside with arms crossed, waiting. "Are you afflicted with this anomaly?"

"You think you got the chops to tackle something like this?" McAlister said.

"I cannot conduct genetic research, Sir."

"Answer the damned question, Korvali!"

"There are always unknowns with genetic engineering," Eshel said. "And I would need access to a proper laboratory. But I believe I can repair your anomaly."

"Report here tomorrow," McAlister said. "1800."

The following day, while the others ate, Master Chief McAlister transported Eshel to one of the Corps laboratories. The place had no one else around, and McAlister ordered him to remain within the laboratory until late that evening, when McAlister would retrieve him so he could sleep in the barracks. They followed the same schedule the following day, and the day after that. Eshel didn't know how McAlister had managed this, or what he told others about Eshel's evening whereabouts. And Eshel asked no questions.

Within a couple of weeks, Eshel had developed a prototype therapy.

"This concoction gonna hurt me?" McAlister said when Eshel showed it to him.

"No," Eshel said. "It will either work, or not work. If it does not, you may experience some visual anomalies that will pass after a day or two."

A day later, Eshel administered the color tests to McAlister. "How many colors do you see?"

"One," McAlister replied flatly, getting up and walking away.

"This is only a prototype," Eshel told him. "But if I am to succeed, I will require more time."

The next day, Eshel worked through the night. When finished, McAlister let him sleep at his home until the lab workers left for the day, and Eshel would begin work again. After another week of this, and two more failed attempts, Eshel showed McAlister the matrix of dots again. McAlister peered at it with dark eyes until, suddenly, his eyes grew big and round.

"Two colors," he said. "Blue and green! I see blue and green!" He turned to Eshel. "I'll be goddamned!"

"How bright is the blue?"

"Not that bright."

"It may get brighter," Eshel said. "But even if it does not, the flaw has been corrected."

Master Chief McAlister, pacing around as if too many thoughts pressed upon him, turned back to Eshel. "I can't send you back to camp now. They think I got you in special training. You got studyin' to do?"

Eshel nodded.

Catherine began to laugh. "So you only spent part of your boot camp time in actual boot camp?"

"Yes," Eshel replied. "Perhaps Middleton's resentment about my receiving 'special treatment' was justified in this case."

Catherine laughed even harder, imagining Middleton's rage if he learned the truth. "Did the Chief get his pilot's certification?"

"Eventually, yes."

"Wait," Catherine said, dodging a tree root. "How does this explain how you know Herr?"

"I spent my remaining boot camp time at the Chief's home, studying. His young son was what the humans call a 'hacker.' He showed me a few things and led me to a hacker community, where a user contacted me to play a game. It was a very complex game, but I learned quickly and prevailed over him. Somehow, this user figured out who I was, based on my location and the way I communicated. We began corresponding in private, after which I learned his true alias: Herr Sycophant. For reasons I still do not understand, he decided he liked me and offered his services if I ever needed them."

Catherine shook her head. "At least that cranky bastard likes somebody."

They crested a hill, below which an expanse of civilization spread out before them, the shining white of Fallal Hall rising above all in the distance. After Catherine put on her gray robe, they engaged their devices and descended the hill. They passed white stone dwellings, each similar to the next, nestled under giant trees that protected them from the elements. The dwellings were simple, even austere, containing no shutters or other window adornments, and no arches, dormers, or other architectural embellishments. Yet, such austerity was more than compensated for by the dwellings' giant windows and, even more so, their extensive gardens that rivaled those belonging to royalty on Earth. Tall grasses flowered into furry plumes that swayed in the wind next to yellow disc-like flowers, small ponds lined with floating orange plumes, and trees with their white hanging fruits. Stone pathways wound throughout and tiny bridges crossed trickling rivulets. There wasn't a weed or a plot of manicured grass to be seen. Occasionally, a person in a pale gray robe could be seen tending the gardens.

Catherine still had difficulty imagining Eshel gardening, or doing any physical labor. But he told her that when he'd taken rest from his work and had finished swimming, he too had tended the gardens of his family home, even planting trees in childhood that now stood at nearly full size. He'd even planted the rare koshac tree, caring for it until it began to take hold. But once the malkaris found out, she had the tree pulled from its roots.

A loud shriek sounded from above. Catherine, recognizing the sound, stopped and looked up. Two of the great white-winged seabirds headed south toward the sea, their wings making the fooming sound as they cast a brief shadow over her and Eshel. Eshel also beheld the creatures for a moment, until recovering his rapid pace. Her feet, tired and blistered, longed for the sleek train that moved silently in the distance. But they needed to stay on foot; a train would greatly increase the risk of colliding with others or their devices creating distortions that others would see.

At last, they reached a large park with tall trees that surrounded a cluster of stone buildings. Eshel led Catherine to a door and retrieved his decoder. The console went blank and, after a moment, the door unlatched. Once inside, Eshel shut the door behind them. Catherine reached into her pocket to shut off her device, but Eshel, able to see her due to the altering of his vision, stopped her and motioned for her to stay put. He went to survey the area, the light from the high windows offering illumination, before he disappeared behind a partition. Soon he returned and told her she could shut off her device.

Catherine removed her robe and took a look around. The equipment sat silent and the computer screens were black. The refrigerators emitted no hum, a light coating of dust covered the tables, and the walls, with their giant boards for drawing plans, schemes, and models, stood clean and unmarked. "Where are we?"

"One of the Osecal laboratories."

"Why isn't anyone working?"

"Elisan curtailed their funding."

Eshel turned on one of the computers. The screen flashed and blinked for a few minutes before appearing to function. They wiped dust from two stools and sat down at the computer. Eshel navigated through several screens before pulling up a command line and typing a series of commands. Blocks of text displayed on the screen. Catherine, despite having learned a little of the Korvali written language, had never seen so much of it all at once. Eshel read, scrolled, and read some more.

He turned to her. "I will need your assistance here."

"What are you planning to do?"

"It is better that you don't know."

"Esh, I don't know your systems. I can barely read your language."

"I will teach you what you need to know," he said. He wrote several more lines, after which the screen changed to a column of single words. "What you see here... it is a list of addresses for messaging. Can you translate any of them?"

Catherine shook her head. "I remember the symbols you taught me, but I don't recognize some of these."

Eshel explained them to her, then tested her knowledge by scrolling to the top of the list and pointing to the first address.

Catherine studied it for several moments. "That's Elisan's address."

Eshel pointed to another.

"Minel," she said, recalling the name. One of Elisan's aides, who'd initially come looking for Eshel after his escape and who'd attended meetings with the Alliance to discuss Eshel.

Eshel pointed to the next one.

"Ivar," she said. The malkaris's now-eldest son. She paused, moving down the list. "Moeb. Vashar." Ivar's younger brothers. She peered at the next one. "Lakli. Who's Lakli?"

"The malkaris."

Eshel pulled out a small wad of wires and connected something Catherine didn't recognize to the computer. Several lines of code appeared on the screen.

"I have downloaded a file." He showed her where to retrieve the file and how to send it to the listed addresses. "Wait until I message you. When I tell you to, send that file to Elisan. Ensure it completes. If you do not receive further orders from me within thirty minutes, turn off the computer." He stood up and began gathering his things.

"Where are you going?" Catherine said.

"To Fallal Hall."

"Esh, they'll expect that," she argued, feeling worried.

"That is why it will work." He looked over at her pack. "I will need some of your equipment."

Catherine reluctantly handed her pack to Eshel and he removed its contents, taking the items he needed.

"Wait here, until I return," Eshel said. And he put on his pack, engaged his device, and left.

Catherine stood up from her chair and paced around the idle lab once more. She'd heard nothing from Eshel. Enough time had passed that she'd begun wondering about his progress, but not so much that she'd begun worrying. She checked her communicator from time to time, and the computer as well, ensuring that each still functioned. For the first time, she understood Tom's complaining about waiting around, hoping for news while someone else took the lead in an operation.

A beep sounded. Catherine's stomach jumped as she looked down at her communicator.

Send it.

Catherine hurried over to the stool and sat down at the computer. She followed Eshel's directions and located the file, sending it to Elisan's address. When her cursor shifted to the next line, a jolt of excitement ran through her. She waited 40 minutes before shutting down the computer.

Unsure what to do with herself and too restless to sit, she began checking out the facilities, wandering deeper into the lab, examining each piece of equipment and trying to ascertain its function. How strange, how big and clunky it all appeared compared to the modern technology she was used to. She peered into the coolers, their empty interiors emanating no blast of chilled air. Feeling a need to keep an eye on the door, she decided to head back, preparing herself to sit tight until Eshel returned. Just as she approached the partition, she heard a sound.

The door latch.

Catherine froze. Could it be Eshel? No. He couldn't have returned from Fallal Hall that quickly. She glanced around before she reached into her pocket and engaged her clandestine device. Knowing her device would create noticeable distortions, she stayed away from solid matter, tiptoeing closer until she could see past the partition. A strip of light appeared where the door had been opened. As she inched forward a bit more, a blue robe appeared. And then a second one.

Catherine's heart raced. She spotted her bag near the stool by the computer, her gray robe slung over it. She had no way out, other than through the strip of light. The two men walked slowly, their pale eyes scanning in various directions. Each held a metal rod in his hand, and each swung it back and forth, like a blind person using a cane to locate unseen objects.

One of them halted, his eyes fixated upon her pack. The other followed suit, as his hand reached into his robe pocket.

CHAPTER 13

Every system has a weakness. People think the more complex systems are the toughest to crack, but it's the simple ones that get you. Not because it's hard to get in, but because there's always some fucking surprise you didn't see coming because you already called it easy and let your mind lapse into efficiency mode.

- Herr Sycophant

Eshel checked his clandestine device, knowing that even when adjacent to Elisan's office—located at the north end of Fallal Hall—the koshac tree would still take its toll more quickly than he preferred. He stood aside while the others found their way into Elisan's office. And once they did, Eshel followed, crossing the doorway's threshold just in case Elisan decided to shut the door. Fortunately, he left it open, likely confident that only his trusted associates could roam that portion of the Hall. Eshel retreated just a hair and planted himself as close to the doorway as possible. Given Catherine's estimates from when she'd rescued him, he gauged he had, at most, another thirty minutes before his clandestine device failed.

Eshel looked around Elisan's light-filled office as rain pattered upon the vaulted glass rooftop. His workspace contained numerous flowering plants—potted, hanging, big and small—far more than Eshel would have predicted for someone like Elisan. The sound of trickling water came from a contained waterfall in the rear of the room, next to a tree that nearly reached the glass.

Elisan stood quietly in his blue robe while the malkaris, her mate, Ivar, Minel, and another one of Elisan's aides joined him. Eshel felt a wave of revulsion at seeing Ivar and his pale reddish hair, and perhaps more so at seeing his mother, a thin, frail woman who mostly kept to her apartments and never swam or gardened. Elisan pulled up an image onto his screen, rotating the screen so the others could see. It was an image of Eshel... talking to Fashal and another robed figure, the figure's sleeve exposing some of his branched marking.

"He collaborates with the Osecal, as we suspected," the malkaris's mate said.

"Are there other images?" Ivar asked.

"Only this one," Elisan said coldly.

"Did Volen send this?" Minel asked.

"The message came to me, but it lacked his moniker," Elisan said. "It may be Volen, but it contained no message."

"It could have come from the traitors," Minel said.

Volen.

Eshel recalled his gaunt, scarred face, his questioning him about Mosel at Station 15. Volen, of course. Yet, if Volen had betrayed them, what about the evidence—the damning evidence—he'd received about his mother? Despite having the information he needed and knowing he should leave, Eshel lingered.

"How does this murderous traitor come to our planet without our knowing?" the malkaris sneered, her chilly expression focused on the image of Eshel, her branched marking peeking out from her sleeve.

"We do not know," the aide said. "The Guard reported another breach seven days ago. However, an Inferior ship appeared to cause the disturbance and it retreated without incident."

"I do not like it," Minel said. "I believe the Inferior ship served as decoy to allow the traitor or others to enter our space undetected, using the same cloaking technology they used previously."

"Yes," Elisan said. "That is it. I suspected those blustering Sunai idiots were involved, despite their protestations, and that they would contrive with the humans to take what is not theirs."

"And what of this redheaded human?" Minel said.

Eshel froze.

Elisan's eyes glimmered. "I believe I have located her."

Eshel left the doorway, hurrying through the quiet hallways until he came upon the stairwell. Once inside it, he sent Catherine a transmission.

Leave immediately. Go to the cliffside. Confirm.

When the light on his clandestine device began to blink, Eshel turned it off. He descended the marble stairway until he reached the ground floor, exiting the much quieter north side of the Hall. Wearing a blue robe he'd taken from his mother, Eshel strode through the gardens with the hood up, making a concerted effort to maintain a normal pace, rather than a hurried one. He glanced down at his communicator again. No response from Catherine. Once beyond the Hall grounds, he headed east, keeping his head down and walking more swiftly, growing increasingly frustrated at how long it took to return.

Eshel spotted a train approaching from afar and stopped, sending another message to Catherine. He received no response. Eshel pulled his hood down further and boarded the train, ensuring no one saw his face. He remained near the door, ready to assault anyone who came near him. The train moved smoothly, advancing him toward Osecal territory. When his stop came, he exited the train and found an open grove of trees. Behind them, Eshel reengaged his near-spent device only long enough to change into his gray robe. He sent a transmission to Ashan.

Volen. Retrieve him, his mate, and any children. Tell the others. Contact me when it is done.

Eshel continued on, his concern for Catherine increasing with every step, with every moment she offered no response. Darkness began to fall, and Eshel was thankful for it. But when he finally arrived at the cliffside, he saw no sign of her.

He searched the area, hoping to see Catherine's red hair, or at least a gray robe on a person of shorter stature, appearing as a child to the uninformed. She was nowhere to be found. Concern turned to dread as he considered the worst, that they'd captured her. Elisan would know that if Eshel were willing to violate Doctrine to become intimate with Catherine, he would also go to considerable effort to protect her. He knew Eshel would sacrifice himself to spare her, if such an option existed, and that meant Eshel would have to leave Ashan and his mother to continue, with the hope that Ashan's bridge to the outsiders was enough to finish what they'd begun. It would set them back, and would inflame their war… but it would be necessary to protect Catherine.

Eshel left the cliffside and headed to the laboratory. Upon getting closer, he changed paths and went around the development so he could approach from the rear. He walked slowly in the darkness, looking all around him, gliding through the tree grove until he came upon the lab facilities. He stopped near a tree, seeing nothing suspicious before resuming his path toward the entrance.

Before he got far, he heard the rustling of leaves above. He looked up, reaching for a weapon as something descended from the tree and landed with a thud.

It was Catherine.

Eshel gaped at her, dumbfounded, as she stood smiling in her field gear, her hair braided and her pack on.

"Why did you not respond to me?" he hissed.

"My communicator's down," she whispered, appearing to take no offense at his surly tone. She handed him another clandestine device.

Eshel said nothing, relief flooding him. He wanted to put his cheek to hers, to put his arms around her. But eager to get away, he engaged his device and motioned for her to follow him, leading her east. Far beyond the lab, they stopped.

"What happened?" he said.

"Two Shereb men got into the lab. They were swinging rods back and forth, looking for invisible people." She demonstrated. "They stood between me and the door. I planned to grab my gear and run, but they saw my pack sitting there—"

"Where were you?"

"In the back, looking around."

"How did you get out?"

"I sucker punched one, then the other. Then I grabbed my stuff and ran. Once I got far enough away, I realized my communicator was down. I think I clipped the doorway on my way out... it must have broken it." She paused. "How did they know we would be there?"

"I do not know. I told no one of my plan."

Catherine gazed at him, her expression changing. "Did you find out? Was it her?"

"There is another traitor."

"Who?"

"Someone I should never have trusted." Eshel began walking.

"Eshel..." Catherine said. "It wasn't Ashan, was it?"

Eshel stopped walking.

"Don't worry," she said, her tone conciliatory, knowing it would bother him that Ashan revealed his identity to her. "I won't say anything."

"It is not he."

Eshel's communicator beeped.

It is done.

Imprison her as well, Eshel replied. *Then take the next step.*

Of course.

"What is it?" Catherine said.

"Ashan has the traitor."

"Are you back in business?"

"Not yet. We have laid a trap for any others. We will know within two days."

"And then what?"

"You will be cleared to leave," Eshel said. "And once you do, you cannot return."

Catherine trekked over damp leaf litter, doing her best to avoid occasional muddy spots as she hustled to keep up with Eshel's pace. They'd left the developed areas, travelled east by boat in the night, and again traveled on foot until hidden within the forest canopy, away from danger for now. After getting some sleep, they continued east.

Later, they came upon a stream, where the water trickled its way south to empty into the southern sea. The rocks were arranged in such a way that the stream formed a small pool. An opening in the forest canopy offered some light, which shined upon the pool and gave a hint of sparkle to the surrounding rocks. Eshel stopped and removed his pack.

"The pool will be slightly warmer than the others due to its exposure," Eshel said. "It is a good place to bathe."

Catherine, glad for the opportunity to clean up, even if it meant getting into more cold water, removed her pack and then her clothes. Feeling self-conscious, she looked around.

"This is uninhabited territory," Eshel reminded her.

She squatted down at the pool's edge and sat upon a rock while her legs dangled in the pool. Once she dunked herself under, a chill consumed her as she stood waist deep, scrubbing herself while goose bumps formed on her arms. Eshel, after sinking into the pool and appearing almost visibly happier, came over and put his arms around her. Catherine warmed immediately, grateful for Eshel's heat and his still recognizing when she required it. Yet, unexpectedly, she experienced something else… something that reminded her of the time Eshel had come to her quarters and kissed her. Like she'd forgotten everything and everyone, immersed in him. She shoved the feeling away, knowing Eshel could only warm her, and would soon pull away for reasons they both understood. However, Eshel remained.

Catherine looked up at him. He stared at her with his sea gaze. Suddenly, the desire for him to kiss her became nearly overwhelming. She looked away, retreating from him, fear coming over her.

"What is wrong?" he said.

"We can't, Esh," she said, still not looking at him. She could feel his eyes on her.

"No," he said. "But it is not because we stand upon my homeworld, that doing the unspeakable here is worse than elsewhere." He paused, his expression changing. "Catherine… I will not return to *Cornelia*. I must remain here, where I am needed."

"I know."

They stood for what seemed an interminable period. Without warning, tears began pooling in her eyes. She took a deep breath and blinked them away, letting out her braids and dunking herself underwater again. She squeezed the water from her long hair, looking for the small towel that sat upon one of the rocks. But just as she reached for it, a warm hand touched her shoulder. And before she could hope to contain it, she burst into tears.

Eshel nudged her around until she faced him, and put his arms around her. Tears streamed down her face as she pressed her lips together to squelch a sob. Eshel pulled away a little and looked down at her. "I do not like when water falls from your eyes."

"I'm sorry," she said, stepping back and wiping her face. "I know… I know you need to be here. And I know we'll adjust to your absence. It's just…" She shook her head, tears pooling again. "It will never be the same without you."

Eshel said nothing, his eyes clouded.

An abstract of mottled blue and green appeared in her mind. "Esh… did you have that piece of art, the one you gave me, the entire time when I was searching for it?"

"Yes."

Catherine smiled a little, reaching up to kiss his lips. He made an effort to return the kiss. She touched his face, his small ears, his arms, his long-fingered webbed hands. She brought her hands to his chest and caressed its tough smoothness, the skin that could withstand being in water for hours or even days at a time, gracefully existing at sea or gliding from island to island. Eshel took her arms and stopped her. He turned her around until she faced the rocks and brought himself close to her, his warmth against her backside and his cheek pressed to her head. His arm surrounded her, holding on to her while he entered her.

Catherine placed a hand on the rocks for balance and closed her eyes, forgetting where they were, forgetting everything but how Eshel felt. And soon, she was so overwhelmed that she cried out, clutching the smooth rock. Eshel's grip on her tightened, until he quit moving. But instead of pulling away, he remained, holding her within his grasp, his heat making her sweat. Finally, he let up on her. He sat upon on a rock within the small pool and took her hand, pulling her to him and seating her between his legs. Catherine nestled against him; and they sat there for the day's remainder, until nightfall came and they slept under a koshac tree merely because Eshel knew that Catherine loved the ancient trees and that, when the morning came, he must return her to her craft.

CHAPTER 14

Catherine made her way through the forest, the straps of her pack digging into her shoulders as she trod upon damp soil cushioned by layers of decaying leaves. The darkness of the dense forest gave way to a clearing, where knee-high grasses brushed against her pants. Something unusual caught her eye: dots of bright white, all around her. Flowers... dozens of wispy beauties sprinkling the area.

She bent down to behold one of them, marveling at their shiny black centers and wondering how, despite countless hours trekking the land's interior, she'd never seen them before. At that moment the sun peeped out, its ephemeral glow warming her hair and encouraging the petals to open wider. She smiled at her fortune, recalling Ashan noticing her appreciation of the "Gernoly star" when it made a rare appearance.

"They aren't as pretty as gentians, but I like them," a voice said.

Catherine turned, and there stood a middle-aged woman, green-eyed and ginger-haired, her face tired but her eyes crinkling as she produced a smile. Catherine blinked several times.

"Mom."

The word came out quiet, almost a whisper, as a warmth flooded her body.

Her mother came closer, her fluffy white bathrobe hanging loose upon her frame, thinned from too many attempts to curtail the aggressive cancer cells. "Sexual relations with a Korvali," she said, her right eyebrow arched like it did whenever Catherine surprised her. "And on their own planet. You were always adventurous, like your father."

A giggle escaped Catherine. "I'm not sure Dad would call that adventurous."

"Typical soldier," her mother said, bending down to pick a white bloom. "They join the Corps to see what's out there, but then seem so untrusting of the others." She stood back up, her nose in the flower before she pulled it back and inspected it.

"That's what Eshel calls aliens… others," Catherine said.

"There's us, and then there are others. It's the way of pack animals."

The sun dipped behind a cloud and the clearing darkened. The flower petals folded against one another.

"Are you in danger here, my little scientist?" her mother said.

"Some. But Eshel protects me."

"So I'm told," she said. "So I'm told." She paused. "It's been too long since you've written your father. He's worried. And you know how angry he'll get when he finds out you're here."

"He won't find out, Mom. He doesn't have clearance to know about… this."

"You should be doing science," her mom admonished, but with a gleam in her eye.

"I am, Mom. I promise. I've never given up on that," she added, tears gathering.

Her mother looked beyond Catherine with tired eyes, her smile fading. "Is it time to leave?"

"You, or me?" Catherine asked, turning to follow her mother's line of sight. But she saw nothing except dark forest. When her mother gave no answer, she turned back around to ask again.

Her mother was gone.

Catherine awakened, abruptly sitting up and looking around her. The blue dappled light of dawn shone upon the koshac tree's leaves. Tears blurred her vision.

"What is wrong?" Eshel said.

"I had a strange dream," she said, blinking the tears away. "I was talking to my Mom. It felt so… real."

"It is the trees," he said.

She peered up at the ancient trees, with their gnarled spreading branches and their shimmering silvery leaves. "What is it about these trees? Do they give off some kind of EM radiation?"

Eshel glanced up. "That is a Korvali secret. You cannot know everything about us."

She shook her head, laughing a little. "Promise you'll tell me someday."

"I will," he said, standing and putting on his robe. "They also affect me, and it is not uncommon to see the dead. I saw my father last night; he was attired as a Shemal, with a spear in his hand."

Once dressed and packed, they ate Eshel's food and resumed their journey east. After dark, Catherine and Eshel encountered a horde of Shemal patrollers. They formed a semicircle around the two of them, their great height making even Eshel seem small. And as with Ashan, they kept their spears lowered and listened intently to all that Eshel had to say. Catherine hoped that, by now, one of them might speak to her. But other than a watchful glance or two, they took no interest in her. Soon, they broke formation and allowed Catherine and Eshel to continue.

After reaching Catherine's ship, they still hadn't heard from Ashan, and so they set up camp inside the Pokey. That night, when the rain had ceased, Eshel climbed up to the top of a tree, encouraging Catherine to follow him. When she did, they poked their heads out of the canopy, where the forest spread out before them. To the south, the moonlight shone upon the sea.

"Eshel, look!" she said, gazing at the sky. Eshel looked up, trying to see what she was excited about. "Stars! You can actually see something besides rain clouds!"

"If the clouds clear, they often do so at night." He pointed to the west. "Do you see the stars that form a circle, with a stem-like protrusion?"

"Like a flower," she said.

"At this time in our annual cycle, it will guide you west."

Eshel pointed out a couple more celestial landmarks, taught to him by Othniel, that also served as navigational beacons for the primitive tribes who must find their way at sea. The tips had come in handy for Eshel... once when he and Elan had swum so far at night that they lost their way, and again when he and his mother took Othniel's body east by boat along the northern sea to the Elliptical Isles, where Othniel was born and where they released his body to the sea. Just as Catherine started to ask more about the sher memeshar and the wailing she'd heard among the Shemal, Eshel's communicator sounded.

Ashan had sequestered Eshel's mother, and their traps had yielded no other traitors. After climbing down from their perch, Eshel made contact with Station 14; less than an hour later, he received a transmission from Grono Amsala, instructing Catherine to leave immediately. Eshel ensured that Catherine fed the correct rendezvous coordinates into the Pokey's computer before gathering his belongings. And then they stood there, looking at one another.

"You sure you don't want to come with me?" Catherine quipped.

But Eshel didn't respond to the joke. He only stared at her. After some time, he spoke. "When you were in sick bay, after the abomination attacked you, you were... distressed. You said 'I love you so much.' What did you mean?"

Catherine raised her eyebrows. "You don't know what that means? After all this time?"

"It is not an expression I have heard before. I researched it, but it is only spoken, never explained."

She hesitated, feeling suddenly self-conscious, her emotional wellspring threatening to return. "To love someone is to convey that they're special to you... the most special. Like a mate, or a child or family member."

"And you feel this for me," Eshel concluded.

"Of course I do," she said quietly.

Eshel gazed at her for a moment. "And I you."

Catherine put her arms around Eshel. They held each other until Catherine finally got into the Pokey, engaged her device, and navigated the craft into the open. As she ascended through an opening in the forest, she looked back down: Eshel stood aside in his gray robe, watching her leave. As she got higher and higher, and Eshel appeared only as a small figure on the ground, she waved goodbye and blinked any tears away before turning to her console. She instructed the Pokey to retrace its previous course past Station 14 and beyond Korvalis's net, where she was assured she could pass with no incident other than a Guardsman quietly stifling the resulting alert. And onward she went, disappearing into the cloud cover before leaving Korvalis's atmosphere, and its people, behind her.

Once out of Korvali space, Catherine received several messages, including one that reiterated the coordinates at which she would rendezvous with Koni and allow him to return her to *Cornelia*. Another stated that *Cornelia* was expecting her, while yet another reminded her that she must maintain the ruse that she'd been on Suna the entire time. However, the messages didn't come from Captain Ferguson or Commander Yamamoto; they were text messages, relayed through the voice of a computer. At that moment, Catherine began wondering what she would return to. Given that communications had shut down after Elisan discovered Eshel's plan, Eshel could transmit no information to Koni… and Koni no information to Eshel about the fallout among the Alliance and the Corps.

After numerous hours of space travel, during which Catherine was so tired that she took stims to stay alert, she approached the coordinates. A Sunai ship waited for her.

"It is excellent to see you, nonaii," said a guttural voice over the com.

"And you, my friend."

Catherine docked the Pokey. When she opened the hatch, something about Koni seemed different. He appeared smaller somehow. Then, she recognized what was wrong: his rust uniform no longer displayed even a single decoration. She forced a smile and went to meet his palm, greeting him as "Grono Amsala" as he put his meaty hands upon her shoulders.

After briefing Koni on all that Eshel had authorized her to share, Koni relayed important information to her as well.

"Much has occurred while you served Eshel on Korvalis, nonaii," he said. "Your Captain and Executive Officer sit imprisoned at Sundani Headquarters, and they will soon return to your planet for punishment. However, their imprisonment is for Elisan's benefit, and they do not endure the discomforts of high security prison. You will report to new leadership. I would provide more information; but the Alliance also knows I am a willful collaborator, and I no longer have the detailed knowledge that my position would otherwise command."

Catherine wondered why Ferguson and Yamamoto went to prison, even if for show, but Koni didn't. But she decided it better not to ask. Later, after the stims wore off, Catherine fell asleep. She awoke upon their entering Suna's atmosphere, its rings shining outside her window. They landed in Jula's military shipyard, a massive structure that, much like Sundani Headquarters, submerged much further underground than one imagined. No one stood waiting for them.

Koni spoke into his sleeve before turning to her. "Your uniform," he said, his amber eyes shifting to a linen bag. "You must change into it and hide your field uniform in your pack."

Catherine nodded and changed her clothing while he waited outside. She paused to smooth her hair and put it back into a ponytail before she gathered her belongings and stepped out of the ship. Koni stood, legs spread, as if he had something important to say.

"Your Captain and Executive Officer request to speak with you before you report to duty."

"Is it safe?"

"Yes. They are allowed to receive guests, and we shall say you merely sought to visit them before returning from your duties on Suna."

Catherine nodded.

He pressed a few buttons on his arm and barked an order in Sunai, and they left the dark bay and took an elevator up numerous floors, where a transport arrived and took them to Sundani Headquarters. As she followed Koni through the busy place, the uniformed men they passed spoke loudly, arguing with one another and staring at Catherine with curious eyes. At times, the Sundani men walked too close to them, one or two even cutting them off as Koni offered a growl. Another officer bumped into her, grunting at her as if she were in his way, rather than vice versa. Had she been on Korvalis so long that she'd forgotten what Sunai males were like? But then she realized the truth: the men behaved that way because Koni, without his decorations, no longer garnered respect. And thus, neither did she.

After an elevator transported them deep into the ground, Koni led Catherine down a dimly lit hallway, the absence of his metallic jingling unnerving her a bit more. They reached a door. Inside, Ferguson and Yamamoto sat at a small black table, both wearing field pants and Corps t-shirts. Without their decorated uniforms, they seemed younger and less intimidating. She saluted.

"At ease," Yamamoto said. He motioned to a chair and Catherine sat down, while Koni took a seat at the table's head. "Are you well, Lieutenant?"

"I am, Sir."

"Catherine," Yamamoto began, "you no longer report to myself, or the Captain. Thus, you are not obligated to report information to us. However, we convene with the Alliance and their leaderships tomorrow, at sunset. If you have promising intelligence to offer, now is the time to do so." He leaned forward. "Does the vokalis continue with their plans?"

"I believe so," Catherine said. "Just before I returned, they'd found their rats and taken measures to ferret out any others."

"Does Elisan know you were on Korvalis?"

"Yes, Sir," she replied with less enthusiasm.

"Does he know how you got there?"

"They figured out that we used a Sunai ship as decoy, but they haven't figured out a way to detect the cloaking devices yet."

Yamamoto nodded. "What else?"

Catherine told them everything, omitting those few details that Eshel asked her to keep secret. She also told them about having met Ashan.

"Good work, Lieutenant," Ferguson said. "Glad to have you back safe."

"Thank you, Captain."

Yamamoto spoke again. "Your knowledge of Ashan's existence and location must remain secret. Also, the timing of your 'assignment' on Suna has raised many suspicions. Prepare yourself for questioning. If Elisan chooses to reveal that you were on Korvalis, speak to no one but Admiral Scott about it."

"Understood, Sir," she said.

Koni stood up, and Catherine saluted and left.

Back at the Pokey, Catherine contacted *Cornelia* and announced her ETA. Koni had already informed them she would return from her assignment that day. She was glad to hear Shanti's friendly voice welcome her back and direct her to one of the bays. As the Pokey drew closer to the ship, its console beeped.

"Lieutenant Finnegan," a deep male voice said. "When you arrive, report to the bridge ready room immediately." It sounded like Commander O'Leary.

At the shipyard for otherworlders, Catherine spotted *Cornelia*. Next to it sat another Corps ship. A warship. When she got closer, she made out the ship's name: SCS *Victoria*. Once landed, several MAs greeted her in the bay to scan her and check her in, after which one of them escorted her to the bridge ready room. Her heart began to pound. Upon arriving, she immediately spotted an older, blue-eyed man. Admiral Scott, whom she recalled from Eshel's trial so long ago. Milling nearby were Commanders O'Leary and Marks, and another officer she didn't recognize, likely their new XO. She saluted and stood aside, staring out the window and waiting for the new Captain to arrive. After a few moments, O'Leary and Marks stood at attention. Catherine turned; when a tall man with a Captain's decorations stepped through the door, Catherine stared.

Their new Captain was Jim Finnegan.

CHAPTER 15

"Dad?" Catherine said, hardly believing what she saw. The room seemed to quiet even more, and Catherine, remembering herself, snapped to attention. "Sorry, Sir," she muttered.

"At ease, Catherine," Jim said, his brown eyes twinkling just a little.

Catherine glanced at the others, her face growing hot.

Jim motioned to a chair. "Have a seat."

Catherine sat down, as did the others. Her father took his place at the head of the table, while Admiral Scott sat at the other end.

"Anything discussed here is classified," her father began. "Understood?"

"Yes, Sir," Catherine replied.

"Did Grono Amsala—or whatever he goes by now—brief you on what's happened while you were gone?"

"He did. He told me the Captain and XO are in prison, due to some operation involving the Korvali."

"Involving the Korvali, himself… and Eshel."

Catherine gave no reply, stifling a frown at her father's tone.

"Catherine," Jim said. "Elisan has made some serious threats and we may lose our membership in the Alliance. If there's a time to be up front, it's now. Regardless of your answers, you'll bear no punishment. If you engaged in activities other than those reported to us, we'll assume you were following orders. Understood?"

"Yes, Sir."

Jim's stare bore into her. "Did you know Eshel was on Korvalis, and not Suna, once he left *Cornelia*?"

"No, Sir."

"Were you involved in the operation your former Captain and XO were engaged in, at any time?"

"No, Sir."

"Were you aware of such an operation?"

"Not until I returned, Sir."

Commander O'Leary chimed in. "What was the nature of your scientific work on Suna?"

"Genetics," Catherine replied. "I can't specify beyond that, Sir."

"Why not?" Commander Marks demanded.

"It's what the Sunai wanted, Sir."

Marks smirked. "It's what the Sunai wanted, or what Eshel wanted?"

Catherine made a face at his remark.

"Don't make that face, Lieutenant," Marks ordered.

Catherine's anger flared. "If you don't like my face, or my answers, you can talk to the Sunai, *Sir*."

Marks glared at her before shaking his head. "This is a fucking waste of time."

"Shut it," Jim told Marks, who clenched his jaw and remained quiet.

Catherine took a deep breath. She felt like she had when Eshel questioned her, when she'd lied to him. But lying to her father seemed worse—not just because he was her father, but because unlike Eshel, her dad seemed to believe her.

The new XO, whose uniform identified him as Commander Templeton, spoke up. "It seems too big a coincidence that this assignment of yours took place just after Eshel left *Cornelia*."

Catherine nodded. "I know, Sir. And you're right... it's not a coincidence." She paused, gathering her thoughts while they watched her, hoping for information that would confirm their assumptions. "Grono Amsala is a good friend. After the clone attack, and especially after Eshel left, I was... unhappy. I think he found the assignment to get me out of the house, so to speak."

At that moment, she felt Admiral Scott's eyes upon her, and she wondered if he knew she was lying. The Admiral knew of her role as COO, but this assignment wasn't sanctioned by Headquarters. However, the Admiral remained silent. Commander Templeton, appearing not entirely convinced by her explanation, merely looked at her for a couple of moments before turning to Jim. The others, out of questions, did the same.

"You're all dismissed," Jim said. Catherine and the brass stood up from their chairs. "Not you, Catherine."

She sat back down while the others filed out of the ready room. Jim stood and approached her. Not knowing what to do, she remained seated, until her father motioned for her to stand up. When he merely hugged her, Catherine put her arms around him, relief mixing with the guilt she felt.

"You alright?" he asked.

She nodded, and they sat back down. "I mean no disrespect, Dad. But what are you doing here?"

But the moment the words left her lips, she knew. Of all the Captains they could've assigned to *Victoria*, they sent Jim Finnegan, despite his not having served active duty in some time. And they did so because they strongly suspected her involvement in the unsanctioned op and knew that facing her own father would increase the odds of gleaning the truth from her, knowing she would otherwise have to lie to protect Eshel and the others.

"They needed someone on short notice… among other reasons," Jim said. "You're under a lot of scrutiny, kid. And Commander Steele is extremely angry about your extended absence. He seems to think you're up to something you shouldn't be."

She rolled her eyes. "Dad, he's always that way."

"I know he's an asshole, but he's got a point. You're one of his scientists and Ferguson allowed you to neglect your regular duties for too long. Do what you can to keep him happy for a while, will you?"

Catherine gave a cursory nod. "What happens now?"

"The Alliance meets tomorrow. Ferguson and Yamamoto head back to Earth after that. Then, we figure out some way to kiss Elisan's ass."

"What about Eshel?"

Jim hesitated. "He's done, Catherine. He acted against us, just like your leadership did. He also violated the terms of his asylum, which means he'll never be one of us again." He paused. "I'm sorry."

Catherine wanted to argue, to spew the numerous arguments that bubbled up inside her, but she stopped herself, knowing they would fall upon deaf ears.

"Did you know?" he said, looking at her. "Were you involved in any of this?"

"No, Dad. I didn't know." She felt awful, cursing Headquarters for knowing just how to manipulate her. Then, another thought occurred to her. "Dad... has anyone talked to Eshel? To find out more about what's going on? I mean, I know what he and the others did was wrong, but what if... what if it succeeds?"

Jim sat back in his chair. "Still sticking up for him, huh? Even after he left without telling you in person?"

She let out a frustrated breath. "Come on, Dad. If you knew him, you would feel differently about this. Have you even talked with Yamamoto or Ferguson?"

Jim gave no reply, which Catherine recognized as a sign that no argument would convince him.

Catherine, eager to get away, said, "I've got work to do, Dad. Good to see you."

Jim nodded. "You too. You're dismissed."

Tom glanced at the time just as he arrived at the starboard bar. 2140. He spotted Jimmy Finnegan sitting at the bar, sipping his beer as he waited. When Tom sat next to Jimmy, Soren greeted him with his big Derovian smile. Tom pushed away thoughts of "Smiley," slang for a Derovian and a word the Derovians hated.

"Thanks, Soren," Tom said, as Soren gently placed a beer in front of him. He took a sip of the hoppy brew and relaxed a little, turning to his friend's father, who he'd known since the Academy. "What's up, Captain?"

"A day's work," Jimmy said.

"Any news?"

"Not so far. After the Alliance meeting, your Captain and XO go home and you're stuck with me for the remainder of the mission."

Tom hesitated, considering the right words to say. "Look, I don't know the details, and I know the Captain and XO acted out of turn. But if Eshel's involved, and it sounds like he is, maybe it's worth considering their plan."

Jimmy gave Tom a dubious look.

"I know it sounds crazy. But, Sir, I know Eshel. That guy never does anything unless he's plotted it a hundred moves in advance and thought about everything that could go wrong. If anyone has a chance of pulling that asshole Elisan from power, it's Eshel."

"Even if that's true, it's a new game now that Elisan knows. Their power came from their secrecy; that's gone, and now that asshole threatens all of us. Headquarters wants to calm him down and move forward, and I agree with them. The safety of our people comes first."

"What does Catherine say?" Tom said.

"You know I can't give her opinion much weight, even if she is my kid. This isn't her area. But you know her... she takes up for Eshel no matter what he does."

Tom, surprised that Jimmy would be so dismissive of Catherine, said nothing. Then he realized the truth: Headquarters hadn't told Jimmy about Catherine's status as an operative, when someone in Jimmy's position would normally have that clearance. Jimmy probably also believed Catherine had been "doing science" on Suna during her absence. He wondered if Headquarters kept Jimmy in the dark for a reason, perhaps because it would make him far more likely to carry out their orders.

Tom shrugged. "She cares about Esh. She looks out for him."

"She's being stubborn," Jimmy argued.

Tom scoffed. "I wonder who she gets that from."

Jimmy gave a reluctant chuckle and took another sip. "Speaking of stubborn, I hear you blew it with Maria Trujillo."

Tom felt a pang in his gut as he looked down at his beer for a moment. He shrugged again. "You heard right."

Jimmy gave him a strange penetrating look, one that had an eerie resemblance to Eshel's. "Tom, how you conduct yourself off duty and in your private life is your business. There's no rule that says you need to settle down with one woman. But if you want to get promoted, you might want to grow up a little."

Anger surged through Tom. "With all due respect, Sir, where the hell is this coming from?"

"I'm not trying to insult you, Tom," Jimmy went on. "I liked having you under my command in the past and I've always thought you were a good kid who didn't let his background keep him from achieving his potential. I just don't want to see you piss it away."

"You know my service record," Tom said defensively. "You know my skills. What does Maria have to do with any of it?"

"It's not Maria. It's involving yourself with too many women while on mission… showing you can't stick with anything because there's always something better around the corner—"

"Hey, I don't know what Catherine told you—"

"I get my information from a lot of sources, Tom," Jimmy went on. "It's not just the girls. It's flouting the rules when you feel like it, showing up ten minutes late to meet your commanding officer, even if only for a beer…" He paused. "There's talk about another round of promotions, and I think one or two others might beat you to it."

"Like who?" Tom cried, unable to imagine anyone at his level more qualified to step up.

"Like Ferrars, for one," Jimmy said.

Tom frowned, pushing his cup away. Not expecting a lecture, especially from someone who'd always supported him, Tom found himself without words as a confounding mixture of aggravation and shame washed over him.

Jimmy took his final sip and stood up. "Think about it, Tom. See you tomorrow."

Tom nodded, barely giving him a glance. "Goodnight, Sir."

Snow, feeling better after his brief shower, dressed himself in pants and a t-shirt before he sat down at his computer and turned on the viewer. After a minute or so, Jooni's face appeared onscreen. Snow smiled.

"How is my friend Jooni?" he asked.

Jooni smiled too, lowering her eyes briefly. "She is well, but ready for moon season to end. And how is my friend Snow?"

"Snow could use some coffee, but he's glad to see you."

It took some time, but Snow had managed to convince Jooni to talk with him over video. He'd apologized for getting angry at her, for not understanding her concerns as well as he thought he did. They engaged in a video friendship, with Yamamoto's approval, where Snow helped Jooni research the interplanetary exchange program that the Alliance promoted.

"Any news?" Snow asked.

"Some," she said. "I went to consulate. Only to ask of exchange program. They say program for teaching language to human, but no music. Yet, they speak of wanting music program, too."

"Good," he said. "I did some more research, too. For the most part, only the Derovians have taken part in the program. They've come to Earth to teach Derovian and primary Sunai, and humans have gone to Derovia to teach English, Spanish, Chinese, and a couple of other languages. It looks like we teach other stuff, too… information about different cultures on Earth and such…"

"No human come to Suna?" she said, puzzled.

"Some, but only to learn primary Sunai."

"And no Sunai go to Earth," she surmised.

"Right," he said. "Did you propose the idea of teaching music on Earth?"

Jooni looked down. "Yes. I say Sunai should teach music to human, and teach of Sunai music history and lore. But they argue, say woman teach music on Suna, not Earth."

Snow gave a wry smile, having expected that response. "Don't worry. We're just getting started. I've got a lot of ideas, and we just have show them that you'll be safe on Earth and that you'll be doing something that honors your uncle and honors Suna. Maybe we can find an Alliance delegate to host you and look after you, and there are also the Derovian immigrant communities."

Jooni looked up, surprised. "You begin to think like Sunai male."

Snow made a face at that. "And we need to consider a time limit for your exchange... maybe six months. It's easier to get people to agree to something temporary. Then, later, when they see how well it works, you can request a longer stay."

"An excellent idea, Snow."

"I should warn you, though," Snow said. "This shit that went down with the Korvali... they excluded the Sunai brass, so your uncle and others won't feel too generous toward humans right now. I'd wait and see what happens at the Alliance meeting before you talk to anyone else."

A look of worry crossed her face. "I know my uncle... such exclusion will enrage him. And that will make my request more difficult."

"Don't worry," he said. "Only a couple of humans took part in this, and they're being punished. This will pass."

Despite his encouraging words, Snow still struggled with it all, with the stupid and hypocritical rules the Sunai had, with feeling like he and Jooni's efforts would come to nothing. But he realized that trying to have a good attitude, even if he had to fake it now and again, helped Jooni. And that was his job now... to help her. Truth was, as much as he missed her, the situation plagued him less now that they weren't romantically involved.

"Snow," Jooni said, strumming on one of her guitars. "Before we play, tell me more of your parents."

"My parents?" he said, scowling. "Why?"

"Just tell me."

He shrugged. "Well, like I mentioned before... they were very religious. Extreme, in their beliefs. To them, there was no other way except theirs."

"Give me example."

Snow paused, thinking up an example he could easily explain to someone from another culture. "Where I come from, most kids use foul language, but not in front of their parents. If they did, they'd get punished in normal ways, like having to do chores or not getting to go outside. If I cussed, my folks would hit me with a belt, wash my mouth out with soap, I'd go without dinner, and then I'd have to apologize to both parents and ask them for their forgiveness."

"Forgiveness?"

"For them to stop punishing me and move on."

She made a face. "They put soap in your mouth, to make your words clean?"

"Yeah. It worked fucking great."

She gave a smile, recognizing his joke. "Did they let you drink coffee?"

"Oh, hell no. And I had to eat whatever they put on the table. If I didn't, they'd made me sit there until I did."

"What if you did not eat it?"

"Well, either Tom would come over and eat it when my mom wasn't looking, or punishment would commence."

"More soap?"

"Nah. But I'd have to stay in my room without food for one day."

"Perhaps that is why you are so skinny, yes?"

Snow laughed, pushing the unpleasant memories from his mind.

Tom left the mess after finishing second meal. As he made his way back to Weapons, Maria appeared from another hallway and headed straight toward him. She smiled, giving him a wink.

"What's up, Trujillo?" Tom said, grinning.

"Oh, you know," she said. "Relieving our numbers one and two of duty, a potential war with the Korvali… the usual. You? Saw you talking with Catherine's father last night."

He rolled his eyes. "Speaking of that… you mind meeting me for a beer tonight? I want to run something by you."

"Run what by me?"

"I want your advice."

"Really," she said. "Mr. Know-It-All wants my advice."

Tom shook his head, crossing his arms as he tried to squelch his smile.

"What time?" she said.

"Is 2200 too late? I'm on duty until then."

"That's fine. See you then."

That evening, Tom found his way to the starboard bar. He greeted Soren and ordered his usual beer; but instead of sitting at the bar, he found an empty table and took a seat. When Maria walked in, dressed down and with her hair loose, Tom couldn't help but stare at her, not believing that she could still look so beautiful to him. She finally spotted him, a look of mocking confusion on her face as she sat down.

"Are you actually early?" she said.

Tom shrugged. "What are you drinking?"

"I'll grab a beer."

"No," he said, standing up. "I'll get it."

Tom headed to the bar, returning with another cup of beer. He set it down in front of Maria and took a seat.

"What's up?" she said.

"Be honest, okay? What do you think the chances are that I'll get promoted next round?"

Maria sat quietly for several moments, tapping her finger lightly on their table. "Pretty low," she said.

Tom shook his head, any warm feelings he'd had draining away.

"You said to be honest."

"I know. It's not you." Tom leaned back. "Finnegan senior… he said the same thing, in so many words."

"Did he?"

Tom nodded. "He really let me have it. My being late, my 'flouting' the rules—his word, not mine—and… and my lack of commitment with women, including you."

She frowned. "He doesn't know what happened with us."

"He knows enough. And he knows me."

"Not like I do."

Tom hesitated, wanting to reach out and touch her hair, to lean over and kiss her soft lips. He shooed such ideas away, irritated that he still had them at all. "What do I do, Maria? How do I change their perception of me? I can be better about time and tighten up my rule bending, but I'm single. Single people date lots of people."

"It's not that you're single, Tom," she said. "It's… how you're single. It's like… it's like you're afraid of what might happen if you settle down."

"Oh, come on," Tom said, irritated.

"You said to be honest," she reminded him.

"I know, but… why does everyone keep trying to call me a fucking coward because I don't want to do the family thing?"

"I never called you a coward."

"But Yamamoto said the same thing, that I'm avoiding fatherhood out of some fear. Why the hell can't I just want what I want without it making me a coward?"

"You're not a coward, Tom," she said. "You never have been, not as long as I've known you. But I think Yamamoto's right."

"Why?"

"I don't know. I just do."

Tom let out a breath. "There are two kinds of people Maria. People who let the shit they face ruin them, and people who let the shit they face make them stronger. And I've seen my share of both among the service kids who grew up in the system like I did. I've never let it ruin me. I've done everything I've wanted to do, and that's what I'll keep doing."

Maria nodded. "Okay."

Tom took a last swig of his beer and glanced at the time. "Well, it's time for LC to get his ass to bed. Thanks, M."

She nodded again.

CHAPTER 16

After the eyeshaded Sunai guards scanned her, Catherine entered the dimly lit subterranean room and took a seat along its perimeter, next to Koni. In the room's center, a shiny black table formed an incomplete ellipse, surrounding by numerous empty chairs that would seat each of the Alliance delegates and their respective leaderships.

The familiar delegates milled about the room in their Alliance sashes, shaking hands, performing the meron, meeting palms, and even grasping shoulders, the sound of their unique voices echoing off the cavernous walls. Tallyn stood near two other Derovians in bright yellow gowns, a male and female, both older and lined with age, smiling as they gently grasped the hands of the others. Toq signed to two other Calyyt, both also older, their slitted black eyes darting back and forth at the bustle in the room as they sniffed through their nasal orifices. Gronoi Sansuai and Grono Jonili stood in their hefty uniforms with their shining decorations, meeting palms with those who extended them. Soon, Jim Finnegan walked in with Admiral Scott. Ferguson and Yamamoto followed, back in uniform but sans decorations; after briefly greeting the others, they joined Catherine and Koni at the room's periphery.

Catherine wondered what today would yield, fearing the Alliance would persist in its desire to appease Elisan and knowing that Eshel, Ferguson, Yamamoto, and Koni's actions only reinforced that persistence. But before she could think any more about it, a hush fell about the room. A hulking Sunai male walked in, the jingling of his numerous decorations resounding throughout. Catherine recognized the man who could silence even a gathering of leaders: Gronoi Okooii.

Catherine glanced at Koni, whose chin rose as he stood to acknowledge his superior. She recalled her initial—and only—encounter with Okooii way back, when the forceful leader grilled Eshel about what he owed the Sunai and made Eshel earn the right to walk on Suna's volcanic soil. At that moment, Catherine understood why Jooni experienced such difficulty with her desire to leave Suna. She'd forgotten just how much power Okooii wielded. Finally, Tallyn broke the silence and rushed over to welcome Okooii, the Derovian leaders on her heels, while the others waited for their turn to greet him.

After the delegates and leaders took their seats at the elliptical table, Gronoi Sansuai stood. "Let us begin!" He stepped into the ellipse's opening, raising his chin. "Leaders, delegates, and comrades of our great Alliance: I welcome you! The Sunai thank you for traveling such a distance, for allowing us to host all of you on our excellent planet! It is with difficulty that I address the topic that brings us together this day."

He paused. "It is for many sun cycles that this great Alliance has desired to acquire the Korvali as a fifth member, to have them unite with us as allies. Such a goal has eluded us, as these inhabitants of the small oceanic planet do not find trust with ease. Meetings with their leadership have not achieved the success that we desire. Squabbles have arisen, and promises have been broken. We have faced conflicting messages from the Korvali; some, including the refugee that has lived among the humans, claim they desire inclusion in our Alliance. Their leadership, however, despite words that tantalize, has found many excuses not to join us. Most recently, and perhaps of greatest importance, the Korvali leadership has acted against this Alliance by sending a clone to attack the human military, as punishment for not returning the refugee to his homeworld."

Sansuai gestured around the room. "Those who sit here today have quarreled over how we shall respond to such an attack. If we retaliate against this treachery, we shall lose progress in achieving the peace that is the goal of our great Alliance, and we shall risk losing many excellent soldiers in unnecessary war. If we allow such treachery, we set a precedent that suggests weakness and a tolerance of that which this Alliance regards with outrage!" He paused, recovering from his anger, looking around at those sitting at the table. "Yet, a third option exists... in which we put our outrage aside and maintain peace until the Korvali address their unrest, fight amongst themselves, and join our Alliance when they are ready, when they come willingly and able to atone for this treachery.

"After much discussion with our delegates and leaderships, it was the recommendation of this Alliance that we abide by this third option." He eyed Ferguson and Yamamoto. "And this decision has been violated by Captain Ferguson and Commander Yamamoto of the Earth Space Corps, and by our own Grono Amsala, all of whom conspired with the refugee himself to override the wishes of this Alliance and act independently. The refugee is afoot on his homeworld, plotting against his leadership and defying this Alliance. Elisan has discovered this trickery, and has made threats that endanger us all."

He paced some more. "Now, we have many decisions before us: how we shall manage Elisan and protect our peoples. How to punish those who defied this Alliance. Whether Earth and even Suna shall remain in this Alliance, or be removed for an agreed upon period in which they shall prove they are trustworthy. And, finally, what measures to take with the refugee himself, who this Alliance has sworn to protect, but who has defied the terms of his asylum and who, in his desire for power, has put his protectors in danger." He gestured to them all. "Speak!"

There was a rap on the table as Toq began signing furiously. His Sunai interpreter spoke. "We must show Elisan that the schemers acted on their own, without the knowledge of the Alliance. We will show him they no longer hold their positions of power and cannot act against us again."

"Toq is correct," Tallyn said. "We must assign punishment to those who violate our rules… not only for Elisan's benefit, but for our own. We are an Alliance; the rules, to which we all agreed, are quite clear about punishment for disobedience!"

Many of the others spoke their agreement.

Admiral Scott stood. "I think we all agree that Tallyn is correct, that those who acted against the Alliance's decision should be punished. I don't mean to create trouble here, but my comrades have sat in Sundani prison for a week, while Grono Amsala has never seen the inside of a cell." He motioned to Koni, who stiffened at the comment.

"We have removed Officer Amsala from his regular duties and he wears no decorations," Grono Jonili said, throwing a surly glance at Koni, who grunted. "Until these proceedings finish, punishment for these defiers is the domain of their organizations, not this Alliance. For future punishment, I will speak now and say that each of these dissenters should lose their rank and privilege as officers."

A few others agreed.

Dannia, the female Derovian leader, stood. "The dissenters shall face punishment, but perhaps the punishment does not need to be so severe as it appears to Elisan."

Another rap on the table, as one of the Calyyt leaders began signing to the interpreter. "Do you suggest we deceive Elisan, or offer only minimal punishment for such a transgression?"

"I suggest only that we do everything in our power to soothe Elisan's outrage, Qyto," Dannia said. "Protecting our people—all our peoples—from his vindictive actions is most important. We will punish the rule-breakers, but the punishment that Elisan believes is more important than the one we employ." When no one argued with this, she went on, her six-fingered hands clasped before her. "With regard to revoking membership in this Alliance, I suggest that we do not punish Earth, or even Suna, for the individual actions of Captain Ferguson, Commander Yamamoto, and Grono Amsala. Every people has those citizens who violate the rules when they believe, no matter how foolish their belief, that their actions will serve their people better than those of their leadership. I offer that Suna's military and Earth's Space Corps may themselves assess whether such defiant acts have served their respective organizations."

"Well said, Dannia of our sister moon!" Gronoi Sansuai boomed. "Very well said. Who shall agree?"

Most of those sitting at the ellipse agreed to Dannia's proposal, and she took her seat once more.

"Excellent," Sansuai said. "We shall let the Sunai and human militaries offer those punishments they believe correct. We shall continue ensuring Elisan knows of the demotions of Amsala, Ferguson, and Yamamoto. And what of other protections against Elisan's threats?"

"The Korvali will no longer visit the Alliance worlds," Grono Jonili said. "The Sunai allow no vessel to enter or leave our space without Gronoi Okooii's approval, and Earth has instituted a similar restriction. Our scanners now detect clones, a technology that shall be shared with all. Such actions protect us against Korvali treachery."

Qyto rapped again. "And what if these Korvali target the most vulnerable of us—my home, Calyyt-Calloq—and for something in which we had no involvement? You banter as if we speak of the Fights, rather than the real threat my people face."

"We can protect your people, Calyyt," Grono Jonili said. "We will send warships to your planet on your request, to remain as long as necessary."

Qyto signed his consent, sitting back down.

"We have addressed protection against Elisan's threats," Sansuai went on. "Now… what of the refugee, who has also acted in defiance of this Alliance and who has violated the terms of his asylum?"

Tallyn stood. "Eshel is an Alliance member and an officer in the Space Corps. He should face punishment in a similar manner to that of his comrades."

Many showed their agreement.

"And how do we do that if he's on Korvalis?" Jim Finnegan said.

"Leave him there and forget his punishment," Grono Jonili growled. "He chose to leave those who protected him. His punishment shall be to lose that protection and the privileges he enjoyed."

A rap on the table sounded, as the interpreter spoke for Toq. "What if Eshel inflicts damage on their leaders with human or Sunai technology? No matter what occurs, they will blame us."

"Did the refugee bring Sunai or human technology with him to the ocean planet?" Sansuai called out to Ferguson and Yamamoto.

Ferguson stood. "He uses our communicators, to transmit updates to us. He also uses a cloaking device created with our technology, but only he knows how it works. He has no weapons or anything else they could come after us for."

When the others seemed satisfied with this, Tallyn spoke. "We have protected Eshel, and do not want to forsake him. Yet, he chose to act against this Alliance and return to the place he escaped. It is, perhaps, what he wanted most. And his return will please Elisan, who has sought it from the beginning."

Catherine sighed, knowing that whether they chose to punish Eshel or not, Tallyn was right. Eshel did choose to return. And, none of them knew the full truth yet, that Eshel had no intention of living among them again, even if the Alliance forgave his actions.

Ferguson stood back up. "Gronoi Sansuai… may I speak?"

Sansuai gave her the nod.

She looked at the others. "Many of us have faced suffering at Elisan's hands, including Eshel. Elisan had Eshel's father killed, and Elisan's attack on our crew had a strong impact on him. He returned to Korvalis to right those wrongs. He didn't turn his back on us; he knew it was the only way to prevent Elisan from inflicting more harm. Punish me if you choose… punish us all, including Eshel. But don't make the mistake I did and assume Eshel only does what serves him. He gave up a lot to leave his people, and he gave up a lot to return." She paused, her blue eyes glimmering with anger.

"Elisan killed two of my soldiers and put fourteen others in sick bay. Say what you will… but I'm tired of cowtowing to that asshole, and I hope Eshel and his comrades take Elisan down."

Grono Jonili stood again. "You lost two soldiers. We lost eight, for merely advancing on Korvali space. Now you too can suffer and have no recourse!"

"Your soldiers were warned to stay away," Ferguson said. "They ignored it."

"They warned you as well, yes?" Grono Jonili said, his chin rising. "You chose to keep the refugee."

Before Ferguson could strike back, a high voice sounded.

"We chose, Grono Jonili!" Dannia said, standing again as her face and arms blued. "Did we not agree, as an Alliance, to aid any Korvali who would survive his escape from Korvalis? The humans kept him, rather than the Sunai, but we allowed this. Did Eshel not defy his own leadership by leaving Korvalis? Did we not give Eshel shelter and support his rebellion? Did we not let Eshel roam our lands freely?" She looked around at each of them. "We chose this."

"We chose to protect the refugee," Qyto signed. "We did not know Elisan would behave with such vengeance."

"And we've tried to appease Elisan to the point of absurdity," Admiral Scott said. "Not letting Eshel do science, giving Elisan information when he wanted it, sitting in negotiations that went nowhere…"

Grono Jonili gestured with his arms, raising his voice even more. "Whether or not we chose to protect the refugee, he and these others defied this Alliance to follow their own plan, excluding those who deserve to be part of such decisions!"

"We tried to work with you!" Ferguson cried. "You wouldn't listen. No matter what we argued, you chose to appease Elisan!"

Grono Jonili responded in anger and, all at once, the room erupted into a cacophony of voices, many of the delegates and leaders shouting to be heard over the others as the Calyyt rapped on the table. It was then that Gronoi Okooii stood, anger in his face.

"Silence!" he roared, so loudly that it reverberated off the walls of their cave room.

The uproar ceased, and the others turned to Okooii, perhaps more shocked than impressed by the Gronoi's anger. Okooii marched into the ellipse's opening, his decorations rattling wildly as Sansuai made way for him. Okooii glared at all of them. "This squabbling… it is a waste of time! This plan, this defiance you all speak of… it is in operation not because the refugee or these other collaborators defy us like Kotui youth… but because I made it so! It was I who authorized this mission. It was I who plotted with Grono Amsala, with the female Captain and her officer, with the refugee himself. And, most of all… it was I who concealed the first Korvali to escape his planet, who protected him and collaborated with him for nearly seven sun cycles."

Catherine let out a gasp at Okooii's admission. Those sitting around the table glanced at one another, speechless.

"Yes," Okooii growled. "The escapee known as Ashan lives. He accompanies the refugee on Korvalis to avenge the deaths of eight excellent soldiers of Suna and two soldiers of Earth, to ensure that these Korvali will join this Alliance! You ask who claimed authority to engage in such an act? I did! I decided!" He brought his meaty fist down upon the metal table, giant eyes peering at them, daring anyone to argue. When no one did, he went on. "Such a decision may appear reckless, may appear as if we do not respect the agreements of this Alliance. And you are right to be angry. Yet, we maintained such secrecy not out of insolence, but to protect all of you and to protect a plan that would benefit this Alliance and every citizen we represent. To reveal such a plan, to make it widespread knowledge, would be to allow it to fail. And, my comrades, this plan shall not fail!"

Okooii paced. "We have reached the place from which we cannot return, where such damage cannot be undone. The Korvali will wage war if we do not act quickly. Gone are the days of reasoning with Elisan, of waiting for him. I have known many Korvali, perhaps more than any who sit among us today. They are cold, they are bloodless, and they are selfish. But they are not evil. Elisan has acted with villainy, with the evil of criminals! And this Alliance humiliates itself by not recognizing this for what it is! Elisan is a disease to our peoples, and we must destroy him like any disease! And to destroy him, we must stand with these Korvali rebels." Okooii paused, glancing at each of them. "You may speak now."

Tallyn went first. "Dear Gronoi Okooii, this Ashan, this first escapee... he lives? You have known this for all these sun cycles?"

"Yes, Tallyn of our sister moon," he said, his tone gentler. "I did so to protect him, to protect us, and to protect our great Alliance. With the help of excellent Sunai women, we falsified his death and sent images to the Korvali."

"Elisan must know he's alive now, Gronoi," Jim Finnegan said.

"Eshel assures me he does not, Captain."

Dannia spoke. "Where has Ashan been all this time, Gronoi Okooii?"

"Waiting, Dannia. Unlike Eshel, Ashan was reticent to act, embittered by the actions of his leadership. Yet, I knew Ashan's presence would wield power one day. With time, another would escape, and then another, their keen minds working together to forge an alliance with us. But as chance would have it, the next escapee wound up in the hands of the humans." He glanced at Admiral Scott. "Therefore, much time passed before we could arrange a meeting between the two men."

Silence filled the room, as people contemplated Okooii's words.

Admiral Scott spoke. "Assuming we decide to support what you propose, Gronoi Okooii... what now?"

"What now, Admiral?" Okooii said. He looked over at Ferguson and Yamamoto, then at Koni. "We make Elisan believe we will punish these conspirators, that we will appease him at any cost, that we will turn our backs on the refugee. Then, we combine our great intelligences and aid these Korvali to do what they must!"

"And what if it fails, Gronoi Okooii?" Dannia said.

"Then you shall punish me," Okooii said. "If it fails, I do not deserve to be Gronoi!"

More silence, as Catherine and everyone else pondered the gravity of Okooii's offer, that he would renounce what every male on Suna would sacrifice everything for. Koni, however, looked down at something that had caught his attention. He stood up.

"Grono Amsala," Okooii called out. "You may speak."

"I have word from Eshel," Koni said. "Their rebellion grows… and they have a plan to move against Elisan."

CHAPTER 17

What is betrayal? To humans, it is a disloyalty, a bond of an emotional nature that is broken. But to the Korvali, it is a duplicity of truth, of ideas and beliefs, in which a person claims one ideology while adhering to another.

- Othniel, Shemal clan

Eshel peered through the small window at the gaunt, gray-robed man with the mottled scar. When he turned around, Ashan stood there.

"Traitor," Ashan said coldly, staring through the window at Volen. "This… this is why I left Korvalis. That a member of my own clan would align with Elisan."

Eshel, understanding Ashan's anger all too well, said nothing.

"He should sit in that room until his years complete," Ashan said.

"No," Eshel said.

"He is a threat."

"We cannot act as Elisan would," Eshel said. "He will face trial and serve as an example of what we represent, of honoring Doctrine." He paused. "For now, we will glean information from him."

"He will not offer information."

"He will if we utilize the proper incentives."

"What do you propose?"

Eshel glanced at the window again. "It is possible Volen dedicates himself to Elisan and the malkaris. However, he is Moshal, and Elisan likely coerced him to serve as informant."

"Moshal are not so easily coerced, Eshel. The traitor must have had another reason."

"Then I will find it."

"What if you don't?"

Eshel turned to Ashan. "Then we will utilize his mate and children."

"Elan had a mate and child. It didn't stop him."

A vision of Elan holding a young Alshar appeared before Eshel. He brushed it away. "Elan believed himself beyond punishment. And I believe he experienced some coercion as well. He lacked the nature of his mother, of Ivar, and merely did what he must until he could rule."

"Let us hope you are correct."

Eshel unlocked the door and they entered the small room, closing the door behind them.

Volen sat quietly upon a bench, his head against the wall and his hood pulled up. His eyes had the vacant stare of someone experiencing visions, the kind of visions one sees after having endured loss. Upon hearing the door, they shifted to a chilly glare as he glanced at his captors. His hand, bearing the circular crest, disappeared under his sleeve.

"Volen," Eshel said, sitting down with Ashan. "Tell me information I will find useful."

Volen gave no response.

"You will find it beneficial to speak to me," Eshel said.

"I will tell you nothing," Volen replied.

"You will speak. Perhaps today, or perhaps years from now, while you sit alone in this place. But you will speak. And the sooner you do, the sooner you may receive something you value."

"Do not attempt to coerce me," Volen said. "You have nothing I value."

"You do not value your mate? Your children? Because I have them, here."

Volen's face swelled with anger. "Do not threaten my family. They know not of this."

"They know," Ashan sneered. "They know, because I told them. They know you collaborated with Elisan and betrayed your clan."

"Do not speak to me of betrayal, absconder," Volen hissed to Ashan. He turned back to Eshel. "They deserve no harm. I ask only that you inform them of my whereabouts after you take me to the remote territories."

Eshel stared at him. "I will do no such thing. If, however, you provide useful information, you will see no harm, you will have contact with your family, and you will merely face trial and a tolerable imprisonment." He leaned closer to Volen, who backed away. "This is the way of Doctrine."

"You Shereb…" Volen said. "You are all alike, never to be trusted. If only Mosel had known this." And he leaned against the wall once more, and resumed his lost stare.

Eshel gave Ashan a Calyyt sign. They stood up and left.

"Such manipulation is not working," Ashan said.

"Not yet."

Ashan paused. "Your mother… she waits for you."

Eshel stepped into yet another room, windows surrounding them and rain drumming upon the glass rooftop. His mother stood up from a wooden bench, her expression cold.

"You dare imprison me," she said angrily.

"I had to. I know you collaborated with Elisan."

She said nothing for several moments, her gray eyes focused on his. "I did."

Eshel gritted his teeth. "Volen told me a Shereb cannot be trusted, a sentiment I have heard before. We have Elisan, the malkaris and her useless offspring, Elan, and now you. What will I learn next, that Father secretly supported Elisan?"

"You are like your father," Fashal said. "You embrace ideals, but you know nothing of what it is to govern."

"I learn quickly, Mother," Eshel sneered. "Teach me about governing our people, about how to represent one set of beliefs while embracing another, even with your own son."

Her eyes narrowed. "Do you believe I would betray my son to the people who murdered my mate? It is I who conveyed the truth about your escape to the vokalis, who worked with them before your return." She paused. "My beliefs have not changed, son. If your methods of questioning Volen had any success, you would know this."

"What do you mean?"

"I did not reveal the vokalis, or your return, to Elisan. Volen did, some time ago. I merely sought to mitigate the damage, to work with Elisan at a solution that may benefit all."

"I have evidence of your collusion that predates my having learned of Elisan discovering us," Eshel said.

"Yes," Fashal said. "I have an informant among the Shereb, who told me of the betrayal. However, she did not know the betrayer's identity. I met with Elisan on two occasions to attempt to negotiate with him and learn who the betrayer was."

Eshel, feeling some relief that his mother's story matched the evidence he had, said nothing for several moments. "Why did you not tell me?"

"You would not have considered working with Elisan."

"You are correct. I wouldn't have."

Fashal stepped closer to him. "Son… what we do here, it is important, and necessary. But it is radical. People will not respond well to our overthrowing the leadership, despite its failings. I planned to come to you and Ashan after I discovered the betrayer, when I had an offer to present. It is often better to work with an enemy who is more powerful that you, and hope to vanquish him later."

"That enemy murdered your mate and other Shereb. He attacked the humans and killed two of theirs. He attempted to murder Catherine with an abomination bearing my face, and even plotted to harm her when she was here—"

"That is your doing," Fashal said. "You shouldn't have involved yourself with her, and you shouldn't have brought her here. You have put her at risk."

"Do not tell me what is my doing," Eshel said through his teeth. "I know what is my doing. If not for her, what excuse would you then have for Elisan's treachery? If you had the audacity to leave Korvalis and all that you know in order to live among the others, you would face choices you did not imagine and see things differently than you ever thought you would. You would then live with the consequences of it all. And until you embark on such a journey, I will listen no more to your disparagement and condemnation." He paused, calming himself. "You seek to compromise with Elisan not because it is best, but because you fear what is unknown."

Fashal stood quietly. "Perhaps so. But so do others. If we act too rashly, they will rebel."

"The others don't know of your collaboration. You must tell them and present your arguments. They will decide how to proceed."

Eshel turned and left the room.

Eshel stood at the window, watching Volen. Waiting. When Volen's eyes glazed over, Eshel entered the room. He carried a portable screen, which he set down upon the bench. Eshel sat and turned on the power; the screen lit up, and a woman and two children appeared.

Volen's expression changed. His eyes brightened and he sat up straighter. But before Volen could speak, Eshel promptly closed the screen. Volen blinked a couple of times, staring at the apparatus before turning away.

"Why do you resist?" Eshel said. "You are Moshal. You are a protector of Korvalis. Why do you serve Elisan, when Doctrine states that the kunsheld shall come from a different clan than that of the monarchy, when his greed led to Mosel's death?"

"Mosel violated Doctrine by leaving Korvalis without permission. She sought to live amidst outsiders. She caused her own death."

"And why would she leave her people, leave you and her kin, to live among Inferiors? Why would she choose this?"

Volen said nothing.

Eshel leaned forward. "Do you believe she desired to leave? To live with those who do not understand her, to eat strange foods, to endure atmospheric temperatures that would harm her, to face the blustering Sunai or the irrational humans, to be hunted for the remainder of her life? Do you, Volen? Because that is what she would suffer. She did not want that; she wanted what I did, to create change."

"To create this 'change,' would she have done the unspeakable with a human?" he sneered. "Whom shall I trust, Shereb? A villainous leader, or one who would dishonor his people?"

Eshel paused, unprepared for Volen's admission. "So it is this violation that convinced you to collaborate with the man who would ruin Korvalis. This was your concern when you detained us at Station Fifteen and pretended to feel concern for Mosel."

"That was no pretense," he said. "Elisan came to me, after he learned that someone breached our net. He knew of my connection to Mosel. And he informed me of your involvement with the redheaded human, showed me images." He paused. "Mosel… she would not have done this, what you did with such ease."

"Perhaps not," Eshel said. "However, I did not do this with ease. I resisted it. I struggled with shame, with doubt. Yet I was able to surmount such feelings, to bond with her in a way I did not expect. She was the only outsider who understood me, whom I could trust, in a place where I could not swim or share the food of the sea with my people. I severed my relations with her to protect her, myself, and others… but also because I knew it was wrong."

"Did you see her after this severing?"

"I did."

"Do you see her now?"

Eshel paused. "I do." He sat for several moments. "Perhaps I deserve punishment for my actions. Yet, punishment or not, you will still have to contend with Elisan." When Volen offered no argument,

Eshel went on. "Do you know of my father? He was murdered, at Elisan's order. He was murdered for his liberal views, that we should maintain relations with outsiders, even if only limited relations. He was liberal, yes. Perhaps too much so. But where in Doctrine does it say that one must be murdered for such beliefs? I ask this, knowing that you have probably never read our Doctrine. You listen to the words of a corrupt leader, who instills fear that those who seek connection to the outerworlds will lead us to ruin. You believe him, share in his disgust at my violation, hoping that doing so will ensure you do not suffer like the Osecal have for defying him." Eshel stood up. "You have a choice, Volen. You may tolerate what I have done and lessen your punishment, or you may spend your remaining years knowing you dishonored the Moshal and allowed Elisan to continue his ruin of Korvalis."

Volen sat perfectly still, his cool gaze resting upon Eshel's face. He then turned away and resumed his vacant stare. Eshel reopened the portable screen, leaving it there as he left.

Eshel entered the room, the rooftop window casting a gray light upon its interior. He sat down on the wooden bench, where his mother and Ashan waited for him.

"Elisan plans an attack," Eshel said.

Fashal, her expression growing cold, sat silent for several moments. "Where will he target?"

"That is unknown," Eshel said. "We only know he plans to strike by air, from the stations."

"How can we defend ourselves without knowledge of where they will strike?" Fashal said.

"They will avoid Moshal territory because they require the help of the Guard," Ashan said. "Targeting the remote territories offers no deterrence for us. That only leaves the Osecal."

"Perhaps they know we are here," Fashal said.

"They don't," Eshel said. "They don't need to. Any attack will hurt us because they know we will crumble when we witness our citizens perish."

"Defending against an air strike will prove quite difficult," Ashan said. "Even if victorious, it would reveal the identities of our Ground and Air Guard, which will result in their losing access to Guard resources. If that occurs, we are defeated."

Fashal looked at Eshel. "How do you know Volen shares no trick?"

"I don't," Eshel said. "But I believe him. He could have revealed that Ashan is alive and among us, but he hasn't. He detests Elisan; I needed only to remove the barrier that separated him from us."

"What of the Shemal?" Ashan said.

"Elisan has no cause to harm them," Fashal said. "The Shemal are the most populous clan on Korvalis, and even Elisan knows that angering them is unwise." She paused. "We may speculate all that we will. We cannot defend against such a threat, and we must negotiate with Elisan."

"You would still work with him, when he plans such a maneuver," Eshel said.

"Especially then," Fashal said. "Volen's betrayal has weakened us. We have no other option. I know Elisan; one strong concession will purchase more time for us to plan our next move."

"There must be another way," Ashan said.

They continued to discuss their ideas, considering every possibility to counteract the impending attack. But as they did, Eshel soon realized the truth... the truth he didn't want to face. And that's when an idea came to him.

"There is another option," he said.

Fashal's eyes narrowed, already knowing what he would say. "No."

Eshel said nothing.

"You seek the aid of the others," Ashan said. "What is your idea?"

Eshel told them. Ashan signed in approval, but his mother still appeared unconvinced.

"We must do this ourselves, without the aid of outsiders," she said.

"It cannot be done without them," Eshel said. "It will render us victorious, and will do so without violence."

"The vokalis will resist," Ashan said.

"Let them," Eshel said. "But they too will see that we have no other choice."

"Including the outsiders is a compromise we cannot avoid," Eshel said to the group. "We either accept this, or we allow Elisan to remain in power indefinitely."

"Perhaps that is better," an Osecal woman said. "Joining this Alliance is one thing. Garnering outside aid and allowing them to trespass upon our lands is quite another. We have remained separate from the Inferiors for good reason."

"But at great loss," Eshel countered. "I have lost my father, my mother her mate, Ashan his mate. Others have died in similar ways. The Osecal laboratories sit unused and atrophying, instead of conducting the science that gives us our power. Osecal and Moshal perish in their escape attempts. Most of the clans have lost their voices in the assembly. The outsiders continue to assume we are weak, because they know a world with competent leadership would not drive its citizens to escape. And all of this within half a generation... imagine what another half generation will do."

"But to look broadly..." a Moshal man said. "The problems you have stated, while egregious, may seem small compared to the unknown problems that could arise when allowing outsiders to influence us. It is foolish to remove one enemy, only to acquire a larger one."

"I do not believe the outsiders are our enemy," Eshel said. "However, if they are, or become so in the future, they will have no power over us that we do not give them."

"Eshel is correct," Ashan said. "The humans, the Sunai... they will not prevail in war. There are many, including the Shereb, who have ensured this."

"I have no concern with our power to defend and protect Korvalis," the Moshal went on. "But we cannot allow the influence of outsiders over our Doctrine, our way. Elisan and the malkaris are corrupt and should be removed; but they too want our way preserved."

"You have lived amidst these outsiders," an Osecal scientist said to Eshel. "You did so for the betterment of our people, but such actions violated Doctrine. It is said that you did not conduct the science, instead choosing to train for war. You have formed an alliance with a Sunai Grono. You even speak differently, and use strange gestures. It is also said that you did the unspeakable with a human female, that you have attempted to mate with her." He paused, as more eyes shifted to Eshel. "Fashal's secrecy was questionable. Volen's betrayal was wrong. But both served a belief that every person here understands. What you have done does not."

Eshel looked at them all. "What you say, it is all true. I engaged in each of these behaviors, some of which violate Doctrine. However, they were necessary to achieve the goals my father discussed with me and my mother. I have returned now, with the goal of eradicating Elisan and this malkaris, the same goal I have always had. These actions you speak of… they are the only reason we have any chance of achieving our mission." He looked down momentarily. "The exception was that of involving myself with a human. As I told Volen, perhaps I should receive punishment for this. But such a violation isn't what is most important now. We will be attacked, and we must thwart this attack. We can negotiate with Elisan and hope he will desist… but Elisan has proven his untrustworthiness many times. My plan forces him to negotiate without pushing him too far. However, it also requires bringing two operatives here: one to assist with the technical aspects, and another to offer protection in case we are detected." He paused. "To address your concerns about outside influence… if we succeed in our mission, the degree to which we allow ourselves to be influenced by outsiders will be something we decide as a people, with a properly functioning government."

"Eshel is correct," another Osecal said. "We no longer thrive because we allowed the Shereb takeover, the breakdown of our government, and the shutdown of our labs. Eshel's absconding allowed him to learn from the others and gain a different perspective. His actions have illustrated why we need contact with outsiders, so that we do not perish from an inbreeding of ideas."

Another Moshal spoke. "Yes... but aid from outsiders means they will expect something in return."

"They will," Eshel said. "That is how alliances work. But I believe we can offer that which is agreeable to us and to them."

"There is one thing I do not understand," the Osecal woman said. "Why haven't the outsiders—these Sunai and these humans—attempted to take advantage of us during our weakness, after they learned of our difficulties? Is that not what their history shows? War, and the conquering of other peoples?"

"Such fortune results from their current leaderships," Eshel said. "If they had discovered Korvalis decades earlier, before Gronoio Vahara rose to power, or during the human-Sunai wars, we would not enjoy such restraint from them."

The group was silent for some time.

"If you allow these operatives to come here, how will we bring them in? We cannot utilize the Sunai decoy again without risking detection."

"There is another way," Ashan said. "I will coordinate it." He turned to Eshel. "You will bring Catherine, of course. Who is the other?"

"Not Catherine," Eshel said.

"Why not?" Ashan said, glancing at Fashal.

"She is a target, and I will not endanger her again. We must bring two others, and I know who will serve us best."

The Osecal woman spoke. "Bring them here. Utilize them, then ensure they leave."

The others agreed.

CHAPTER 18

After teaching one of Yamamoto's self-defense courses, followed by a long training session, Catherine picked up her towel to mop the sweat from her face. She looked around the studio, realizing how much she missed her mentor, how lackluster the studio seemed without his disciplined presence.

Despite the progress made during the Alliance meeting, and despite the impact Gronoi Okooii's diatribe seemed to have upon the others, Ferguson and Yamamoto still remained imprisoned. Catherine didn't understand the purpose of this, given that the delegates seemed to agree that each leadership would issue punishment as they saw fit. Yet, despite her service on Korvalis, she was still not privy to such information.

Catherine's contactor beeped. She glanced at it, not having heard that sort of beep in a long time. She'd received an encrypted message.

Catherine,

You will find a file attached. Do not decrypt or open. Eshel instructs you to forward it to your mutual friend, and that you will receive another file to return to me. Please do this by tomorrow.

Koni

Catherine's eyes narrowed. She grabbed her things and returned to her quarters. Once there, she sat down at her computer, pulled up a command line, and delivered her series of passwords, still committed to memory but a couple requiring her to think hard for several moments. She could almost hear his chiding at her slowness.

HerrSycophant: *What do you want?*

Soobooii: *Our mutual friend sends a file. He needs something from you. And he needs it by tomorrow.*

HerrSycophant: *Of course. It's always fucking urgent.*

Soobooii: *Sending it now.*

Herr disappeared. Late that night, Catherine logged on again.

HerrSycophant: *Here you go. Don't bother trying to look. The encryption is beyond your pay scale.*

Soobooii: *What's your other half, Herr?*

HerrSycophant: *Sweetheart, if you haven't figured that out by now, you aren't worth sharing it with.*

Soobooii: *Great talking to you, as usual.*

HerrSycophant: *Tell the Filthy Mutant good luck. And by the way, Boris and Natasha seem to be making good progress.*

And once more, Herr was gone.

Boris and Natasha? And then she got it. Steele… and Albert Vanyukov.

Catherine shook her head, her annoyance at Herr's surliness quickly supplanted by a far bigger aggravation: Steele was making progress. With Eshel's data, obtained without his permission. Other thoughts ran through her mind… including those that would upset the limited peace treaty she and Steele had enjoyed for a while now.

But she pushed such disturbing thoughts away. Now wasn't the time to cause trouble. She relayed the message and file to Koni, and went to bed.

Catherine emerged from her office, stretching to remove the stiffness from her body. Holloway slouched in his chair, mindlessly scrolling through screen after screen of genetic code. Varan sat forlornly at his desk, working alone instead of next door with Dorel, likely waiting only a bit longer before coming to her office to see if she had any errands he could run. She glanced at Holloway, tempted to tell him what Herr had told her, knowing he wouldn't ask her how she knew or care if she refused to tell him. But she couldn't dangle a temptation in front of him now, when their mission would soon come to a close, when he had more to lose than she did.

She retreated to her office to finish her report for Steele. As she sat back down, her contactor beeped. Koni.

Nonaii: We must speak. You will join me after your duty? I will pick you up.

Of course, Koni.

That evening, Catherine stepped into the transport and Koni took off. She didn't bother asking where they would go, soon realizing they headed in the direction of Sundani Headquarters. Catherine's mind immediately went to Eshel. Something must be wrong. Fear washed over her as Koni set down, her mind racing with thoughts of Eshel imprisoned by Elisan.

She turned to Koni. "Please tell me Eshel's okay."

"Do not worry, nonaii." Koni said. "Eshel is unharmed. But he has learned that Elisan will attack the vokalis, and he requires aid to foil the plan. The Alliance has agreed to offer this aid."

She broke into a smile. Okooii had convinced them! That's why the Captain and XO lingered in prison, as one of many ways to fool Elisan into believing they would continue appeasing him.

Koni went on. "Eshel has requested that Lieutenant Commander Kingston and your Executive Officer come to his planet."

Her smiled faded. Tom and Yamamoto? Catherine exited the transport, muttering a curse to herself at being sidelined. But then she remembered Eshel's promise… that he would get her off Korvalis and keep her out of harm's way. "What else?"

"Your XO wishes to speak with you."

She nodded.

She followed Koni into Sundani quarters, once again noting how differently the other males regarded them now that Koni remained undecorated. When one officer with a Gro's decorations walked too close to her, assuming she would make way for him, she maintained her position and braced herself, colliding with him. He growled at her. She growled back, and kept walking. When she glanced over at Koni, wondering if her behavior would offend him, his eyes remained forward, but she swore she saw a hint of amusement in his face.

It was at that moment that she felt the need to bring up a difficult topic.

"Koni…" she began. "You know that Okooii Jooni wants to teach music and primary Sunai on Earth, as part of interplanetary exchange."

"A more favorable idea than joining your military, nonaii," he said, his chin raising slightly. "But she will not succeed."

"She wants to teach, something many Sunai women do. And she wants to do so in a way that honors the Sunai, that shares Sunai culture with humans."

He grunted. "I do not disagree. But this… it is not my decision."

"Come on, Koni," Catherine said. "You've been working with Gronoi Okooii this whole time. You have his ear now."

"A Grono does not anger a Gronoi he respects!" he growled. "Not if he wants to lead!"

"A leader thinks differently than his peers, Koni! You provided Okooii a different option for dealing with Elisan... you can do the same with this."

He grunted again, and said no more about it.

After descending deep into the earth, Koni led her down a hallway of closed doors until they stopped at one of them. When they entered, Yamamoto sat in his small chair, reading. He looked pale and a little tired.

Yamamoto set down his reading pad and stood up, while Catherine saluted him. "Grono Amsala," he said. "May I request ten minutes of privacy with Catherine?"

Koni raised his chin. "Of course," he said, exiting the room.

Yamamoto turned to her. "We don't have the luxury of time, Catherine, so I will be quick. Eshel plans an operation of considerable ambition, for which he has requested the aid of Tom and myself." He paused. "However, I am increasingly concerned that the operation may require more skill than I possess."

"Did Eshel tell you anything about this operation?"

Yamamoto told her the overall plan, including a few details. She nodded in awe. Eshel never thought small, and never the way others did.

He went on. "Eshel excludes you out of fear that you will be harmed. However, I believe he puts the operation at risk by doing so." He began pacing. After a minute, he spoke. "I believe you need to go to Korvalis with Tom, in my place."

Catherine looked down, chagrined at the idea of going against Eshel, of doing something that would not only infuriate him, but would hurt him. And she didn't understand why Eshel had admitted his fears to others, why he'd revealed even as much as he had about the operation, giving others the opportunity to pick it apart or to know more than they ought about Korvali defenses. It was so unlike him.

She shook her head. "With all due respect, Sir, as much as I want to help, I trust Eshel's judgment. If he says the op doesn't need me, then it doesn't. And if I may speak freely, Sir... if you doubt him, it's probably because he hasn't told you everything. To be honest, I'm surprised he told you as much as he did."

Yamamoto stared at her. "You are correct. Eshel has not provided details... Ashan has. Ashan relayed a message to us, concerned that Eshel places their operation in danger in his desire to protect you. He wants you there, and has pledged that he will protect you himself from any danger."

Catherine gasped. Ashan had gone behind Eshel's back.

"I too was concerned by Ashan's back-channeling," Yamamoto said, seeing her reaction. "However, given the technical nature of the operation, Ashan encouraged me to consult a trusted expert. I contacted your trainer; he claims the technical aspects are far from complex, but agreed that you should accompany Eshel in the event something goes wrong. And you know by now that, in the field, something often does."

Her "trainer"... Yamamoto's name for Herr. She bit her lip, recalling the encrypted file Eshel had sent, and the file she'd sent back to Koni. Herr knew. And for all his insults, even he thought she should go.

"What does the Captain say?" she said.

"She agrees with Ashan."

She nodded. "I'll go, Sir."

"Good. However, there is one problem. The Corps does not agree with us on this, your father included."

"My dad doesn't know I'm a COO—"

"He does now, but he still doesn't want you there. In fact, he raised quite a stink when we sent you to Korvalis for Eshel's rescue, and I suffered an earful from him. He's even unhappier now that he knows of your recent unsanctioned operation on Korvalis, and your lying to him about it."

Catherine let out a breath. *Fuck.*

Yamamoto approached her. "Catherine... this must succeed. If it doesn't, the vokalis will suffer a blow from which they cannot recover. I have limited power in this situation. Speak to your father.

Share your experiences and enhanced knowledge with him. Once he hears it from you, he may very well agree."

She gave a faint nod.

"You have until midnight. We cannot afford further delay."

Catherine glanced at the time. It was nearly 2145. She got up and left.

"What brings you to *Victoria*, Lieutenant?" a beefy MA asked brusquely. He stood rocket straight and stared down at her.

"I need to see Captain Finnegan," she replied.

The MA spoke into his contactor. "Sorry to bother you, Sir. Your daughter wants to speak with you."

"Send her in," her father's voice replied.

Another MA scanned her. Once finished, the first MA said, "Follow me, Lieutenant."

The bulky soldier led Catherine down a narrow hallway, passing more bulky men until they reached a ready room. The MA buzzed the door. Once it opened, Jimmy Finnegan sat at his desk, still in uniform. He nodded at the MA and the door shut behind her.

Jimmy's expression turned colder as he leaned back in his chair. "Have a seat."

Catherine sat down, her palms beginning to sweat. She cleared her throat. "Dad, I know about the Korvalis operation—"

"If you're here to talk me into persuading the Corps to let you go, don't waste your breath."

She sighed. "Dad, I'm sorry about lying to you about the op. I knew Headquarters kept you in the dark about my role as COO, and I suspected they sent you here to get information out of me. I took part in that op because I felt it was my duty." When her father seemed less angry, or at least no angrier than before, she went on. "I know you don't want me to go, and I understand why." She went on to tell her father those things she couldn't share with him before: the skills she'd gained, the problems she'd surmounted, and more about Eshel and his concerns. She wrestled with how much to tell him, knowing more would achieve greater impact, but also knowing she faced an impending deadline. Her father listened without interruption until she finally ceased, having said all she believed necessary.

"Catherine," he said. "They're putting you at unnecessary risk for their own gain, just like they have all along."

"Oh, come on, Dad!" she cried. "I'm trained for this!"

"Lower your voice," he warned, giving her a menacing look. "We have others who can do this op, and you know it. Okooii got the Alliance to join his party, and the Corps is okay with that... but Ferguson and these others, they lied to us, acted behind our backs. They're trying to save their own asses and using you as a pawn."

"Dad..."

"Even Eshel doesn't want you there. You're a target. We'll find another field operative."

Catherine stood up and began pacing. "Dad, I understand why you see things that way. But I've met Ashan, and I know Yamamoto. If they say I'm the best qualified for the op, then it's my duty to go. Yes, it's risky. But if they fail, imagine what will happen! Elisan will—"

"You don't need to tell me the consequences, Catherine. We've talked with Headquarters about this for days. But I have a bad feeling about your going there, and so do others. Whatever they need from you, they can get from someone more qualified to be in the field, and I'm willing to FTL someone from Earth if necessary." When Catherine went to speak, Jim held up his hand. "That's it. Not another word."

Catherine, out of arguments, left.

Catherine glanced at the time. Midnight loomed. She shook her head to Yamamoto, slumped in her chair. "He won't bend, Sir. We'll have to trust that if something goes wrong, Eshel and the other operative will figure it out. Eshel always figures things out."

Yamamoto looked at her. "Catherine, do you want to do this operation?"

"Yes, Sir."

"Do you believe you're necessary for it to succeed?"

"Probably, Sir."

"You don't sound confident. I need you committed to this."

She took a deep breath. "I want to do my duty, Sir, and I'm willing to disobey orders again. But I admit I'm scared. It's not easy to defy Eshel, my father, *and* the Corps, especially if they have another candidate."

"We have no other candidates who know the Korvali language, who have your technical skill, and who we can transport to Korvalis before it's too late." He paused. "If you could get the Corps to back you, would that put you at ease?"

Catherine nodded. "But how, Sir?"

"Go to Admiral Scott. You might find him more persuadable than your father."

She pressed her lips together as a chill ran through her. "You mean go over my father's head."

Yamamoto gave a nod.

CHAPTER 19

Catherine and Tom, in full field gear, peered at Korvalis in the distance. At Koni's word, they'd grabbed their gear and climbed into the Pokey, engaged their clandestine device, and exited the Sunai ship. They slowly made their way toward the Forbidden Planet, even Tom saying nothing other than to confirm the coordinates of their destination and the path that they must take to get there. This time, both ships utilized the technology that obscured them from Korvali eyes. And this time, Ashan had assured them no Korvali Guard would pursue them, that his Guard comrades would squelch the alert.

Catherine gritted her teeth as they crossed the border near Station 9. *Not now. Not today.* Silently they floated closer and closer to the cloud cover that, today, had gaps revealing the vast blue ocean beneath.

"So are you gonna tell me how these clandestine devices work, or what?" Tom said as they entered the cloud layer.

"If you want to know, ask Eshel," she said coldly.

Tom made a face. "What's with you, Grouchy?"

"Not now, Tom."

"Jimmy still pissed at you?"

She sighed. "He wouldn't talk to me."

"At all?"

"Nope."

Tom shook his head, a bit of laughter escaping him. "Yeah, you dug a nice hole for yourself on this one."

Catherine gave no reply.

"Hey, look," Tom said. "You did your duty. If Ashan is anything like Eshel, you probably need to be there and the Admiral was the guy to persuade."

"Maybe. But I feel lousy about it."

"Yeah, well, Eshel isn't going to be too happy either when he sees you."

"Thanks for the reminder."

Tom shrugged. "Duty means dealing with lousy shit sometimes. Welcome to a soldier's life."

Tom was right. When offering her the COO position, Yamamoto had said her allegiance to the Corps would have to supersede any others. But never did she imagine she would have to disrespect her father.

"Anyway," Tom went on, "it's good to see Jimmy knocked down a little."

"Why?"

He shook his head. "He gave me a hard time, saying I'm too irresponsible to get promoted. Maybe he had a point, but he was pretty harsh."

She nodded. "He can be that way."

They emerged from the clouds and altered their heading, aiming for the forested land mass. Before long, it began to get dark and Catherine directed Tom to land under one of the weeping trees, a different one this time.

"Holy shit!" Tom said as they set down under the tree. "This is the broadest damned tree I've ever seen. You could live under here!"

Catherine smiled. "Tom, keep your voice down. We don't need to attract any trouble."

He pressed his lips together and made zipping motion. "I guess we just sit and wait, huh? At least that bastard isn't sidelining me this time."

Catherine scoffed. "Which means we don't have to listen to you complain anymore."

Tom waved his hand at her. He opened the hatch, stepped outside, and approached the drooping branches that enclosed them.

He pulled out a pair of teleglasses and began peering through the branches.

"You can't see shit with all these trees," Tom remarked. He walked the entire perimeter of the tree's branches, surveying the area around them. Then, he stopped. "Whoa," he said quietly.

"What?"

"I see one of them."

"Where?"

"One o'clock," he said. "Three of them, actually, up in the trees, watching us."

Catherine peered through the branches in that direction, but saw nothing. "Do they have spears?"

Tom looked for a few moments. "Oh, yeah. Yeah. Perched in the branches."

"They're patrollers."

"Why aren't they coming over?"

"I don't know."

"This is awesome!" Tom said in wonder.

A short while later, Catherine heard the snapping of branches. She stood up again, afraid that the Shemal had changed their minds.

"Can you see anything?" she said in a hushed voice.

Tom searched the area. "A guy in a gray robe. Never seen him before."

"Let me see." Catherine peered through the teleglasses. She smiled. "It's Ashan."

Catherine and Tom stepped back as Ashan approached their tree, parting the weeping branches and entering their hovel. He immediately made eye contact with Catherine. "You have come."

She nodded, seeing perhaps a glint of gratitude in Ashan's expression. "Ashan, this is my friend Tom."

Ashan stared at Tom, a chilly look on his face.

"How you doin', Ashan?" Tom said.

Ashan continued examining Tom. "Eshel has spoken highly of you."

"Don't believe everything he says," Tom joked.

Ashan said nothing.

"Catherine told me you had a better sense of humor than Eshel does," Tom chided.

"I await something humorous," Ashan said.

Tom shook his head, looking a little deflated.

"Now it is I who jokes," Ashan said, his blue eyes with a hint of twinkle.

Catherine burst out laughing as Tom grinned.

"We must go," Ashan said.

Once they crossed the riverlands, Ashan led Catherine and Tom to a shuttle hidden in the western forests. A gray-robed pilot who never acknowledged them raised the shuttle above the forest canopy and headed northwest. Catherine peered out the window as they flew, the moonlight illuminating the white stone homes and streamways below. Ahead, a large stone edifice loomed, as blocky and gray as the compound of Felebaseb had been. The ground Headquarters for the Guard.

A knot formed in Catherine's stomach. She didn't know what she feared more: the unknowns of the operation and the consequences if they failed, or Eshel's reaction when he saw her. She looked over at Tom, who sat quietly, staring out the window himself, his lack of chatter only increasing her unease. They flew into a small bay on the east side of the building and the bay door shut behind them.

Ashan spoke something to the pilot, who got out of the shuttle and went to secure the door that led inside the building. When a beep sounded, Ashan glanced at his communicator. He signaled to the pilot and the bay door began to rise, a dark gray robe appearing behind it. Even before the door rose high enough to see a face, Catherine knew it was Eshel. She waited, her hands sweating as Eshel's face appeared.

Eshel entered, the door shutting behind him. When he spotted her, he froze. He stared, his eyes bright with emotion that Catherine could not decipher. He turned his gaze to Ashan.

"Why is she here?" he said in Korvali.

"You know why."

"You orchestrated this," Eshel said.

"I did."

"Why? Why do you put her in unnecessary danger, when she is not needed?"

"She is needed," Ashan replied. "And it is your attachment to her that blinds you."

Eshel's expression grew colder. "I made myself clear, Ashan. Catherine is a target for Elisan and I will not risk her again. If you do not take her away, I will have the Shemal imprison her."

"And you will delay our operation, risk what we have planned in order to return her to the eastern territories? You will begin anew?"

A chill ran through Catherine. Ashan had known just how to trap Eshel.

"You idiot," Eshel sneered.

"Your concern for Catherine is unfounded," Ashan said in English, still undaunted. "I protected her once; I will do so again. Now, do you want to undergo this operation, or do you prefer to continue engaging in a dispute that you cannot win?"

Eshel turned to Tom. "You knew of this?"

Tom puffed up his chest and removed any signs of guilt from his face. "Look, Esh, you have every right to be angry. This is your gig, and we went against your orders. But we thought hard about this. Everyone insisted that Catherine do this—Yamamoto, the Captain, even Admiral Scott, for Christ's sake. She's the best person for the job, Esh." When Eshel offered no argument, Tom went on. "Your desire to protect Catherine interfered with your ability to strategize. It happens to everyone. That's why we have our comrades to question us and look out for us, man. We'll do this thing, we'll hide Catherine in a hole somewhere, and then we'll leave. And if any shit goes down with Elisan… you have me. You know I could level this fucking place to the ground in a matter of seconds, if you wanted me to."

"She is a target, Tom," Eshel said. "You are not. Yamamoto is not."

"We're all targets now, Esh," Tom said. "If you're not on the enemy's side, you're a target! We're here to help; let us do our jobs."

Eshel stared at Tom for a moment. He glanced at Catherine. "Then we must begin."

Tom grinned. "Good. Same plan?"

"Yes," Eshel said. "We will breach the Guard's computer network… and completely disable it."

Under a tree that protected them from the drizzle that fell from the dark sky, Catherine and Eshel prepared to leave. Ashan had left to keep watch from a different location, while Catherine, Eshel, and Tom went over their plan.

Catherine and Eshel engaged their devices and approached the door that would take them inside Guard Headquarters. As Eshel decoded it, she glanced behind her, at the tree. She could no longer see Tom, and adrenaline began to course through her. Inside, Eshel and Catherine tiptoed their way through the thankfully wide hallways, dodging an occasional Guardsman and heading toward the location that Ashan had given them.

Eshel halted. After decoding another door, they entered a dark room. Eshel produced a tiny light, and she followed him until they came upon some stools and sat down. Eshel turned on a computer, rotating its screen until it faced away from the door. He pulled up a command line and typed in a series of commands. Catherine stared at the screen, still baffled by the strangeness of Korvali in its written form.

"I have found it," he said.

"The pathway to the central network?"

"Yes. However, it is as I feared: six different networks, and none are connected."

"That's okay," she said. "We'll just have to go after them one at a time."

Eshel's eyes narrowed. "That will take far longer."

"Not necessarily. Open more command lines."

Eshel did so, after which he retrieved a portable device and inserted it into a port. When the file took several minutes to upload, Catherine looked around nervously. Korvali information systems were easy to invade, but they were slow. Eshel began typing again. Finally, having broken into his first network, he ran the malware Herr had created.

He glanced at her. "Let us now see if Herr's arrogance is justified."

Catherine chuckled. "Go to the next network. And be sure to save the network we're on now for last."

Eshel broke into a second network with similar ease and delivered the malware. He did the same with the third and fourth networks.

Only two more to go, Esh.

The fifth took more time. Eshel stopped typing, his eyes scanning the screen until he typed a couple more commands. He paused again.

"What's wrong?" she said.

"This network... it is configured differently than the others," Eshel said, his face glowing from the computer's lighting.

A shadow passed the small window. Catherine's stomach jumped as she instinctively froze. Eshel looked toward the door.

"Someone walked by," she whispered, her heart pounding.

As Eshel struggled with the network, Catherine became increasingly nervous and frustrated, knowing she could probably figure it out if she'd spent more time learning their written language. She watched the window until she heard rapid typing. Eshel had broken in. When Eshel went to tackle the last network, Catherine stopped him.

"Before you do it, let's make sure the malware worked."

They pulled up the first command line. It sat, lines of unreadable code unmoving, frozen midway through. Two sets of eyes stared at the lack of movement, waiting for it to continue and complete its duty. Nothing. Eshel checked the others; all ran, but eventually they too stalled, hesitating on the same line of code.

"What is wrong?" Eshel said.

"It's hung up," she said. She found another computer, rotated the screen away from the door, and turned it on. "What line?"

"Eighteen twenty-two."

"Let me take a look."

Eshel gave her the file. She scrolled through it, worry coming over her at the prospect of trying to debug code created by someone well beyond her skill level. They located line 1822, both sets of eyes scanning the code. With what little she could translate, some of it looked familiar… but the rest of it made little sense to her.

"What's this?" she said, pointing out a few commands. Eshel translated. "And this?" Eshel translated again. But there were too many unfamiliar elements, too many things beyond her "pay scale," things that only Herr could understand. She muttered a curse. As she tried to rein in her increasing frustration, she looked again, this time only at the code's structure, without trying to translate it. And that's when she saw it… something that didn't look right. A command without a closing, creating an endless loop.

"Kill it," she said. "Kill all of them."

Eshel stared at her.

"I found it," she said.

Eshel got to work while she sat at the second computer, corrected the mistake, and gave Eshel the updated file. "Run it again, on all but the last one." She deleted the file from her computer as Eshel reran the malware on each of the five networks.

A buzz sounded; Eshel looked down at his communicator.

"What is it?"

"Tom," he said. "A ship from the Air Guard has arrived."

"Is that bad?"

"Yes. We must leave."

"Start running the malware on this network," she said.

Eshel did so. Code ran and ran in the background as they collected their gear. Just as Eshel's communicator buzzed again, Catherine heard a voice call out from down the hall. Before she could react, Eshel grabbed her and pulled her back, away from the light of the screens. He relayed a message, glancing at the small window before he received a response. "Put on your mask. Use whatever force necessary to exit the building. Then, prepare to run east."

They donned their masks and reengaged their devices. Suddenly, both computer screens went white. She blinked a couple of times and looked at Eshel, who eyed the blank screens before he opened the door.

Black-robed Guard filled the hallways and Catherine got ready to defend herself. However, the Guardsmen coughed and put their hands over their eyes, and Catherine and Eshel wove their way past them through the long hallway. "Clear the area," a voice called out in Korvali, as Guardsmen headed in either direction to escape the toxin. Catherine and Eshel slipped by them and made their way toward the door. Outside, rain came down as more Guard coughed and hurried away from the area. Catherine and Eshel took off running and splashed through the streets, past train tracks and stone residences and gardens. Tom caught up with them and led them further away, until they reached a grove of trees, the shuttle hiding within it. Catherine and Tom scrambled into the rear of the shuttle and sat down, dripping water all over the seats and floor. Eshel sat in the copilot's seat while Ashan took the shuttle east.

"How'd you get Eshel's weapon into the building?" Catherine asked Tom, trying to catch her breath as she yanked off her mask.

"I forced my way in the door and deployed the rest of it. To make it easier for you to get out." Tom took off his own mask and shook the water from his pack. "They had the place surrounded."

"Good thinking."

"How'd it go?" he said.

"I think it worked."

He held up his fist. Catherine bumped it, a smile reaching her face as she let herself enjoy their triumph.

When the craft set down in the forest just west of the riverlands, Catherine and Tom put their packs on as the door opened. Eshel followed them outside, where the rain had faded to a drizzle.

"So I guess this is goodbye, huh?" Tom said to Eshel.

"Yes," Eshel said. "You are in safe territory, but Ashan will still accompany you to your ship."

Catherine shook her head. "Elisan will have plenty to keep him busy now, and even you said no Shereb would dare travel this far east."

Tom chimed in. "Not to mention that between the two of us, Catherine and I can do some pretty serious damage to anyone who messes with us."

Eshel hesitated. "You must not linger. If the Shemal accost you, ask to speak with Koriel. Do not resist them." They nodded. "Thank you. For aiding us."

"Anytime, Esh," Tom said.

Catherine looked down, glad that Tom's presence would make it easier to say goodbye to Eshel again, probably for the last time.

"Take the route I have provided you," Eshel said. "It is the fastest way to your craft. Coordinate with the Grono for your exit."

They all stood there, fidgeting and glancing at one another.

"I hate goodbyes," Tom said. He walked over and gave Eshel a quick hug, slapping him on the back.

Catherine did the same, giving him a smile. And she and Tom turned and began their trek east.

Eshel followed Ashan into another dwelling, this one large and spacious, a sizable tree in the glass atrium that stood in the middle of the home. They entered the atrium and stood near a bench under the tree, the sound of rain echoing off the glass above them. He looked at Ashan expectantly.

"You may be angry if you choose," Ashan said. "But first tell me, was I correct in bringing her?"

"Yes. But you shouldn't have acted without my knowledge."

"I made a choice."

"A risky one," Eshel said. "I behaved with irrationality, but you behaved with callousness, showing little concern for Catherine, perhaps because you have forgotten what it means to protect someone."

Ashan, instead of getting angry, simply returned the stare. "I took measures to ensure her and Tom's safety, including having the Shemal track them and informing the Guard of their estimated departure time. I would have escorted them myself, as you know. I did all of this because I know her importance to you. Just because I walk our lands alone does not mean I have forgotten the strength of the mating bond."

Eshel finally sat down on the bench. "She is not my mate."

Ashan sat down as well. "Mate or not, you have bonded with her. This is why you need myself and your mother, who have no mates to consider, to keep you on the correct path."

Eshel was silent for some time. He knew Ashan was right.

Fashal appeared in the atrium. "I have received word. Their systems are fully disabled." She looked at Eshel. "The humans have gone?"

Eshel gave a single nod, breaking eye contact with her to discourage any commentary that would anger him.

"They have done much for us," Fashal said.

Eshel looked back at his mother. "Yes."

"The Guard cannot act until their systems are restored," she said. "And they cannot coordinate with Elisan without meeting in person. Our patrollers are on watch for such meetings."

"Then it is time," Ashan said. "To face Elisan."

"We will go in the morning," Fashal said.

"Eshel."

Eshel heard the distant voice of his mother. He looked around the laboratory, seeing his father busy at work, wondering what his mother needed. Othniel looked over at him with the green-eyed gaze of a Shemal.

"Your mother needs you," Othniel said.

Eshel's eyes opened. His mother stood before him. "What is wrong?" he said, sitting up.

"Someone has come," Fashal said. "She wishes to speak to you."

Eshel stood, retrieving his robe from a nearby hook and putting it on. He followed his mother past the atrium and into another room, where Ashan and a few others waited. When Eshel peered at the group, attempting to determine whom his mother was referring to, he spotted her. A woman in a blue robe stepped forward, her hands out and fingers spread to indicate she had no bioweapon. She put a magenta-crested hand to her shoulder.

"I bring word from Fallal Hall," she said.

"How did you find this place?" Eshel said coldly.

"I contacted your mother," she said. "She had me escorted here."

"What do you want?"

"Elisan desires to speak with you."

"We planned to speak with him in the morning," Eshel said.

"No," the messenger said. "Elisan requests to speak only with you. He will come to the southern sea, where the shore meets the cliff. He will bring no entourage, no weapons."

Eshel was silent for several moments, feeling the eyes of his comrades upon him. It was highly unusual for any Shereb to leave their territory, but for Elisan to do so was unheard of. It was said that Elisan swam only in the western waters, walked only in the gardens of Fallal Hall, and had never touched dark rock in his life.

The messenger went on. "He will meet you at sunrise, if you will agree."

Eshel stood for several more moments. Then, he approached the Shereb woman and stared her down.

"Tell him I will come."

CHAPTER 20

In the pre-dawn darkness, Eshel and two Moshal made their way to the crescent bay, where the cliff began. As they drew near the shoreline, he spotted the others out at sea, one dragging a buoy bag along with him as they approached a small islet with no more than a tuft of grass to adorn it.

Eshel checked his communicator. Nothing. Their sea patrollers indicated no sign of the Guard or Elisan's minions. However, they indicated no sign of Elisan, either.

Eshel stood ashore, the two Moshal going to hide themselves. The first signs of light hinted in the partly cloudy skies. At Eshel's request, Fashal had not come, nor had Ashan. Those who occupied their dwelling the previous night had gone elsewhere, with Ashan and Fashal heading in separate directions. If something should happen to him, the vokalis could not afford to lose them, too. Many, especially his mother, had fought him on his decision to meet Elisan alone. But Eshel had insisted, only agreeing that he would allow others to accompany him if they kept their distance.

As it grew lighter, Eshel looked out at the sea dwellings, the white rocks, and the nearby islets, searching for a boat bearing blue-robed occupants. Water lapped at his bare ankles, a small ray of light peeking over the horizon. But Eshel saw no one resembling Elisan... and he glanced at his protectors, beginning to acknowledge what they already suspected.

Then he heard a high-pitched cry. One of the sea patrollers pointed west. And there, on one of the islands, stood Elisan. He wore no clothing, and carried nothing but a small buoy bag. He looked at Eshel for a moment before diving into the sea and swimming ashore, toting the bag with him. One of Eshel's comrades did the same, while the others remained on the islet, ready to follow if necessary.

Elisan quickly reached the shore and rose from the sea, water beading up on his body, his skin looser and musculature somewhat atrophied with age and inactivity. Eshel stayed where he was, watching him.

"I will cast my bag aside," Elisan called out, "if he will do the same."

Eshel motioned to his comrade, who set the bag down on the grass and slowly distanced himself from it. Elisan followed suit, putting his bag down and approaching Eshel, his hands out in front of him, fingers spread. And once at the appropriate distance, Elisan stopped and gazed at him with cold grayish eyes.

"Eshel," he began. "I have hoped you would return to our homeworld. It is unfortunate that it must be under such circumstances."

Eshel gave no reply.

"Your father would do that," he went on. "He would offer no reply to even a grand statement that would seem to demand one. I believe he enjoyed watching what the other would do in response to such silence."

"Perhaps that is why you had him killed," Eshel said.

Elisan's eyes narrowed slightly. "Such combative words, when I have left my domain and come all this way, with the hope of meeting you."

"What do you want, Elisan?"

Elisan looked out at the southern sea with interest, as if seeing it for the first time. "You have attacked our information systems. A clever maneuver, I admit." He paused, still eyeing the sea, which glimmered in the dawn's light. "I have not yet decided whether your dependence on outsider technology is your strength, or your weakness."

Eshel still gave no response.

"I imagine you plan more attacks," Elisan said.

"We do not plan attacks, Elisan. We thwart them, as we did last night."

Elisan stared at him for several moments. "And perhaps we devise more maneuvers, to which you devise more counter-maneuvers. We act against you, and you against us, and on such things go while we place ourselves at risk for invasion and allow what makes us a great people to fall into ruin. One does not have to serve among leadership to know that such ways make us no better than the humans, with their stupid wars, or the Sunai, with their constant inter-provincial conflicts. You and I do not agree on many things, Eshel, but even we must agree on this."

"I assume that somewhere behind this persuasive speech lies a proposal," Eshel said.

"Yes. There is a better way."

"What way is that?"

"The way your mother has proposed," Elisan said. "I want you to take a position in our government, in our assembly. You may elect five others to join you, one of whom may be your mother, if she is still inclined. I will propose the same to the Osecal and Moshal."

"Of course, Elisan. We will put on our blue robes and begin tomorrow."

Elisan's eyebrows rose. "Again, mockery. Another gift from living among the others."

Eshel gave no reply.

"And more silence," Elisan said. He peered out at the ocean again, at the rising sun behind only a puff of clouds, at the silent group who watched them from the islet. He turned back to Eshel. "Let us begin again. You do not agree with my decisions, with the methods we have engaged in to govern Korvalis. But you, Eshel, have the ability to think far beyond the immediate, even more than others of our kind. Every decision I make, every action I employ, I do for the long-term betterment of Korvalis." He paused, gathering his thoughts. "We are a superior people, Eshel. I say this not out of conceit, but to speak what we both know is true. We are scientifically superior to the others. We keep our planet and people under careful regulation by managing our population levels, our sick, our pollution, our conflicts. The Inferiors, particularly those who are most powerful... they do not." He paused again. "I am told you have spent time with the Shemal. Perhaps they, or your father, have told you the legends of the ancients. It is said the ancients traveled to the outerworlds and observed them, that they have known for centuries that we are not alone among the stars."

"I have heard such legends, as a child."

"They are not legends, Eshel. They are truth."

Eshel's eyes narrowed. "What do you mean?"

"Our progenitors disliked what they saw among the others, and refused to make contact with those they deemed untrustworthy. With time, however, the others advanced. They found us, and we have spent the current era protecting ourselves from those with whom we never wanted contact. We have even chosen to forgo technological advancements, of which we are more than capable, to preserve who we are." He looked at Eshel. "That, Eshel, is what I seek to protect."

"I would not have imagined you subscribing to the myths of primitives, when you are surrounded by people of science," Eshel said. "But I admit this persuasive tactic of citing the old legends is better than most, especially knowing my father was a primitive. Quite an eloquent and convincing speech, Elisan, given that you and the malkaris rose to power illicitly and murdered those who did not agree with this spectacular vision."

Elisan, whose pensive expression turned cold again, hesitated, as if choosing his words carefully. "Do you believe, Eshel, that these Osecal and their extended monarchial family were superior leaders? Do you believe they differed from the stupid, shortsighted minds of the current monarchy? Why do you think the Osecal monarchial line was more susceptible than others to disease that afflicts the young, which even science could not rectify? I know why, Eshel. I know the truth that most Osecal scientists did not, that their inbreeding coefficients had surpassed acceptable levels, that they had mismanaged their mate pairings and disregarded Doctrine too many times and for too many generations during their 'peaceful' rule. I know that they maintained their power by intimidation and for far longer than they should have, when it was time to relinquish Fallal Hall to a new clan. You lead a rebellion, Eshel, one that seeks power and leadership. This, what I have told you… this is what it is to lead in a system that allows people to rise to power merely because of who spawned them." Elisan took pause, his sneer more pronounced. "We chose such drastic actions for Korvalis, to create change for our people while still maintaining who we are, who we have always been, without influence from outsiders who are too stupid to protect their own people from the ravages of war or poverty."

Eshel paused for several moments, his skepticism and disgust diminishing somewhat. "Even if what you say is true, it does not justify your actions, and you must think me stupid to believe it would. You have murdered those who were guilty of opposing ideas, restricted research funding for those who didn't do your bidding, even created an abomination that killed innocent outsiders and nearly killed Catherine, among other offenses. These people, they are not the enemy of this vision of yours. Even my father… why was his differing vision, his desire to connect with outsiders, so harmful to you?"

"Othniel did more than keep a vision, Eshel. He surreptitiously collected samples of monarchial DNA and conducted experiments that were forbidden, including the work that allowed you to survive your escape. He conspired against his own government. If such truth offends you, it is only because it is truth." He paused. "Perhaps some of our actions were malevolent, even beneath us. But we did what we did for Korvalis… just as you do now. Do not believe you are different, Eshel, with your band of rebels. Even if you succeed, you will only face the problems I have, until another band of rebels rises up to usurp your power."

Tired of pointing out Elisan's errors in logic and his manifold violations of Doctrine, knowing that arguing with the intractable only made for more intractability, Eshel spoke no more, and the two men remained silent for some time. The cloud layer thickened as the sun disappeared for what would probably be the remainder of the day.

"Consider my offer, Eshel. We disagree on many things… but we must agree that of all the vagaries we face, engaging in war among our own people is the worst of them."

"I will consider it," Eshel said.

Elisan hesitated, gazing at him. "You murdered Elan in the tradition of the sher keltar. And perhaps it was correct to do so. Yet, Elan was the only member of that family worthy of rule, and now he is gone, leaving a weaker mind for us to contend with when his mother passes. You may find it interesting that others suspected your traitorousness and attempted to convince Elan to kill you as well. He made excellent arguments against such a move, excellent enough to convince most. But I knew… he killed your father because he must, but he spared you because he could." Elisan turned and left. But before he got far, he turned back around. "Go to coordinates 74.17 by 12.44 in the remote territories, in the high latitudes, where rain becomes snow. There, you will see."

And with that, Elisan picked up his buoy bag, walked into the sea, and dove in.

"I do not believe it wise to accept Elisan's offer," an Osecal scientist said. "However, what Elisan said of the Osecal monarchy… it is true."

"Why did you not speak of it?" Eshel said.

"My brother did," she said. "His research funding was curtailed until he recanted his statements publicly. There are many who believe the monarchial system is beneath us, a relic of our primitive past. We cannot blindly adhere to ancient ways that do not serve us, Doctrine or not. Even the Sunai ignore the bonds of genetics when choosing leaders, selecting only the best."

"They choose their leaders based on their physical traits, and many misuse science to increase those traits," another reminded her. "And they experience constant conflict."

"Because they are combative by nature," the Osecal scientist argued. "My point is, someone such as Lakli, who betrayed her own clan, was never fit to rule despite her valid claim to the malkaris's seat. We hold elections for assembly members… we can do so for kunsheld, kunsheld's aides, and even a board of elders to replace the monarchy."

Ashan interjected. "Regardless, we cannot join with Elisan. Even if his offer is genuine, he is duplicitous. At some point, we will all end up strewn about the remote territories."

Fashal spoke. "I have spent more time around Elisan than any of you. He is duplicitous, but what he conveyed to Eshel—regarding his frustration with the monarchy and his desire to elevate us to that which we are capable—is genuine. With opposition in the government, he can no longer achieve such duplicity. Not joining with him will only lead to more conflict."

"Yes," said one of the older Osecal, a former assembly member. "Elisan detests weakness, and he behaves with tyranny because he is surrounded by the inept. He will bend if we join him."

"We cannot trust someone who has done what he has," a Moshal man said. "We must seize Fallal Hall, as we planned initially."

"No," Eshel said. The others looked at him.

"This is the opportunity," the Moshal said. "When they are vulnerable, when Elisan believes you to consider his offer."

"No," Eshel said. He turned and left the room.

Tom strode through the dark forest, Catherine easily keeping pace with him as they made their way east.

"Why do we have to walk all this way again?" Tom said, shaking his head, sure he could feel blisters forming.

"No aircraft allowed east of the riverlands. We'd be easy targets for the Guard."

Soon, they came upon a forest unlike the others, unlike any Tom had ever seen. It had enormous, sprawling, gnarled trees that seemed ideal for climbing. Unexpectedly, his mind returned to a place from his childhood.

"Look at these trees," Tom said in wonder. "They remind me of an old tree I used to climb as a kid."

Catherine stopped. "Turn off all your devices. The trees will drain their power."

Tom gave her skeptical look. "What?"

"Just do it," she insisted.

Tom shut off his equipment, checking the surrounding area with his teleglasses to ensure they weren't being tracked. They began walking again; but within a few minutes the wind kicked up, and soon afterward a powerful gust came through and knocked them sideways. Rain began to fall. Catherine stopped and began looking around.

"What's up?" Tom said.

"We need to take cover. A storm's coming."

"C, it's rained almost the entire time we've been here."

She shook her head. "This is big one."

They found a tree where both could easily sit upon its enlarged roots, and took out their rain gear. Tom, still not convinced of Catherine's prediction, took another look around to ensure they were alone. But before long, the rain came down in sheets, pounding the forest floor and forming rivulets beneath them.

He hadn't seen a rainstorm like this since he was a kid, since he and Snow would play outside all day long during summer, until someone ordered them to return home. On some days, a big storm would come with deafening thunder and buckets of rain that soaked him through. He and Snow would run around in it, stomping their feet in puddles to see who could yield the biggest splash, ignoring the calls to return to their adoptive homes and take cover from the lightning. Tom would wear a metal cage on his head, hoping lightning would strike him and bestow him special powers. Snow always told him he was an idiot and that he was going to die, but he'd remained convinced the right strike would make him special. He shook his head and smiled at the long-forgotten memories. He rarely thought about the past. What was the point? The future... that's what mattered.

Tom dug into his pocket and pulled out a tiny flask, taking a sip. His throat burned momentarily until his chest and stomach warmed from the swill he'd borrowed from Snow. He nudged Catherine, offering her the flask.

"What do you think?" she said over the din of the rain, taking a sip. "Of Korvalis?"

He shrugged. "It rains too much."

"You finally get to walk on the Forbidden Planet... and all you can say is it rains too much?"

He shrugged again. "If I actually got to interact with the people, I'd have more to say."

"You look tired," she said.

"Just a little sleepy. The rain always does that to me."

"Take a nap," she said. "We have a while until it lets up. I'll keep watch."

"Nah," he said. "I'll be fine."

Tom leaned against the hearty trunk and took another sip of his flask, his thoughts going to Maria. Despite all that had happened, he still felt the same sense of calm joy at the thought of her. Seeing her with Ferrars... it still irritated him, but not as much as it used to. Losing her had been tough; but if he couldn't give her what she wanted, she deserved to have it with someone else.

His mind drifted back to the tree, the one he and Snow would sit under on really hot days or during big storms, out and away from their dull government housing, beyond the retaining wall they weren't supposed to climb over. On days when Snow's foster parents wouldn't let him leave the house, Tom would sneak out there alone. When he got big enough, he would climb the tree and watch everything from up there. Sometimes, he would sit under it and read. No one ever knew he was there, except the one time. And he never went back after that.

Tom heard leaves flapping, like when the wind blew against the cottonwoods during summer. He peeked out from his hood, but saw nothing. He heard it again. This time, in the darkness, someone approached. He reached for his weapon.

It wasn't there.

Tom sat, frozen, waiting for the shadowed person to reveal himself. And when he did, it was a human male. He was perhaps 40 or so, with a short beard and blue eyes. He'd seen the man before, somewhere.

The man smiled. "Hey, Tommy. Out beyond the wall again today? Don't worry, I won't tell anyone."

The man came over and sat down near him, closer than even Snow sat. Then, he put his hand on Tom's leg. Tom's breathing increased as panic flooded him. When the man reached for his crotch, Tom yelled out and hit him.

"Tom!" a voice said, as the man faded away.

Tom blinked numerous times. Catherine was there, leaning away from him, both her hands in defensive posture.

"It's me," she repeated.

"What the fuck is going on?" he said, his heart still pounding.

"You must have had a nightmare."

Tom looked around; the man was gone. He looked back at Catherine, who stared at him, her hand on her cheek.

"What's wrong with your face?" he said.

"Your breathing was labored, and you looked terrified, so I tried to wake you. You hit me."

"Jesus fucking…" Tom leaned over and pulled her hand away from her face. It had begun to swell. "Fuck. We need to get you a cold pack."

"I'm fine. We have one at the Pokey." Her brown eyes still watched him. "What was the dream about?"

He shook his head, checking around them again. "Nothing. Just a bad dream. Sorry… I didn't mean to fall asleep. If Yamamoto found out he'd probably pull my privileges."

"I won't tell him," she said. "I had a strange dream here, too. It's the trees."

When the deluge gave way to a typical rain, they gathered their gear and trekked east. Tom shook off the eerie feeling that haunted him and focused on getting them off this planet and back home.

Later, perhaps an hour from the Pokey, Tom began to feel like himself again. But when he heard something above, something that didn't sound right, Tom put his hand on Catherine's shoulder, urging her to take cover with him behind some trees. He pulled out his teleglasses, searching in the direction of the noise. And that's when he saw it.

"Shit," he said.

"What is it?"

"A Guard ship." When the craft drew closer, Tom saw its underbelly, spotted with small, regularly dispersed circles. "It has these little pod things. They just opened… but they don't look like weapons."

"Tom," she cried. "They're going to disseminate a bioweapon!"

CHAPTER 21

Tom immediately pulled out some equipment. "My sensors show infrared to the south. Run," he said, pointing. "Warn them and get them as far away as possible. Go!"

Catherine took her mask from her pack; once on, she fled to the south, dodging trees and tightening her pack to keep it from bouncing. It wasn't long before she saw them... a group of patrollers with spears and other weaponry. "Go!" she shouted in Korvali, pointing east, her voice muted from her mask. "Go! The Guard brings death!" She motioned to the sky.

'How many?" said one of them.

"One ship. My comrade... he will help you," she added, pointing in Tom's direction.

"Tell the others to flee," the patroller ordered.

Catherine took off running. When she began seeing villagers, many of whom looked up to the sky, she shouted at them to flee and pointed to the east, away from the ship and its path. They stared at her only momentarily, until she heard a loud sound, like an animal in pain. Someone had called out a warning. More joined in, until all could hear the call. Shemal emerged from their huts, their expressions calm but their bodies moving hastily. Others scurried down the ladders, while some even jumped directly from the tree homes above. Catherine kept motioning them east, away from the craft. Even with the flurry of activity, it was still quiet enough to hear the ship.

It was coming their way.

The villagers fled… but instead of going east like she'd instructed, they ran south. To the sea.

Catherine, her throat stinging from her shallow breathing and from shouting, looked all around, searching for anyone else, wondering where Tom was and what the patrollers were doing. The village now deserted, she began running again, making her way back toward Tom. Suddenly, she heard a loud "fump" above her, followed by a bright flash of light. She covered her head and ducked against a tree. Everything became quiet. Too quiet.

Have I gone deaf?

She raised her head and looked around, but saw nothing unusual. Then the fump came again, with another flash of light. More silence. She resumed her way north, only walking this time… until a far louder sound stopped her in her tracks. The clang of clashing metal, and loud booming sounds she couldn't decipher. She began running.

She headed toward the sounds, encountering tree after tree, but seeing no sign of Tom, the patrollers, or the Guard ship. She stopped, glancing around again, checking her positioning device to ensure she headed in the correct direction. The screen was black. She remembered she'd powered it down in the koshac forest, and turned it back on. After running some more, she finally saw it in the distance: the Guard ship, half demolished along with several trees it had taken down with it. She took out her energy weapon. But before she even reached the ship, she halted.

There, on the ground, lay six patrollers: four in front of her and two further in the distance, their spears still in their hands. The ones she'd warned, who'd told her to alert the villagers. She approached them and dropped to her knees, checking each of their pulses. But she already knew. They were dead.

A painful sense of dread came over her as she stood and looked frantically around for Tom. She advanced toward the ship, weapon in hand. Its fuselage torn open, Catherine peeked inside and immediately saw a black-robed Guardsman slumped on the floor, the side of her head bloodied. Another sat in the pilot's seat, head lolled to the side and eyes closed.

She backed away from the sickening sight. "Tom!" she shouted. She shouted his name again, and then a third time. Hearing no reply, she searched the area, knowing Tom must be nearby, hoping he'd emerge from behind a tree with an expression of victory upon his face. She called for him again.

She heard something. A muffled voice. Catherine stumbled along, following the voice… until she saw him. He lay on his back, his pack awkwardly lifting him above the ground, his legs pinned beneath a tree trunk.

"Tom," she whispered, running over to him.

He tried to sit up and push the tree trunk off him, but before he could barely grasp the tree, he gave up and slumped back down. Catherine attempted to lift it herself, but it proved far heavier than she'd expected and she could barely get it to budge.

"My legs," Tom panted, his voice muffled through his mask. "They're broken. Both of them."

She knelt down in front of him. "Just your legs? Everything else okay?"

He nodded, grimacing.

Catherine loosened the straps on Tom's pack and removed them from his arms. She lifted him enough to pull the pack out from under him, setting the pack aside as she lowered him to the ground.

"I need to find help… to get this damned thing off you," she said.

"They're gone," Tom said, his voice faint. "Use your energy weapon. To cut it. But do exactly what I say…"

After Tom told her what settings to use, Catherine made her first cut on the long side of the tree, which fell to the ground. She knelt down to get under the remaining trunk, grunting as she lifted it, still amazed at how heavy it was. Tom cried out in pain as she pulled the trunk to the side and heaved it away from them until it landed with a thud. A panic came over her as she looked at Tom's lower legs, both of which appeared flattened, making her consider whether

Tom would bleed out… or if he bled internally. She took out her laser and cut away at Tom's pants, sighing with relief when she saw bruising and abrasions… but no bleeding.

She rifled through Tom's gear until she found his scanner, giving Tom's legs a thorough onceover before scanning the rest of him. "Tib-fib fractures, both legs. The left leg has been mostly crushed in three places. No arteries cut, no internal bleeding. The rest of you is okay." She dug through his other gear and found the painkillers, feeding him some of her water to wash them down. "I need to get the med kit. The ship is a few kilometers from here, so it'll take me a while. Keep your mask on."

She retrieved her blanket from her pack, placing it under Tom's head. She glanced all around and above her, ensuring no other ships were coming. She took out Tom's energy weapon and placed it in his hand.

"Don't harm the Shemal," she said. "But if you see any blue robes, kill them."

"Yes, ma'am," Tom said.

Carrying only the essentials, Catherine ran off. Soon, sweat poured from her and her blisters screamed at her, but she didn't care. She kept going until she reached the Pokey, collected what she needed from the med kit, and made the journey back. She was relieved to find Tom still there, still conscious, weapon in hand. She began unfolding the braces she would use to stabilize Tom's legs.

"Aren't you going to ask me what happened?" Tom said, a grin forming beneath his mask.

"What happened?"

"I took down the ship," he said proudly. "Torched it… took out its engine."

"You saved their lives, Tom."

His grin turned to a grimace as Catherine set his left leg, sweat beginning to bead on his forehead. She retrieved another pain pill and helped him take it. She set his other leg, ran another scan, and made adjustments to the braces. "I have to make some minor repairs on the breaks. Brace yourself."

Tom grimaced again as she worked on his legs, hoping to prevent further damage until a physician could work on him. Afterward, Tom caught his breath while Catherine sat down to send a message to Eshel.

Guard attacked the Shemal. Tom's legs broken. Need a physician.

She scanned the area, hoping the bioweapon had diffused enough to be safe, but knowing it was probably too soon. When results came back positive, she resumed scanning Tom, hoping she didn't miss anything, but knowing if they didn't get help soon, Tom's legs would never heal properly.

"I'm going to lose my legs," Tom said, his voice flat.

She shook her head, leaning over to touch his curly hair. "Don't say that. You're alive, and that's what matters."

"Okay, M," he whispered, his eyes closing as the medication took hold.

When Catherine received no reply, she sat down and began to think. She could run back to the Pokey and bring it back… then she'd just have to figure out a way to get Tom into it. Koni could bring a science ship with a physician aboard to meet her, which would take a day or two. And the Shemal… maybe they'd help her get Tom into the Pokey, especially given that Tom had protected them. She didn't want to leave Tom alone… but she had no other choice.

She stood up and gathered what she needed. She scanned the area again… this time, the result came out negative. She removed her mask, and then Tom's. Tom came out of his stupor, mumbling something, his blue eyes looking beyond her.

"What?" Catherine asked him.

"Here they come."

Catherine turned around. A horde of patrollers headed their way, while another gathered in the distance, staring at the ground, at the six who'd died. Another group veered toward the wreckage.

"Christ," Tom said foggily. "They're huge."

Once they got close enough, Catherine spoke in Korvali. "The ship is broken," she said. "Two inside, dead."

She received no reply. Instead, they raised their spears at her and advanced toward her. She pulled out her weapon and aimed it at them. "Stay back," she hissed. "He is injured. He needs treatment."

They ceased their approach, tall men and women staring down at them. "You may kill us," one of them said. "But others will kill you… and him."

"What do you want?" she said.

"You must come with us."

Angry, but knowing she was outmatched, she lowered her weapon. "Tell Koriel we are here," she snapped. "I have contacted Eshel."

One of the patrollers produced a platform made of tree branches, held together with twine. He laid it upon the ground next to Tom; Tom somehow managed to hoist his upper body and hips onto the platform, while Catherine carefully moved his legs. Several of the patrollers squatted down, raised the platform by its wooden handles, and began carrying Tom away. Catherine gathered their gear and followed, the remaining patrollers right behind her. The sky above seemed to grow lighter. Dawn drew near.

Before long, they were at the village, which still appeared abandoned. The patrollers led them to a small wooden structure, similar to the one she'd visited previously. They carried Tom inside and set him upon the wooden platform. One of them approached Tom, inspecting his legs as Tom gaped at him in curiosity. After several moments, he turned and left. Another patroller aimed his spear at her and Tom's gear. Catherine sighed and gave it all to them, including the contents of their pockets, keeping only her communicator. The patroller pointed at that, too.

"I need it," Catherine said. "Eshel might contact me."

The patroller gestured again.

Catherine cursed and gave it to him. "I need technology back! For him!" she said, pointing to Tom.

And they left, shutting the door behind them.

CHAPTER 22

Eshel's face turned cold. "When did this happen?"

"Only hours ago," Ashan said.

"Who disabled the Guard ship?"

"I do not know. Reports only say it is down, fallen in Shemal territory, and the villagers have fled the area."

"Why does Catherine not respond?"

"They are being held captive."

Eshel felt some relief. If they were captive, they were alive... and safe.

Elisan, you worthless filth. You waste my time with your speeches about the betterment of Korvalis, pretending you will compromise.

"Did you believe Elisan would follow through on his offer?" Ashan said, as if reading his thoughts.

"I did not know," Eshel said. "But I didn't believe him capable of this, of punishing the Shemal or any primitive clan, who are defenseless in such attacks."

"Did you not?"

Eshel said nothing more, putting Elisan out of his mind as he stared out the shuttle's window. One of theirs disobeyed the law and flew him and Ashan beyond the riverlands, to the eastern forests. With them was an Osecal physician who offered no objection to treating a human. Soon, Eshel saw it: a clearing in the forest created by the grounded ship that had destroyed two trees, one of which appeared to have taken out a third tree. When he looked closely, the third tree trunk showed a clean cut, as if performed by a person... then, he knew the cause of Tom's broken legs.

Once landed, the physician went to find Tom, while Eshel and Ashan inspected the Guard ship, both surprised to find it not only disabled, but destroyed. Eshel circled the ship, recognizing residual signs of a blast from an energy weapon. It appeared someone had aimed at the ship's engine, disabling it and causing it to crash. When they peered inside, nobody was there.

"Where are the Guardsmen?" Ashan said.

"Likely burned by now," Eshel replied.

From his peripheral vision, Eshel saw movement. The patrollers had come upon them, spears in hand, surrounding them. Without a word, they led Eshel and Ashan to the fire pit. And there, on its surrounding stones, sat an elderly woman.

"Koriel," Eshel said. "Are your people safe?"

"They begin to return," she said. "However, six patrollers are dead."

Eshel closed his eyes, anger rising in him. He'd hoped that the demolished ship and the emptied village meant that all had escaped in time. Yet the dead patrollers, along with the fact that the ship's weapon disseminators had been open, confirmed to Eshel that Elisan had done what no one had ever done on Korvalis... deployed a bioweapon intended to harm the masses. His first thought was that Elisan must pay for such an act. But he pushed such thoughts aside, realizing he no longer had the luxury of such thinking.

"May we attend the sher memeshar for your dead?" Ashan said.

"No," Koriel said, slowly getting to her feet until she too stood over them. "You will take your outsiders and the dangers they bring, and leave us. They draw the attention of Elisan and bring death to our people."

"We will take them if you wish," Ashan said. "But tell me: how is it only six perished?"

"The others escaped before it was too late."

"They escaped because the humans warned them and disabled the ship," Eshel said, staring at her. "If they had not, this village would have no survivors."

Koriel stared back, her faded green eyes acknowledging the implications of his words. "Why would these humans help us?"

"Because they are my friends, and our allies."

"Perhaps. But they should not be on our lands," Koriel said.

"They should not," Eshel said. "But the vokalis agreed they must come, to gain an advantage over Elisan. You were informed of their presence."

Koriel looked beyond them, her gaze settling upon a small hut, where they'd likely imprisoned Catherine and Tom. "We do not seek to live as you do, with your trains, your stone dwellings, and your technology. We seek only to live as we have, and without the influence of outsiders."

Ashan spoke. "To preserve that which you value, you must prepare to retake your place in the assembly, and inform the remote clans to select representatives who will do the same."

"Not I," Koriel said. "Someone younger shall take my place… perhaps my son, or his daughter. They know what is best for the Shemal." She turned to them again. "And what of Elisan now?"

"We move to seize Fallal Hall," Ashan said. "And we do so tonight."

Eshel and Ashan approached the wooden structure and opened the door. Catherine sat in the corner, out of the way, as Tom lay unconscious. The physician turned to him.

"I am limited here," she said. "A fallen tree has crushed his legs and he requires surgery. We must take him to our facilities, or the red-haired one must return him to his ship, if he is to walk again."

Eshel glanced at Tom's battered, splinted legs, hardly able to imagine his active, energetic friend without the ability to walk. Ashan and the physician watched him, awaiting his decision.

"We must transport them to the Sunai ship—the one that brought Ashan and me here—and Catherine can take him. I will contact the humans and instruct them to rendezvous with Catherine."

"Why not treat him here?" Ashan said. "That is faster."

"It is not safe," Eshel said.

"I can't pilot a Sunai ship," Catherine called out in Korvali.

Eshel closed his eyes for a moment. "Of course. Then we will retrieve the Pokey, and you will take it to rendezvous with a medical ship. It is not as fast, but it will work."

"Will his legs withstand the delay?" Catherine said to the physician.

The physician hesitated, taken aback by Catherine's fluency with their language. "I believe so. It is better for his own people to treat him."

Eshel turned to Ashan, who stood in the doorway. "We need clearance."

Ashan nodded, stepping away to send the message.

Eshel got on his communicator, after which he turned to Catherine. "I would prefer to accompany you and ensure your safety, but I cannot." She nodded, in that way she did when she understood that his refusal was for an important reason. "Grono Amsala will provide coordinates for you to join your people."

She nodded again.

Later, after returning with the Pokey, Eshel and Ashan hoisted Tom's wooden platform while Catherine gathered all their belongings. Once outside the hut, several patrollers stepped in and aided them in carrying Tom to the Pokey. Once they got Tom situated inside, Eshel's communicator beeped.

"*Cornelia* comes this way," Eshel said. "Grono Amsala will retrieve you and take you there. However, you must await clearance, which should come very soon."

"Got it," Catherine said. "Thank you, both of you."

"Catherine," Eshel said. "We will need some of your equipment."

She motioned to her and Tom's gear, and Eshel and Ashan went through it quickly, taking what they needed.

"Where is Tom's extra clandestine device?" Eshel asked her.

She shrugged. "It probably fell out of his pocket at the crash site. Take all of mine."

216

Once finished, Ashan left and Eshel turned to Catherine. He hesitated for a moment, gazing at her, disliking that he must again say goodbye and face another onslaught of visions that would plague him for months to come. He wished he could put his cheek to hers.

"Be safe, Catherine."

"Something big is about to happen, isn't it?" she said.

"Yes," Eshel said. "That is why you must leave Korvalis, and why we must leave now."

She nodded. "Be careful."

Eshel looked at her a moment longer, before turning and heading back to his shuttle.

Eshel engaged his clandestine device and instructed his comrades to do the same. One behind the other, they walked through the gardens of Fallal Hall, each with a hand on the other's shoulder since they couldn't see one another. Eshel, his vision unaffected by the devices, led them past the weeping seshac trees silhouetted against a fading sky and past the rivulets filled with the magenta flowering plant, to the north side of the Hall. That entrance saw less traffic, which meant less likelihood of collision with others. Once clear, Eshel decoded the door. But when he went to enter the password, the door remained locked. They'd figured out how to defend against his device. Prepared for such a likelihood, Eshel retrieved Tom's weapon and cut the door open. By the time anyone reported the damage, it would be too late.

When he opened the door, he found the area clear and pulled the others in behind him, letting it shut. Soon, three Shereb came their way. Eshel and his comrades scattered to avoid the oncoming people, as he'd instructed them to. Once the Shereb passed and approached the door, Eshel reconnected his comrades and led them up the stone steps until they reached the top floor, where Elisan and his minions gathered and spent their days plotting the ruin of his people. When they arrived at another door, Eshel halted, as did the others behind him.

Eshel listened, but no noise emerged from behind the door. However, given its sturdiness, one would have to listen quite carefully to hear anything. He gave the tactile signal to each of his comrades before decoding the door. This one unlatched, so loudly that he worried he may have ruined the element of surprise. That sound— that tinging clatter of metal releasing—was the sound Eshel had known from their plan's inception would represent the moment of commitment. As his comrades waited silently, Eshel opened the door.

He would look first for Minel, who was quickest with a weapon, stunning him if he had to. He would then disseminate the weapon before he quickly exited the room and barred the door. With ample time and no ability to escape, the Osecal-designed weapon would render them unconscious, after which Eshel and his comrades would give the signal for their Guard to seize Fallal Hall and take the unconscious leadership to Felebaseb for imprisonment.

Eshel stepped through the doorway, the tiny weapon in his hand and ready to deploy, his other hand on Catherine's energy weapon. Suddenly, he halted. He stood motionless, gaping at what he saw, forming a visual memory that would perhaps be one of his more powerful.

Remembering his comrades, who stood outside awaiting his signal, he backed up and shut the door.

"Disengage your devices," he said to them.

They did, glancing at one another and looking at him in puzzlement. Eshel opened the door wide, stepping into the room so they could enter. And when they did, they too stared, their pale eyes fixed upon the sight before them.

In the room stood a rectangular table of white stone. And around it sat six people: Elisan, the malkaris and her mate, their now-eldest son Ivar, and two others Eshel recognized. Each sat perfectly still, resting against the backs of their chairs, eyes open. And through each chest, and through each chair they sat upon, was a single spear.

Eshel stood with his mother in one of the government offices. Guard surrounded Fallal Hall, Elisan's aides had been taken into custody, and government business had come to a standstill.

"What threats do we face?" he said.

"Supporters of Elisan, some of the Hall Guard," Fashal said. "However, our Guard has sequestered them."

"You have informed the assembly and the Shereb of what has happened?" Eshel said.

"Yes," Fashal said. "They know of the deaths, and they have agreed to gather in order establish a temporary government, to be replaced by an elected one in the future."

"The other clans… will their representatives join the talks?"

"I have already informed them of the circumstances and invited them to join. Koriel will inform the remote clans."

"And what of the Shemal?"

Fashal's face clouded over. "They must be held accountable for this. Doctrine is very specific about the sher keltar; the dead, they did not themselves murder those Shemal patrollers."

"No, they merely ordered others to," Eshel said. "They are responsible for the Shemal deaths."

"I do not disagree, son. But Doctrine says otherwise." She paused. "This unrest we have endured… it has fostered violations of Doctrine among many, yourself included. The people must decide whether such violations will incur punishment, or if Doctrine requires amendment. I imagine this topic will comprise much of the initial talks."

Eshel nodded, impressed by his mother's wisdom, and even more so by her acknowledgement that perhaps their Doctrine did require some amendment. Before he could comment any further, Fashal's communicator beeped. She glanced at it, staring for some time. When she looked back at Eshel, her expression changed.

"What is wrong?" Eshel said.

"I have word from Koriel. She will attend the meetings, and states that the remote clans will send their representatives. However, she reports disturbing news."

"What news?"

"Catherine has gone missing."

CHAPTER 23

When Catherine opened her eyes, her body hurt. Everything appeared blurry and a mild nausea fell over her, reminding her of how she felt when she rode amusement park rides that catapulted her upside down.

"Tom," she said. It came out gravelly. "Tom," she said, louder this time.

Tom gave no reply.

Shit. Tom might need more painkillers. Maybe he's just sleeping. Leave him alone.

But I have to get him back to Cornelia. Vargas needs to work on his legs or they won't heal right.

Jesus. I'm so groggy. What the hell kind of COO falls asleep at a time like this? Maybe we're under one of the koshac trees. Maybe the effects are worse than I realized.

But as her fog lifted, her eyes began to clear. And when they came into focus, fear washed over her. She wasn't with Tom in the Pokey; she was in a Korvali shuttle. When she glanced at the copilot, he wore a blue robe. Something about him... his profile... seemed familiar.

She struggled to move, soon realizing she was bound. A strange contraption encircled her, pinning her arms to her sides. It was tight. And for such a rudimentary mechanism, it worked very well. They were flying somewhere, in the darkness. No one said a word.

She didn't ask any questions. She knew better. No one would answer her; and even if they did, they'd tell her nothing she wanted to hear. She knew. She knew where she was going, and why.

Finally, the copilot stood and faced her, staring at her with pale gray-blue eyes. She knew that face. Knew it. But she couldn't place it. He put out his webbed hand and raised it, motioning for her to stand up. With some effort, she rocked herself forward and managed to get to her feet, catching herself as she almost fell forward. The familiar man merely stood there, his chilly gaze on her. She wanted to get angry, but she was too befuddled. And it was too late for anger.

The shuttle slowed, seeming to descend, as if it would soon land. However, it never touched down, seeming to only hover midair. The familiar Shereb approached her. She stiffened as he got closer.

He loosened the restraining device. Catherine felt relief at her increased freedom, and she began planning several potential maneuvers against her captor. *Strike before he expects it, and worry about the next move later.* However, he didn't remove the contraption. She considered some kicks, some takedown maneuvers requiring only her legs, and even a head-butt. But before she could execute any of them, the shuttle door opened. The blue-robed Shereb grasped her restraining device and yanked it, thrusting her from the shuttle.

Catherine cried out before she hit the water with a thud, the device smashing into her face as she submerged. She'd swallowed some water, and a panicky feeling rose in her as she began to thrash. Somehow, her fruitless flailing about reminded her of Yamamoto's calm and what he'd taught her, which quelled her panic and the desire to cough from the water she'd inhaled. She yanked the device up, scraping it along her clothing as she sunk further, until she could push it over her head, and within moments she was free of it. She swam up, feeling bogged down by her clothing, hoping the distance to the surface wasn't far as her lungs begged for air and desperation clawed at her.

When she surfaced and inhaled that initial breath, a bout of coughing burst from her. She treaded water, still rasping, looking around and seeing only darkness. She searched the sky for the shuttle, finally spotting a faint light in the distance and tracking it until it disappeared. She began heading in that direction.

The ocean was quite calm, which Catherine realized was lucky. Light was minimal, but seemed to get slightly brighter as the moon shone through a thinned cloud. After swimming for a while and seeing nothing at all, a blast of fear gripped her. With everything she and her friends had been through, she was going to drown on a planet of swimmers and never see the results of all they'd done.

Shut up. You aren't going to die, for fuck's sake. You're going to conserve your energy and tread water, all night if you have to. Just survive the night; then, when it's light, see what there is to see and figure out what to do next. And with that, she removed her heavy boots, watching them float for a moment before disappearing into the black sea.

She swam easy, occasionally turning on her back to calm herself and to conserve energy. From time to time she would look around, hoping to see something... an island, a rock, a tree. But she saw only darkness.

After swimming for an indeterminate period, possibly hours, hoping she still headed in the correct direction, she began to feel fatigued. Not the sort of fatigue that came after an extended period of exertion, but rather the drained fatigue one faced when epinephrine wore off, taking important sources of energy with it.

Whatever Eshel had planned... it was probably over by now. And if she knew Eshel at all, he would have succeeded, or at least put a major dent in Elisan's plans. But then again, her being dumped into Korvalis's remote territories like one of Elisan's enemies suggested otherwise. She pushed such thoughts away. *Keep going.*

Her arms tired, Catherine flipped onto her back again and floated. When she gazed up at the sky, she realized the clouds had cleared, as Eshel said they often did at night. Stars greeted her, sparkled at her. She searched for familiar patterns within the dense speckling. And then she spotted it, the circle with the stem, the constellation that would steer her west. She smiled, never more glad for Eshel's teachings, for the wisdom imparted to him by Othniel, who perished at the hands of a Shereb. She corrected her direction, having drifted to the south quite a bit, any fatigue she'd been feeling gone.

After more time swimming west, getting as far as she could before the clouds obscured her astral compass, she saw something. Something dark. Soon, she realized it was a rock, and as she drew closer, relief flooded her. The rock stood upon a small island, and there were several more in the distance.

Once at the shore, Catherine pulled herself onto the island and lay there, the smooth rocks pressing against her. Eventually, she picked herself up and walked gingerly over the rocks in her bare feet, her socks long lost to the sea. She stubbed her toe on one of them, letting out a curse. A chill swept over her as the ocean breeze cooled her wet body and clothing. She was tempted to get back into the water, but realized that, with time, she would become hypothermic if she didn't get dry. After removing her clothing and squeezing the water from it, she laid it all out on the jutting dark rock, her teeth chattering as her body hair stood on end. She squeezed the water from her hair and brushed the drops from her body, still shivering but hoping she would warm to a temperature at which she could survive the night. What the hell time was it and how long would she have to wait until dawn?

As she began to dry and warm up, she surveyed her small island. The big dark rock took up most of it, its walls too steep to offer any solace. The big rock led to jutting talus, which gave way to smaller rocks. The best place for her seemed to be a flattish rock that sloped a bit but remained above the water, at least for now while the sea was calm. She was grateful for the calm sea and lack of rain, knowing her fortune wouldn't last. She perched herself upon the cold, unforgiving stone, turned on her side, and curled into a ball.

When the first light began to appear, Catherine stood and took a good look around, her body stiff and tired from swimming and spotty sleep. The sky had clouded over, but her sense of direction remained intact as she looked west, seeing what she couldn't see in the darkness: islands, lots of them, dotting the horizon. She put on her damp clothing and began to swim.

She island-hopped, using each islet as a place to rest and reorient herself. As she picked off isle after isle, fatigue eventually found her. She nonetheless kept going, as swiftly as she could, knowing that conserving her energy would have no value if she didn't reach the mainland or encounter the primitives, who supposedly inhabited the eastern archipelagoes. But she saw no one, not even any sea creatures.

Later that day, she spotted something on a nearby islet, something that looked out of place among the uninhabited isles. White, perhaps metal, certainly manmade. When she reached the islet, she recognized the object: it was a restraining device, like the one used on her, its body bent and mangled. She momentarily wondered if it was hers, having drifted in the same direction she'd swum. Yet, its weathered and beaten appearance suggested it had been at sea for some time, since Elisan's last victim had been discarded to perish in the land of the lost. She shook off the lousy feeling that crept in, found the westerly landmark that she'd aimed for, and resumed swimming. The rain did come; but it was no more than a drizzle that lasted only a few hours, making Catherine's journey easier but providing her nothing substantial to drink.

By the time darkness set in, Catherine's stomach grumbled and her mouth began to feel parched. She ignored her fatigue and plodded on, glad that the cool humid conditions would slow her rate of dehydration. But as the night wore on, her mind began to wander. She thought of Eshel and his people, their struggle to right themselves, and the price many had paid for such change. She thought of her mother, who'd looked into the face of death for months before she passed. She remembered her mom's red hair, brighter than hers, and her green eyes, and the way she could wither you with just a look. People always thought Jimmy was the intimidating one, with his stern expression, his temper, and his being Space Corps brass. But it was her mother who could really silence you. Her mind wandered to her father, who'd refused permission to let her come here, who'd sought to protect her, who she'd hurt in order to help those she cared for. She thought of Koni, remembering their initial greeting, when he'd called her "an angry one" because she'd been so surly with him and Grono Amui. How strangely ordinary he appeared without his decorations! She thought of her work, how Holloway could handle things if she didn't return, would make sure the work completed and got recognized, no matter how much he feared Steele. And she thought of Eshel, of the first time he'd put his hands on her, the first time they'd "done the unspeakable," and the first time she'd shown him the pleasure of what the Korvali didn't even do with one another. Such thoughts occupied her mind for some time, until the realization came that she would never see Eshel again. Even if she survived this, Eshel would remain at the place from which he'd come… the place he belonged. A layer of tears covered her eyes.

She shook such thoughts from her mind and forced her tears to dry.

Keep going. Swim west. Stroke right, then left. Right, then left. Rest on your back. Just keep going.

When daylight came, Catherine woke, having allowed herself a brief rest upon a grassy islet. She resumed her journey, feeling somewhat reenergized. However, after more hours passed, her progress slowed as she slogged her way from one deserted islet to another. Hunger had turned to nausea, thirst to exhaustion. But when the wind kicked up and rippled the gray sea, she saw what she hadn't noticed before: the tides had shifted. They now worked against her, forcing her to work twice as hard to get half as far. She contemplated stopping and resting until they shifted again, but something told her to keep going.

At dusk, when Catherine reached a small landmass, she pulled herself from the sea onto soft earth covered in crunchy sea grass. As she stood upon it, she began to teeter. The earth, her very surroundings, seemed to be moving. She knelt down and waited for the sensation to pass. She removed her clothing and rung it out as much as she could, her skin burning from the chafing of her wet clothes against her. Her body shivered, uncomfortably cold as she stared at the water for several moments, its dark gray-blueness beckoning to her. She bent down to scoop some up, its coolness refreshing her parched mouth. But as she swallowed it, she made a face and spit out the rest, its saltiness waking her from her stupor.

Keep moving.

The landmass was no more than a thin, two-meter wide finger. She walked upon it, still feeling unsteady from having spent so much time swimming, but glad nonetheless to walk upon firm ground. She kept going, her eyes down to avoid anything that could injure her feet, until the narrow landmass came to its end. And there, resting upon the shore, sat a small wooden canoe with one oar.

Smiling, her fatigue and dehydration forgotten, Catherine pushed the old worn canoe offshore, hoping it would float. When it did, she stepped into it and began oaring her way west-southwest, maximizing the tides as much as she could. If she was where she thought she was, she would eventually reach Shemal territory. Like her or not, the Shemal would help her.

As she rowed, her tired arms nearly dropping her oar twice, it occurred to her that people would wonder where she was. Eshel would look for her. Ashan too. Maybe they'd find her. She looked up periodically, patches of clouds revealing now-familiar constellations as she made corrections to her course.

She paddled and paddled, the distance she'd spanned completely unknown to her, but likely far less than it felt like. She cursed the dry conditions and the lack of rainwater to drink, when it seemed like rain fell constantly during her forest treks. Then, strange lights appeared ahead of her. Lights!

She jerked her head up. The lights were gone. She'd nodded off.

Wake up, Catherine. No time for sleep.

She paddled on. Soon, she saw the familiar face, the blue-robed man who'd spoken not a word before shoving her from the ship to test her mettle in the place where long bodies and webbed hands ruled.

Such sick motherfuckers you are. Never killing those you deem as enemy, only placing them in impossible circumstances, where they struggle in vain to survive, knowing their terrible odds but nonetheless jumping from the window of a burning building in the hopes of surviving the long fall to the unforgiving ground.

The familiar man sat nearby, peering at her from under a blue hood.

Her head jerked up again. Only darkness this time. And it hit her... the familiar Shereb had been on the train, in Ronia, so long ago. He and another had stared at her. She didn't know who he was... but he knew her.

So tired.

Catherine again debated between resting on one of the islands and continuing in pursuit of the water she would need if she were to survive. She'd drunk no water in two-and-a-half days, and her pathetic efforts to find civilization had certainly taken some of her reserves.

Keep going. You can't linger.

She shouted into the night, screaming until her lungs emptied and her throat was raw. And she took her clothes off, jumping into the water once more to ensure she stayed awake and didn't damage her boat on some rock. More alert now, Catherine resumed rowing. More memories of her friends and loved ones began racing through her mind, as if hoping to obtain recognition before it all shut down permanently. Finally, her mind settled upon those of her and Eshel at their intimate moments, repeating themselves over and over in her mind like a video.

"Why such thoughts?" she said. "You dirty girl. You and an alien, doing dirty things. Doing the unspeakable!" And then she laughed, her laughter all raspy hoarseness from her parched throat.

They'll think you're crazy if they see you talking to yourself in the night.
Good. They should.

More laughter.

Knock it off, crazy. Keep going. Go west-ish. West-southwest, I mean. To the shoreline, where the primitives will carve you up and use you as fertilizer.
Please... take my nitrogen!

She laughed some more. And Eshel, sitting across from her in the boat, smiled, in his way where he didn't actually smile, but barely changed his expression, where his mouth turned upward and his eyes seemed to glimmer momentarily when he found something amusing.

"Find that funny, do you?" she chided.

Catherine's head snapped up. She blinked. Eshel was gone. There was only the quiet of the night, the breeze, and the mild chop of the sea. She set her oar aside and splashed water on her face to wake up.

Find an island and nap. At dawn, we go.

Catherine awakened at dawn, still shivering from a chill she couldn't shake. *Did I sleep at all?* The shivering continued as she got to her feet, until dizziness came over her. When it subsided, she looked around. Something seemed different. Ominous. The clouds had thickened, the air had become unsettled. The gray sea chopped and roiled, nearby islands disappearing briefly under swells. A storm was coming.

Fuck.

Tears came to her eyes.

She climbed up the jutting rock to get a better western view. And in the distance, she saw something near the horizon. Movement. A boat, perhaps. Then another. And strange dark shapes. Rocks?

She scurried down the rock and jumped into her canoe, her fatigue momentarily forgotten. Rain began to fall. She oared herself that direction as quickly as she could against the challenging tide. When she topped out on the increasingly large swells, she saw that her eyes hadn't deceived her. Boats, rocks, all getting bigger. Civilization! But after ascending a particularly large swell at the wrong angle, she capsized and plunged into the water. She grabbed the boat before the sea stole it away from her, and managed to flip it back over. It took several tries before she successfully climbed back into her vessel without tipping it. After catching her breath, she reached for her oar.

It was gone.

Catherine frantically looked around. And there it was, partially floating nearby, threatening to sink into vastness. She jumped into the water after it and dragged it back toward her boat, tossing it inside. Too exhausted to climb back in, she clutched the boat, resting against it, dizziness coming at her again. Just as she prepared to haul herself into the boat, another swell overcame her, flooding her nasal passages with salty water as she desperately held on. After it passed, she pulled herself into the boat, nausea making her dry heave several times. She grabbed her oar and paddled sloppily as she began to shout, spewing curse words and orders at herself, sounding like her father at his most angry, or her drill instructor at his most passionate. She repeated them, fighting over the swells, hoping she headed in the right direction, knowing she must keep going and hold on to her boat before the cruel sea carried it off forever.

As she rose upon another swell, she spotted them again, closer this time. People. Primitives. Korvali. Someone. The sea calmed momentarily as she oared her way closer, her shoulders and chest burning with lactic acid but rewarding her with good progress.

You can't see me yet, but I'm almost there, Shemal people!

Noise. Strange, loud, familiar noise. The unmistakable foom, foom, foom. But the cadence wasn't right… there were more of them, all fooming at once. Three of the giant white seabirds headed out to sea and would soon fly right over her, casting their giant shadows.

Hello, beautiful winged creatures!

She craned her head around, wondering where they headed. And that's when she saw it: a massive swell, as big as a building, as tall as a mountain. She dove from the boat just as the wave crashed down upon her.

Catherine held her breath, the intense power of the wave's underbelly tossing her this way and that. Once the tossing waned, she swam to the surface and took in a deep breath, immediately looking for the next wave. And there it was, in the distance. To the southwest, she saw someone swimming. Perhaps many of them, arms everywhere. The jutting dark rocks seemed to take the shapes of animals, as if coming alive. Catherine began shouting for help, her desiccated throat letting out hoarse, shrill screams that tore through her voice box. Seawater rushed into her mouth and she swallowed its saltiness. She screamed some more, in Korvali too, and in her sick, dizzy state she flapped through the water, to the pale people and the terrifying rock animals, hoping the next tsunami would push her the rest of the way because she had no energy left to make it herself.

And when the wave came, she took a giant breath of air and surrendered to it, saving her energy and hoping it would steer her somewhere safe, somewhere where she could rest and sleep in the blackness that overtook her.

CHAPTER 24

"Catherine should have left Korvalis yesterday, which means she has been missing for a day," Eshel said. "Why did they not inform us sooner? And why does no one have information?"

"No one witnessed her disappearance," Ashan said quietly, his expression clouded. "They are still searching the area. I have word out to the Guard, and Koriel will get word to the northeastern shores and the remotes."

"This would not be happening if you had not operated to bring her here," Eshel said coldly.

Ashan gave no reply.

Eshel sat down while he waited for transport, a terrible dread fallen upon him. After everything, after all their precautions and all the times Catherine had been in far more danger, that she would go missing now, that she may be harmed, or dead. What had happened to her? Why did no one have information? The lack of knowledge from which to make decisions tortured and angered him even more.

His mother entered. "One of our Guard will search the remote territories. It is unlikely the enemy would risk taking her there, given the recent attack on the Shemal. However, if they did, a Korvali is unlikely to survive the tides, the storms, and the paucity of edible fish in the remotes. A human surviving is even less likely."

Eshel closed his eyes for a moment. "This… it is Elisan's final act of cruelty, the one that punishes me for my rebellion, just as he punished the Shemal for theirs."

Fashal stared at him for several moments. "Son, the attack on the Shemal... it occurred without Elisan's permission. He'd developed the plan, but had refused to execute it after meeting with you. He'd intended to honor his offer."

Eshel's eyes narrowed. "How do you know this?"

"I spoke to him, just before his death."

"And you believe him."

"Others, my informant included, confirmed it. Elisan went to considerable effort to persuade the malkaris." She paused. "When I saw him, he appeared tired... tired of fighting that which is inevitable, tired of managing a wretched monarchy. He knew compromise with us would yield the better result. Someone else ordered that attack, and has likely orchestrated Catherine's disappearance."

Eshel said nothing in response, glancing at Ashan, whose expression showed surprise. Elisan had been forthright with him, had not engaged in trickery. In his own way, he'd prepared for change. And for a moment, Eshel's disgust at the ignoble man dissipated as he understood the burden of leading in a disrupted system.

Then numerous visions assaulted Eshel. They were mostly of Catherine, both recent and past.

"You see her," Fashal said.

He gave a single nod.

"There is one who was not present in that room of speared leaders," Ashan said.

"Minel," Eshel said coldly.

"He has yet to be found," Ashan said.

Minel. That sneering man who'd visited Suna, who'd come looking for him initially. He was the culprit, and likely the one who'd acted outside Elisan's wishes. Minel had shown considerable disapproval at Eshel's relations with Catherine, enough to mention them at an Alliance meeting. "He likely took her to the remotes, and that is where I will search."

"I will join you," Ashan said.

"You cannot," Eshel said. "You are needed here. The others

know who you are now, know what you represent by returning to Korvalis."

"If you wish," Ashan said.

"No," Fashal said. "Ashan must accompany you. The more who search, the better. The others… they will help maintain stability here."

Eshel suddenly remembered Tom. "What of Tom?"

"He is still among the Shemal," Ashan said. "They have cared for him, and his injuries remain stable after the physician's treatment."

"Have you told the humans of Catherine?" Eshel said.

"No," Ashan said. "I have said only that we experience delay in receiving clearance to leave. However, the Sunai ship will arrive soon, and the humans come this way. They will begin to question our delay."

Eshel nodded. "I will inform Grono Amsala. Then, we search the remotes. If we do not find her, I will transport Tom myself. Catherine may be dead; I cannot also allow Tom to be maimed for lack of proper medical treatment."

Ashan signed in the affirmative.

Eshel sat in the shuttle's copilot seat while the vokalis Guardsman transported them east. Eshel had instructed her where to go, while Ashan's shuttle headed in a different direction. Neither pilot offered any argument, despite both violating the rule about taking aircraft east of the riverlands. The shuttle hovered low, making it easy to see all that was below them. Once beyond the forests, they arrived at the northeastern sea, where landmass gave way to cape, which gave way to the archipelago that curved like a spiral, beyond which it broke into numerous scattered islets that became fewer and fewer until, finally, giving way to open gray sea.

Eshel scanned the cape, the Spiral Isles, and the rocks, shorelines, and sea for any sign of Catherine, for any boat, oar, or pale skin cast upon the dark eastern rocks. For hours they searched. Eshel was grateful for unusually good weather that day, where the sea was calm and rain only came as sporadic drizzles, allowing their instruments and eyes maximum detection ability. However, as the day wore on and dusk encroached, they saw nothing and no one.

"We must return," the pilot said, when visibility had diminished. "At dawn, we will search again."

Eshel said nothing, continuing to scan as the shuttle turned around. He contacted Ashan, already knowing that if they'd found any sign of her, Ashan would have contacted him. And, sure enough, their search had yielded nothing.

Sleeping across from Ashan in one of the wooden huts, Eshel barely slept that night, his night visions a confounding slew of memories of Catherine along with visions of her in a boat, rowing alone among tides she didn't understand.

When dawn came, they returned in the shuttle, searching farther out this time, far enough that Catherine couldn't make it to the mainland without a good boat, even in this fine weather. But before long, the cloud cover darkened and the sea began to chop. A storm was coming. Eshel knew this would be no ordinary storm, but instead a squall of considerable proportion. It filled him with a nauseating dread, knowing that a human could never survive at sea during such a squall.

They searched on, still finding no sign of Catherine. Then the pilot spoke. She'd spotted something in the distance, and Eshel saw it a moment later. Something white, upon the rocks. As they descended, Eshel lowered himself to the tiny island, realizing that the white object was a restraining device, just like the one the Guard had used on him when the Sunai had abducted and brought him back to Korvalis so long ago. The device had only minor abrasions, as if it hadn't spent much time at sea. Eshel wasn't sure whether such a discovery brought him hope... or despair. They searched the surrounding area even more carefully, looking for any sign of Catherine. However, again, they found nothing other than the churning sea and bare dark rocks. And when darkness descended upon them, the Guardsman suggested they return.

Eshel refused, knowing now would be the time that Catherine needed help the most and that if he didn't find her soon, he would never find her, as she wouldn't survive the kind of storm that formed waves as high as trees and roiled the ocean senseless. The swells alone would overtake the islands, would beat upon the rocks, would send the outlying clanspeople to shelter. They searched until the Guardsman insisted they return, for safety reasons. Eshel put his head in his hands, sick with dread and enraged at not knowing where she was, but fearing the worst, that she would die and he must bear the responsibility for her death.

The following morning, they searched again, looking not for a human woman rowing a boat or taking shelter upon an islet, but for a corpse floating amid the gray seas, or nudged ashore on some island, much like her restraining device. If Catherine perished, he must find her body and return it to her people for proper burial. He must.

But as with the previous days, they found nothing. When they arrived at the Shemal village, Eshel, having received no news about Catherine's whereabouts, strode past Ashan and the others until he reached the shore. He snatched off his robe, soaked by the rains that flooded him as he marched into the sea and dove into its dark moonless depths, knowing the tides did not favor him but not caring. He swam until he saw nothing but blackness, blackness that swallowed him up until, hours later, he relented and went ashore to the agony of land and safety. Again, Eshel lay down to face a tortured sleep, this time with visions of Catherine drowned and bloated with death.

Eshel shot up from his lying position, visions of the sea still blinding him. Someone had spoken to him. Someone familiar. When his vision cleared, Ashan stood above him, holding a robe.

"We have received word," Ashan said. "A human has been found among the Tobeb, at the Spiral Isles."

"Do you have coordinates?" Eshel said, immediately standing and grabbing the robe, the haunted visions ceasing as hope flooded him.

"Yes," Ashan said.

Eshel began gathering his gear. "You will accompany me?"

"We cannot go to the Spiral Isles alone," Ashan said. "When they see your marking, they will kill you. We must bring Koriel."

Eshel gritted his teeth. "Will she come? For this?"

"Catherine's actions prevented more Shemal deaths. Koriel will come."

One of their pilots shuttled Eshel, Ashan, and Koriel to the northeastern sea. Eshel felt a strange sense of pride at Catherine, at her ability to once more overcome danger, at her courage and resourcefulness. He now imagined her not rowing the seas or bloated with death, but sitting with the Tobeb, who had known not to kill her. Would she smile, happy to see him? Would her brown eyes darken in anger at his allowing such suffering to befall her? Or would water stream from her eyes in an explicable outpouring of complex feelings that he could not understand?

When they arrived, the shuttle set down on the thin strip of the cape that stretched into the spiral that gave the region its name. Koriel stepped out of the shuttle first, while Eshel and Ashan followed. Tobeb patrollers stood nearby. Their stature was shorter than that of the Shemal, their hands marked with the dotted spiral, their hair dark and their eyes varying shades of pale, pocketed strips of fabric strung across their chests that held more daggers than Eshel could easily count. Each watched Eshel and Ashan, who put their hands to their shoulders. Just as their eyes settled upon Eshel's marking, Koriel began.

"This Shereb and this Moshal… these are the leaders of which I have spoken," Koriel said. "The outsider is here?"

"Yes," a golden-eyed man said.

"Where is she?" Koriel said.

A silence hung among the Tobeb as they shifted their pale eyes back to Eshel. The patroller spoke again.

"She is dead."

CHAPTER 25

Eshel's chest tightened, making it more difficult for him to breathe. He closed his eyes for several moments before gathering his thoughts. "Did you kill her?" he demanded in Old Korvali.

"No."

"Did you put her out to sea?"

"It is not yet time."

"Take me to her," Eshel said.

They followed the dagger-laden Tobeb, his musculature especially sinewy from most days spent at sea. In the darkness, they walked up the cape, heading inland and beyond a village of wooden sea huts until they reached the forest, its tree trunks covered in vivid green moss due to the region's heavier rainfall. Well beyond the village, only firelight illuminating their path, Eshel spotted it in the distance. A cloth shroud.

When they reached it, Catherine's enshrouded body lay over tidy bunches of grass and leaves, only her red hair showing. It lay smooth on each side of her, as if someone had arranged it that way. Instead of burning her body or pulverizing it to use as fertilizer, as they would any unwelcome outsider, they had treated her like one of theirs by laying her upon organic matter to aid the decomposition process. The only difference was where they kept her... farther away than they would a Korvali.

The patrollers stood aside as Eshel lifted the shroud, exposing Catherine's face and torso. She was nude and pale, paler than a Korvali, and her vulnerable human skin showed abrasions and bruising. When he placed his hand upon her, she felt cold. He could see her ribs and the bones of her pelvis and shoulders, and her face appeared gaunt. Eshel turned away as nausea came at him. He took several deep breaths before facing her pallidness again. Upon closer inspection, Eshel noticed scratches on her sides, as if an animal had clawed her.

"What do you know of her arrival, of her death?" he asked them.

"Patrol saw her at sea, when the squall came," one of them said. "They heard her shouts, but she went under. It is said the basarac lifted her from the sea, that patrol sent rocks to basarac until it released her. But when they found her, she slept. We removed her water, but life left that evening."

The basarac. The great white seabird, the one Catherine had said was the most spectacular creature she'd ever seen. His father had told him that many of the remote primitives, those who lived beyond the Shemal, viewed the basarac as an honored creature, and he wondered if they'd preserved Catherine not because they'd received word from Koriel to do so, but because the bird had raised her from the sea.

A series of visions of Catherine flooded him, so many that he kneeled to keep from losing his balance. The visions overwhelmed him—of her red hair, her standing under the evening light of Suna's rings on Derovia, her amusing slurred words after her first CCF match, her slapping him in the face, her expression when she stood above him at Fallal Hall, her bruised breast after the fights on Calyyt-Calloq, the sight of her at the sea dwelling and how glad he'd been to see her, her soft body pressed against his on what would be far too few occasions, her tears, her laughter, her fury, and many others, more than he could possibly see in those moments of swelling pain.

He heard soft footsteps on the forest floor. The others formed a circle around him and Catherine, and turned their backs to them. Eshel, after sitting upon his knees for several more moments, felt the pressure build in him until he let out a massive wail, more visions flickering past his consciousness as he remembered Catherine, as he even recalled the last time he performed the sher memeshar, when his father had been killed.

After some time had passed, Eshel was silent as he remained on his knees, next to Catherine's body. When the visions subsided for the time being, he stood. And when he did, the Tobeb, Ashan, and Koriel turned back around, staring at him, likely taken aback by his reaction, that he would suffer the loss of a human as he would one of his own.

"I must take her to her ship," Eshel said. "I will return her to her people, so they may bury her according to her customs. I ask your assistance in carrying her."

One of the patrollers retrieved something nearby, a platform made of woven branches, which she laid next to Catherine's body. Knowing they wouldn't feel comfortable touching Catherine, Eshel went to lift her onto the platform himself. But before he could begin, the others stepped in, each taking a different part of Catherine and transferring her to the platform. Several of them took a handle and, all together, raised her and began carrying her to the shuttle.

As they walked, Eshel considered what must happen next. He would need to relay the bitter truth to Grono Amsala, informing him that he would convey Catherine and Tom in the Sunai ship that remained hidden at Station 14. Grono Amsala would inform *Cornelia* and set rendezvous coordinates. He would explain to the Corps, to whomever, what had happened. He would assume full responsibility. Despite Ashan's contriving to bring Catherine here, it was he—not Ashan—who put Catherine in danger. She was in danger the moment she had befriended and trusted him.

Tom. His legs remained stable, but Eshel could only imagine how Tom would react to such a delay, to having no English-speaker to explain Catherine's absence, but knowing that her absence was no good sign.

When they arrived at the shuttle, they placed Catherine's corpse inside. The shroud fell away, revealing her nude body once more. Eshel quickly picked it up and began covering her. But as he did, he took pause, examining her again. Thin, pale, and abraded she was... but she somehow seemed otherwise serene. Given the time of her death, her corpse would show at least minimal signs of decomposition by now, given what he'd learned from Dr. Vargas when he'd taken measures to delay decomposition of the two dead Corps soldiers. She died in the evening... had Eshel only slept a couple of hours before he'd received word? In his tired, addled mind, he recalled searching for three days. The first was calm, the second had the squall, and the third...

The third. Hours hadn't passed since her death... more than a day had. Had they been mistaken and lost count of the days since the squall, or otherwise assumed she was dead when she'd actually been unconscious for longer than they'd realized?

He asked one of the patrollers to repeat how they'd found Catherine. Her story was identical to that of the other: she'd arrived during the squall, and died that night. That meant she'd been dead more than a day. She should've begun decay by now, particularly in such a humid environment.

Ashan's voice interrupted his jagged thoughts. "We must go. I will inform Grono Amsala."

Eshel ignored him, grabbing Catherine's wrist and checking for a pulse. Nothing. But he held on nonetheless, waiting. And finally, after a lengthy delay, he felt something. A bump, barely detectable to his fingers. He waited... until he felt another.

His mind cleared as a realization came to him, one he should've already considered. "Obtain clearance to retrieve the Sunai ship at Station 14. Do it now."

"What is wrong?"

"Catherine is alive."

At Station 14, several black-robed Guard assisted Eshel and Ashan as they put Tom into the Sunai ship. Eshel was surprised at how heavy Tom was, despite being considerably shorter than they. Tom had said little during the entire process, which meant he was still in significant enough pain to require a stupor-inducing dose of painkillers. He also suspected that Tom's silence came from his concern over Catherine, as the sight of her deathly pallor had drained the color from Tom's face. Tom lay upon a platform on the ship's deck, his legs wrapped and stabilized, clutching his canister of pills.

Eshel, Ashan, and two Guard carefully transported Catherine next. Eshel had started an IV for her and scanned her with the Sunai scanner. She was alive, but barely.

"What is happening?" Ashan said. "They said she was dead."

"She is in stasis," Eshel said. "She altered her genetic material to survive, as I did when I escaped Korvalis."

"You showed her how?" Ashan said.

"No. She utilized the data from my stasis and discovered the rest herself."

"Then she will live?" Ashan said, a sliver of hope in his expression.

Eshel glanced at Catherine. "I do not know. Her readings concern me. No one else has ever done this." He glanced at the ship's instruments. "What is *Cornelia*'s location?"

"I still await Grono Amsala's response. However, we requested they come days ago, and they've been waiting for report from us. I imagine the humans are nearby, but remain at a safe distance because they do not know whether the Guard can be trusted."

"I must contact my mother."

"I already have," Ashan said. "She and the others will take over in our absence."

Once everyone was situated, the bay door opened and Eshel, cleared to leave, took the ship out of the bay, past the Korvali border, and toward the Grono's last known coordinates.

A beep sounded.

"*Cornelia* has received your transmission," Ashan said. "We should rendezvous with them in two hours."

Once he engaged the ship's FTL, Eshel, never one to be impatient to arrive somewhere, at last understood the value of the technology.

However, even with the FTL, their travel time seemed interminable.

Eshel left the helm and knelt down by Catherine's body, scanning her again as Tom lay asleep. She was still very dehydrated, but she was alive.

You are safe, Catherine. I will be here when you awaken.

When approaching the rendezvous coordinates, Eshel dropped out of FTL and scanned the region. To his relief, his sensors picked up *Cornelia* as well as Grono Amsala's ship. However, they also picked up a third. Before he could inquire, he heard Shanti's voice over the ship's communicator.

"Ensign Eshel, set your heading for *Cornelia*'s starboard bay two," Shanti's voice said. "Don't mind Starship *Victoria*."

"Wilco," Eshel said. "ETA nine minutes. Medical emergency. Have two gurneys ready, one with an IV, and ensure Doctor Vargas is present."

"Wilco, Ensign," Shanti said. "Good to hear from you, Sir."

Once they landed in *Cornelia*'s bay and the door shut, Vargas and a slew of medics flooded the bay along with several other officers, none of whom Eshel noticed or acknowledged. He thought only that he must prevent Catherine's shroud from falling away. They must not see her nude. Two MAs scanned all of them, confirming their identities. Ashan, along with Vargas and two medics, lifted Catherine onto a gurney, Eshel carrying her IV pack and ensuring her cover remained. One of the nurses tried to take the IV pack from him.

"Do not touch it," Eshel barked.

The nurse backed away and looked to Vargas, who shook his head at him and motioned to Tom. "Take care of Kingston."

They left the hangar deck, took the elevator to the first deck, and proceeded down the hallway, Vargas's large build lumbering at a quick pace.

"She's in stasis?" Vargas asked gruffly. "How the hell did that happen?"

"I will explain later," Eshel said. "She is very dehydrated and her life signs are weak."

Vargas shouted at oncoming crewmembers to clear a path as they headed to sick bay, passersby staring at Catherine as they pressed themselves against the bulkhead. Once there, they moved her to a medical bed and got her on a regular IV just as the others rolled Tom in.

"Pinkney, deal with Kingston," Vargas bellowed. He turned to a nurse. "You... you're with Pinkney. The rest of you, get out of my sick bay." After the others made their hasty retreat, Vargas turned back to Eshel. "You have some explaining to do."

"She is in stasis, as I was when I arrived on *Cornelia*. One of Elisan's aides left her in the remote territories to die... she must have dehydrated and fallen into stasis."

"How the hell is that possible?" Vargas said.

"Give me your scanner, and access to your software, and I will find out."

Vargas handed Eshel the scanner. After downloading the results, Eshel began examining Catherine's genetic material on the viewer. He searched the software's analytic options and found an epigenome scan. When he got the initial results, he saw what he expected to see: clear evidence that she'd altered her epigenome. He gave Vargas enough explanation to satisfy him before sitting down to rest briefly and consider his next step.

The doors to sick bay opened. When an officer he'd never seen before strode toward them, Vargas stood at attention. The officer said nothing, eyeing Eshel before going to Catherine's bedside. He paused, staring at her pale, unresponsive face. Finally, the officer turned to Eshel.

"What the hell happened to her?" the officer demanded.

Eshel grew irritated at the officer, who seemed to demand an answer only to satisfy his curiosity and exert his power. "Who are you?"

"Is that how you address your superior officer, soldier?" the man barked.

"Look alive, son," Vargas called out. "This is Captain Jim Finnegan… Catherine's father."

Eshel looked back at the man, seeing his brown eyes and hard expression, both of which looked remarkably like Catherine when she became angry. Dumbfounded, Eshel raised his hand in salute.

"I asked you a question, Korvali," Catherine's father said.

"She is in stasis. Sir. She has been injured, but she lives. She should awaken in the next few days."

"Stasis?"

"She has genetically altered herself to survive in low resource conditions." Eshel said nothing more, unsure what to say to Catherine's father, having never expected to encounter him. He knew he would face difficulties upon returning to *Cornelia* with Catherine and Tom compromised… but he hadn't prepared for this one.

Captain Finnegan's glare remained. "I want hourly reports," he said to Vargas.

"Will do, Captain," Vargas said.

Captain Finnegan left.

As Eshel reviewed his analyses, he felt a strange sense of relief upon being in sick bay, in the place he used to dread, around the physician he used to dislike. He appreciated the calm quietness, appreciated Vargas's gruffness and his desire to find a solution. After analyzing their initial data and stabilizing Catherine, they had nothing left to do but monitor her… and wait.

"Well, kid," Dr. Vargas said, stroking his thick mustache. "I don't know whether to praise you or condemn you. Your science saved her life, but she wouldn't be lying there half dead if it weren't for you."

"I believe she will make a full recovery."

"I hope you're right. You don't want to face Jim Finnegan if this doesn't go well." He paused, a look of amusement on his face. "Catherine didn't tell you he took over for Ferguson, did she? You should've seen your face when I told you his name!"

"Catherine said nothing of it. There was no time for such discussion. Where are Captain Ferguson and Commander Yamamoto?"

Vargas leaned back against the counter. "A lot's happened around here. They're still here, for the same reason we allowed Catherine and Kingston to go to your planet."

"Gronoi Okooii."

Vargas nodded. "Was that Ashan with you in the hangar bay?"

"Yes."

Eshel recalled Okooii's loud bluster during *Cornelia*'s first visit to Suna, his demanding that Eshel pay a debt to Suna and his chastisement that Eshel chose to live among the humans rather than the Sunai. He hadn't believed that the Gronoi, regardless of his position, would have such persuasive powers over the Alliance. He was somewhat impressed, and acknowledged that perhaps he had underestimated Okooii.

Pinkney emerged. "The Korvali physician did a good job on Tom's legs. I had to do regenerative work, especially on the left... it was crushed in multiple places. He'll need some time to heal, but he'll walk fine."

"May I see him?" Eshel said.

Pinkney shook his head. "He's sleeping."

Eshel sat down to examine Catherine's genomic data further. Hours later, he scanned her again. Nothing had changed. Vargas's gruff voice interrupted him.

"Go back and get some sleep." He tilted his head toward the recovery beds.

"I am fine."

"You're fatigued. And you aren't useful when you're fatigued. Sleep. That's an order."

Eshel, knowing it was useless to argue with Vargas, headed back to one of the recovery beds. Suddenly, he heard a voice.

"What's up, Esh?"

Eshel turned toward the voice. A few beds down lay Tom, his face tired and without its usual grin.

"How's Catherine?" Tom said.

"Still in stasis," Eshel said.

"Is she going to be okay?"

"I believe so." Eshel paused. "I am sorry, Tom, that I put you and Catherine in danger."

"It's our job, Esh. I'll be fine, Catherine will be fine. Get some sleep, man." Tom closed his eyes.

Eshel selected the bed next to Tom's, and lay down.

A few hours later, Eshel rose and immediately went to scan Catherine.

"Same readings," Vargas said. "Pinkney will be back on duty soon, and then I'm going to get some shuteye myself. If anything changes, call me immediately."

Eshel nodded.

Much later that evening, Catherine still hadn't awakened. Vargas, back on duty, ordered Eshel to sleep again. After talking to Tom for a while, too many ideas rattled around in his mind and sleep evaded him. But eventually he drifted off.

When Eshel woke, the lights had dimmed in sick bay. He wondered if Vargas had lowered the light levels so they would sleep better. He stood, letting his robe fall to the floor. Vargas and Pinkney were nowhere to be found. When he emerged from the rear of sick bay, he spotted Catherine lying on the bed, seeing only her auburn hair as her head faced away from him. Eshel searched for a scanner, locating one on the counter. He picked it up and approached her.

When he viewed the scanner's readout, it showed her heart and respiratory rates at zero. Eshel scanned again. Same result.

He searched for another scanner, but saw nothing that would help him. He picked up Catherine's cold wrist, glancing at her face. He dropped her wrist, which fell to the bed with a thud.

Her face had taken on a purplish hue.

Eshel sat up on his bed, his breathing labored. The lights were bright again. Vargas, having seen him, lumbered over.

"What's the matter?" Vargas said.

Eshel got up and went over to Catherine. Her face was pale, but not purple with death. He reached for a scanner.

"I just scanned her," Vargas said. "She's fine."

Eshel scanned her anyway. Her readings hadn't changed. "We should see change by now. Her metabolic readings should show signs of recovery."

"Maybe it just takes her longer than it took you," Vargas said.

"No. Something is wrong. And if I don't find it, she will die."

CHAPTER 26

Do not kill those who attempt to abscond from our world and share what is not theirs to share, and do not kill those who betray our principles. Yet, do not forgive such transgressions, either. Instead, strike at their ability to survive and let them observe the end of their years with great clarity. And those who surmount such futile odds, who possess the cleverness or merely the tenacity to survive... they deserve to live, and without punishment.

- Elisan, Shereb clan

"I have to tell the Captain," Vargas said.

Eshel gave a reluctant nod, dread coming over him. He would rather face an angry Sunai, the disapproval of his mother, or even a resurrected malkaris, than face Catherine's father. Especially now, when he had no good news or explanation to offer. He, a Korvali geneticist, an expert in the very thing that had saved Catherine's life, could not explain her readings. He had no knowledge of what she'd done to achieve this. He only knew that she'd made substantial progress, that she and Holloway had...

Holloway. Eshel turned and left sick bay, ignoring Vargas's gruff voice calling after him. He flew up the stairs, not noticing or acknowledging anyone he passed. When he reached the fourth deck, he proceeded to the science section and burst into one of the labs.

Holloway and Varan looked up from their work.

"Eshel!" Varan exclaimed.

"She will not come out of stasis," Eshel said to Holloway.

Startled, Holloway stood up. "Varan, would you mind if I speak to Eshel alone?"

"Of course, Ensign!" Varan said, jumping up and scurrying from the room, the door shutting behind him.

"Stasis?" Holloway cried. "I thought she was merely injured!"

"Her epigenome has been altered," Eshel said. "Her metabolic activity has not reestablished itself. If it remains, she will begin to atrophy. You worked with her on this; you must know what she has done."

Holloway's face reddened. "You knew what we were doing?"

"Yes."

"We put it aside months ago to avoid any more trouble with Steele. But it wasn't finished... we hadn't finalized the model yet!"

Dread came over Eshel. "Where are the data?"

Holloway motioned for Eshel to follow him. When they arrived at the library, Holloway approached one of the computers, looking around and seeing a couple of other crewmembers. Eshel moved to block Holloway from others' view while Holloway pried the computer open and retrieved a portable storage drive. They hurried back to the lab.

"Wait here," Holloway said before he disappeared. After a couple of minutes, Holloway returned. "Anka said Catherine used her lab just before she left for Korvalis. She must have constructed the therapy then."

"If the model had an error, the therapy would not work properly. I will need every detail."

"My quarters," Holloway said.

Once at his quarters, Holloway pulled up a series of files. He then took the portable from his pocket and displayed its contents, letting out a sigh. "We agreed to leave it until after the mission ended. She must have worked on it in secret."

Eshel sat down and began reviewing all the files, asking questions when necessary.

"A unique approach," he finally said. "It is... data driven, rather than driven by theory."

"That was Catherine's idea. You didn't do yours that way?"

"No," Eshel said. "We lack the computing power for this. It is innovative... but unnecessarily complex." Eshel's contactor chirped. Vargas. "Yes, Doctor."

"Where the hell are you?" shouted Vargas.

"I believe I have found a possible solution for Catherine. I will return soon."

"You do that!"

Eshel stood, putting out his webbed hand so Holloway would give him the data.

"I know the model better than you do," Holloway said. "Let me look for the error. The problem isn't our original model, but with our adapting it to the human genome. It worked beautifully in the mice and they're still alive. I can find it from here."

"No," Eshel said. "That will take too long. It is more efficient if we both search from sick bay. We must tell Doctor Vargas the truth."

Holloway nodded, looking apprehensive but offering no argument. "What about protecting the work?"

"I will ensure the files are cleaned from sick bay's backup networks."

Holloway raised his eyebrows. "You know how to do that?"

"Yes."

Back at sick bay, and still no change in Catherine, Eshel and Holloway combed over the code, searching for errors. After reviewing their model, Eshel reasoned that the error must lie with metabolic regulation, rather than regulation of the survival systems themselves. She'd entered stasis and remained there without complication; the problem was that administering fluids hadn't signaled her body to resume normal metabolic activity. Some epigenetic pathway had been overlooked. Holloway agreed with Eshel's conclusion and focused his attention there first.

Upon their return, Vargas had given Holloway the evil eye until Eshel told him he needed Holloway's help and would explain everything later. Given that Holloway was a geneticist, Vargas gave no argument, which bought Eshel more time to consider what he needed to reveal about the illicit project and what he could hide.

"You can't create a new therapy to treat her with?" Vargas said. "Just give her what you gave yourself back then?"

"No," Eshel said. "It must be adapted to a human genome and that would take too long."

Eshel combed over Catherine and Holloway's extraordinarily intricate model, both frustrated and impressed with what they'd come up with, unaided by himself or any Korvali scientist. But as time passed, dread crept in again, knowing that if they didn't find the error soon, Catherine would lapse into a coma from which her brain would never fully recover. After reading line after line of unfamiliar code, his powers of concentration undermined by fatigue, Eshel's frustration began to rise. Just as he turned to Holloway, the doors to sick bay opened. When Vargas announced the Captain, Eshel closed his eyes momentarily before he stood up, saluted, and braced himself.

"Why isn't she awake yet?" Captain Finnegan said through gritted teeth.

Eshel hesitated. "There is an error in the therapy she took, Sir. We're reviewing her work in order to find it."

"Reviewing her work?" he said. "I thought you were the expert on this."

"Catherine developed this on her own. It is extremely complex."

The brown eyes bore into him. "If it weren't for you, Korvali, she wouldn't have developed it at all. If you hadn't brought her to Korvalis to deal with your problems, she wouldn't be lying there, half dead, waiting for you to figure it all out. Every time I hear that Catherine's in trouble, you're somehow involved. You've put her at risk, for your own selfish needs."

Eshel paused, attempting to keep any barbs to himself. "I did not want her to come."

"But she did, going over my head to get permission. And you didn't send her back, because your civil war was more important."

Eshel's patience began to grow dangerously thin; but he remained quiet, hoping Catherine's father would finish his tirade and let him do his work.

Jim took a step closer to him. "When this is over, assuming she recovers—and she had better recover—you can take your science and your fucking arrogance and leave this place. Because if I see you again, you're going to wish you'd never crossed my path."

Eshel, his forbearance having run out, flooded with anger. "I see where Catherine gets her temper," he sneered.

Jim's eyes lit up. "Oh yeah? You want to see where she learned to fight, too?" Jim took another step closer to Eshel, so close that Eshel would normally have backed away.

Before Eshel could respond, he heard shouting. Holloway stood, his cheeks flushed.

"I've found it!" he cried. "I've found the error!"

Eshel went to Holloway. "What is it?"

"An error in mapping, in adapting the model from mouse to human," he said, his words rushed. "A regulatory pathway, in the metabolic module, like you proposed!"

"Begin constructing a therapy to correct it," Eshel said. "I will review the pathway."

After Holloway left, Eshel sat down to examine the error, forgetting Captain Finnegan and everyone else. Holloway appeared to be correct. Such an error could keep her in stasis, regardless of the changed conditions. He went over to Catherine and scanned her yet again. It wasn't too late. Not yet.

He felt eyes upon him. Catherine's father. But he didn't return the stare. He couldn't. He continued reviewing the model for any other potential errors, hoping the Captain would leave. However, he remained, standing aside. After what seemed an endless amount of time, Holloway returned with the vial.

He handed Eshel the vial, his hand shaking. "Are you sure this is right? We only have one chance."

"Let us review once more," Eshel said.

After another careful review, they agreed and administered the therapy to Catherine. Soon, many lingered nearby, watching: Holloway, Vargas, Pinkney, and Tom, who'd woken up and whom Pinkney had assigned to a wheelchair. And Catherine's father, his hard look replaced by an expression that even Eshel recognized as profound concern. Eshel didn't know if he recognized Jim's expression because he'd come to understand humans better, or because Jim's feelings mirrored his own, the sickened worry that Eshel had shoved away while he'd worked toward a solution to bring Catherine to full metabolic status again. Now, with no more work to occupy him, the worry consumed him.

After an hour of tense silence, in which Jim had begun to pace, Eshel ran a scan. The readings had not changed.

"Give it more time," Holloway said. "When Catherine and I experimented with less complex phenotypes, like hair color, even those could take several hours to work."

In the following two hours, their scans began showing a rise in Catherine's heart and respiratory rates, and changes in her metabolic functions. The others' faces seemed to convey the hope that rose within him. Then, Catherine twitched. They watched her, rapt, but nothing else occurred. Eshel, no longer able to tolerate the waiting, sat down to review the model one last time, to ensure they hadn't missed anything else. The others began talking amongst themselves.

After another couple of hours, Eshel heard mumbling. It had come from Catherine. Everyone jumped to their feet. Her eyelids fluttered and then opened, revealing her brown eyes. She seemed to look right at Eshel. But then her eyes rolled back and her eyelids shut again.

"She's waking up," Vargas said. "Her readings look good, although I'm seeing elevated body temperature and T-cell readings."

He looked at Eshel, giving him a hard slap on the back. "When she comes to, maybe she'll be less of an asshole than you were."

The others snickered.

Eshel only watched Catherine. And soon, when Catherine opened her eyes again, they remained open, appearing more lucid than they had previously. Everyone gathered around her. Her eyes scanned them, seeming to recognize those who watched her. But despite her lucidity, Eshel could see that she didn't look well.

"Talk to me, Lieutenant," Vargas said. He held up two fingers. "How many fingers?"

"Two," she said, her voice barely a whisper. Her face crumpled into a disturbed expression. Before Eshel could ask what was wrong, she leaned over the side of her bed and vomited. The others quickly backed away as vomit splashed upon the deck. She lay back down, her forehead glistening. She looked at Eshel.

"What happened?" she said.

"You just emerged from stasis. You are back on *Cornelia.*"

"I feel horrible."

He scanned her. "It is the viral vector, to deliver the therapy. Your weakened state made you susceptible to its effects."

Catherine gave a faint nod and closed her eyes.

"Let her sleep for a while," Vargas said. "I'll get someone to clean this up."

"I will clean it," Eshel said.

The others stared at Eshel for a moment, until Vargas gave the nod. Eshel retrieved the equipment and began cleaning the mess.

Eshel sat at Catherine's bedside, running the scanner over her. "You are improved, but not yet well. It will take time to repair the damage to your systems."

It was late, probably later than she should've been awake. But she was so happy to see Eshel, so relieved to be among those she loved once more, that she didn't care. And Dr. Pinkney had given Eshel permission to stay later.

Eshel took a long drink from his canteen. "Tell me what happened."

"I don't know what happened," Catherine said, tucking her tangled hair behind her ear. "I was waiting for clearance to leave Korvalis… and next thing I knew, I woke up in one of your shuttles, bound." She told him the rest, at least as much as she could recall of her jumbled memories from the three days she spent at large. "The man who tossed me from the shuttle… I *knew* he looked familiar, but I couldn't place him. Then, in some exhausted fog, it came to me: he was one of those men I saw on the train, in Ronia."

"Minel," Eshel said.

Catherine gasped. Him. "Did the Shemal find me?"

"No. You were much further northeast, among the Spiral Isles. The basarac… they lifted you from the sea. The Tobeb made them release you."

The giant white birds… the ones she'd admired. She broke into a smile. "I saw them. I saw huge waves, and people, and…" She paused, trying to sort out the disjointed memories. "I was so tired, so dehydrated… I was hallucinating. I saw you, I saw others… I was even convinced those dark jutting rocks were giant animals."

Eshel gazed at her. "I can assure you I was not there… but the animals, they were no illusion."

"What do you mean?"

"The Tobeb… they carve the rock into the shapes of animals. It is said the carvings take years to create. My father told me that Elisan wanted one brought to Fallal Hall, but the Tobeb refused him."

They were real! Catherine shook her head at the memory, then giggled at Othniel's story. Even the primitives hated Elisan. "And now he's dead."

Eshel nodded, but didn't seem to feel the triumph she did.

She looked at Eshel, at his sea green eyes, his brown hair, his stoic face. "Thank you for finding me. For repairing my mistake."

"Thank Holloway. He discovered the error." She nodded at that, before he went on. "Why did you take the therapy, especially when you hadn't finalized it?"

She took a deep breath. "I was willing to help, no matter what the risks. But when both you and my dad went to that much effort to keep me off Korvalis, I knew I was in danger."

Eshel's clouded expression softened. She smiled, and closed her eyes.

"Slow down, Kingston!" Vargas shouted. "This isn't a speedway!"

Tom eased off the chair's accelerator, grinning at the only joy he'd experienced in what seemed like forever.

"Maybe it's time you got your ass out of here and slept in your own quarters," Vargas said.

"Fine by me, Sir!" Tom called out, swinging around and pulling up to Catherine's bed. Catherine sat quietly, playing a tune on the small Sunai guitar that Koni had given her. "You look better, Finnegan."

"So do you," she said.

"You scared the shit out of me," he said. "You were all but dead."

She gave a half smile.

"We did good, huh?" he said with a grin.

She nodded.

When the doors to sick bay opened, they turned to see who'd come to visit. Tom assumed it would be Eshel, who'd gone to talk with Ashan and the brass. But instead, Jim Finnegan walked in. Despite having patched up their disagreement about Catherine going over his head, Jimmy looked unhappy. Tom's only relief was that Jimmy and Eshel wouldn't have to cross paths again.

"At ease," Jim said to them, giving Tom a nod before turning to Catherine. "Feeling better?"

She nodded.

Jim, a wrinkle in his forehead, paused for a moment.

"What's wrong, Dad?" Catherine said.

He let out an exasperated sigh. "Look. This thing... this genetic therapy that saved your life... it violates the Alliance's rules about

Eshel or anyone else commandeering intellectual property that belongs to the Korvali. Given the circumstances, I'm willing to overlook it, and so is Vargas and the few others who know… and for the sake of making peace with the Korvali, we thought it better to not tell the Alliance."

Catherine nodded, she and Tom waiting for the bad news.

"Someone—we don't know who—informed the Alliance, said you've been working in secret this whole time and provided pretty damning evidence. Which means you and Holloway will face charges."

CHAPTER 27

Yamamoto listened to Catherine's story, nodding occasionally and offering no interruption. He and Captain Ferguson had been released from Sundani prison, their court-martial postponed until *Cornelia* returned to Earth. When she finished talking, he sat for a few moments, absorbing all of it.

"So…" he began. "You and Ensign Holloway spent considerable time attempting to reproduce Eshel's work—the work that allowed him to survive his escape—throughout the bulk of this mission?"

"Yes, Sir," she said, a smattering of shame coming over her at Yamamoto's tone.

"And you began this course of action only after discovering that Commander Steele had been engaging in such research with this professor Vanyukov from Stanford University?"

"Yes, Sir."

"And you have evidence of this discovery…"

She handed Yamamoto a portable with the files Eshel had sent her: the emails between Steele and Vanyukov, and two copies of Eshel's genome. "The earlier copy of Eshel's genome comes from the scans we took during Eshel's stasis. And the second copy… ask Eshel if he gave Steele permission to obtain and use his genomic data."

Yamamoto narrowed his eyes. "I will. But I believe I know the answer to that question. And who sent you these files?"

"I don't know, Sir. They came anonymously, and encrypted. I even enlisted Holloway to help me figure it out, but he couldn't."

"Care to hazard a guess?" Yamamoto said, his keen eyes watching her.

"Eshel was the obvious choice, given his motivations. I also wondered if Holloway sent them, as a sneaky way to persuade me to take on the project with him..."

"But Eshel, despite his willingness to take risks, lacked the necessary technical knowledge to accomplish this back then," Yamamoto surmised. "And we both know Holloway, despite his technical skill, is not the sort to take such risks."

Catherine, taken aback at Yamamoto's neat assessment, only nodded. It was the truth, all of it. However, she failed to mention that Eshel eventually admitted to having sent her the files.

"Fortunately," he went on, "the worst of this—how the Korvali will react—has its own solution, given that your work provides them with a valuable offering to the Alliance during negotiations. Such a therapy will have immense value to the Alliance, as long as you and Holloway relinquish the data to the Korvali."

"Of course, Sir."

"What about the evidence that it was Commander Steele who informed the Alliance of your undertaking?"

"It's on there, too," she said. "And, Sir... the Commander did make a threatening advance toward me once. I defended myself... but you should know the truth, in case any others complain about him."

He nodded, leaning back in his chair. "You and Holloway will take no space missions or visit any of the Alliance worlds for one Earth year. The Alliance will issue this punishment, and the Corps will support it."

"Yes, Sir."

"And, as you abused your privileges as COO to learn that Steele had informed the Alliance... you may no longer serve in that capacity. However, given that our mission is nearly finished, and you have expressed a desire to pursue a civilian science position, this should be no great punishment."

Catherine blinked a few times. "Yes, Sir."

"You're dismissed."

When Catherine arrived at her quarters, Eshel sat in a chair, waiting for her.

"How did it go?" he asked.

"Okay, I think. Holloway said the same. He stuck to the story, and said Yamamoto didn't challenge him or ask that many questions."

"Do you think the XO believes you?"

She cocked her head. "Hard to say for sure with him. He never asked if you'd given me files or if you were involved, which tells me he knows there's more to the story but has decided not to pursue it."

"And what punishment will you incur?"

"No space missions and no visiting the Alliance worlds for a year. And they'll pull me from COO duty."

"That is unfortunate."

She looked down for a moment. "Yeah. But the truth is, I got tired of lying to people I cared about. As for the rest… it's no big loss. I could use the break, and Holloway could too. He's planning to propose marriage to his girlfriend and we both want to get jobs doing real science with real scientists."

Eshel hesitated. "It is still unfortunate, as it means I will not see you for at least one year."

Catherine felt a pang in her gut. She hadn't thought of that. Eshel would soon return to Korvalis, and she to Earth. After several moments of silence, Eshel spoke again.

"Will you find it acceptable to suppress this information about your experiences with Steele, to know you lied to Yamamoto?"

"I have to. So does Holloway. And what choice do we have, really?"

"The full truth would reveal Steele's real treachery, would end his career," Eshel said.

"And mine too. And Holloway's."

"Not necessarily. Steele was the instigator. He broke into your quarters, stole your data, blackmailed Holloway, threatened you, and even attempted to assault you. Your actions served only as defense against his."

"And to get what I wanted, Esh," Catherine said. "I could've blown the whistle on Steele ages ago, and I probably should have... but then we'd never have completed the project. And divulging the truth would implicate a lot of other people: Tom, Koni, Anka, Herr... and you. It would've violated the sher keltar, where I promised I'd keep this secret."

"You remembered," Eshel said.

"Of course I remembered. In the end, it would've come down to my word against Steele's. He would've lied, and all those people who helped us would face punishment for no good reason. This way, no one gets in trouble, Steele will face court-martial, Yamamoto and the brass will know what a hypocrite he is... and we did something scientifically worthwhile. Something my mom would be proud of." She paused. "In the long term, this was the best way."

Eshel gazed at her. "It is unfortunate that you cannot return to Korvalis."

"Why's that?"

"You have begun to think like one of us."

She started to laugh. "How terrifying."

Eshel smiled.

Tom eased himself into bed from his wheelchair, careful to avoid bumping his legs. He reclined and took a sip of his beer, glad to be back in his own quarters, sleeping in his own bed, and able to drink as much beer as he wanted without Vargas giving him a hard time. Good old Soren: upon hearing that Vargas had released Tom from sick bay, the friendly bartender brought him a canister of his favorite beer in a cold bucket. When his door sounded, Tom glanced over at the screen, hoping it was Snow or Catherine or Esh, and not the brass coming to question him again. But to his great surprise, Maria's face appeared. He voiced her in.

Maria strolled in wearing her uniform, her hair pulled back neatly. She had the fresh appearance of someone just about to report to duty. He felt a surprising self-consciousness about his busted legs, about having to sit there like an invalid. He pushed those thoughts away.

"Hey, M," he said. "Working redeye?"

She nodded, pulling up a chair and taking a seat, concern in her dark eyes. "How are you? I've been trying to visit you for days, but Vargas wouldn't let me in."

"Yeah," Tom said, knowing Vargas would've made an exception if Maria had been his girlfriend. "Finnegan was in pretty bad shape. She almost died. You know how Vargas is."

"She's okay?"

"Yup," he said, sipping his beer. "Scared the piss out of me, though."

She glanced at his stabilized legs. "How are they?"

"Doc says I'm down for a little longer..." He motioned to the wheelchair. "But I'll have full mobility again."

"Good. They said a tree crushed you. How did that happen?"

"I took down the ship, ship took down the trees, and I made sure I stayed out of their fall trajectories. But it was dark, and I tripped and fell. Turns out one of the fallen trees took down another tree... that one got me." Maria grimaced. Tom changed topics. "So... what's up with you, Trujillo?"

She shrugged. "Not much. Just winding down the mission. I just... I wanted to see how you were. I was worried about you over there."

"Could've been worse."

"Is Korvalis pretty?"

He nodded. "Yeah. It rains all the goddamned time, but you wouldn't believe the trees. They're huge, and the forests are dark and dense and pristine... and they go on and on. In one place, there were these giant old trees that sprawled in every direction. It was like... Fangorn forest. Or what I imagine it would look like."

Maria broke into a smile. "I love those books."

"I know. I remember."

"Have you ever read them?"

"I've never been much of a book guy. I tried to get through them… I'd take Snow's reader and sneak out of the compound to sit under this big tree, where we weren't supposed to go…" Suddenly, he remembered the dream. The dream he'd had on Korvalis, while he and Catherine waited out the storm.

Maria's smile faded. "What's wrong?"

He shook his head. "Nothing. Just reminded me of a bad dream I had on Korvalis."

"I thought you never remembered your dreams."

"I don't. But this one…" Tom waved his hand. "Never mind. What else is new?"

Maria talked about her work, her career plans for when they returned to Headquarters, her excitement about going home. But as she talked, Tom heard less and less of what she said. He only saw the tree again. And the man. Before he knew it, he interrupted Maria.

"Listen, Maria."

Maria stopped talking, taken aback by the sudden interruption.

"I was molested as a kid."

Her eyes widened. "What?"

Tom, not knowing what had come over him, just started talking. "That's what the dream was about. Finnegan and I were sitting under one of those trees, waiting out a storm, like I used to as a kid. I'd go to this tree outside the compound. Sometimes I'd read, but I was such a slow reader. We weren't supposed to go out there, but it was the only peace and quiet I ever got in that damned place. One day, some guy with a beard came around… said I wasn't supposed to be there, but that he wouldn't tell anyone. And he…"

"He what?"

"Touched me."

"Jesus, Tom. Did you report him?"

"No. I was too afraid. I never told anyone. Until now."

Maria put her hand to her mouth, tears in her eyes.

Tom reached out for Maria's hand. "Hey, no tears, M. I don't want to upset you. I'm just tired of holding on to that secret and I didn't realize how much it weighed on me until I had that dream." He paused. "It almost happened again, a few years later. Different place, different guy. This time, I beat the fucking daylights out of him and told him if he ever touched any kid, I would kill him. Looking back, I should've reported him. I didn't know better. They always taught us about that in school, that it wasn't our fault, but they never told us how to speak up or how to deal with it. You knew it wasn't normal, but that's it."

Maria blinked several times, wiping away an escaped tear or two. "I'm so glad you told me."

"Me too."

She came over and sat on his bed, putting her arms around him. Tom embraced the woman he now called friend, whose hair smelled like flowers from the special shampoo she always brought on missions rather than using the Corps-issued stuff. He'd learned to love that smell.

"Promise you won't repeat this," Tom said.

"I promise."

Snow opened the shop door, the pleasant odor of wood and kala spice bringing back pleasant memories. Tom followed him inside. When Jooni emerged dressed in her winter gown, metallic jewels on her neck and hands, Snow smiled at her.

"Lieutenant Snow," she said, lowering her eyes and extending a palm to Snow, which he met. She turned to Tom, raising her palm to him. "Lieutenant Commander Kingston."

"Hey Jooni," Tom said with a grin. "How's business? Have any instruments for a guy with no musical talent?"

"Perhaps this, Mister Kingston," she said, motioning to a small wind instrument, designed for young children.

Snow and Tom erupted in laughter. When the laughter subsided, Snow stared at Jooni, who again cast her eyes down.

"You two go ahead and talk," Tom said, turning away. "I'll be over here, guarding the door."

With Tom out of earshot, Jooni and Snow faced one another.

"You wear the ear jewels again, the ones I gave you," Jooni said. Snow nodded.

"When do you leave for Earth, my friend Snow?"

"In a few days. I don't want to make things difficult, but I had to see you in person before we left."

She smiled. "I am very pleased that you did."

Snow, feeling awkward, changed topics. "I decided on my next tattoo."

"What will it be?" she said, excited. "Something of Suna?"

"Yes. Something beautiful." Snow took out his contactor and projected an image of what he'd drawn.

Her eyes grew larger. "My name, in Sunai lettering! I do not deserve such an honor," she said, taking his hands.

"Yes, you do." He paused, seeing a hint of sadness on her face. "You don't want me to?"

"No, I do."

"Then what's wrong?"

Her eyes remained down for some time, until she finally looked at him. "They are still being difficult and stupid. No matter what offer I bring, they make more argument. They quibble over detail. I don't believe they will ever grant me permission to leave Suna. They have no reason to." Her face scrunched up.

Anger welled up in him. Snow had seen Jooni upset, but he'd never seen her in that much pain. He urged her to the back of the shop, where he put his arms around her. He'd accepted that their romance was unrealistic, knowing there was little future for them. She knew it too. But to see her unhappy, to see her not fulfill the wish that mattered so much to her… it still angered him.

"Don't give up, Jooni," he told her. "Change takes time. Look at Eshel, how long he kept at it. He never gave up, and now their corrupt leaders are gone and they're talking about change. Keep coming up with ideas, and I'll do what I can from my end." He paused. "I had another idea: come visit Earth, to one of the Derovian communities. Just a visit. Bring one of your brothers with you, if you have to. Let them see for themselves."

Her face softened as she looked up at him. "A good idea, my friend Snow." She paused. "I will not see you again."

"Not for a while. But once I get reassigned, we'll be back."

"I look forward to it." She glanced at her guitar. "Shall we play? Perhaps teach Mister Kingston of Sunai music?"

Snow nodded. They emerged from the back, Jooni carrying her guitar as Snow grabbed another. And they played and sang together while Tom listened, until Snow kissed Jooni goodbye and they left.

When Catherine walked into the noisy mess, she eyed the meat offering that Snow and Tom would choose, but instead chose ornon and sea vegetables.

"Catherine."

She turned around. There stood Eshel, who'd snuck in behind her. She smiled. He too chose the ornon and vegetables, and they found Tom and Snow. Tom grinned at them from his wheelchair.

"Hey, you two! Welcome back to the table, Esh." Watching Catherine dig into her food, Tom added, "Good to see you eating again, C. Better than barfing all over sick bay, right?"

"Man, I'm eating," Snow groused.

Tom laughed. "How much longer are you and Ashan around, Esh?"

"We meet with the Alliance tomorrow, and return to Korvalis the day after," Eshel said.

A silence fell over the table. The four of them glanced at one another, then began focusing on their meals.

Eshel turned to Snow. "What is the status of Jooni's request for interplanetary exchange?"

Snow shook his head. "I found some places that would house her, including a school in England where she could teach the kids music and primary Sunai... but those assholes won't let her go."

Catherine shook her head.

"What a bunch of hypocrites," Tom said, stabbing more meat with his fork. "I'm telling you, they're always yammering about open borders and welcoming outsiders... and they've hovered around the Korvali border for years, waiting for an invitation. But when one of their women wants to leave, suddenly they're the Korvali." He looked at Eshel. "No offense, man."

Snow shrugged. "We did all we could. Like I told her, change takes time. If I've learned anything, it's that."

The others nodded.

"Do you look forward to returning to your homeworld?" Eshel asked them.

Catherine hesitated, as did Tom and Snow.

"Yes and no," Tom said, as she and Snow nodded in agreement. "You? You looking forward to going back?"

Eshel said nothing for several moments. "Yes and no."

"Won't be the same without you, man," Tom said.

Catherine and Snow nodded again. Her eyes blurred just slightly as she recalled having said those very words to Eshel when he'd told her he wouldn't return.

"Likewise," Eshel said.

Before much else could be said, someone approached their table. When they looked over, Catherine gasped. It was Captain Ferguson. Tom immediately rolled his chair back a little, pulling his hand up in salute. Catherine, Snow, and Eshel stood. Ferguson stood before them, her hair in a neat bun and her blue eyes sparkling once more.

"It's good to see you out and about, Captain," Tom said.

"You on the mend, soldier?" Ferguson said, glancing down at Tom's legs.

"Yes, Ma'am," Tom said.

"You too, Lieutenant?" Ferguson asked Catherine.

"Yes, Ma'am," Catherine said.

"Excellent work, both of you." Ferguson turned to Eshel. "Walk with me, Ensign?"

Eshel strolled alongside Ferguson in the hallway, waiting for her to speak.

"How are things on Korvalis?" Ferguson said.

"There is still unrest, but no incidents. My mother has gathered representatives from every clan to discuss the appointing of temporary leadership, until we can organize elections."

"I think the Alliance is looking forward to meeting tomorrow."

"As am I, Captain."

"How do you think it will go?" she asked.

"It is difficult to say. My mother is less... liberal... than I am. However, you will find her more reasonable than Elisan."

"That's a start." They entered a stairwell and climbed up one deck. "This thing with Finnegan and Holloway... can you contain it?" She gave him a sidelong glance.

"Do not worry, Captain. The Alliance, and my people, will see only the benefit of such a breach."

Once at Ferguson's office, they sat down.

"I'm told you won't be returning to duty," she said, eyeing him. "I would've preferred to hear it from you."

Eshel hesitated. "I did not know the proper procedure for such an announcement, given the change in leadership. However, I do not want to dishonor what you have done for me by ending my service dishonorably."

She waved her hand at him. "You need to be there. I'll make sure you get an honorable discharge. You've earned it."

"Thank you, Captain," Eshel said.

She took a sip from her canteen. "We made a difficult choice by taking you on. We angered the Sunai, who in many ways had more rights to you. Headquarters was divided. Elisan certainly didn't approve. I admit I was wary myself... but I believed something worthwhile would come from giving you a home here."

"It did not seem that way," Eshel said.

"I know I've been hard on you. I don't always trust scientists, especially when they're arrogant."

"Science is an important part of this organization, Captain," Eshel said. "I intend no disrespect… but without scientists, the Space Corps does nothing but defend Earth's borders." Eshel waited for Ferguson's anger to surface. However, Ferguson only watched him.

"Never underestimate the importance of that protection, Eshel. You wouldn't have succeeded without it."

"That is true."

She paused. "Has anyone ever told you about my father?"

"Your father? No."

She leaned back in her chair and took another swig from her canteen. "He was a scientist. A physicist, and a good one. He hated soldiers, hated the military, hated anyone who didn't understand his science. He would drill us on quantum mechanics or relativity, staring at us until we answered, berating us when we didn't get it right." She paused. "I never cared much for science after that."

Eshel, taken aback by Ferguson's admission, said only, "A good scientist inspires others. Your father's behavior did science a disservice."

"Yes, it did." She stood. "I'm proud of you, Ensign. I wish you well on Korvalis."

"Thank you, Captain," Eshel replied, standing.

"By the way… you'll do something about that clone of me, right?"

"It is already done," Eshel said.

She nodded. "See you at the meeting. You're dismissed."

CHAPTER 28

Gronoi Sansuai stood up with his usual amount of ceremony in the softly lit room, his decorations clinking as he strode to the place from which he would orate. Eshel and his comrades, along with Sunai, Derovian, Calyyt, and human delegates, sat waiting for Sansuai to begin. Among the Sunai delegates also sat Grono Amsala. Days ago, Eshel had met briefly with Koni to thank him for his crucial role in their operation, and had found the Grono's unadorned uniform strangely disconcerting. Today, he was pleased to see Koni properly embellished once more.

"Comrades, friends…" Sansuai began. "We again gather at the Alliance's table. This marks an occasion of great significance, where we welcome new leadership from Korvalis." He turned to the Korvali. "Our comrade, Eshel: the former refugee who was instrumental in creating the change that allows us to engage in real negotiation with the Korvali." He turned to Fashal, who wore the blue robe of the Shereb. "New to this table, Eshel's mother, Fashal, who served in Korvalis's assembly for many sun cycles and who will continue to serve among this new leadership." Gronoi Sansuai's amber eyes settled on Ashan. "And, perhaps most notable of all, Ashan, who escaped his homeworld and informed our Alliance of the unrest on Korvalis, who planted the seed that has become the tree that grows here today!" He paused, glancing at everyone. "We shall discuss the terms upon which our Korvali neighbors will join our great Alliance. Eshel," he boomed. "You may speak now, and tell us what you will offer!"

Eshel stood, as Sansuai sat back down. "Korvalis still faces reorganization of its government. Thus, the offer we bring will be a simple one, perhaps even a paltry one. However, you will find it more equitable—and more genuine—than those offered previously." Eshel paused. "We will provide genetic medicine, with terms very similar to those offered by Elisan. With the aid of the Sunai, Korvali scientists and physicians will travel to the other worlds at regular intervals to provide treatment for those we have the technology to treat."

"Eshel," Tallyn said, her gown a bright blue. "How will you develop such treatments without consulting our scientists and medical professionals?"

"We have studied your scientific and medical literature for years," Eshel said. "The exception is the Calyyt, who have no formal science program. Thus, we must request permission to collect samples from their citizens, both healthy and ill."

There was a rap on the metal table as Toq gave a brief sign. "You will receive this permission," his Sunai interpreter said.

"And what diseases can you treat?" Admiral Scott said.

"We are still gathering that information, Admiral. Some treatments are quite straightforward, but others, such as most cancers, are far more complex. And they will differ from species to species. We must decide where to put our resources first; as such, our initial offering will be limited until we are able to develop more."

"If you require funding, supplies, or manpower…" Admiral Scott said. "We can provide it."

"As can we," Grono Amsala chimed in. "Whatever aid you require, the Sunai will give you."

"Thank you," Eshel said to both men.

Grono Jonili spoke. "And this offering, will it include this therapy created by the geneticist… the one she violated Alliance rules to develop?"

"She has been punished for her violation, Grono," Eshel said. "And the offering does include this therapy, which will save many more lives, and will be modified for Sunai, Calyyt, and Derovian peoples." When Eshel glanced at the delegates' faces, he saw that this satisfied them. "As for our other terms... we are not prepared at this time to share our scientific methodology. However, I believe that will change with time." He turned to Grono Amsala. "It is often the case that superior innovations arise through competition. When it comes to our science, the Korvali will welcome such competition."

"You will have it, Korvali," Grono Amsala said, his big eyes gleaming.

Laughter filled the room.

"What of allowing outsiders into your space?" Grono Jonili said gruffly.

Eshel looked at his mother.

"We will allow no outsider to visit Korvalis at this time," Fashal said. There were muffled groans in the room. "The Korvali still do not trust outsiders. You know this about us, and it does not change simply because we choose to join your Alliance."

Toq rapped on the table again as his interpreter spoke. "Joining the Alliance means making concessions. The Calyyt have strict rules about visitors, but we allowed your son to visit and gave Ashan a home for many years."

"I do not disagree," Fashal said. "But Korvalis has already experienced significant change. We cannot offer more, particularly not until we reestablish a representative government and put such issues to vote. This is our way, the way of Doctrine."

Tallyn spoke up. "The changes Korvalis has experienced are significant, Fashal, and your offering of medicine is quite generous. Yet, a world that remains closed to outsiders does not feel like it is part of this Alliance."

Fashal turned to Eshel.

"It may appear as such, Tallyn," Eshel said. "However, if you are to honor our taking a seat at this table, you must accept our limitations. Our current leadership has agreed to the terms we bring you now, but they do so with trepidation. Our isolation... it is our way, and has been for millennia. I cannot ask my people for more than they give now." He paused, glancing at his mother and Ashan. "However, we have discussed the possibility of inviting a select number of outsiders to visit Korvalis briefly, as a beginning."

"Who will you invite, and when?" Admiral Scott said.

"We do not know that yet."

"And what of emigration?" Grono Jonili said. "Will you allow your citizens to live among us if they choose?"

"We have not addressed that either, Grono," Eshel said. "Those who've escaped Korvalis have only done so in response to a corrupt leadership. However, we acknowledge that some may still choose to leave Korvalis, temporarily or perhaps even permanently. This is another issue we will attend to on Korvalis."

At last, their questions sufficiently addressed, the delegates grew silent.

Gronoi Sansuai stood again. "If there are no more questions for these Korvali, then we shall take recess. We will reconvene to finalize this agreement and amend the code of the Orion Interplanetary Alliance."

With that, the delegates stood and began talking amongst themselves.

Eshel entered through the large doors, each opened by an eyeshaded guard. The spacious room had a sweeping view of Jula's volcanic peaks, the massive window tinted to reduce the glare that so easily offended the Sunai eye. He was overtaken by the odor of an unfamiliar spice, sweeter and less pungent than the one that pervaded Jula.

As he walked, the hard stone floor under his feet gave way to something far more forgiving. He glanced down; a woven rug encompassed the majority of the spacious room, its rust, brown, and black fibers intertwining in an intricate pattern. At one end of the room sat a table; but instead of the usual sleek black metal, the table was constructed from a golden red wood, carefully carved by a Sunai craftswoman. As Eshel drew closer, the top of the table had a pattern carved into it, the same as that of the rug. And behind the table, in a wooden chair with a tall, ornately carved back, sat Gronoi Okooii.

Okooii raised his chin, watching Eshel approach, his large eyes taking note of everything Eshel looked at as well as any subtle signals relayed from the nearby guards. He remained seated, and silent, until Eshel reached his desk, after which Okooii stood and met his palm.

"Sit," Okooii said.

Eshel took a seat in the less ornate but still impressive chair across from Okooii.

"I am told you choose to leave us and return to Korvalis," Okooii said, his powerful voice resonating throughout the room.

"Yes," Eshel said.

"I do not understand such a decision," Okooii said. "You now have such power, have made such progress. This is due to your living among outsiders, working alongside the Sunai and the humans. Now, you cast off such advancement to return to the familiar."

"I have a duty to Korvalis, Gronoi," Eshel said. "My living among the others created the conditions for change, but my return to Korvalis fueled the change itself. My leaving, my violations... they have troubled many. Now, I must show my people I put their interests above those of outsiders."

Okooii waved his arm dismissively. "Such violations... if they had any importance, your people would not have supported your rebellion. Some of your men... your men of science... should take residence on Suna. We may embark on great achievements together, with your superior knowledge of the map of life and Sunai technological advancements. We will not succeed at such a great distance. Your men must come here, and ours must go there."

Eshel felt a sliver of amusement at Okooii's bluster, at his insinuating that Sunai technology was superior to that of Earth's, or Korvalis's for that matter, assuming what Elisan had told him was true. He also wondered if Okooii truly meant to include only men in the invitation, or if he merely said as much out of habit. However, he refrained from sharing such thoughts, saying only,

"Such collaborations will not yet occur, but I hope they will in the future, Gronoi."

Okooii stood from his chair, his russet uniform crunching as his myriad decorations clanked against one another. He went to his sizable window, peering out at the mountains. "The Sunai gave your escapees proper burial. The Sunai gave Ashan a home, protected his identity for so many sun cycles. And the Sunai collaborated with you on your mission to unseat your despicable kunsheld, when the others sought to appease him."

Eshel knew Okooii well enough to know that when he began listing ways in which the Sunai had served the Korvali, he expected something in return. Mere flattery and recognition would often suffice... however, Eshel sensed that Okooii wanted more this time. "Your protection of Ashan, your vision of how we would come to join the Alliance... it is most impressive, Gronoi. If there is something that you want, now is the time to speak."

Okooii approached his kingly chair and sat back down, his chin raised and his pupils expanding. "When the time comes that you invite outsiders to Korvalis, the Sunai shall visit first. Before the Derovians, before the Calyyt... and before the humans. We shall go to this forbidden planet, speak with your leadership, see your treasures, and sit in your great Hall. We shall be first."

"Such a request dishonors the humans, given that they have provided me a home, training, and protection."

"You dare compare this to what the Sunai have done?" Okooii boomed.

"Perhaps not," Eshel said. "I will honor your request... if you agree to one stipulation."

Okooii raised his chin. "What is it?"

"That you allow your niece, Okooii Jooni, to participate in the interplanetary exchange program and teach Sunai music and language to humans on Earth."

Gronoi Okooii stood again, a growl escaping from him. "How do you know of this?"

"My human friends told me of it."

"Yes," he said angrily. "Your male friend with the markings, who would attempt to consort with her."

"They are only friends, Gronoi," Eshel said. "Such friendship is good for both peoples, as you've seen with Grono Amsala and Catherine Finnegan."

Okooii waved his arm, his decorations clinking again as he paced. "Yes, Grono Amsala said this, too. But Koni is male. Our women do not leave the protection of our males, do not go alone to other lands where they will face harm."

Eshel stood as well. "You ask the Korvali to allow outsiders on our lands, to allow Korvali to live among you. You ask us to amend our Doctrine. Yet, you will not allow one Sunai female to leave Suna, so that she may teach fundamental aspects of your culture—your language and your music—to humans?"

"You do not tell the Sunai how we will handle our women!" Okooii bellowed, his meaty hand striking the wooden table with a thud.

"I tell you nothing," Eshel said, undaunted. "You want something of value, and I ask for something in return, something which proves the Sunai are capable of the change that they ask of us."

Okooii glared at Eshel. "You ask that I release my brother's daughter from my custody, defying the tradition of Sunai females marrying our males... yet, come tomorrow, no Korvali will live off his own planet. You return, Ashan returns, all return. What do you really offer this Alliance, other than treating the most ill among us?"

Eshel gave no response.

"Let us banter no further," Okooii said. "Such important decisions are not decided in a moment."

"Agreed," Eshel said.

At Okooii's signal, the guards opened the doors and Eshel left.

Catherine sat up in bed as Eshel entered her quarters and put his cheek to hers.

"Have I awakened you?" he said, noting her tired appearance.

She shook her head, putting aside her reading pad. "Just reading."

"How are you feeling?" But instead of answering, Catherine began to giggle. "What is humorous?"

"You never did get used to asking that question, did you?"

"Perhaps not." Eshel pulled one of her chairs next to her bed and sat down.

"How'd the Alliance meeting go?" she said.

"Well enough. They want more than what we offer, but I believe they find the agreement tolerable."

She smiled. "Congratulations. What does your mother think of all this?"

"She is cautious. But she approved the offer."

"And what does she think about being offworld for the first time?"

"She prefers Korvalis and looks forward to leaving tomorrow," Eshel said. "I told her Suna is the worst of the Alliance worlds, that she should visit the others before reaching any conclusions. But she did not seem convinced."

Eshel considered whether to bring up his mother's cold treatment of Catherine at the sea dwelling, whether it required justification. However, his mother's behavior, while perhaps unnecessarily distrustful, was no different from that of most Korvali when it came to outsiders. Given Catherine's lack of complaint about it, Eshel decided she understood and thus remained silent on the issue.

Catherine sipped her tea. "Well, we're more similar to you than you might think. We leave for Earth in a few days, and I admit I'm looking forward to it. No matter how much I love to explore, there's something about home."

"Your father and the *Victoria* crew will escort you back?"

She nodded, her expression changing. "Tom told me my dad was pretty hard on you. I'm sorry about that."

Eshel hesitated. "I was… disrespectful. He was worried for you, and so was I."

They gazed at one another for several moments, neither speaking.

"When does Koni arrive to take you home?" she said, glancing a the time.

"0530." He paused. "I will sleep here, if you prefer."

"Only if you do me one favor."

"What is that?"

"In the morning, leave without a word. I can't say goodbye to you again."

Eshel stared at her. "I will."

Early the next morning, Eshel quietly put on his robe. He took one last look at Catherine as she slept, her auburn hair strewn across the pillow, before he left. After returning to his quarters and gathering the remainder of his belongings, his contactor chirped. When he glanced at the message, dread came over him. Catherine's father had called him up. The prospect of facing another inquiry, particularly from Jim Finnegan, didn't sit well with him. He could've ignored Jim—he'd relinquished his uniform and contactor, and no longer reported to anyone—but he refused to give in to such cowardice. Fortunately, Catherine had recovered from her harrowing experience on Korvalis; thus, there was only so much her father could level at him. Eshel left *Cornelia* and headed toward the *Victoria*.

When Eshel entered Jim's office, Jim motioned for him to sit.

"So… the deal is all but carved in stone," Jim said. "Korvalis will be part of the Alliance now.

"Yes. Sir."

"And Vargas tells me that Catherine will fully recover."

"Yes."

Jim sat back in his chair. "You're leaving soon?"

"Yes. Grono Amsala will arrive in ten minutes."

Eshel sat before Jim's probing eyes, making him wonder what difficult topic Jim's small talk would lead to. Finally, Jim spoke. "I'm not happy with some of the difficulties Catherine has faced since knowing you. I think you've put her at risk unnecessarily, and for selfish reasons."

Jim paused for several moments. Eshel, knowing Jim had more to say, remained quiet.

"This is the part where you reply, soldier."

"I do not know what reply is necessary," Eshel said. "You have made your dislike of me very clear, and I believe I understand the reasons for it. Catherine has endured significant harm since knowing me. I did what I could to protect her… however, perhaps such protection was enough to meet Captain Ferguson's approval, but not enough to meet that of her father."

"And you understand why that is?"

"I do."

Jim paused again. "She's my only kid. I lost my wife… I don't want to lose her, too."

"If you seek apology for my disrespect in sick bay, I offer it now."

Jim gave a nod. "I know some of the trouble she's gotten into is her own doing. She's always been a risk-taker, and I can't blame you for that. She takes after me that way." He paused again. "Good luck over there. You're dismissed."

Eshel stood up to leave. Before he reached the door, he turned around. "Permission to speak."

Jim nodded.

"Perhaps I took more risks than I should have with Catherine. However, my influence on her was not intended to be selfish. I chose to involve her because she was only the human I trusted, the only one who understood me, and because I knew she was capable. Perhaps any lapse in judgment was because… to use a human phrase… I loved her."

And with that, Eshel left.

CHAPTER 29

Eshel sat quietly next to Ashan in the Guard shuttle, while his mother sat in the copilot's seat. They soared past Stations 14 and 15 before heading toward the cloud cover. He still marveled at the ease of it, at Grono Amsala taking them to their border, at their transferring to a Guard ship, at their entering Korvali territory without having to outmaneuver the Guard or risk any lives. And, when necessary, they could leave Korvalis with similar ease—without trickery, without risk, and, most of all, without shame.

Much had changed, and there was more to come. The Alliance wanted more, had hoped that the shift in Korvali leadership would mean granting the concessions they'd sought. But Eshel knew that even the vokalis, many of whom would serve among the new leadership, still didn't trust the Alliance, and the humans in particular. Fortunately, Eshel had begun to see what his people hadn't yet, what most humans hadn't yet. Catherine was correct: the humans weren't all that different from them. Neither trusted the unfamiliar, the alien.

Now, the Korvali would focus on its greatest challenge: establishing trust among themselves. Many didn't trust the Shereb. The Shereb didn't trust the Osecal. And now, many distrusted the Shemal due to their daring act of rebellion, the culprits of whom had never revealed themselves. Those who took over Fallal Hall had the technology to begin tracking down the murderers; however, no one had pursued such an investigation.

"It is still disconcerting," Ashan said.

"What is?"

"Sitting here, rather than there." He eyed the pilot's seat, where a black-robed Guardsman sat.

"You are no longer Guard. You will serve in other ways." Ashan, his hair still unfaded and his eyes bright, appeared perhaps younger than he had previously, while cooped up in the hidden caves of Calyyt-Calloq. "All of this... it would not be, if not for you."

"One could say the same of you," Ashan said, gazing at Korvalis's oceanic surface, his expression without the chilly cynicism he'd had when they'd first returned.

"Ashan." Ashan faced him. "I should not have blamed you for Catherine's disappearance."

"Would you have come to the same conclusion if she had perished?" Eshel hesitated. "I do not know."

"Nor do I know if I would experience resentment toward Elisan if my mate had survived her illness, despite receiving no treatment."

Eshel gave no response, knowing that Ashan, once more, was correct. "Perhaps it is time for you to mate again."

Ashan returned his gaze to the view outside the window. "Perhaps."

When Eshel arrived at the gates of Fallal Hall, he entered the code his mother had sent him and opened the heavy wooden door. He took in the gardens, his usual visions of Catherine replaced by fleeting ones of his father and Elan. The sun had peeked out from the clouds and the foliage of the giant, weeping seshac trees glistened, still moistened from a rain shower. The gleaming white of Fallal Hall and its sculptures and bridges, once normal to him, now seemed a strange contrast to the dark rock of the east, where he'd spent so much time. He crossed a small bridge, stopping and peering down at the bright magenta plant that grew in the shallow waters babbling their way south. He glanced at his tattoo; for the first time, he felt no flicker of dishonor upon seeing it, upon seeing the bright color and ornate design that once seemed to represent an undeserved self-importance. Yet the magenta plant, as with the gardens themselves, brought him no real joy.

He walked on and entered the Hall, where people strode this way and that, their robes of various colors. The koshac tree rose grandly before him, its small silvery leaves having grown and begun greening. So quickly they changed with the proper feeding and care that only the Osecal were capable of, now that they were allowed to work in the building again. Visions of Catherine interrupted his sight as he recalled her admiration for the great trees and her desire to understand their powers. She would appreciate the tree's transformation; yet, she may never see it in person. Such an invitation wouldn't receive the others' approval, as any invitation received consideration only out of political necessity, not beneficence. If it were up to him, Catherine would be invited first. Certainly her contributions to the Korvali amounted to as much as those of the Sunai or human leaders, if not more. But politics… it was something he must consider now. To join this Alliance would mean taking into account the desires of the demanding Sunai and the distrusting humans. Such things never mattered before, when the Korvali had no one to answer to but themselves, and when his own days were filled with the wonders of science.

Eshel glanced at the time and made his way upstairs to his mother's office. As he passed a window, he stopped, looking down at the plainer stone buildings to the north. The research labs. After gazing at them for some time, he resumed his way and entered his mother's new office, already cleaned and rearranged. It looked different with her occupying the space, despite the same tree that grew under the glass roof and despite Eshel recognizing many of the plants from when Elisan resided there.

"Are you rested?" Fashal asked. "You slept much on the journey home."

"I am," Eshel said. "Negotiating with outsiders is tiring."

His mother gave a small smile. "And you thought science was complex." She paused. "How was Okooii? Did he make demands, list the ways in which we owe his people?"

"Of course."

"And what does he want?" she asked warily.

Eshel related the exchange to his mother, including Okooii's request to visit Korvalis before the others, and Eshel's stipulation regarding Jooni.

Fashal narrowed her eyes. "Why would you challenge his request, over such a trifle for a human friend?"

"It is no trifle. He asks us to change a fundamental tenet of our Doctrine; he must show he is capable of such change himself. Allowing Korvali to live among them, protecting Ashan... these are not sacrifices for the Sunai. He wants to walk on our lands, where no Sunai has ever walked... let him make a similar sacrifice by letting one Sunai woman live among humans for one Earth year."

His mother stared at him for several moments. "What if he refuses?"

"He won't."

Her expression softened, reminding him of how she would gaze at him before all had changed, before his father had died. "Living among outsiders has not changed you as much as I'd feared." She paused. "The leadership will offer you a seat in the assembly, until we can hold elections. They will also offer you the primary delegate seat once we finalize the agreement with the Alliance."

"Of course."

"I want you to refuse them," she said.

Eshel raised his eyebrows. "Refuse them? Why?"

Fashal stood up. "Let us walk in the gardens."

Eshel followed his mother as they descended the white stone stairs and exited the Hall. The sun had disappeared, and a breeze blew past them as they strolled along the stone pathway.

"You must leave Korvalis," she said. "You must leave and live among the others. You do not belong here."

Anger rose in him. "I have worked for years to bring about this change. You cannot continue to chastise me for actions I took when living among the others. Either punish me or remain quiet on the issue... but do not attempt to exclude me from my own people."

"No," she said. "You misunderstand. I attempt not to chastise you, son." She stopped walking. "Ashan has called you a 'Spirited One,' a label the Moshal give to those who adapt well to the novel, who seek to explore the outerworlds. He is correct. You are one of these, as was your father. The Korvali must maintain a connection to the outsiders, especially now that we will join this Alliance. The others... they trust you. As Ashan has said, you have power here, but you have far more among them. And you have proven, to myself and to many others, that you will protect Korvalis." She paused. "You may remain here, son, and govern our people or even conduct science... but you will serve your people better there, where your presence will convey our willingness to change and where you can ensure the protection of Korvalis."

Eshel, taken aback by his mother's words, said nothing. His mother resumed walking again.

"Ashan can take the primary delegate seat, if you will serve as secondary," she said. "He has the trust of the Sunai as well as the Calyyt, and he has no interest in representing the Moshal in the assembly."

"He won't take the seat."

"He will. I already offered it to him."

Eshel stopped again, staring at his mother. "You offered this without speaking to me first?"

"I made no promise to him, son. It was important that I secured an appropriate candidate to represent Korvalis before speaking with you."

"And what is Ashan's opinion about my leaving Korvalis?"

"It was his idea."

Eshel walked over to a stone bench and sat down. His mother joined him, her gray eyes meeting his.

"It was my hope," she said, "my very plan, that you would escape this place and its corruption, that you would create change. But never did I imagine how rapid the change would be, and how profound... for you, and for our people. I hoped only that you would survive your journey to the others, that you would merely tolerate living among them until another escaped and joined you."

"Change happens quickly among the others. It is we who move slowly." He paused. "There is much to be done here. I cannot leave now."

"You have done what you needed to do."

"The others... they will resent my leaving again. It also violates Doctrine."

"Some will not like it. But too many now see how your living among them has benefited us. They will overlook the violation, and I imagine we will amend Doctrine someday to allow others to do as you will, for the betterment of Korvalis." She paused. "You are always Korvali, and you are always welcome here, whenever you wish to come. You will have a voice in our government. But to remain here... it is not what your father would have chosen, had he lived to witness what has come to pass."

Eshel and his mother sat for some time among the seshac trees and flowers, the rivulet burbling behind them and weeping branches swaying in the breeze. Finally, Fashal brought her warm cheek to his. And she turned and walked away.

CHAPTER 30

Fight by my side, earn my unwavering loyalty.

- old Space Corps adage

Catherine lay upon the chaise with her reading pad, sipping her beer as the aroma of pine trees wafted over to her again. Feeling the high altitude sun encroaching, she sat up and adjusted the umbrella to protect her fair skin from sunburn. Just as she resumed reading Dante Stravinsky's *Evolutionary Astrogenetics*, she heard a door shut from inside the house. Soon, her dad emerged onto the deck wearing shorts and a Corps t-shirt.

"Still feel strange? Being back home?"

She nodded. She certainly appreciated sleeping in a real bed, taking long showers, breathing fresh air, and having easy access to the great outdoors. However, even those perks couldn't displace the lost feeling she had.

"That's normal," he said. "It can get pretty bad after your first long mission, but it passes." He paused. "Think you'll do another one?"

Catherine recognized her father's tone, knowing he would understand her taking another tour but that he secretly hoped she wouldn't. "I still want to get a job and be a real scientist again. But... another part of me wants to see more of the other worlds, especially if they assign a decent Research Chief."

Her dad shook his head. "The *Alexandria* deploys in November. You're grounded for a year, and they won't change their minds."

"They grounded Yamamoto and Ferguson for a year, too, but they're already planning the next mission and Yamamoto offered me an assignment. It sounds like the mission could include a visit to Korvalis, even if just to one of the space stations."

Jimmy rolled his eyes. "That crafty bastard. He knows just how to persuade you."

She smiled but said nothing, understanding her father's concern. The Korvali still hadn't located Minel. But Catherine wasn't worried. Minel had acquired many formidable enemies… and it was only a matter of time until they found him.

Jimmy changed topics. "Did you talk to Doctor Edelstein? Do they have a position at the Peloni Institute?"

"I did," Catherine said. "I think that last therapy worked… he looks much better, at least over video. And it sounds like they'll have funding for a position starting in September."

"Good. Will you work on that Eshel project, the one that kept you alive?"

"No. We gave those data to Eshel. It was part of the agreement with the Alliance."

"You don't get any credit for the work?"

She shrugged. "I don't care. I learned enough from doing it to generate tons of future projects… good ones. And Eshel will find a way to give me credit."

"I'm sure he will." Jimmy glanced out at the foothills, blanketed in green conifers. "You up for a hike tomorrow?"

Catherine grinned. "Sure. High country? I need to see some wildflowers. Just nothing too strenuous… I'm still out of shape."

He nodded. "Talisa will be here soon. Grilled steaks for dinner?"

"Sounds great. Let me finish this chapter and I'll come in and help."

Her father went inside, and she resumed reading. But before she'd finished more than a couple pages, Catherine heard the door again. She put her reader aside so she could greet her dad's girlfriend and start shucking the corn. Just as she put on her sandals, the screen door opened. Catherine looked up… but it wasn't Talisa who stood before her.

It was Eshel.

She jumped to her feet, gasping with broken laugher. "Oh my god! What the..." She rushed over to him, throwing her arms around him with probably more vigor than Eshel would prefer. He returned the hug. She stepped away and looked him up and down, still hardly believing it was really Eshel. He was dressed in pants and a t-shirt. "How did you get here?"

"On a ship," Eshel said, face expressionless. But then he gave one of his almost imperceptible smiles.

She giggled. "Look at you! They actually let your kind walk among us. Things have definitely changed!"

"It was rather difficult, actually," he said. "The humans have not instituted any formal changes to the law that forbids the Korvali to visit. But the Corps requested an exception for me, as long as I allowed them to track my whereabouts."

"How ridiculous..." she said, shaking her head. "So what are you doing here? Why didn't you tell me you were coming?"

Eshel gave no reply, his expression unreadable.

Fear came over her. "What's wrong?"

"Nothing is wrong."

Catherine continued watching Eshel, not understanding his strange expression, his tenseness. Eshel squinted in the intense sunlight, ducking under the umbrella and sitting down on her chaise.

"You're overheated," Catherine said, finally understanding that the July heat and strong sunlight would wilt any Korvali. She left and brought back a cup of chilled water for Eshel, sitting down on the other chaise.

Eshel took a long drink. "Catherine... I have left Korvalis."

Catherine gaped at him. She wanted to ask questions, so many of them. But she knew to be quiet and let Eshel speak.

"I will live here, on Earth," he went on. "I have received approval, and funding, to start a genetics institute."

Catherine broke into a big smile. "Holy shit! Where?"

"In England, near the coastline. It was the only location to have both the infrastructure for a proper laboratory and a climate I can tolerate."

"That's perfect for you." A thought came to her. "Holloway's from England. When he finds out, he'll be vying for a job."

"I already offered him a position," Eshel said. "He accepted."

She began to laugh, joy overwhelming her at Eshel—and Holloway—getting what both have always wanted. "Esh, how did you make this happen? What about Korvalis, and Ashan, and all that's going on?"

"I will explain later." Eshel paused, gazing at her. "Catherine, I want you to come live with me."

Catherine's smile subsided as she returned his gaze. "You want me to live with you?"

"Yes."

"As your girlfriend?"

"As my mate."

She blinked a couple of times. "What about my work?"

"You will work at the institute, if you choose. I may be able to obtain permission for you to continue the project you and Holloway worked on, if it still interests you."

Catherine felt tears come to her eyes.

"Your eyes water again," Eshel said.

She nodded.

"Are you sad?"

"No. I'm happy."

"Then you will come with me?"

"I will."

EPILOGUE

February 8th

Hi Dad,

Sorry to write you the old-fashioned way… our emitter went down again and we haven't had time to repair it. Eshel's been really busy with work and the pregnancy has wiped me out. Eshel warned me that while Korvali women don't get nauseated or moody like human women when pregnant, they do sleep a lot more. I'm nauseated and still sleeping 12 hours a day. Lucky me. The other scientists at the institute keep asking to scan me and study the first human-Korvali baby, but Eshel won't let them. He scans me daily and keeps a log of the baby's development and he's insisting on overseeing the delivery. I told him I don't want to know the sex until the birth. If it's a boy, we'll call him Othniel, after Eshel's father. If a girl, we'll call her Kate, after Mom.

Before the emitter failed, I chatted with Gronoi Amsala for quite a while. Do you remember Koni? He and his wife are also expecting their first child, and he's very excited. He's completely confident their first will be a boy, of course. Eshel hopes they have a girl and, to be honest, so do I! Koni has already begun the search for another wife, and I gave him a hard time about that. He only replied that it's important to have more wives because more wives mean more children, which is expected of a Gronoi because he'll hopefully sire more superior military candidates to follow in his footsteps. Also, and you might know this already, Gronoi Okooii will get promoted to Gronoio soon, which will make him a demigod on Suna and, according to Eshel, even more insufferable. Despite Okooii's hatred of Korvalis's heavy rainfall, he's hounded Eshel at Alliance meetings, vying for another visit to Fallal Hall.

Eshel reports that the Korvali leadership has made more progress. After an attempt to break into Fallal Hall, Moeb and Vashar (the late malkaris's surviving sons) sit imprisoned along with Minel and the others found guilty of crimes committed during Elisan's time. The newly elected government has settled in, and although Fashal isn't the warmest of people, even the Alliance has found her to be a far better kunsheld than Elisan. Since the deaths of the monarchs, the new leadership has allowed no one to replace them at Fallal Hall. Eshel said there's more talk of abolishing the monarchy altogether, that such a system promotes inbreeding and puts the undeserving in power. But he doesn't believe that will happen for a while. The Korvali have gone without a malkaris for a year and a half now; maybe they'll realize they don't need one and make an amendment to their Doctrine. I will say that when Eshel returns from an Alliance meeting and puts away his sash with the new Alliance insignia, I can't help but think how much better it looks with five symbols, instead of four.

Tom's doing great and seems glad to be redeployed again. Maria wasn't keen on another mission, even a 9-month mission, but I think that engagement ring Tom surprised her with convinced her another few months couldn't hurt before they settle down. Tom told me the other day that he's planning to "knock her up" when they get back in August. His words, of course. I also talked with Snow's girlfriend recently, who's thinking about pursuing a PhD in genetics. Snow was worried his 9-month absence would upset her, but she said it's given her time to finish up her BA and find PhD programs to apply to. I like her; she's outgoing and gets Snow out of his shell. And I think she has as many tattoos as he does.

We had Jooni over again recently. She really likes England, and I think her being stationed near Eshel was what sealed the deal with Okooii. Eshel said the kids like her so much that the school has begun begging the Sunai to let her stay longer. Eshel jokes about what concession he'll have to give Okooii this time to get him to agree. I suggested that, when school gets out, maybe Jooni could stay here and help with the baby while she works on her own music. Eshel likes the idea, so we'll see.

Oh, some science news. But don't skim this, Dad... you won't believe it.

First, it looks like Eshel, Holloway, and I will receive recognition for the survival project. We've finalized the model in humans and begun testing prototype models for the Calyyt, Derovians, and Sunai. We're not eligible for a Nobel since the work is based on Korvali technology, but we landed the cover of Science, *which is pretty amazing. But that's not the interesting part.*

Dad, you have to promise that you'll stay quiet about this until Eshel and his people are ready to reveal it.

Remember me telling you about that conversation between Eshel and Elisan, just before Elisan was killed? And Elisan telling Eshel of those legends about the ancient Korvali having visited the outerworlds, believing himself that they were true? Eshel didn't give it much credence, what with Elisan's deceptiveness and the fantastical nature of the legends. But on his trip to Korvalis, Eshel and Ashan finally visited the coordinates Elisan had given him, in the northern polar region. Dad, you won't believe this: there was a ship buried there, preserved over time. It was advanced... and FTL capable. And it was old, Dad. Older than you can imagine.

Also, remember me telling you that one of the Shemal patrollers could see me even with my clandestine device engaged? On that same trip, Eshel took DNA samples from some of the Shemal, with their leader's permission. Some of them have genetic variants... get this... that link them to humans. To us, Dad. Dante Stravinsky postulated that humans and Korvali may have a common ancestor, but everyone thought he was crazy. Holloway has become obsessed with this idea, and Eshel has given him permission to run with it. I look forward to seeing what he comes up with... to say the least.

Anyway, I've attached some images of me with my increasingly large belly, Eshel and Holloway working, and our Science *cover. And yes, please come stay when the baby comes, for as long as you want. We have plenty of room. Just know that, at some point, Fashal will visit. Eshel got permission for her to visit Earth and stay with us. He didn't think she would come, but apparently even a Korvali-human abomination has the same appeal that a Korvali baby does in their culture!*

Talk to you soon…

Love,

C

THANK YOU!

Thank you for reading *The Forbidden Planet* and the Korvali Chronicles series! If you enjoyed the series, feel free to check out my other works on my website (5280press.com).

Also, if you would like to be notified when I release new books or when I'm going to make an appearance at an event (such as a Comic Con), please sign up for my email list (5280press.com home page, bottom right). Don't worry: these emails will be infrequent!

You probably already know that book reviews mean the world to authors, especially indie authors. If you're up for posting an honest review on Amazon, I would be very grateful!

And finally, if you want to delve more into the Korvali Chronicles world, check out my Author's Notes about the series (http://5280press.com/category/authornotes/korvali-chronicles/) where I offer insight into the story and its characters.

ACKNOWLEDGEMENTS

So many people to thank.

Those of you who took the time to read the manuscript: Nick, James, Corinne, David, and Ken… each of you offers a unique perspective that is invaluable to me, and I'm grateful for you.

My Handsome, for your beautiful covers and your unwavering support… it's amazing to come home to such a creative but grounded person!

And, finally, those who read and loved *The Refugee* and *The Operative*… your eagerly awaiting the final book made me work all the harder and obsess over every detail, just so you would love it as much as I do. Thank you.

ABOUT C.A. HARTMAN

C.A. Hartman specializes in writing science fiction. Recovering from her years as an academic scientist, she's refocused her overactive, analytical mind on writing thought-provoking sci-fi with memorable characters. Her *Korvali Chronicles* trilogy tells the story of the fallout that occurs when an alien scientist escapes his corrupt, xenophobic planet and comes to live among humans on a starship. She's also glad to report that she's working on more sci-fi stories, some of which you could even call sinister...

A graduate of the University of Colorado (CU), Hartman earned her PhD in Behavioral Genetics and worked as a scientist for 15 years. She lives in Denver with her husband and has a special fondness for good film, the desert, aviator sunglasses, and dark roast coffee (decaf, of course, because you DON'T want to be around her when she's caffeinated). Doc Hartman is an introvert but she does like engaging with readers. Here's how to find her:

Her website: http://5280press.com/
Her blog: http://5280press.com/blog/
Her events: http://5280press.com/events/
Twitter: @5280_SciFi
Goodreads: C.A. Hartman
Pinterest

GLOSSARY

Admiral Scott: Captain Ferguson's commanding officer at Space Corps Headquarters.

Alliance: Formally known as the Orion Interplanetary Alliance, the Alliance is a coalition of four of the five known inhabited worlds (Earth, Suna, Derovia, and Calyyt-Calloq).

Alshar: Elan's daughter.

Anka Henriksen (Lieutenant): Molecular biologist in the lab next door to Catherine's.

Ashan: A former Korvali Guardsman and the first person to successfully escape Korvalis.

Basarac: The giant white seabirds of Korvalis, sacred to some of the remote clans.

Biocracker: Information thieves who steal and/or deal in biological information and patents.

Bulkhead: A wall on a ship.

Calyyt-Calloq (CC): Planet that is home to the Calyyt people.

Captain Ferguson: Captain and commanding officer of Starship *Cornelia*.

CC: Calyyt-Calloq.

CCFs: Calyyt-Calloq Fights.

CO: Commanding Officer.

Commander Marks: Chief Operations Officer on *Cornelia*.

Commander O'Leary: Chief of Engineering on *Cornelia*.

Commander Steele: Chief of Research and Catherine's commanding officer on *Cornelia*.

Commander Ov'Raa: Chief of Administration on *Cornelia*.

Commander Yamamoto: Executive Officer (XO) and second in command on *Cornelia*.

Commander (Doctor) Vargas: Chief Medical Officer on *Cornelia*.

Coran: Eshel's former Derovian bunkmate and brother of Dorel.

Dannia: Female Derovian leader.

Derovia: Moon that orbits Suna, inhabited by the Derovian people.

Dr. Pinkney: Ship's doctor, often in charge during redeye shift.

Doctrine: Korvalis's constitution, outlining their laws and how Korvalis shall be governed.

Dorel: Eshel's former Derovian bunkmate and brother of Coran.

Elan: Eldest son of Korvalis's malkaris and Eshel's long-time friend. Dead, due to Eshel murdering him as part of the sher keltar.

Elisan: Korvalis's kunsheld.

Fashal: Eshel's mother.

Ferrars (Lieutenant Commander): Operations officer and boyfriend of Maria Trujillo.

FTL: Short for "faster than light." Refers to a starship's engine that can travel at speeds beyond the speed of light, allowing for time-efficient space travel.

Gogooi: A large, aggressive predator on Suna, particularly in the highland regions.

Gro: The lowest rank among officers in Suna's military government. By increasing rank, Gro is followed by Gron, Grono, Gronoi, and Gronoio.

Grono Amsala (Koni): Sunai military officer and friend of Catherine.

Grono Amui: Sunai military officer and friend of Grono Amsala.

Grono Jonili: One of Suna's Alliance delegates.

Gronoi Sansuai: Officer in Suna's military government, and an Alliance delegate.

Gronoi Okooii: Officer in Suna's military government and one of the most powerful of the Gronoi rank.

Gronoio Vahara: A highly respected top military leader on Suna. His unexpected death meant postponing *Cornelia*'s visit to Suna until after the Thirty.

Guard: The Korvali Guard.

Guardsman: Member of the Korvali Guard.

Gumiia: On Suna, non-military male thugs who wear rust-colored vests.

Head: Bathroom on a ship.

HerrSycophant: Alias for the hacker who trained Catherine for her biocracker op.

Holloway (Ensign Patrick): Geneticist, and Catherine's subordinate in the genetics lab.

Ivar: The Korvali malkaris's second born son.

Jooni: Sunai female and musician, and Snow's love interest.

Jula: Major city on Suna and location of their military headquarters.

Kala: A traditional sweet and spicy fermented beverage of the Sunai.

Koni: Grono Amsala's given name.

Koriel: Shemal elder and leader.

Korvali Guard: Korvalis's military that protects their borders from outsiders. Further divided into Ground Guard (ground military, including the Hall Guard that protects Fallal Hall) and Air Guard (those who work at the 21 space stations that surround and protect Korvalis).

Korvalis: Oceanic planet and home of the Korvali.

Koshac tree: On Korvalis, ancient sprawling trees with mysterious properties. Rare, with only one or two known forests left, along with the single tree that lives within Fallal Hall. The Osecal clan chose the koshac the tree as its symbol, and their crest represents its branches.

Kotui: The people of the Kotui region of Suna. Known for being rebellious and warlike.

Kunsheld: Korvalis's non-monarchial leader.

Lakli: Korvalis's malkaris.

Lava nigger: Extremely vulgar slur for a Sunai person.

LC: Lieutenant Commander.

Leshe: Among the Korvali, the meeting of cheeks, performed only with loved ones.

LT: Lieutenant.

Mahoney (Lieutenant Michael): Operations officer, pilot, and Catherine's friend.

Malkaris: Korvalis's monarchial leader. The current malkaris is Lakli, a former Osecal. After her cousins died and she inherited the throne, she split from her Osecal mate and mated with a Shereb to put the Shereb clan into power.

Maria Trujillo (Lieutenant Commander): Operations officer and friend of Tom's.

Mellon: The southern (and less populous) continent of Derovia. Those from Mellon have the "Mel" prefix in their family names.

Meron: Derovian greeting, where both hands are used to grasp the other's hands.

Middleton (Petty Officer Mackey): One of the poker regulars and friend of Zander. Works in Engineering.

Minel: Korvali (Shereb) government official who visited *Cornelia* after Eshel's escape and met with the Alliance at a later date.

Moeb and Vashar: On Korvalis, the malkaris's two youngest sons.

Mosca (F-1): A Space Corps fighter ship. Small, maneuverable, and FTL-capable.

Mosel: Air Guardsman and one of the nine who died during Eshel's escape. Volen's sister.

Moshal clan: Ashan's clan and the clan that most of the Korvali Guard belong to. The Moshal have a simple, circular crest.

Moyyt-toq: Large, reptile-like animal that resides in the rocky outcrops of Calyyt-Calloq.

Mutant: Slur for a Korvali person, referring (somewhat erroneously) to their genetic abilities.

Neuter: Slur for a Calyyt person, referring to their being genderless.

Nonaii: Sunai word for woman.

Noob: Slang for someone new or uninitiated, short for noobie or newbie. Unlike newb, noob is specific to the tech world.

Ornon: A common Derovian sea creature, edible to humans and Korvali.

Osecal clan: The clan whose monarchy ruled Korvalis before the Shereb takeover. Their branched crest represents the ancient koshac tree.

Othniel: Eshel's father.

Ovlon: The northern (and more populous) continent of Derovia. Those from Ovlon have the "Ov" prefix in their family names.

Pokey (T-1): A Space Corps shuttlecraft designed for transport over short distances. Easy to pilot and not FTL-capable.

Qyto: A Calyyt leader.

Redeye shift: Night shift.

River valley (riverlands): An uninhabited and unforested region on Korvalis's main inhabited landmass, east of the developed regions and west of Shemal territory. The river and its tributaries flow south, into the southern sea.

Ronia: Capitol city on Derovia, on the northern continent of Ovlon.

Seshac tree: On Korvalis, large trees with weeping branches that often reach the ground.

Shanti (Petty Officer Patel): One of the poker regulars. Works in the communications center.

Shemal clan: The most powerful of Korvalis's primitive clans, and the largest clan of the planet's inhabited landmass, covering the eastern forests, the eastern and southeastern shores, and nearby islands. The Shemal have many sub-groups, each with a differing dotting pattern in their tattoos, representing maps of the region in which they live. The Shemal protect the more remote primitive clans to the east and northeast. Othniel (Eshel's father) was Shemal before mating.

Sher keltar: An ancient Korvali rite where a murdered person's family member may legally kill the perpetrator.

Sher memeshar: The death rite among the Korvali, in which the mate or closest genetic relative of the dead wails over the body. Once the body shows signs of decomposition, the body is taken to sea and released.

Sher mishtar: Among the Korvali, the rite of secrets, where two Korvali stand in water and share secret information.

Shereb clan: The current ruling clan of Korvalis and the clan Eshel belongs to. Their crest is the magenta leaf, representing the tiny plant that grows in the rivulets of Fallal Hall's gardens.

Smiley: Slur for a Derovian, referring to their tendency to smile a lot.

Soren: A Derovian bartender who works at *Cornelia*'s starboard bar.

Suna: Planet that is home to the Sunai people.

Sundani: Military police on Suna.

Tallyn: Derovian Alliance delegate.

Tobeb clan: On Korvalis, a primitive clan that inhabits the Spiral Isles. The Tobeb are ancient descendants of the Shemal, and their crest is the dotted spiral.

Toq: Alliance delegate from Calyyt-Calloq.

Toor: Catherine's Calyyt opponent in the CCFs. Also means windstorm.

Vanyukov (Dr. Albert): Geneticist at Stanford University and Commander Steele's research collaborator.

Varan Mel'Kavi: Derovian lab tech who works in Catherine's lab.

Vokalis: The multi-clan faction of Korvali who oppose Korvalis's current leadership and plot to remove them from power.

Volen: Air Guardsman and vokalis member. Brother to Mosel, who died during Eshel's escape from Korvalis.

Whitecoat: Soldier slang for a scientist.

XO: Executive Officer. Second in command on the ship.

Zander (Private Javier): One of the poker regulars. Works in Weapons.

www.ingramcontent.com/pod-product-compliance
Lightning Source LLC
Chambersburg PA
CBHW060404260626
47160CB00006B/2426